DREAMS OF YS AND OTHER INVISIBLE WORLDS

Jonathan Thomas

DREAMS OF

YS

AND OTHER INVISIBLE WORLDS

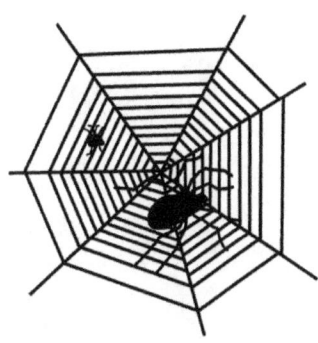

Hippocampus Press

New York

Published by Hippocampus Press
P.O. Box 641, New York, NY 10156.
http://www.hippocampuspress.com

Cover art © 2015 by David C. Verba. Regarding the cover painting, Verba
has stated, "To me, the first story in the collection pictures the sky and sea in
a prominent way; plus death, a sense of age, and a world inside the mind, an
interior landscape . . . which, to me, plays a large part in this author's writing."

Cover design by Barbara Briggs Silbert.

Hippocampus Press logo designed by Anastasia Damianakos.

First Edition
1 3 5 7 9 8 6 4 2
ISBN 978-1-61498-134-3

contents

DREAMS OF YS AND OTHER INVISIBLE WORLDS

three dreams of ys

Survivor's guilt is ridiculous, for crissakes. Mom was ninety, smoked a pack of clove cigarettes every other day, fried breakfast, lunch, and supper, and took pride in spending $10 tops on a weekly liter of vodka. Miraculous that she held out so long.

Too bad ornery spirit didn't inhabit self-reliant flesh. Till she died my life was on pause, and the transparency of this to us both couldn't have enhanced her sunset years. Must be my view of death as positive outcome that eats at me sometimes, like now, as I roam Breton tidal flats instead of sizing up the hotel where I contemplate sinking my inheritance.

The tidewater in this plaza-sized basin has dwindled to a silty channel. Skiffs, dories, and shallops lie tilted on glutinous sand till incoming sea refloats them. They form an unruly horseshoe within the hoofprint outline of the basin. Sure, the collective tonnage of small craft rests stably atop the slime, but that's no guarantee one wrong step wouldn't mire me knee-deep.

Besides which, the pickings are slim for any self-respecting beachcomber. Maybe motorboat traffic discourages shells and other marine oddments from accumulating. On this blank slate of a beach, the merest suggestion of a half-buried nub, casting a thimble's worth of shadow, looms conspicuous. It lures me out between the semicircle of boats and the shallow cleft of the channel. Water oozes up around my loafers as they indent potential quicksand.

I'm already queasy at prospects of engulfment before I bend low and start digging, and churn up the dizzying ferment of seafloor muck. I gag haplessly as grubbing fingers free a tetrahedron the width of outspread hand. Its angles and heft suggest I've salvaged a chunk of cornice. I stop to swab off gunk with a handkerchief only

9

after slogging back past the cordon of high-and-dry vessels.

Stubborn grains cling, but the wet sheen on bluestone helps me distinguish traces of carving. Over how many centuries have ocean currents smoothed bas-relief designs into tentative line drawings? On one face the letter S has been rotated in series to constitute a pinwheel, and alternating spirals and triskelions fill the loops of each letter.

The adjacent face startles me when I recognize it is, in fact, a face. Oversized eyes are round with pinpoint irises, as if in goggling trance. The nose has eroded to a tiny bracket, like an upside-down upholstery staple, and the mouth is a somber hyphen. Sufficient hatch marks rise from crescent forehead to suggest bristly hair continuing beyond my fragment's broken edge.

No matter how I tilt and squint at these faint incisions in April sun, they won't resolve into a familiar style. I should have paid more attention in Art History class, not that it would have materially aided my two decades hawking real estate. I give up and drop my arm. Maybe ask at the hotel if similar rubble has ever cast ashore.

Quavery, singsong French spins me around. "Please do not discard that! I know where it is from!" Despite my bilingual upbringing, lilting dialect takes some seconds to process.

Has black-clad codger been sitting on the nearest dory all along, practically a silhouette merging with dark hull? His thin jacket flaps in the nippy breeze. A patch of sun on one knee reveals pinstripes in woolen trousers. Hat with circular brim and round, shallow crown puts me in mind of country priest or ancient Roman peasant. I try to soft-pedal skepticism as I shout back, "How can you tell where it's from?"

He waves cavalierly at unburied treasure. "I would know that face anywhere!"

My skepticism lingers. The codger must be thirty feet away and would need sharpshooter vision to spot abraded features that fade into random scratches at arm's length.

But meanwhile, where are my manners, forcing a pensioner to strain vocal cords? I tread closer till his patronizing smile unsettles me. Gap teeth lend him the mordancy of a jack-o'-lantern. "Your little *objet trouvé*," he volunteers, "it is from Ys, of course!"

"From where?"

Now the pensioner gapes in disbelief. "You are here in Douarnenez and know nothing of Ys?"

"Should I?"

He feigns mild umbrage at my ignorance. Or is he feigning? "Ys was the most splendid city ever in Brittany, the richest, the oldest. It became great eons ago when the bay itself was young, not yet fully grown." He nods oceanward. "You could have stood here and seen dry land out to the horizon, and on that horizon were the shining bronze and silver roofs in the port of Ys. Douarnenez was among its beggarly suburbs."

He rattles off fairytale spiel like a tour guide. "But in later centuries, every king had to rebuild ramparts and dikes as the waves invaded and then surrounded their city, whose foundations came to be fathoms below the surface of the bay. Finally men could not prevail against God's will. Before the birth of Charlemagne, the pitiless sea destroyed the palaces, the counting houses, the temples, and plunged them into the deep. Some blame a spoiled and wicked princess for tampering with the sluice gates." He shrugs as if recommending I digest this one detail with a grain of salt.

Sounds like Atlantis envy to me, a Chamber of Commerce ploy to enliven dull boondocks with contrived lore. Saying so to earnest informant, though, would be cruel. Or will he slyly parlay his lecture into a plea for cash, as seems the case whenever characters accost me? I proceed on a sensibly even keel. "Shouldn't I surrender this artifact to the authorities? Isn't it considered state property?"

He sagely shakes his head. "The government does not believe in Ys."

"So keep it? Is it supposed to be lucky?"

His narrow gaze appraises my piece of legendry. "It is too big to go under your pillow. Still, you should dream of Ys if you put it under your bed. This I learned from my grandmother."

"Have you had such dreams? What was the city like?"

The codger purses bloodless lips. "Nobody believes the dreams of a penniless fisherman like me." A line, if ever I heard one, to tug at the heartstrings of a soft touch.

Let's save us both some time and shilly-shallying. "I appreciate this information and your generosity in giving me this relic. But it's more rightfully yours, and I'd rather not be an ugly American. What would you like for it?"

At first the codger regards me quizzically. What the deuce am I talking about? Then he gets it and blows up at perceived insult. My apologies, my appeals for calm make no dent in the wall of bellowing indignation. I back away, prattling futile amends, reluctant to turn around lest he boil over and charge after me. Halfway up rocky path to the cliff-top hotel, I check on his position. He hasn't budged. Perhaps waiting for the tide to raise his vessel. Is that his laughter amidst the almost human cackle of gulls, or simply the gulls?

The vista from the hotel ranks among its less perishable assets. It occupies a headland, cloverleaf-shaped in aerial view, which probably won't crumble away and deposit it next to Ys for another century or two. In that respect, the hotel's a sound investment.

The site presents another underutilized advantage. Research indicates tourism on the upswing in Brittany, and the *Auberge des Falaises*, at its slight remove from the village, should attract upscale guests averse to mixing with the hoi polloi. However, that fails to factor in the current owner and his larval complexion, earth-tone wardrobe, and midlife dejection plainer than mine.

Architecturally this is a diamond in the dirt. Sheer façade, narrow multipaned windows, a row of pointy dormers in a steeply pitched roof cry out for allusions to "petit chateau" and "manor." Sadly, such grandiosity is moot behind tarnished green eaves and maroon walls mottled with white spackle patches. Blatant disrepair, dead rhododendrons out front, and a "For Sale" sign beside rusty-hinged door aren't helping. A less demoralized hotelier than Monsieur Kervigo might have summoned the wherewithal to cease operations, but here I am, with the staff and facilities all to myself.

E-mails in flawless French spelled out why I was coming. Yet on my arrival, reminding Kervigo I was the prospective buyer rated the blandest acknowledgment, as if I'd declared myself a pipefitter or a dentist. How depressed he must have been not to brighten at golden chance to unload his depressing business. And ever since, I've been left on my own, like any other lodger. No, I won't be soliciting his opinion about my fistful of enchanted debris.

My first afternoon on the premises, I begin to tally deficiencies inside and out. Obsolete furnace, leaky plumbing, rickety fixtures, threadbare carpets, mold in the vents top the list after cursory once-over. The kitchen's little more than a pantry and couldn't handle half-capacity in the dining room, even if can-openers do most of the prep work. None of the employees qualify as spring chickens, and they mope as if to one-up the boss's apathy. Not a curtain rod or banister but would flunk the white-glove test.

I'm too discouraged at the number of shortcomings in pocket notepad to put them in perspective by sorting the cosmetic from the profound. At suppertime I brave the dining room, where the staff and I at separate tables partake of ratatouille with no seasoning beyond the nagging tang of metal. Hard ciders, then snifters of calvados, help blunt my critical edge. They also break down resistance to nudging bluestone in among the dust bunnies and grit under my creaky bed frame.

I hunker beneath multiple tatty blankets against April drafts and unsoberly challenge the bluestone, "Okay, what have you got for me?" Should I credit the power of alcohol, of suggestion, of an emergent wish to be elsewhere? After negligible gap in my awareness, the drab, fusty room switches to dreamland. I'm pacing along, still in the dark, yes, but moon and stars suffuse brothy sea mist around me with a wan glow.

My legs follow preset course, as I take stock as best the atmosphere allows. Faint in the befogged distance behind me is a monumental stone wall, high as an arena's, in which a stitchwork of iron plaques optimistically binds a crack together. Ahead of me is a gleaming zigzag boardwalk, less a street than a gulch between houses.

The houses, whether of quarried blocks or vertical planks, under clay tile or stoutly thatched roofs, bulk large as mansions. Their eaves, riding rugged beams well past gable ends, form dramatic overhangs. Stone piers and timber stilts elevate many of the foundations. The milky damp hides details of any ornament, yet accentuates the glitter of silver leaf on walls and on the boardwalk, which changes to flagstone pavement on a sudden upslope. I neither meet nor hear anybody. Where am I if not in Ys, a metropolis curiously devoid of nightlife? Or is the city deserted?

Toward the hilltop, houses and pavement peter out, and the incline merges with irregularly spaced stone buttresses against a precipitous white mortared wall. Like the iron plaques, they come across as ad hoc reinforcements against generations of floods or structural fatigue. The mist thickens with increasing altitude, concealing the scale of this edifice, though its eminence hints it's a citadel.

No gates or windows compromise the blank mortar corresponding to the first and second floors. Higher up till they're consumed in fog, a smattering of glassless narrow windows is scattered randomly, like slots in a punchcard. They affirm the city isn't abandoned because yellow light flickers in them all, and in one at the lowest level a woman, to my chagrin, peers down at me.

The mist veils her like gauze, but as she brushes luxurious sable hair aside and leans out with supple confidence, I decide she's young and gorgeous. I can just distinguish dark crisscross lacing down the center of ample bodice in translucent gown. She stretches a slim, bare arm into the night and beckons me with leisurely forefinger.

I'm not ready for such direct attention from a vision of loveliness. At the back of my mind hovers the knowledge I've been dreaming all along. I grab at that knowledge, to awaken with a jolt under motheaten blankets. The room now smells of stale kelp, instead of stealthy mildew.

My coastal excursion east to Carnac is theoretically multipurpose, to flush cobwebs and fantasy from my brain, to better acquaint myself with the region, to preview the joys of tourism in which I might soon be immersed. This entire trip is also, by default, my closest approach to a vacation since Mom went into death-bound tailspin. At day's end, I exit Carnac with both food for thought and culture shock.

The sprawling Neolithic alignments occupy more village territory than its shops and homes, and are too incredibly much to absorb on one visit. About a dozen standing stones abreast, ranging in size from hassocks to upended Winnebagos, troop by their thousands for more than a mile, through scrubland, lawn, and glades, across a stream, and onward. Those glades allegedly contain the country's last wild-growing woad, the weed with which naked Celts stained themselves fetid blue before battle.

I rove the landscape overwhelmed, but only in part by the monuments. This is the off-season, though some Euro equivalent of Spring Break is pointedly underway. There must be three tourists for every menhir, climbing, bunny-hopping, or hammering for mementoes on these pillars of bygone sanctity, of superhuman devotional exercise. In French, German, English, Dutch, they jabber at companions to snap their photos, and collectively the loudmouths are like a polyglot flock of starlings. Do I really want a career catering to entitled Eurotrash?

By municipal parking lot where the alignments begin, a whitewashed cottage with slate roof and stubby chimneys serves as visitor center. I yearn to complain about the yahoos abusing cultural heritage, but the personnel are too busy selling them postcards, key rings, snow globes, T-shirts, and anyway, what could they do?

Similarities of Carnac to other far-flung archaic achievements like Stonehenge I dismiss as facile, coincidental. Not necessarily so, argues a flyspecked diorama in a neglected corner. Six millennia back, when megaliths were all the rage, a maritime Atlantic economy was already well-established, circulating goods and ideas between Portugal and the Hebrides. And peninsular Brittany was like a natural fulcrum, situated to tilt the balance of trade for the whole shebang.

Cruising west to the hotel along shoreline Route D781, I open my windows and endure chill winds to sniff salt water and pine groves. I try to picture this pastoral, sparsely settled geography as the center of a world, and wonder where its urbane elite could have dwelt, and speculate, Why not Ys? If Brittany was the hub of a coastal trading network, Ys, in a sheltering bay close to land's end, could have functioned as its lynchpin. If Ys existed, that is.

The name itself suggests profound antiquity, in common with others chaffed by epochs of repetition into one brief syllable, like Aix or York or Ur. And why shouldn't oblivion have swallowed the reality of Ys along with most of its name? Volcanoes erased memories of Pompeii. Tremors drowned the glories of classical Alexandria and Jamaica's swashbuckling Port Royal. Venice and not Ys might be the esoteric footnote today, had "sea change" and engineering knowhow ordained differently.

What a fabulous realm I've rebuilt from one battered chunk of rock. Still, speaking intellectually, I believe no more in Ys than in any other useless dream. Vis-à-vis my dealings here, it's as irrelevant as anything under sludge at the bottom of a gulf. I've come too far to let Monsieur Kervigo delay negotiations further.

Tonight's supper of savory crêpes and mussels demands a level of freshness and skill evidently reserved for special occasions, a beloved saint's day or someone's anniversary. I fairly insist my host join me at table, and to offset impression I'm a pushy philistine, I attempt small talk about Carnac, about the stunning amount of prehistory there, and inquire after Neolithic remains in Douarnenez.

He blinks as if clearing film from his eyes and snaps, "Some things are older than dolmens." I'm both gratified and taken aback at prickly core beneath passive skin. Without expanding on cryptic remark, he excuses himself to preside at the employees' table. Any pretext for our celebration dinner goes unannounced.

I retire on the logy side, thanks to rich and heavy Breton butter cake and cheese platter and chalices of Bordeaux. Upstairs, misgivings that my piece of Ys would have vanished prove unfounded. The pillow's been fluffed and the blankets tucked in, but of course nobody's cleaned under the bed.

From her exquisite hand to my lips, she feeds me orange segments one by one, as if they're precious, exotic commodities. Yet they're scrawny and bitter, and despite the seductive touch of her fingertips, I almost say *No thanks, I'm too full,* as if I'm dreaming with the same midriff bulge I took to bed, as if it's minutes later in the same continuity. But no, mine is a dream self with appetite intact.

Roman affectation vies with less obvious provenience. My couch is firm like a futon and most resembles a prop from *Satyricon.* Silk cushion on shallow-angled headrest supports my neck while the lady lounges on a backless chair with its legs of crisscrossed ivory tusks. Blue glass bowl of oranges, grapes, and pomegranates rests on delicate checkerboard of a table. Terracotta lamp impersonates a gliding crow, and hangs at the end of a chain bolted into massive ceiling beam. Between couch and narrow window, a beehive-like censer balances on a three-footed pole.

Aromatic haze from oil and incense can't obliterate every whiff of kelp, but obscures much of water-stained, flaking murals, excepting a naked archer with antlers, herons preening on the shoulders of bulls, a girl astride a dolphin. Thanks to the haze, I've also yet to see my affectionate hostess with pinpoint clarity. But she projects a grace, a glamour, a nobility radiant as the pure white of her sleeveless gown. How can she not be a princess?

Since I'm well aware this is a dream, I don't bother questioning why royalty would dote on me, or how I gained entry to this sanctum. The slipshod logic of REM state must also account for Dark Age lady's acceptance of my casual American attire and her impossible understanding of modern French when I look from my muddy loafers to her sky-blue eyes and ask, "Are you a princess? Is your kingdom older than the dolmens?"

She nods pensively, stacks leftover orange wedges on curly peelings, and slides another checkerboard table from under the platform of my couch. The straw upon marble floor bunches up around spindly table legs. She hunts among the clutter on the checkerboard for a petite soapstone figurine, which she presents as if it certifies eons of venerability.

Its workmanship is both painstaking and crude, and it's worn and polished like my bluestone. Quizzical, bald homunculus squats with knees up and wide apart, and arms snake under them to assert gender by tugging open a hyperbolic vulva. Porn accessory or fertility fetish? As if they're mutually exclusive? A token of age immemorial, yes, but of an age sordid and debased. I quickly replace figurine on the table.

If my revulsion shows, the princess is too refined to acknowledge it. She's busy pouring blackish wine from a sleek bronze flagon, its spout a swan's long-necked head, its handle a leaping hound. Our cups are of burnished grey metal, each fashioned into three repoussé faces, side by side, beetle-browed, imperious.

I sit up as she passes me a cup and raises hers in wordless toast. I reciprocate and, before a trial sip, reflect warily on metallic bouquet that hearkens back to hotel ratatouille, and that I hope comes from cup and not beverage. But the princess smiles beatifically as if she's tasted nectar, prompting me to forgo caution. I'm instantly sorry. The consistency is syrupy and granular, the flavor at once sour and oversweet, as if honey could remedy spoilage.

To drink more is unthinkable. As is the prospect of offending my hostess. I plant feet on the floor, nod courteously, mosey past the censer, and pretend to swig again while gazing out the window. Maybe put my cup on the sill and forget about it? No, not yet anyway, she's already by my side.

"It's a wonder of the world, isn't it?" I gesture toward the city outside. She nestles into me, and full-body contact persists as if she couldn't share the view otherwise. Her point-blank scent blends sweat and musk. I'm not positive I like it, but it arouses me all the same. Still, even in a dream, to smooch her on raw impulse would be déclassé, so I focus on Ys from royal vantage.

The mist has condensed to a fine, lucid drizzle, in effect stripping the town's cosmetic veneer. Starker moonglow demotes the luster of silver leaf into moisture beading up on pitted surfaces or leaching out of cracks or glistening on streaks of luminous fungus. And ominously, a thin skin of water covers the boardwalks fanning out from the foot of citadel hill. Rising tide must seep in through chinks in the towering barrier. How bleak to witness an Ys antediluvian in terms of more than showing its age.

Her probing gaze draws me like a flare in the dark. I haven't noticed until now she only comes up to my shoulders, as if regal presence made her seem taller. She reads and mirrors my melancholy, her gaze sidelong toward urban decay, and she murmurs, as best I can discern, "Nisudo ardanny groz." Is that Breton? Gaulish? Something more remote?

She takes another demure swallow from metal vessel, and her uplifted face may be seeking or dispensing sympathy, I can't tell which. To perch my unwanted cup on windowsill at this solemn juncture feels apropos, self-serving or not.

Her smile is bewitching, bidding me forget sorrow, live for the moment. With businesslike ease, she tugs at crisscross lacing to loosen her bodice well past functionality. One expert hand exposes right breast and cradles it, and as it nudges my shirtfront, resignation leavens her irresistible smile, as if she fulfills a sad duty.

Fierce itching distracts me. A titan among fleas is battening on my forearm. I slap it off and wake sitting up at bedside, in the middle of furiously transcribing noblewoman's lament, vandalizing the lacquer of wobbly nightstand with ballpoint pen.

Borderline erotic dreams of mythic city, as foretold by a moody fisherman, I can handle in stride. To find a new guest at breakfast, however, strains credibility. He hunches frowning over a brie omelette no greasier than mine, and his head hangs too big for his torso, barrel-chested though he is. A furrow like that on a saddle spans his bald crown and competes for prominence with wicked black monobrow. I can't quite ID the cartoon character he resembles. Nobody memorable enough to click.

Newcomer petulantly shoves substandard meal around his plate, then hollers for the sluggish waitress. By the time his breakfast is inedibly cold and mine's a memory, she's fetched Kervigo, who leans inert against the nearest table through most of diatribe about abysmal cuisine. Just as well the coffee goes unsampled. Finally the customer, patently more riled the longer Kervigo listens unfazed, raves, "I have friends at the departmental level who will hear of this!"

The owner then erupts from lethargy to laugh in the face of outrage. "If you have such important friends, what are you doing in this dump?" Kervigo's temper, in fact, brings to mind a happy dreamer's after rude awakening. He slouches off to leave cartoonish adversary sputtering.

What kind of twerp expects gourmet cuisine at a self-professed dump, anyway? The same kind, I reckon, who'd try enlisting me as sympathetic ear. I keep my head down, pretending to enjoy wretched coffee, and with pen I repeatedly scribble "Nisudo ardanny groz," as if it meant something, on green paper placemat. Just think, that hotelier with the shitty attitude could soon be me.

The placemat's almost out of space before I reconsider. In spite, or actually because, of this customer's ill-humor, I ought to engage him, as practice for the heroic forbearance I'll have to cultivate daily in Kervigo's shoes, an order of magnitude greater than realty sales required. Too late. Not only has the complainant decamped, but Kervigo has returned with a plastic basin to clear the dishes.

I'm nowise tempted to bring up my business with him. Annoyance still fuels his body language, and he might well spew vitriol at me for aspiring to buy his dump. Meanwhile, why am I loath to admit aloud my waning interest in the place? Then our sightlines lock, dammit, and someone has to say something. To my relief, he intones, "I am sorry to startle you." He arches an eyebrow. "You were dreaming, perhaps?"

At mere mention of dreaming, I'm even more tongue-tied, for no conscious reason, than at outlook of buying the inn. I have to clutch at any change of topic. "Do you speak Breton?"

"No, not fluently," he concedes straightaway, as if I haven't jumped the conversational track.

"Nisudo ardanny groz?" Rising inflection conveys wishful thinking this is some of the meager Breton he knows.

Sallow brow crinkles as he shakes his head. I tear off a strip of placemat with several renditions of the phrase, and thrust it at him on the off chance my accent is the problem.

He curtly glosses my scrawl and remarks, "An acquaintance of mine may be of assistance. You and I will meet later." He voices no interest in where or how I encountered this text, as one ordinarily might. Has a dream state begun to pervade my waking life here?

Hiking the couple of miles to Douarnenez proper for lunch might contribute to a new grip on normality, a reality check. Maybe I'll even hit upon a better hotel for sale. I make it as far as the cliff's edge where footpath descends to the beach. The tide is out, boats are marooned, and Kervigo is giving my scrap of placemat to the volatile fisherman, reseated on oblique dory.

I can't verbalize why I don't want them to see me. I just don't, as if they're in nefarious cahoots. I whip around and retreat to the inn, all the better, I tell myself, to intercept Kervigo with the fisherman's answer ASAP.

Another item for my list of demerits at *Auberge des Falaises* proves inescapable. Aside from eating, there's nothing to do here, nary a shuffleboard nor boules court nor library nor even stash of board games. Nothing helps the already quiescent staff wile away breaks and downtime. Like a pinball down the drain, I meander into the dining hall, to partake of the same mushroom soup as the early birds among the crew. Nobody else acts bothered by a soupçon of mold, a smell akin to that from crusty heating grates.

Kervigo slinks in, and I welcome the excuse to put spoon aside. He surveys my dubious fare askance. "You should have received bread. I will reprimand those at fault." He lays my green shred next to red luncheon placemat. "No easy job, but undoubtedly, this translates, 'We sink beneath the cross.'"

What? How does prayerful sentiment fit with soft-core scene I experienced? I'm slack-jawed with bewilderment.

"I am instructed to explain that Christians forbade trade with pagans. And that sea walls crumble without silver to uphold them." Kervigo as disinterested messenger gives me a second to absorb that. "You have spoken before with the person who provided this information, yes? Therefore, he felt sure you would understand."

That made one of us. Blindsided by this glut of revelation, I remember my manners only after a foundering silence. I thank Kervigo and request he thank our mutual acquaintance for me. Kervigo asks if he can be of further service.

Here's my golden ticket to a serious discussion about buying him out. Now or never, likely enough. In his blasé eyes I glean, rightly or not, that we're on the same page. Yet I'm unsurprised, and neither is he, when instead I impose on him for a hard cider. He retrieves it and I drink alone, shunning even the company of wandering thoughts, as I fear they'd lead to grief about my mother.

The bottle's empty, my mind's an enduring blank, and I've pushed the soup into the position of stone-cold centerpiece when fiftyish waitress with frizzy blondish hair and sagging waxen features lumbers over. She smacks a plastic basket of quartered baguettes in front of me and departs, with the eloquent scowl of someone rousted at 3 A.M. for nothing.

The alternative to plain bread is no lunch at all. I finish it off and decide a nap is in order. Or more to the point, I'm at a loss for what else to do. Maybe I should leave that up to the princess of Ys.

Her bodice is laced up again. We stand apart in separate contemplations of the vista, as if we've retracted into shells. My triple-faced cup still rests on the sill. I retain nothing of whatever's transpired between dreams.

Dank, stiff gusts skirl off the bay and through the window. I shrink a little from the cold, but mostly from the fecal stink. No mistaking raw, festering sewage. I'd sniffed well over my quota while inspecting subprime properties. So where else during Dark Ages would an island's waste go except straight into the sea? And how could dysentery, cholera, et cetera not breed rampant among the islanders, princesses included?

I covertly scrutinize her with new perspective, half pitying, half squeamish. Undismayed by the odor, she gazes out tenderly, proudly, as if she always has beheld and always will behold a brilliant silver metropolis, stupendously rich, eternally true to its legend.

She homes in on sneaking gaze and turns, stalwart with civic pride, then adopting a more playful mode. Big, wide-set, sky-blue eyes fix upon me; she pouts coyly and sips her wine. Subtle sexual charge gets under my skin. Without letting me out of her sight, she sets her cup beside mine. She rakes lazy fingers through abundant sable hair, and ignoring vagrant streaks of grey is easy.

Behind more expansive smile her teeth peek out, and heaven help me, I shudder and fight to maintain deadpan appearance. Enamel is stained dirty blue, the crowns are down to a crooked serration, and inflamed, receding gums frame yellow snippets of roots. Should I really be shocked? The water supply is a virtual Petri dish, and daily flagon of acidic wine is the lesser evil, centuries from the invention of toothpaste. Her bid to cajole, to enmesh me, has miserably backfired. My God, her breath must be atrocious.

"Can we take a walk along the battlements, now that the fog's lifted?" I stammer. "To see your beautiful city?"

She nods brightly, glides over to the couch, sits and reaffixes coquettish look at me. She pats the firm cushion right next to her. I can't move. All I've ever said to her was gibberish, wasn't it?

Epiphany arrives like a lead sinker in my stomach. No, she wouldn't be suspicious of a weird foreigner spouting nonsense and wearing flannel shirt and khakis. Nobody here can afford suspicions. Royal chambers have to double as brothels in this guttering pagan economy. And academic, I surmise, whether she's a princess duty-bound to prostitute herself, or a palace courtesan leased out to every visitor.

This isolated outpost of a relict world, this pariah town on the edge of Christendom, is one tremor, one hurricane shy of final inundation. Please let it be now, to abort this excruciating situation! She bares rotten teeth again and, with faint sigh as if I couldn't be denser or more bashful, spreads her knees in unmindful imitation of profane soapstone fetish and hikes white gown with both hands above her hips.

At first I assume she's partial to a Dark Age equivalent of fishnet hose. And then to flinch away is no longer an option, though I hate myself for gaping horrorstruck. From shoeless feet to naked loins, a scabrous disease like none I've ever seen mars profuse swaths of creamy skin. Overlapping ranks of brittle, black-tipped flakes recall the scales of water moccasins or salmon, as if she's undergoing piecemeal transformation into marine species.

Her womanhood per se isn't visibly afflicted, and she persists in smiling sweetly, as if intact womanhood is all that matters, and her fingers perform a salacious, kneading dance with bunches of her kilted gown. She's prepared to wait the whole night for me, isn't she?

Already, though, encouraging smile is tightening toward sardonic rigor, and in the blue pools of her eyes wild insanity begins to surface. Whether staving it off or in submission to it, she croons a nigh inaudible tune, with the maudlin contours of an Irish lullaby.

I can't allow that singing to go on. I'm sorry she's trapped in such untenable straits, which doesn't imply I'm willing to be trapped with her. My panic rapidly escalates. She's a prostitute, right? She might desist if I pay her, yeah, but paper money won't exist for a thousand years. I trawl around left hip pocket for every coin and scoop out pennies, nickels, Euros, dimes.

Now what? I don't dare venture closer, especially as stifled sobs intrude on whiny melody at ever briefer intervals. With shaky arm I aim a gentle underhand pitch at the upholstery beside her. Jangly cluster lands bursting at her feet instead, and roughly fourteen cents rebound against her midcalf scales. Her shriek could put a banshee to shame, and I've scarcely questioned how intercourse could occur amid such sensitivity when she springs at me, still shrilling away, and where the hell had she hidden that silver dagger in upraised fist?

Instinctively I raise protective arm and steel myself to feel defensive wound through flannel sleeve, and then that arm is straining against the bedsheet I've soaked in sweat, and I'm thankful to wake where no one cares if a guest is screaming for his mother at 2 P.M.

Am I packing to avoid overhauling this derelict hotel and kowtowing evermore to obnoxious tourists, or to be shut of dismal Ys and grotesque princess whore? Moot point. Circumspect knocking extends the option of answering the door or not. "Come in!" I yell while stuffing dirty laundry into a plastic bag, and there's Kervigo. Who else?

He blinks at open suitcase on the bed. "You're leaving?" Must I dignify that with an answer? No. Without ado, he clears his throat. "About the defacement of your nightstand . . ." It's as if I'd never brought up buying this shambles of a hotel. Thank God!

"Yes, I'm sorry," I jump in. "I'll pay to have it refinished. Right now, in cash. If you can estimate the cost." Fact is, I'll gladly pay extra to vamoose sooner.

He waves dismissively. No, no, I've understood nothing. "I must criticize how amateurishly you dream. Have any of us ever disturbed you? Whatever happens, our bodies sleep tranquilly and cause no damage or noise." He sighs regretfully, as if compelled to address my halitosis or armpits. "You would be well advised to improve your control."

My look must pose the question I'm too flummoxed to verbalize.

"Yes, we all dream of Ys here, with or without an artifact under the bed. What else could be of importance compared with that?"

With or without an artifact? My heart is racing with redoubled urge to hit the road. Is *Auberge des Falaises* a nest of lucid dreamers, adept beyond the need for talismans, for literal touchstones? Or maybe fungal spores taint the soup, the air, and elicit bedtime delirium, shaped by power of suggestion? What will staffers' brains and lungs be like in ten, twenty years? What of my own health after three days?

I nod deferentially. "I'll be down in a minute to settle up the bill."

He takes the hint, bows a token inch, and lurches out.

Kervigo has said his piece and shows himself no more. Reception is manned solely by a gaunt clerk with droopy eyelids and the balky joints of early-onset rheumatism. Itemized bill does not refer to nightstand damage. At the door I turn for one last glance at forsaken investment opportunity, and the clerk watches my exit with mute indifference, probably because I'm the lobby's single moving object.

Anxious as I am to put miles between the hotel and me, I resolve to enjoy the scenery during headlong quest for saner lodgings. I must have a couple of hours till dusk, and the coast is crawling with accommodations.

Oh, fuck. Penniless fisherman is sitting on the hood of my Renault. He flashes jack-o'-lantern grin. All is ostensibly forgiven? He hops off the car. Better and better. I won't have to deal with passive resistance before speedy getaway.

"Please do not presume to judge us," he greets me. Again, I won't approach too near his cavernous grin. "We who receive a portion of Ys build of it what we will. Yours was not a happy place?"

"No," I barely hear myself say.

He clucks in sympathy or disappointment, I can't decide which. "None of us would want to go on living if we could never enter the glorious city again." I suppress an impulse to ask, Is that good?

His grin shines on, but his sentiments kindle overwhelming sadness in me. He adds nothing more, doesn't lift a finger to detain me as I clump past him into the car and ditch my suitcase on the passenger seat. He can readily see his words have found their mark.

Survivor's guilt rebounds as I follow the signs back toward Carnac. What had been wrong with me to envision Ys only at its bitter end, when others routinely navigate the millennia to its golden age? And how unjust of me and my dreary world to grind along when the magnificence of Ys is drowned and forgotten. I brood about Mom and the lifespan of insights and memories forever lost with her, with any person. For a city, a civilization to die, the loss is incomprehensible, unbearable.

I take a curve along rockbound shore a hair too fast and hear a soft thump as something in back tumbles off the seat. I park to investigate where the shoulder widens just enough to excuse signage about "scenic rest area." Paranoia whispers I have a stowaway as I exit the vehicle and swing rear door open.

I anticipate discovering foxy codger's parting gift of my discarded bluestone. It's much worse. Soapstone fetish with yawning vulva smiles coyly from the polyester carpet, looking not a day older after 1600 years. Absurd to think he had a perfect replica of figment from my dream. In any case, the squalid thing must go. I pluck it up and take aim past guardrail at the breakers pounding boulders.

Spasm between thumb and forefinger locks my grip. Kervigo and crew always seemed to have one foot in dreamland, didn't they? Toward the horizon an island gleams brazen and silver, except where towering white citadel casts a shadow. Is it, and the figurine too, no more than spores in my brain? I lower my arm. Do I also blame spores for removing the guardrail, my car, the highway? And for sowing snaggly pine witchwood all around? I may never know what hit me if I premise otherwise, set off anywhere rather than wait for the hallucination to fade. But suppose spores aren't the problem?

Singsong French draws my attention toward a shoreline yards beyond where it just was. The pensioner's dory is afloat at last, in a high tide of yesteryear. "Come, these waters are calm! Join us, or stand there till you starve."

"How do I know you're for real?" I shout back.

He laughs, and I laugh much more self-consciously. If there's a "real" guardrail ahead, I don't trip over it as I advance, whatever that means. Foxy codger, deliver me where the wine is drinkable and the women aren't deranged! Have I a better choice? In any event, I refuse to view death as a positive outcome.

down the hatch

The house had no cellar. None in the development did, said the abrasively perky realtor. Back in the '70s the builders apparently hadn't considered cellars necessary or modern or worthwhile. Nate was about to bail then and there, till Barbara's toxic look shut his mouth. After the walk-through they conferred out of earshot in the attached garage, though Nate wouldn't put eavesdropping past anyone wearing frosted pink lipstick and mustard blazer with black trim.

Yes, he agreed, they'd already wasted three weeks house-hunting. No, he didn't expect anyplace to be perfect. Yes, yes, he started at the Newport division of Raytheon in two weeks, leaving scant time to fast-track a cash sale, ransom their stuff from storage, and move in. Besides, Barb wasn't the only one running out of patience. Their realtor's corporate smile had become brittle enough to shatter if someone tapped it.

To Nate, ever under non-negotiable workplace pressure to keep secrets and meet deadlines, any extracurricular pressures were too much, a perpetual onslaught of last straws. Giving in was his means of ignoring, of dismissing them. Life was too short for nuisance impositions to drive him batty. He wrote the check for a four-figure deposit.

And weeks later, what would he gain broaching how he'd had the reservations beforehand, but hers was the buyer's remorse now? No sooner was furniture for the "family room" in position than both family members suspected their imaginations of playing tricks. In one corner, rustic black hutch with phone-booth proportions couldn't really be inclined to imitate the Tower of Pisa, nor could sturdy Trinitron TV and striped curtains flanking it really be tilting forward as if toward gravity anomaly. But while Nate and Barb lounged on frayed corduroy sofa watching *Ghost Whisperer*, one of Barb's antique wheeled toys, fortunately not the Pre-Columbian clay dog, rolled into the hutch's glass door. Sharp clink startled the bejesus out of them and set off Barb the avenging Fury.

How dare that little snip of a realtor foist off shoddy workmanship, maybe even a defective foundation, on them? A carpenter's level from the garage confirmed the floor did sag toward its midpoint, not so's anyone whose mind was occupied would notice, but once the fact was out, Barb felt a little more off-balance whenever she crossed the room. Nate failed to mollify her by observing if worst came to worst, they had no cellar to plunge into.

By this time he'd been racking up fifty-hour workweeks and had neither energy nor leisure to make a big deal of a flaw he could, with minimal willpower, shrug off as subliminal. Flex-schedule job as pharmaceuticals rep, meanwhile, allowed Barb opportunity galore to bang her head against the wall of realty company indifference to an off-plumb horizontal. In a Colonial-era cottage, she vented at Nate, that would be one thing, but in a newish ranch house there was no excuse. The realtors might have laughed off her threats of lawsuit, but such long-term, costly prospects terrified Nate, spurring him to the heroic measure of addressing a problem himself.

One way or another, excavating beneath "family room" was per se a remedy, because even if he couldn't find or fix the cause of the sinkage, Barb would have nothing to sue about when the floor no longer existed. Back from Saturday shopping, she was speechless to learn of Nate's unilateral move by catching him prying up floorboards in the middle of the "family room." She saw right through talk of sparing her further realtor-based grief, glowered at passive-aggressive interference with her quest for justice. Why else wouldn't he have warned her what he'd be up to? But what was done, was done.

"Well, since you're busy," she finally declared, "I'll have to put the groceries away myself." Why the hell, he silently fumed, does she have to slap a guilt trip on me whenever I show some initiative? He hefted the crowbar and eyed the next board.

She took off to a sale at Macy's without comment on his discovery of a depression in the loose stone fill between joists, as if the builders had misreckoned how much they'd need. She returned to goggle at a virtual construction site around him, as if with malice aforethought he'd gutted, he'd desecrated, her "family room" and all it represented. Tarps covered furniture, dust polluted the air, floor-boards formed a careless stack, and stones ranging from pebbles to cobbles loaded down a wheelbarrow.

Kneeling beside a gap like an extra crinkly outline of the Chevy insignia, aglow with childish excitement, sweaty, grubby Nate announced, "The floor only dipped because there weren't enough stones underneath. Just part of the house settling."

"Then why are you taking more out instead of adding to them?" She was genuinely curious, which made her even madder, as he'd brought her into conflict with herself, with her competing urges to demand when he'd clean this up and how they were supposed to watch TV later. Last week's *Ghost Whisperer* had been the first of a two-parter!

"C'mere, c'mere and look!" he enthused. "At first I thought this used to be a French drain or something because the ground around it was like a funnel, but then I recognized it's a well, must be centuries old, a big hunk of antiquity, and it's all ours! You like antiques!"

How she wished for a simple verbal hatpin to pop his manic balloon on occasions like this. Antiquity on the scale of toys, yes, fine, but this much was too intrusive, out of proportion, threatening to her and her cherished serene domesticity.

"It's an honest-to-God mystery," he raved on. "I must've told you, my family vacationed in Newport when I was a kid. I'm familiar with this area. I remember going by this spot where we're standing now, and it was all cornfields, no houses, and then one summer it was this development instead. What the hell was a well doing out in the middle of the corn?"

Barb hadn't the foggiest, couldn't deign to frame a reply, surveyed topsy-turvy chamber of horrors and her fantasies resorted to an atomizer full of discouragement to quench overexuberant fire in Nate's eyes. This wasn't the Raytheon exec she'd married. This schlub couldn't have earned security clearance in a million years. She did, as proof to them both that she really still loved him, approach the damn pit and peek in, composing placid expression to mask inner turmoil.

Oh Christ, how many barrows of rock must he have trundled away already, and to where? This incongruity of ancient well in ruptured modern floor conjured an image of round peg in square hole, but the masonry was in nowise primitive or hamfisted. Precisely circular brim consisted of paving stones fit tightly without mortar, of a diameter that could have swallowed a sumo wrestler. And below the rim, or at least in that rubble-free zone to the depth of a koi pond, the wall was of rough flinty chunks that all the same projected expertise, unity, permanence.

She stepped back briskly as from the edge of a bottomless, inevitable descent. "I want to send out for Thai food. How long till you empty the wheelbarrow and remove the tarps and vacuum the floor?" Mustering every ounce of forbearance, she spoke in monotone, proud of smoothing inflections that would have read as inflammatory, as admission of distaste at treating breadwinner husband like a difficult child.

During lemongrass chicken and red curry shrimp, they arrived at a truce, without stooping to sympathy for each other's viewpoints. Resolved, he had leave to delve when she was gone pushing drugs, for three days consecutive at most. Resolved, before said delving resumed, he would replace the crevasse in the room (tomorrow, preferably) with a hatch, subject to her approval vis-à-vis looks and safety. Resolved, he would quarry no more than ten feet down or until help was necessary, with strict taboo on showing or describing the well to anyone. What a nightmare if people blabbed and the state busted in with archaeologists and the media and goodbye suburban tranquility!

Nate was mordantly gratified that she was giving in, she had to give in to some degree, by dint of implicit blackmail. If he confided in more sympathetic ear than hers about indoors dig, news would spread eventually—like mold or cellar damp, it always did—and the house would become uninhabitable. And speaking of cellar damp, the hatch was admittedly a good idea, because earthy, fungal, slightly acrid vapors were mingling already with the sachet of the upper air.

Honestly, he wasn't sorry he'd fortuitously hemmed her in, and he abstained from hypocritically putting her at ease. It served her right, goddammit, reflexively cold-shouldering him when he tried

sharing his excitement about this incredible find, to bring them closer together by the one route currently available. No kidding they had
communication issues. He hated how his life from 9-to-5 (hell, 8-to-
6) was classified, precluding normal marital chitchat that began,
"How was work today?" Yet here she was with snooty attitude, making of his curiosity, his wonderment, another wall between them.

Okay then, let the deception proceed; he wasn't the sort of asshole to outright violate the terms of their bargain. That would be abject. But there was the hatch, constant reminder of her lack of
interest in his project, in any revelation pertaining thereto. As such,
she'd never be the wiser, would never raise the lid to learn he'd
cleared ten feet of shaft and kept digging. He'd compromised no secrets ordering zip line and portable winch from Amazon.

When specifying "ten feet down or till help was necessary," Barb
may have entertained ten feet as unlikely maximum, so she had only
lack of vision to blame as he slowly, laboriously, single-handedly
sank the shaft to fifteen, twenty, twenty-five feet. Maybe from that
insidiously rising cairn in the backyard he could someday construct a
wall to replace their rickety stockade fence, another home-front undertaking whose symbolism he alone would know or care to know.

Nate passed as much of his solitude sitting on the lip, inhaling
the funk of history, dangling his legs in the cool effluvium, as he did
hoisting bucketloads. Like his professional self, here was a repository
of secrets, but where his were stifling and overly technical, its were
enticing, invigorating. Ironic, how apropos the poor air quality below
would be for the atmosphere of repressive groupthink in his office.

Some part of Barb's soul must have been missing for her to see
nothing save a threat to mundane, anal tidiness in this mother lode of
mysteries, among which the age of construction was merely the most
obvious. Had the cornfields of his boyhood expunged a farmstead of
the 1700s or even 1600s? Or was he tunneling toward a break-
through that would rewrite the textbooks, vindicate one outsider
theorist or another, and how in good conscience could he then honor
any vow of silence? Hah. He'd have to burn that bridge when he
came to it.

Scraps of info floated to mind like pronouncements in a Magic 8-
Ball. A century before the Pilgrims planted bootprints on Plymouth

Rock, the Portuguese, on the evidence of rusty breech-cannon and basket hilt unearthed by a plowshare, had allegedly sojourned in Narragansett Bay and with missionary zeal erected a church whose eight-arched round tower still presides in Newport. Some diehards, though, persisted in assigning the tower to Norse builders, making it the heart of Vinland, inspiring sundry Viking-themed businesses including a hotel, tux rental, and liquor store. Then again, validating one marginal faction meant refuting others, and Nate didn't relish bursting mythic bubbles that made harmless crackpots happy.

And a month along, he was empathizing with those crackpots because he seemed to be experiencing their putative loopy, untethered mentality. Barb's road trips rarely involved weekends, forcing Nate to open the hatch after long workdays, chronic sleep deficit and fatigue resulting. He did his insufficient utmost to catch up on rest while slaving in perhaps bottomless pit by depleting sick days and personal days, guiltily chipping away at vacation days (but in fairness, Barb hadn't said not to). He pondered the broader significance of wife and coworkers acting none the wiser as he, a conspicuous staggering wreck, went through the motions of normality.

Thirty feet down, spatters of ossified, tawny clay on the stones had proliferated into hateful matrix. Further gains were twice as exhausting as he had to moisten and gouge and chisel at each square inch, snapping two trowels in frustration. The clay, he decided, was good at least for hinting he'd soon hit bottom, and he psyched himself inflating the antiquity of the well, speculating on how many centuries it must have taken for the water table to drop this much.

Whatever the answer, foul claustrophobic shaft as ex-landscape feature, as part of bigger human context, had lain unsuspected for ages. How fully, he mused, do people ever grasp the character, the identity, of their countryside, and how do buried truths affect them and their modern surroundings? One way or another, did the presence, the nature of forgotten habitations influence the developers to dispense with cellars in the 1970s? Damn, but this lousy air was making him philosophical. His trowel, right then, scraped against rough metal in the clay, derailing his reflective train of thought.

He painstakingly sliced around long straight artifact with his trowel and tugged it loose in its jacket of clay. But some wariness or scruples or just plain stupor wouldn't let him transfer it from the glare of cubical LED lamp to the milder light of day till he'd pared away the jacket and picked off clinging flecks and stared quizzically till he realized he held the entirety of an object and not a fragment.

No fancy Portuguese hilt helped define this crude ironmongery as a sword, with lopsided, lumpish grip and snippet of wheel rim, perhaps, for a guard. Its shoddiness would have insulted a child, though this had been a full-grown pauper's excuse for a weapon, judging by the manifest effort invested in welding fractional blades into snaggle-edged composite. Its rust resembled welts and eczema, cosmetic flaws Nate couldn't correct without risk of graver damage.

Was he giddy with excitement or creeped out at this sordid relic, or were the rotten fumes getting to him? If only to restore emotional clarity, he rode the zip line up, sword tucked in his belt. Unscrolling paper towels for a placemat between nasty prize and dining room table, he waited in vain for more orderly feelings. Say that past events colored a locale's present, subconsciously impinged on behaviors or decisions of later generations, what did concealment of a makeshift tool ideal for very sloppy murder suggest about neighborhood ambience now?

In a city, he elaborated, too many incidents, public and private, accumulated for even a plague or nuclear blast to dictate the personality, the spirit of a place overall. But in ranch-style suburbia, with fewer formative strata, drilling peepholes through the terrain toward key moments, as Nate had done, was more feasible, leading him to extrapolate more sweeping cri-de-coeur, *Where are we ever, really?* Subjectively, what more is the heart of a place than the effect it exerts? Of course, in 99.9% of cases, the citizens are in utter ignorance of whatever's shaping them from belowground, from the past.

Patchwork sword on the table served as anchor, as reminder, unsavory or not, of where he really was, for those golden hours till Barb returned. She'd scarcely kicked off her sensible flats when Nate dragged her into the dining room for show-and-tell. Voilà, exhibit A, alias last-ditch effort to sell her on the value, the magic, of their pit in the family room. Yes, unsavory as the artifact was, such that his eyes and fingers had given it wide berth, she had to focus past that, on the richness of history, the promise of revolutionary discoveries still trapped in clay and debris.

Was she blind? Into simple gesture of unclipping tortoiseshell barrette from brunette ponytail she crammed years of exasperation. His disgusting piece of trash, she decreed, was no more a real sword than he was a real archaeologist. Hadn't this play-acting gone on long enough? She assumed he functioned as an adult at Raytheon. He had to summon no less maturity here, or did he take her less seriously than his supervisors? Did home rate less respect than defense contract? And for Godsakes, we eat at that table! Put your filthy thing where I don't have to look at it, before it makes someone sick.

Every time she came back, he'd been more slipshod cleaning up from moonlighting as a mole, flouting their agreement. Strip of rust on the table marked the frontier of her tolerance. She laid down the law and parsed the unabashed shock and disbelief on his face as spoiled, childish. That rockpile out back was going right down the hatch again, and then they'd plug the well with cement and install wall-to-wall carpeting, before something costlier than a vaguely sagging floor happened. Nate, despite red-cheeked dissent, didn't pick an argument, as usual, and Barb wavered as usual between relief and contempt.

To Barb, the hatch amounted to a manhole cover, and by analogy, the contents, the insights within were excrement. That made Nate's "strip of rust" an overrun border, a battle line, no, a Maginot line whose inevitable ruination he'd delay with skirmish and guerrilla tactics. Direct confrontation was unthinkable amidst his "new normal" of bleary, lurching weariness, his low reserves of *compos mentis*. What's more, Barb had fired the starting gun of a virtual "race to the bottom," its course of unknown duration because she hadn't specified when her hirelings would start tromping in. He sure as hell wasn't lifting a finger, not in her service anyway.

Worst-case scenario haunted him wherein the well was bottomless and he could never exhume its truths, as if arrival at an endpoint guaranteed enlightenment. But that endpoint was inches from the tip of his grubbing trowel, an article of faith reinforced by archaic sword enshrined in his socks drawer, and to debate whether he betrayed the letter of a covenant by going for broke in Barb's absence would be a waste of conscience.

Why not laugh out loud when his trowel poked through clay and sounded a startling dull clink? He'd had a boring, stressful workday, spontaneous hilarity was always good medicine, and no one was in earshot, not thirty-plus feet down! Unbidden gales of mirth racked him at odd intervals as he heaved and scrabbled and hacked at the final detritus. All too soon those gales died wheezing ingloriously, along with hopes of more finds coming to light, as he exposed a floor of loose-fitting flagstones.

Yes, here was proverbial, barren rock bottom. Or was it? The paving impressed him as artless, impromptu, no hardship to pry up and check beneath, and if he didn't exploit this perhaps once-in-a-lifetime chance, he'd always regret it. Leveraging the trowel blade to pop the seal between dry clay and slab was surprisingly tough, and tougher as he went along, but in mocha sediment under the fourth slate were three low chalky protrusions, one larger than the other two, like bubbles beginning to surface. The joy burst cackling from him again.

During this crucial, grueling extraction of pearls from dross, anxiety steadily eclipsed his joy at the potential, however remote, for wife's return ahead of schedule as he slogged away in his own private netherworld. Dammit, she didn't even have to be home to be a killjoy. He slammed on the brakes, slowed his breathing, and continued more heedfully after reminding himself of Sydney Greenstreet frantically chipping at counterfeit Maltese Falcon. Not till calm prevailed did it register that the caulked-up eye sockets of a human skull were goggling back at him.

He'd suspected as much at first sight of the protrusion, had banked on no less from day 1, but had to shudder at sudden close quarters with a death's head, and the skin of his hand clutching it had to crawl, while the other hand dutifully picked at encrustations. Don't forget, this formerly belonged to a person! And what the hell had happened to that person to have wound up, at least in part, beneath the bottom of a well, and what about the rest of him?

Nate had ferreted skull and unspecified second bone, still in block of matrix, from under the last flagstone he could conveniently upend. On the remaining few weighed the heap of cobbles and clay he'd tossed aside, and he lacked the energy to gamble that reshifting the heap would be worthwhile. Anyway, why be greedy? He already had fodder for rumination galore.

Lower jaw, for example, was missing, along with a circle the size of a Mason jar lid on one side of the cranium. A smart-alecky smile rose as he inferred, Here was pure skullduggery. How, though, to pin down the exact interplay of brutality, sin, and victimhood through the haze of conjecture? He earnestly regarded defleshed face as if communing with it. Oh, to be an anthropologist or antiquarian, versed in listening to cues whispered by the dead! His throat tickled, and a coughing spell landed a gob of black phlegm inches from his loafers. Ugh! High time he adjourned up top, to environs friendlier to lungs and brain.

Word of his little ossuary was strictly between himself and the socks drawer. Barb he didn't notify about going down the hatch at all, which qualified as a courtesy really, since she was less than uninterested in updates. She, meanwhile, hadn't been forthcoming about day of reckoning for his window onto the abyss, her luck hiring laborers. The option of inquiring point-blank he vetoed as provocative. He'd either hear news he'd rather not or jog her into cementing plans she'd let slide. The atmosphere grew altogether as cloying and repellent as the pit's, too toxic for barrels of sachet to alleviate.

He'd have been no less impolitic to demand when she'd be hitting the road again. Christ almighty, was she home between trips this many days just to torment him? He was itching to descend once more at least, though clueless about what he'd do down there. And come the weekend, he spent hours in the bedroom, for as long as she was elsewhere in the house puttering or bustling or whatever. It defused the tension, he theorized, and perhaps reduced his blood pressure.

He gently transferred rescued skull and that other bone, which had proved to be a tibia, from drawer to bedside nightstand, and contemplated them like a monk from dimly remembered medieval painting. After flaking away lingering accretions, he detected parallel trios and quartets of thin, shallow strokes at 10 and 4 o'clock relative to the hole in the skull, and a thumb's width from the knobby ends of the tibia.

He left off chomping at Saturday lunch of pulled pork sandwich from Whole Foods when mental search latched onto matching footage of these knife marks from Science Channel or PBS or one of a thousand websites. Such signs of shearing meat off bone, whether impelled by famine or ritual, bespoke butchery, cannibalism. Nate spaced out trying to link osteologic forensics with particular docudramas on Neanderthals or Anasazi or survivors of Donner wagon train or Andean plane crash, till that jawless, skinless face, now gaping horrorstruck in his empathic estimation, begged for attention, pity, some salvaging of selfhood, redemption from oblivion.

But was he in a position to promise it anything? Plundering the pit had produced less fodder for rumination than he'd anticipated. He couldn't even vouch for open-and-shut connection of homemade sword with lacerations. Jerry-rigged weapon, a mere few centimeters longer than the tibia, would scarcely have been equal to punching or sawing a cavity out of the cranium, and did that cavity delineate deathblow or postmortem access to a delicacy? Calcium brow and nose and row of teeth seemed more horrorstricken than ever.

If recovered mementoes of trauma were like dowsing rods for the underlying character of a place, what did cannibal leftovers portend for Nate's "bedroom community"? Footage from a slow news night emerged from the Magic 8-Ball of his memories, about moss that revived and flourished after 400 dormant years under a Canadian glacier. How long could the chemical remnants of stress and aggression, the psychic aftermath of murder, survive underground to infect unwitting vectors? Would it be fair to prosecute the misdeeds of those vectors? The sword might have been wielded and discarded under the mute urging of blood already decades old in the muck from which broken skull had stared up.

Nate was acquainted with none of the neighbors, may have crossed their paths unbeknownst time and again at the market or mall. Who could second-guess what went on in their bungalows? No, he could only speak, and with woefully limited authority, of evil tidings on his own premises. And speak of the devil, Barb's Forester pulled into the driveway and parked right outside the bedroom window. Damn her! When had she gone? If she'd said something on her way out, he needn't have stayed cooped up for the duration.

Besides, wherever did she get off laying down the law with him? Values, priorities in collision underpinned their grudges toward each other, and Nate was absolutely positive he was on the side of the angels and acting at the behest of, for the sake of, his soul. His was a crusade for justice, no matter how belated or imprecise. The Forester door slammed like a thunderclap. Hers, meanwhile, was a crusade under the auspices of *Good Housekeeping* at best, and partook of nothing more cerebral or profound than slamming that car door.

In pursuing her shamelessly cosmetic, skin-deep goals, she'd committed herself to literally covering up (wall-to-wall), rejecting, insulting the truth of this place, its suffering and tragedy, the sheer, dizzying fathoms of hidden ages to be illuminated by scholarship, tales of atrocity and perdition to stimulate the popular imagination. Those tales were properly the public's, and neither he nor Barb had any license to sequester them, no more than anyone had the license to sequester history. Through bedroom wall he heard the muffled slam of front door, as if it were worlds more distant than the driveway.

Damned if it wasn't Nate's turn to lay down the law. At work he ate, breathed, and drank reticence, self-censorship, compartmentalization, and he'd no longer submit to the home version of that regimen. He had to get it through wifely noggin that their prior contract was null and void. What were peace and cleanliness next to sharing his paradigm shift with humanity? He idly hefted game-changing skull like a blunt instrument.

Eureka! There in hand was unbeatable argument for "going public." Human remains made home sweet home a crime scene, imposing legal obligation to phone authorities. Brandishing skull and tibia, Nate charged from the bedroom. He harbored guarded optimism Barb would listen to reason, and if she didn't, then shit, that was one more bridge to burn when he came to it. She was in the kitchen, toasting a cheese bagel, and hadn't had the common decency to ask if he'd also wanted one. Never mind that his appetite had run aground at tip-offs of cannibal feast.

Barb directed disapproving frown at Nate, milky-eyed on the kitch-
en floor, breadknife straight up in his throat, and then at the dirty
skull, across the checkered linoleum where it had rolled when con-
vulsing Nate had jettisoned it. What the hell had been wrong with
him, to barge in yammering and getting in her face with those squalid dead things? She had to skewer him, could picture no alternative,
nothing at any rate felt as irresistibly fitting. And though tomorrow
was astronomically distant, she was uncannily clearheaded about today. Whiff of scorching bagel from the toaster oven alerted her to
pull the plug.

A ton of heavy lifting, more or less, was in the foreseeable offing.
The source of all this neck-deep unpleasantness, this pesthole in her
tidy nest, had to be destroyed, and having it done right meant doing
it herself, she'd learned that much from grievous decade with Nate.
The sooner she started, the sooner she'd have her serenity back, and
that would supplant the fever unsteadying her vision, the jitters in
her stomach. My God, his mess had spread right up to the rear fence!
She'd be up all night schlepping wheelbarrows of rubble and dumping them down that cesspit.

But first, rationality dictated she chuck skull and that other bone
and so-called sword into perdition, and Nate as well. Oh, and that
ridiculous mountaineering equipment for dicking around below sea
level, what ridiculous irony. And add a plug for good measure, yes,
she'd have to research mixing concrete. She grinned waspishly. Nate
wasn't the only one who could keep secrets.

Sad about the breadknife, though, pretty much her favorite piece
of cutlery. Would a gusher follow if she set her heel on Nate's forehead and yanked on oaken handle? Heck, she already had a pool of
blood to mop up—what did another pint matter? The worst part
proved to be dislodging the business end from between his verte-
brae, and she likened it to a rite of passage, a minor-scale variant on
Excalibur, entitling her to rule the roost.

Hurray, only a sluggish gob welled from the wound, and how
about that, crumbs of whole-wheat and dill Havarti still clung as if
for dear life to the serrations. Come to think of it, she was starving.
Initially the temptation to sample combo of cheese and bread and
blood revolted her, but was it really so gross, from the broader per-

spective of husband lying there cold and stiff and oozing from auxiliary mouth?

She had no inkling where change of heart originated, but suddenly she saw no cause to disobey the impulse to go on, try a lick, just a little taste, establish whether she liked it, before doing anything irrevocable with the body. As if receiving sacrament, she brought the blade to her lips and stretched out her tongue toward the thickest blood on the dull side.

we are made of stars

He keeps the world as his disguise ... The leader of the starry skies ...
—Tim Smith of Cardiacs

Ira wasted no sympathy on the hack from the Preservation Commission. Photo op or no, who wore three-piece Armani to man a power washer? And with foolhardy bare hands? In sensible navy-blue jumpsuits, Ira and his DPW duo stayed upwind (as did the *Journal* reporter and cameraman) of clumsy assault on defiantly indelible graffiti "We are made of stars" above an illegible signature. From misapplied nozzle billowed a cloud of agitated droplets, and jets ricocheted everywhere.

The gray granite wall of St. John's Cathedral was 200-plus years old, and magenta scribble bloomed beside a padlocked, weathered side door. When laden breeze shifted perilously, the onlookers backed farther among the churchyard's worn and broken gravestones, in even sadder shape than the cathedral. The property had been vacant for months, victim of shrinking congregation and untenable upkeep, a candidate for the wrecking ball. Preservation Commission gesture of solidarity with the Mayor's Graffiti Taskforce was a classic case of too little, too late.

Too bad about historic architecture like this, but why get all sentimental? Progress and omelets alike demanded some breakage, did they not? Meanwhile, the dapper, sopping idiot persevered with pneumatic blaster to laughable effect, and the photographer angled for a spray-free shot, like a jackal angling for a one-eyed wildebeest's blind side.

Wandering attention led Ira's eyes around the cemetery, in its artificial hollow bound south, east, and north by church wall, field-

41

stone retaining wall, and a nursing home. Atop seven-foot retaining wall was a railed promenade accessible to more active seniors, several of whom glumly surveyed the compressor-powered spectacle. A male orderly in turquoise was rubbernecking too, and over everyone's shoulders peered a passerby from off Benefit Street, an artistic type, hardly unusual with RISD four blocks down. Detached, hipper-than-thou demeanor gave him away. In Ira he instantly triggered feelings of affinity and resentment.

He could have passed for Ira's prodigal self, dropping by from parallel universe to taunt him. Same rough age, height, photogray lenses. Skin-deep differences between them Ira chalked up to *plein air* versus deskbound lifestyles. Prodigal self, beneath brown leather jacket, was concave where Ira was convex. Prodigal's sun-kissed tan in April made Ira self-conscious of year-round doughy white, and flippant silver forelock mocked Ira's receded hairline. Hell, the teenage Ira had harbored decidedly artistic leanings, but nobody had to tell him he'd be a damn sight safer majoring in business.

Impatient tap on the shoulder restored him to bleak reality. The two damp, fed-up newshounds were violating his personal space. They'd gotten what they came for, the writer mouthed over the roar of compressor. Goodbye! The so-called preservationist was still at it, venting mercifully private frustrations on unyielding spray paint. Ira signaled his crew to kill the noise. When high-pressure stream conked out, overdressed shoulders slumped as if a trance had lifted. Neo-yuppie turned stiffly, and fastidious beard sparkled with beaded-up water as he wailed, "I'm all wet!"

And dude, you're the last to notice, thought Ira, who said instead, "We're parked in the church lot down on North Main. Should be a towel on the passenger seat."

Photo opportunist's glower projected silent accusation he'd been tricked into dousing himself. Where was civilization headed, Ira pondered, with this level of chronic mistrust between private and public sectors? "Thanks. The Commission's around the corner. I'll change there," victim demurred in frostiest patrician monotone. Cloaked in bruised and shivering dignity, hands red and raw, he tromped up brick path to stone staircase up to the promenade and then Benefit Street.

Ira beckoned at his Taskforce, lounging on tabletop tombs. "Let's show our fans how it's done." During inch-by-inch erasure of "We are made of stars," Ira puzzled at such artsy sentiment's appeal to a delinquent. The audience, including his bothersome, mismatched doppelgänger, had dispersed from the railing when next Ira checked.

By the evening rush, smudgy column of smoke presiding over downtown would have apprised Commission twit his self-promotion had been wasted, even if he'd missed that thud like a piledriver impact, followed by sirens. Damn, it's happened again, mulled Ira during ten o'clock news, not the least heartbroken that everyone would ignore the item about St. John's, assuming the *Journal* ran it at all. Nor could he muster shock at latest attack, only mild surprise at how readily citizens adjusted to a semblance of life in wartime.

Third local pipe bomb this month had destroyed the gondola shed under the footbridge at Waterplace Park. And with what result? Expensive boats were reduced to toothpicks, concrete bridge over the lazy Woonasquatucket had withstood the blast handsomely, and several minor casualties were receiving treatment for lacerations and tinnitus. The park was usually depopulated past mid-afternoon, based on enduring rep as a good place to get mugged, except on WaterFire nights, when too many suburbanites clogged streets and parking facilities.

Yes, the incident would wreak havoc with biweekly WaterFires, or Campfires on the Canal as Ira had it, when the gondoliers were busiest and stacks of hardwood in midstream rows of iron baskets went to blazes. City councilmen vowed on camera they'd approve special funds to rectify this cowardly act of terror. For prize tourist bait, Ira sourly observed, money always solidified up some magic sleeve, but termites were welcome to the 200-year-old wainscoting of historic landmarks.

So in whose manifesto was bombing gondolas an ideological goal? And with zero body count and no serious disruption? Previous sabotage had been equally random, stupid, and thus far untraceable, and Ira was happier than ever to be out of the homeland security loop. He was unclear whether the mayor had dubbed him Graffiti Czar as an honorific or a joke, and didn't care, content to rule his little roost of DPW loaners and two vanloads of cleaning equipment. Let more ambitious politicos risk fucking up where it actually mattered.

In windowless excuse for a corner office, Ira slogged through morning review of voicemail, with near-even ratio of complaints about graffiti and misdirected tirades about potholes. Between peevish messages, he overheard coworkers beyond his partitions react to yesterday's explosion. Their tone rapidly escalated from fretful to rabid, and he stopped listening when a proposal to summarily execute foreign agitators met with cheers.

He'd plead guilty to his fair share of heated discussions, talking trash, around the water cooler. But such outright bloodlust, no, never! This new conversational norm made him cringe, as if people were losing their inhibitions, their judgment, like a milder version of the impulsiveness behind cretinous trend to plant bombs. Or maybe he wasn't exempt from bad graces on the rise. Maybe he could have offered that Preservation Commission clown some pointers on using a power washer. It just hadn't occurred to him.

Then again, absurd targets were blowing up daily in cities worldwide, as if terrorism had been dumbed down, rendered apolitical. That should have been enough to put everyone on edge everywhere, despite most sanguine adjustments to "life in wartime." The mayhem hurdled national, cultural, and religious boundaries like wildfire over white picket fences, too scattershot to blame on copycats or any one organization.

Given the global situation, Ira was grateful for an HQ on the sidelines and off extremist radar, by Allens Avenue waterfront south of downtown, in a city hangar smelling of gasoline, rubber, and paint. This was particularly okay because a faint, embarrassing air of camphor always clung to him, and he was more at ease in pungent surroundings than at City Hall, regardless of loud maintenance on sander and street-sweeping trucks.

Anyway, Ira couldn't wax too pessimistic at grisly headlines. Every generation since Plato's had proclaimed its officials most corrupt, its youth most irresponsible, its ideals most debased, its criminals most heinous. And how often have Jehovah's Witnesses alone had to revise their date for doomsday? No sooner does prophetic handwriting on the wall fade from sight and mind than it reappears, as if for the first time every time, Ira concluded.

He happened to be staring at the crappy linoleum, as if subjecting it to X-ray vision, probing into its past when dispatcher's or mechanic's station might have occupied this corner. The cracked and scuffed flooring was black, with haphazard off-white whorls and ripples like froth on a creek or cobwebs in a drafty cellar or gas clouds adrift in cosmic void. Yes, that was it. Those clouds, he'd heard somewhere, were the last gasp of defunct suns, or the first stirring of nascent suns, or both.

What the hell were they called? Simple English escaped him, even as the cracks and scuff marks faded and a planetarium's illusion of depth surrounded him. He tried to wrap his head around the enormities of distance he'd have to travel to float within that starscape, the enormities of time in which dust became suns and then dust again. Somehow it didn't faze him to dwell on light-years and eons, nor was it strange that these spans weren't intimidating. He felt at home, in fact, within this daydream of deep space.

After a vacant while, the ringing phone brought him down to earth. He reached for the receiver slowly, dreamily, as if under the spell of lingering weightlessness. At the mayor's voice he snapped to attention. His Honor ordered him to drop everything and skedaddle downtown to fix some goddamn graffiti on the Superman Building.

Superman Building was an utter misnomer, but who cared? Since Ira's boyhood at least, Rhode Islanders had cherished the myth of Art Deco skyscraper as model for one version or another of the *Daily Planet* offices, and nothing could disabuse them of it. Might as well try insisting "spa" didn't rhyme with "star." For eight decades, bigger and bigger banks had tenanted the state's tallest high-rise, till the biggest bank in America pulled out and left it like St. John's, derelict and ripe for demolition.

Tagger had scorned unchallenging street level and bas-relief frieze (for which he'd have needed a ladder) of city founder Roger Williams befriending Indians and securing a charter and other iconic highlights. Rather, he'd made straight for the tippy-top, abetted by B&E or human-fly skills, and was obviously the same artiste who'd profaned empty church, because along the entablature below cylindrical cupola was scrawled "We are made of stars." Naturally the mayor was furious. The view of vandalism from his window would have hit him like a magenta slap in the face. Was that the artistic intent?

With leaden heart Ira grimaced upward, deaf to schoolkids and geezers milling around, waiting for buses in scruffy Kennedy Plaza. To undo this product of daring, stealth, and spray paint, Ira had to requisition scaffolding, safety harnesses, netting, and how the hell much else? The mayor would have to cut a lot of red tape, fast-track a lot of permits. Still, based on His Honor's displeasure, Ira was confident of men on the job by noon.

Mayoral ego they could salvage, sure, but the outlook for Superman Building was more doubtful. For Ira's money, graffiti on abandoned property always contained a subtext that solvent couldn't remove. It marked a place as unprotected, vulnerable, the brick-and-mortar equivalent of a sick, lame critter ready to cull from the herd. Sad it had to be the Superman Building, and the repetition of high-flown text irrelevant to the wall it marred was mystifying.

As expected, fully tricked-out Taskforce was soon hustling to the twenty-eighth floor, and by 4:30 the masonry was verbiage-free. Funny how fast the wheels of power spun when self-image was at stake. His Honor, of course, was home long before then, and would mayoral short-term memory extend to thanking Ira tomorrow? In any case, the cupboard in Ira's apartment was bare, so he scouted downtown for a menu within modest civil-servant budget.

He paused at the corner of seedy Washington and Mathewson Streets, leery of presenting a stationary target to panhandlers or worse. Wasn't some organic, local-ingredients eatery hereabouts? Down Mathewson, a mixed company of well-dressed thirty-somethings, with white collars or shiny necklaces, was filing through a doorway. That looked promising. The façade surrounding the doorway was of beige tiles with a sculpted row of blue cresting waves at tiptoe level, which Ira followed past the point of no return, to find himself gawking through picture window at a gallery opening, AKA refreshments gratis. Why not?

The stoop was surfaced in black marble, as was the length of the foundation. It caught Ira's eye and induced brief vertigo. In the black were white veins, webbed and swirling like the linoleum in his cubicle, like the seething stellar gas whose glow wouldn't reach the Earth for a million years. Steady there!

He wrenched his focus toward the unframed canvases beyond the glass. They only unsettled him further. The walls were like windows onto night skies, where stars clotted together as if between folded hands, or were strewn in irregular clusters, on the verge of resolving into patterns purely in the mind of the beholder maybe, like something by Jackson Pollock. These contorted heavens were somehow perverse, sinister, but mostly confounding because their exquisite stippling, their subtle infusions of red and blue and yellow, had been executed in spray paint. Ira would recognize that generally crude medium anywhere.

Refocusing on plate glass an inch from his nose depressurized him till he discovered upon it the press-type lettering "Signs of the Times" above an illegible signature in presumably water-soluble magenta. Were all scribbles too alike to differentiate, or had he erased this one twice in as many days? Out the corner of his eye he glimpsed a pair of upscale hipsters smirking at him on their way in. He shut his gaping mouth and steeled himself. If the culprit was right here and Ira oafishly slunk away, he'd never live it down.

The space behind the glass amounted to an anteroom with a massive reception desk, or did bank of shallow drawers for artwork make it a storage unit where an attendant sat? Anyhow, upon it stood an artist's statement in a clear holder, and Ira skimmed as far as, "My true name is the unreadable name on my work. To reveal it would cede power to others, and moreover, the human larynx cannot pronounce it."

Yep, in each lower right corner was a unique miniature of the magenta squiggle, an insanely narrow-gauge use of the spray can, in keeping with that possibly calculated insanity of the artist's statement. Through square arch was a windowless inner sanctum with more paintings and, with any luck, wine and food.

First, though, title labels below each image might lend insights into the painter as madman, or better yet, as perp. Shuffling along, Ira crinkled despairing brow. "Pack Up Your Troubles"? "Everything Must Go"? "Game Over"? Names were as unrelated to compositions as graffiti had been to historic walls. "The Stars Are Soon Right"? Aha, connection with the subject matter at last, but as usual with modern art, Ira didn't get it.

"It Had to End Sometime." That arrested him, that threw him, as when a passing stranger snickered at his orthopedic Crocs. It had preternaturally singled him out, a rejoinder to earlier musings on the countless postponements of doomsday. He shrank from the label as if that were the same as disowning his outbreak of magical thinking.

Oops! How the hell had someone snuck up behind him, and he none the wiser? He recoiled from jarring contact, with the keenness of repulsion between like magnetic charges. "Sorry," he mumbled, and turned to meet emotional short-circuit. Part of him was shocked, and part was too ready, to confront yesterday's Bohemian from the parapet.

Had the Bohemian bowed more curtly, Ira would have mistaken it for a tic, and he grasped whose reception this was even without benefit of introduction. "An honor to be in the crosshairs of my specialty's most outspoken critic. Call me Ari, why don't you?"

Ira's mental short-circuit sputtered on. How much, if anything, had this Ari just admitted, if that was his birth name? Ira fumbled for words like a skydiver for a misplaced ripcord. "What do you know about that graffiti you saw me erase?"

"I know it was unimportant once it served its purpose." As Ari shifted his blasé weight from right foot to left, tight leather pants squeaked. Ira hated leather pants. "I know you shouldn't fritter away the time we have left."

Jesus, what to address first, the graffiti's "purpose," or "the time we have left"? Ira was still foundering when a plump girl with armloads of jangly bracelets and blue streaks in blond dreadlocks steered the exhibitor away by the puffy sleeve, whispering about a buyer. She betrayed no awareness Ira existed.

Stress was loosing that musk of camphor from his pores. No wonder gallery girl had shunned him. He'd learn no more tonight about tentative suspect. This had been a far cry from his scene, his comfort zone, for decades. Best to steal away, before he attracted further demoralizing smirks.

On the sidewalk, he glanced up repeatedly en route to his Civic. Providence was city enough that its skyglow made for mediocre stargazing. Big Dipper, Scorpio, Orion's Belt, anyhow, looked no different, to his great relief. Had he really doubted they would? And remarkably, sense of kinship with smug painter had also endured, though morphing into sibling envy that yearned to put parallel self behind bars.

Ira lost track of how many days plodded by without local disturbance, but they offered no respite. Spirits didn't rebound, no hopes for lasting calm brightened, definitely not for Ira, and how could he be atypical? Nope, more mayhem had to be brewing, and the longer it held off, the tenser the citywide atmosphere grew. In others, moreover, Ira discerned unseemly, ill-harnessed anticipation, as if they were secretly eager for smoke and explosions, a circus, a festival of calamity. Disappointment lurked under new workplace greeting, "Well, no bombs yet."

Ira deplored this ghoulish hankering, credited strength of character for exempting him from it. Yes, for weeks he'd had crazy dreams, but how was he responsible for those? Actually they'd have qualified as nightmares, except he woke energized, elated, like Scrooge on Christmas morning. But upbeat mood wasn't his fault either, was it?

In fact, the dreams only chafed because he couldn't decipher the remembered chaos so lucid to his dormant self. Ari's jagged signature across chrome gate the width of a canyon had been perfectly legible, and Ira had blithely pronounced its chittering syllables. He was basking in the nuclear fusion at the heart of a sun, in teeming red bursts and eddies and vortices, and he beheld in it a parity with rioting mobs packed into malls and town squares, looting and torching and butchering, and both the solar furnace and the carnage filled his ecstatic regard as if he were in two places at once. The act of looking up had thrust him into black space among white maelstroms of gas broader than any planetary system, and had reminded him that everything material spent more eons inchoate than otherwise, that such was everything's true and normal state, and squinting, he could comprehend the age of each atom as handily as reading a clock. But come morning, the buzz of electric razor dispelled any remnants of epiphany, demoting him to sad sack who'd absorbed too many bad vibes from the zeitgeist.

The mayor had convened a review session of everyone in charge of anything at Public Works, and glowing self-reports droned on at the same pace shadow crept over brick wall across the way from stuffy Victorian council chamber. Rush-hour traffic had ebbed away before a blue-haired secretary barged in and practically brayed, "Bomb scare at the Arcade! Bomb squad's there now! Chief of Police and Public Safety Commissioner both called and said tell the Mayor immediately!"

Meeting adjourned, before Ira could enlarge upon promising efforts to nab the graffitist His Honor most wanted to rot in jail. Stampede swept disapproving Ira along, involuntarily excited as if by osmosis, among seasoned bureaucrats no classier than hungry paparazzi chasing some poor celebrity. The Arcade was a minute's trot from City Hall, but intervening taller structures prevented it from sticking like derisive finger in mayoral eye.

Here was another venerable landmark, its survival till impending two-hundredth birthday in question, a veritable temple of commerce with Ionic colonnades and proportions from the heyday of Greek Revival. Touted as the first roofed shopping mall ever, it had ridden out economic crests and troughs galore until current owner evicted its small-scale retailers to install a single major player, who promptly reneged during the mortgage crisis. For years the mice had had three stories of boutique floorspace to themselves.

Used to be, Ira mused, that prospects of lethal blast and dismemberment and rocketing shrapnel would have frightened the public off. Now, however, his colleagues' bluster and elite rank couldn't even leverage them up to the police cordon, through crowd thicker than pigeons around a hill of crumbs. Thrill-junkies had flocked from college dorms and repertory theatres and barstools, ditching nightlife culture in the dust. Not that city fathers were setting a more dignified example.

Nobody pushed or jostled. Rather, as if by psychic consensus, everyone strained forward en masse, to exert constant, fatiguing pressure on police line, like a starfish on a clamshell, ignoring orders to disperse without specific misconduct to provoke nightstick reprisal. Bomb-squad armored van was parked on slate sidewalk between cops and Arcade steps, and the crew was somewhere indoors. Nothing to see, actually, apart from the crowd itself, and in isosceles triangle below the roofline, the magenta script "The Stars Are," stopping short of a forlorn little Xmas star made of light bulbs at the base of the triangle.

Hey, that was half of a title from Ari's exhibit! Ira drew exultant breath. He had wily vandal dead to rights, never mind how unwily Ari had been to recycle telltale phrase. What's more, the foretaste of guilt-by-association was delicious. Maybe bomb prep had taken Ari so long that police arrived before he could finish tagging.

Logic dictated Ari was already miles from the scene of the crime. Too bad! Ira indulged backward once-over just as streetlamps sank incandescent shafts into the dark, and for once wishful thinking was rewarded by sudden spotlight on Ari, cattycorner on the forecourt of an '80s pink granite office tower. With a nonchalance as if he'd practiced at a mirror, as if his eyes hadn't met Ira's, he about-faced and ambled through the revolving doors into the tower's glass-encased lobby.

Briefly Ira spaced out as he would while watching a seahorse in an aquarium. Then he charged off, without alerting his colleagues, who'd joined relentless mob, or the cops, in no position to assist. He darted through the revolving doors, raised an eyebrow at absence of night guard from receptionist's island in the middle of capacious lobby, and detected Ira on the black rubber ramp to the revolving doors on the other side of the block. Green backpack with a pair of oblong red reflectors sewn into the flap must have functioned as vandal's paintbox.

Ira padded along, a casual stone's throw between them, grateful for de facto tracking device that bobbed away like the eyes of a playful monster skipping in reverse. Soon, he rejoiced, he'd be phoning police from outside Ari's home or atelier or next site of misdemean-

or in progress. Ira trailed him past Superman Building, across nocturnal sideshow of Kennedy Plaza, up more and more desolate streets beside the glass-and-girder impersonality of Westin Hotel, Convention Center, the coarsely christened Dunkin' Donuts arena.

Red-eyed monster was much less worrisome than the foot traffic. There was an awful lot of it, and it only increased dramatically after he and Ari crossed the bridge over Route 95 and headed up Broadway. Lowlife or cleancut, cool or conservative, male or female, pedestrians stalked around with hard, feverish expressions as if out looking for someone to start something and for no other reason, not that this avenue of padlocked cafés, funeral homes, and rundown Victorian mansions provided reasons.

Everyone's bearing was jittery, loose-jointed, as if they had trouble containing themselves. What had gotten into people? Did they even question why they were rambling under the stars? Was tonight a full moon? Ira narrowed his gaze onto Ari's backpack and every so often repressed an urge to bawl, "Where the hell are we going?" Ari was as keen on the way forward as Ira, never glancing aside or behind. Nothing in his behavior let on he knew Ira was tailing him.

Ira had to weigh the dismal possibility he was in the thrall of a cheeky, solipsistic Pied Piper, a story that never ended well. Simultaneously, to break off pursuit would leave him alone in the thick of maladjusted, hostile humanity, as if Ari at close range conferred safe passage.

A knot twisted in Ira's stomach as Ari entered Broadway's final downhill stretch. Yes, they were bound for Olneyville, Ira's least beloved neighborhood, scuzzy, congested, post-industrial bottomland where bottom-feeder shops and businesses and the city's social dregs collected. He was aware of how that sounded, but dammit, who could accuse Ira of snobbery when it was the plain truth? And ironically, though downtown touted itself as the Arts District, substantially more artists resorted to the gutted mills and warehouses of Olneyville for low-rent lofts and studios.

In the basin dubbed Olneyville Square (though it was more an unruly intersection), the locals were at their most reckless, most agitated, in such scofflaw numbers that cars weren't getting through, the net effect resembling a restive carnival midway. He overheard plenty of angry muttering, but saw no conversations. Praise the Lord, Ari veered left before gathering riot entrapped them. Ira memorized the name of the side street and debated whether he'd ever been here, had dined at a rib joint around that hairpin bend, shit, it would have been thirty years ago.

But then, forget the rib joint. Every sensory input engaging his consciousness began to resonate as if with déjà vu, or with the echo of someone else perceiving likewise. It felt like a nitrous oxide high, and maybe the someone else was Ari, halfway through parking lot of rehabbed multistory factory. Most of the windows, shaped like those tablets bearing the Ten Commandments, were lit and filtering giddy cocktail chatter, lapping like sonic waves out to the sidewalk. Ira shook his head vigorously and cleared it for the moment. Wow, tough day was taking its toll on his pragmatic brain, or was he hyperventilating after crosstown hike?

Squatting behind a minivan in the parking lot, he freed his cell from vest pocket of City Hall go-to-meeting suit and had 911 connect him with West Side precinct house. Two dozen exasperating rings later, he rattled off his name and title and the street and the name of the "arts complex" on plywood sign above the dark arch of the entrance. Inside, he announced, was a graffitist the mayor avidly wished to nail, and possibly the Arcade bomber as well.

The desk sergeant seemed inappropriately lightheaded and cavalier when terrorism and mayoral priorities were involved. They were kinda shorthanded at present, he hedged, but he'd try sending a car, and what was the address again? "Okey-dokey," he signed off.

"Okey-dokey?" grumbled Ira at dead phone.

Ari must have gone in by now. Ira scurried to the murky archway, seeking some directory of tenants with Ari therein, or even his true name's unpronounceable zigzags. Instead he found Ari, taking snide, minute bow, and heaving open gray steel door. Ira rationalized he wasn't more startled because he'd grown used to Ari's unpredictability.

"That bomb in the Arcade was none of my doing," Ari greeted him. "In fact, I tipped off authorities when I noticed the break-in while going about my business. I refuse to let anything as rudimentary as fertilizer and brass tubing upstage me, though in light of quick police response, that's exactly what happened." He beckoned Ira brusquely inside. "You'll be safer accepting my hospitality."

Ira was at a loss for what to believe. He would, however, most likely feel safer behind even this lawbreaker's locked door. In short order, cocktail chitchat suffusing night air had devolved into the up-roar of a building-wide drinking game. Ira ducked on ahead, tempted to perform a snippy little bow of his own, but why lower himself to Ari's level?

First-floor offices behind frosted-glass windows were dim and si-lent. Ceiling fluorescents shone dull on worn varnish of floorboards rife with gummy black spots and oily streaks, and Ira could have sworn the lighting pulsed in synch with the ebb and flow of raucous celebrants. At the end of the corridor were stairs and a freight eleva-tor. Nary a soul had sprung from the woodwork yet, for which Ira was profoundly thankful.

Was accompanying impulsive Ari into confined quarters a wise idea? Ira's line of sight tarried on the bottom steps till Ari cleared his throat. "I'm four flights up. Odds are better of running into people on the stairs than in the elevator." Ira nodded haplessly.

Ari bent at the knees to yank elevator door up by a strip of bur-lap trailing in the dust. He slid aside the inner folding gate. Ira meek-ly preceded him into the cage and prematurely fretted over whether forward or rear door would admit him to the fourth floor. Snap out of it, man! Ira had to regain some control before he degenerated into blubbering putty. He hit mental rewind of memories about Ari, stopped indiscriminately. "Do you really think your vandalism will save historic landmarks by publicizing their condition?"

Tarnished brass plaque on the wall had a big red button labeled "Up" and a big black button labeled "Down." The frame for the in-spector's certificate was empty. Ari pressed his thumb against red button and held it there, and shook his head as if Ira were a slow child incredulous about the birds and bees. "We're in 100% agree-ment that graffiti spells a property's doom."

When the hell had Ira told him that? Or was it like Ari's "Had to End Sometime" title as clairvoyant rejoinder to Ira's private musings?

"And I've used innocuous spray paint to hasten the destruction, rather than risk lives with messy explosions."

"But why do you want these places torn down?" Furthermore, how long could this rattletrap take to go up four stories?

"Till quite recently I took for granted a morality that informed great art, an ethical code for artists. Then the dreams convinced me otherwise, and I realized abetting the inevitable would lessen the general suffering."

"But what is it that's inevitable, and what does flattening old buildings have to do with it?" Ira also puzzled at his poor judgment in decamping from the parking lot, since the cops, assuming they ever showed, would be clueless without him.

"You would know our inevitable end, you would know everything I do, if you let yourself." Ira was half listening, half diverted by his blossoming bouquet of camphor, automatically concerned he was offending Ari. No revulsion was evident. "Too many factors are contributing to that end for me to summarize. But would you like to discuss the one in which we've played roles?"

Grinding, squealing gears in the elevator shaft shook the cage and made Ira grimace, which Ari interpreted as yes. "Obviously, 'old buildings' are a tangible part of our history, our cultural memory. Destroy enough, forget enough of the past, replace its traces in enough skulls with the ephemera of today minus all yesteryears, the collective psyche reaches a tipping point, as when infections from separate wounds stage a coup together. Ours then becomes a species deprived of history, mere consumers, just like germs in a Petri dish, devoid of purpose or perspective, often in the name, ironically, of progress. And this is good, this merits expediting."

"This is good?" Ira's weak echo died as the car shuddered and groaned to a standstill.

Ari lectured on, as if oblivious to stoppage. "It's good because it's inevitable, it's the reality of the universe in naked glory, the state in which we'll be beyond good and evil, reveling and merging in a holocaust of ecstasy. Dreams have taught me this, and those like you who've had the dreams but learned or remembered nothing of them, they still awaken your atavistic selves to foment havoc or hatred."

Could blithering Ari still relate to the here and now? "Are we going to be stuck here for long?"

Ari frowned again as if Ira were a pitifully slow child. "It stalls like that sometimes." His thumb released the red button. "Let's retry our luck later." Ari was obnoxiously unfazed. "Ever occur to you that elevator factories are always in one-story buildings? What kind of confidence does that instill?" Ari had to grin for the two of them.

No sooner had ratchety elevator motor gone silent than the bedlam of merrymakers rushed in to plug the vacuum. Between the laughter, banging, shrieks, and breaking glass, the residents were already too ecstatic for Ira's taste. Overbearing racket crimped the wail of approaching sirens into the whine of mosquitoes.

Pragmatic Ira was frantic to debunk this whole evening as an elaborate hoax, a joke, a montage of delusion and coincidence. However, calm and clarity from interior parts unknown assured him his doors of perception needed no cleansing. From out of that same uncharted depth reverberated Ari's soliloquy, a syllable ahead of its delivery aloud, like the pre-echo of first notes on Dad's LPs, further proof of the empathic party line he and Ari shared.

He shied from buying altogether into Ari's endgame madness, but something untoward, something surreal was occurring. As a pragmatist he had to acknowledge sober sensory input. And before pandemonium worsened, he had ledgers to balance, dots to connect. "Ari, you underestimate me. This anarchy erupting around us, I remember it from dreams as well as you do. But since I'm such an ignoramus, please, why is that anarchy mixed up in my dreams with feeling euphoric inside the sun and floating in dust clouds a million light years away?"

"Apologies if I've misjudged you." Again with the minimal bow. "But to my credit, I detected in you a kindred spirit, the fellow beneficiary of an inborn gift." Ari paused as thundering feet and concerted jabbering from somewhere below set the latticework gate to gently vibrating. "We're privileged to observe these preliminaries without engulfment in them. Genetics or more obscure agency has made us brothers in that respect."

Ari and Ira flinched in unison as a flurry of gunshots prompted a spike in the caterwauling, and then a bated hush, and then shriller caterwauling and muffled pounding. Cops in the maelstrom, as per Ira's 911 call? Cops bluntly neutralized? With their blood, and that of their marksmanship, on Ira's hands?

Ari shrugged off his backpack, dangled it by the straps on his forearm. "The rioters, the heart of the sun, the stardust, they are all one. That was the lesson of your dreams, decoded from every cell in your body, had you only been receptive to it. You should have become an artist. Knowledge doesn't always come of logical processes. Or do revelations belong in the same mythic ghetto as Bigfoot and chupacabra?"

While awaiting tongue-tied Ira's reply, Ari lowered backpack to the floor and fumbled in it, and then the dingy bulb in the ceiling went out. In the treacherous dark, Ira went rigid like a panic-struck pillar of camphor, but then, light from a battery lantern next to the backpack tainted the cage wan blue, as if Ari had foreseen this blackout.

That question on revelations must have been rhetorical, for he forged on, "If you'd cultivated a less earthbound disposition, you'd have remembered the sounds of my true name engraved on the chrome gate, you'd have remembered how to write it, and you'd have fathomed it's your true name as well, just as it's everybody's true name."

Ari paused as if forewarned again. Thud! Ira managed to embrace the white lie that a bushel sack of potatoes had slammed into the elevator roof and rocked the cage, in the seconds before a dribble, brownish in the blue light, seeped through the seam around the ceiling exit hatch and pattered onto the floor between them. Ari went on as if such distractions were beneath him, or simply weren't getting past his manic effulgence.

"A more intrepid will than yours would have bypassed the chrome gate, and deduced from tableaux and inscriptions on geometrically indecent monuments the glory of those who flourished before our stars, our sun, occupied the sky. You'd have understood our predecessors can only reclaim bodily existence when the stars are right, those stars that were their stars, which decomposed into dust, into atoms of elements that became our sun, our planets, ourselves."

With a clinical detachment in itself probably symptomatic of mental breakdown, Ira noted a readiness to take Ari at his word, as if he were professing nothing deranged, just as Ira's reaction to blood from the ceiling was limited to a desire to sidestep the widening pool. No dice! His vexing bouquet had vanished, he was no longer a pillar of camphor, but his feet were stuck fast.

"In other words, we are the stars, and now we are right, and in a position to restore the primeval majesty of one who has bided inert and diminished, a relic of his former omnipotence. This is our destiny, to revivify a lord of previous creation, to commune with what we were ten billion years ago."

Initially Ira blamed bleak lantern glow for Ari's greenish complexion, but it overtaxed coincidence that at the same instant he perceived Ari had gone mute, flapping his lips like a stranded fish, or else Ira had gone deaf, for he couldn't hear the orgiastic din either. His nose, meanwhile, still functioned, and in lieu of camphor was the burgeoning stench from a barrel of rotten shrimp. It didn't bother him, though, any more than the blood on his shoes did, and really, it was something to savor.

And now sea-green Ari was calmly, languidly sloughing off human outline and melting out of his clothes, and Ira yearned to liquefy more quickly and coalesce with Ari and flow from the elevator toward the others, and it didn't hurt, without pain receptors it couldn't, those must have been among the first mortal attributes to go. Instead, his disembodiment felt liberating, empowering, and especially natural.

Best of all about becoming one drop in this rising sea, one piece in this global puzzle, he could envision the totality, as if a jigsaw piece could see the finished picture. His interactions with Ari, everybody's interactions the world over, had always been jigsaw pieces too, building up to this moment, and as history ended and the eternal now began, he saw with another's eyes, and with dwindling selfhood, that he would be augmenting the girth of a mountain, a mountain he brought more fully to life by melding with it, a mountain that would live forever and tread among the stars and among the stars that would succeed them. The sound of his true name no longer posed a mystery, except no human mouth could properly pronounce it, and he had no mouth whatsoever.

pests: a provisional translation

They were in again, and not for the first time this temperate cycle. I'd gone to look outward, and there they were, three of them, frantically crawling up and down the surface. How did they get in, and why? Nothing for them on this side but death, whether by starvation or exhaustion, no way to tell which. They eventually ceased to move, in any case, and soon were no more than clingy, oxidized wisps.

What could be simpler than to exit as they'd entered? Sadly, that never occurred to them. They evidently had no capacity for that to occur to them, as if they couldn't perceive an entire dimension and their continuum were limited to four.

I wished they could just blunder out again, resume their infinitesimal lives, do whatever they naturally did, but that never happened. I'd have pitied them had they been less minute and revolting, too unlike us to elicit sympathy.

One of them had been stuck in a corner once, and I'd studied it under a magnifier. Its body plan made me queasy, two lower limbs, two upper limbs, a protrusion between the upper limbs for putative sensory apparatus, and encasement top to bottom in some shiny, crinkly substance, jointed in multiple places, and grossly deficient as protection because the magnifier had set it ablaze. Of course, they were so revolting I couldn't feel too bad about killing one especially hapless specimen.

The relation approached, and before he was altogether beside me he'd followed my perceptions to the little pests and gestured at them, observing as if it were original of him, "They're not even conscious we're here, are they?" That instant, they contradicted him and ruffled us both by stopping in their erratic tracks to wag upper limbs excitedly at each other and point toward us, as if his gesture had somehow attracted them.

We reflexively withdrew; he rebounded first and impulsively reached over as if to make forceful contact, testing or rather teasing them for some response. Nobody would have expected a happy reaction, but I was almost as startled as he when minuscule flames leapt from the ends of their left upper limbs, and he recoiled and yelped, more in surprise than pain, as three barely discernible puncture dots appeared on his person. I refrained from stating it served him right. After his retreat, the tiny menaces twisted about in confusion, as if their oppressor had vanished.

I was mildly worried the relation had incensed my ugly specks of monsters into attack mode, however trivial the danger. His dismay was markedly more acute. "How dare they!" he bristled. Knowing his disposition, he'd hardly have granted the difference in scale between us and them made their boldness admirable. He was already detaching a section of the cleansing matter, lunging with it vengefully and stretching it to cover all three potential fire-slingers. They acted unaware of oncoming retaliation till no chance remained for evasion or anything else.

The cleansing matter sealed flat against the surface and came away with three sparkly black smears. I was sorry the creatures' bravery hadn't served them better, but then, reading purposeful virtues into their behavior was wrong. The relation was correct to lay down the law, to brook no impudence from these miniature upstarts. It wasn't as if they had thoughts or feelings. How could they, and be as they were? Their teensy upper protrusions had no room for bravery.

The relation was both more volatile and more practical than myself. No silly qualms for him about killing vermin! How fortuitous, he asserted, that he was passing through just when proactive decisions were in order. He couldn't stay, but urged me to come out with him as far as the perimeter and perhaps locate where the four-limbs were sneaking in. To oblige him was easier than pretending I was busy inside. We moved forth, he warned me to obliterate every last pest lest they breed uncontrollably, and he was gone.

I patrolled the contours, checking for chinks and disjunctions and vortices. Frustration impended because I'd never verified exactly where exteriors corresponded with interiors at this dwelling. But there, an addition to the contours stopped me, conspicuous because it reflected instead of absorbing the strobing starshine. A tapered cylinder was embedded in the matrix and rife with a baffling array of rods and lattices and discs. If this were the vermin's nest, what irrational drive had bid them attach these features? And considering the nesting material's similarity to their bright coating, had they instinctively excreted this home from their bodies?

I warily sent vibrations against the cylinder to try rousting any denizens, while maintaining a presumably safe distance from spurting flames. I owed the relation thanks—or did I, for making me take stock out here before infestation became too entrenched? That which belongs somewhere tends to have ways of dealing with that which doesn't. The nest wobbled loose at my inducement and began tumbling, hollow and flimsy, fracturing and floating away on ionized currents. The larger fragments bore telltale signs of the fauna that normally frequent the contours. They'd eaten whatever was in the cylinder, and sampled the cylinder as well.

Damage to the contours where the nest had adhered was negligible, but repairs were a priority, to prevent entry by new pests. I pressed up to the peephole rupture for a speck's perspective inward. From this angle, this scant opening, the interior was mystifying, maybe as much to me as to them. How nightmarish if everything were always so chaotic!

I retracted without further attempt to make sense of my own domicile. What would it be like, trapped on a plane of existence confusing to us as ours was to the pests? With a quiver of chagrin I banished this vagrant speculation. If such a transcendent realm existed, might not transcendent inhabitants also exist, able to survey us, and we none the wiser, even as we surveyed the four-limbs? And wouldn't those watchers thus outrank us as masters of the continuum, put us beneath something greater than ourselves? No. That was arrant negativism.

I went back in, vowing to eradicate any future pests on sight. Harmless in themselves or not, clearly they were vectors for thoughts as distressing and pernicious as the onset of any disease. What, discounting almighty chance of course, could ever oust us from our centrality in the tesseract of life? The relation could have me exiled or worse for merely bringing up the possibility.

a quirk of the mistral

Here's how secluded the professor was. From the airport outside Marseille I took a taxi to the midcity train station, and there I bought a ticket for Arles, where I boarded the Avignon-bound bus, from which I disembarked on two-lane blacktop between parched alfalfa fields. The driver, who had a postcard of a cicada taped to his dashboard, was adamant that Domaine St. Jude was two or three kilometers down the unpromising byway before me. I never did resolve whether the road was paved or not, because nothing but rounded tips of tawny stones broke the monotony of pale impacted dust. Let the record moreover state, I had to negotiate this trying geography under the handicap of stupefying jetlag after eight-hour flight from JFK.

Before I'd trudged the first kilometer, I was pleased as ever I'd been with my dedication to traveling light. A backpack tidily under the weight limit for carry-on was it for these two weeks abroad. All the same, the straps were chafing my shoulders raw, and sweat had fused thin cotton shirt to my back. Sycamores and pines and a smattering of palms flanked my route, though arid drainage gullies on both sides kept shade at a maddening remove. And the August sun was merciless, like a scouring pad abrading my scalp. Worse yet, mean, sporadic gusts whipped road grit into my oily face, like drafts from a cindery furnace.

The cicadas, at least, liked the climate, to judge by the welter of buzzing that waxed and waned in the foliage like phantom power tools sawing through one phantom branch after another. It made a fitting soundtrack to my fatigue and dehydration, and on the verge of cursing the heat aloud and deliriously, I plodded into a crossroad and found my second wind. Ahead on the right was a rusty wrought-iron

crucifix atop a truncated brick pyramid, just as the fax had described. This ordeal was near its end! A scant hundred yards would
bring me to the dilapidated gaggle of several farmsteads dignified as
Domaine St. Jude, a name absent from Rand McNally atlas and
highway signage. The closest village on Institut Géographique maps
was Boulbon, where the épicerie must have put a fax machine at the
professor's disposal.

In the year since his retirement and retreat to native precincts,
he'd forsworn phone and e-mail and even pen and paper, so when
the secretary at the Department called about his message for me, I
was elated, although his excited mélange of French and English also
mystified and worried me a little.

Someone he claimed I had to meet was "à la maison," and he be-
seeched me to come "vite! Aussitôt que possible!" This someone he
then referred to as "quelque chose incroyable," and with me alone was
he comfortable sharing this incredible something. Henceforth he would
be incommunicado, but guaranteed he'd always be home to welcome
me, and "don't fail to catch the soonest plane you can. Une farce cosmique! The dogma has exploded." He signed off, as was his custom,
"Take care. Do not hope too much. I'm sure it will be all right."

And here I was, silently mouthing those words at the head of his
bramble-lined driveway, drawn by friendship and concern and, yes,
some twinge of obligation. Thanks to his influence at the Life Sci-
ences Department I'd stepped into his tenured shoes, and couldn't
very well repay him now by ignoring his urgent summons.

I was punchy to the point of mistaking an oversized shed for the
main house, understandably insofar as it boasted a residential-looking
tile roof and mortared walls and green louvered door. I knocked
twice before noticing more substantial candidate for a home up
ahead, and unlike the shed, it had windows, from one of which a
pair of goggle eyes, distinctly not the professor's, was studying me. A
querulous voice, also not the professor's, loosed a babel of syllables
toward the interior of the house.

I hadn't marshaled the strength to move when Hervé Bayard
bounded outside, in cool vanilla linen shirt and trousers, sensibly sea-
sonal but almost alarmingly loose, as if he'd shed too many pounds.
With his perennial vitality he shook my hand and hugged me and

thanked me profusely for indulging an old coot. I was still hemming and hawing a semi-coherent reply in French as he staggered backward and turned away to expel a slew of wracking coughs. He waved away my concerns for his health, which only grew upon observing twin inflamed swaths, of a finely granular texture, along his ocular orbits.

I was in no shape to comment on these tactfully, and anyway the professor was escorting me to a side yard and a rickety square table, with a hole drilled into it for a parasol. He put up the parasol, of the same buttery yellow as the table, and bid me sit while he disappeared into the house and dispensed instructions about readying dinner and guestroom, to which he received the somber Provençal assent, "Très bieng." He reappeared with a tray containing a bowl of reddish olives, a liter of pastis, a pitcher of water, and a pair of shot glasses.

"Relax and be refreshed," he prescribed, and though hard liquor after roughly twenty-four hours on the go sounded counterproductive, what the hell. I was running on fumes already. Adding distilled fumes might even help. Hervé clucked in mock reprimand as I raised the drink to my lips without remembering to add water. Then he quizzed me on my arduous journey and stateside current events and a year's worth of campus gossip. Baffling how my explosive reason for crossing the Atlantic had apparently slipped his mind, but I was tired beyond bringing that up, and the pastis hadn't even begun to hit me yet.

Presently the sturdy owner of the goggling eyes addressed the professor from the doorstep. She was dressed in modest, stifling black woolens, and a black Spanish comb clenched thin gray hair away from coarse-grained face. I garnered from the decipherable snatches of her idiom that dinner was served. To me she remarked, in plainer French, "It is always better the second night." She ducked back inside.

"That is Clairette," Hervé explained as he set our half-empty glasses beside the untouched olives on the tray, and picked up the tray. "She was here when I signed the lease. I cannot find a way to dismiss her." He shrugged resignedly. "And why should I, really?"

We ate cold pork roast and stewed apricots with reheated ratatouille at a worn oak table in the kitchen. It was sweltering, and I wished in vain for the wherewithal to ask politely if this house didn't have a better-ventilated dining room.

Clairette leaned against the gaping iron crevasse of a sink and occasionally swabbed her craggy brow with a dishrag. During a lull in our small talk, she made a rapidfire announcement, which the professor rendered in English. "Clairette says you are in luck. No doubt you were annoyed by the marin, the hot wind, as you walked from the bus, but her bones tell her the mistral is due tonight, and that brings the fresher weather." I thanked Clairette for the encouraging forecast. She regarded me blankly as if my French were gibberish. Then she prepared us a cutting board of bread and cheeses and a platter of peaches and pears and bananas.

I finally contrived an opening to say what needed saying. "Where is this incredible houseguest you were dying for me to meet? Why isn't he eating with us? Is he all right?"

"He is taken care of." The professor wasn't normally evasive, so his answer dismayed me as much as his recurrent coughing spells and the pebbly rash beneath his eyes. "In good time," he amended more affably. "Soon, if you are not too weary from your long trip." He smiled hospitably and poured us more pastis.

With the heels of his hands against the tabletop, Hervé laboriously boosted himself from his chair after we'd finished out third glass, or was it our fourth? "Let us get you situated before anything else," he advised.

I needed a second to figure out what he meant. "Right. I stupidly left my stuff out in the yard. Sorry."

"No, no, it is good." He gestured toward the door. "I will go too." Damn, I'd furnished him yet another delaying tactic on the path to introducing his "houseguest." He commended Clairette for an excellent meal, at which I nodded in hearty but unacknowledged agreement, and he assured her we would be fine now on our own. In the softening nine o'clock light, while I grabbed my backpack, he looked around at nothing in particular and stretched and rocked on his heels. I had the sneaking impression he was steeling himself, limbering up to propose a contentious thesis. This I read as a sign of progress. The din of cicadas was unabating.

He nodded on eventually realizing I had backpack in hand, and I followed him through front hall, past a room blocked off by hefty sliding door, and up a dim stone stairwell. He was out of sight around the bend, and I heard but didn't see him stomping something. As he climbed, he defined the chitin bits in ugly smudge upon a step, "Sometimes in the south you find a scorpion." He glanced behind to appraise my reaction. I must have gone pretty waxy. "Please, it is no big deal. If one stings, you just go to the hospital for six months and you are fine. Then you come home, and the other one stings and you just go to the hospital again for six months. They travel in pairs, you know."

Hervé, I surmised, had reverted to the rustic humor of his youth while readjusting to home turf. I was feigning an appreciative grin in case he checked for therapeutic effects of his jest, but he intrepidly clambered onward.

Mine was one of two chambers off the cramped landing. The professor pulled a cord on a pole lamp inside the doorway and conducted what I inwardly disparaged as a spotty search for the other scorpion. In the casement above the bedstead, twin panes swung in, and green shutters swung out. He set the latches to allow an inch-wide stream of air to enter. "It will stop only the most idiotic of mosquitoes, but you will have air to breathe."

I dropped my backpack onto the bed. The only other item of furniture was a straightback wooden chair. The professor bowed dramatically to peek under the bed and proclaimed, "You are safe for now." Without more ado he ambled out and I trailed after. His bonhomie had withered to a husk before he reached the bottom step.

To initiate me into this mystery, this "cosmic joke" of his, had evidently been a much less fraught proposition from 4,000 miles away. He dawdled outside the sliding door till I caught up. He had two fingers in lozenge-shaped brass indentation to pull the door aside, but first he whispered, "Clairette has been forbidden to go inside. She should be in her quarters, elsewhere on the property."

He retracted the door by slow centimeters. Milking the moment for maximal suspense? No, on his face was a safecracker's degree of concentration, as if he feared triggering any disturbance within, or perhaps destabilizing some cherished illusion. He poked his head through as soon as space permitted, and murmured, "C'est bon."

At that instant a smell lunged out at me, a potent meld of unclean fish tank, fermenting hot sauce, and dead lilies, and something more was wrong with it, a dissociation from the natural world, like a square peg in the round hole of my experience. Hervé went ahead as if perceiving nothing amiss or offensive.

He nudged a dimmer switch on the wall, and a glass chandelier suffused the stuffy, shuttered room with twilight. Here was his salle à manger cum personal museum, cluttered with the Cambrian hagfish skulls, beetles in amber, ammonite shells, and jumbo shale dragonflies of a career teaching invertebrate paleontology. The casement windows were all gaping open, though the green shutters were fastened together, permitting air to circulate through gaps a mere few centimeters wide. Eight brocade chairs, as if they'd wantonly obstructed him, were scattered at a distance impractical for dining from a marble-topped table whose dimensions could accommodate a billiards game. Dozens of hardbound volumes, many of them by Hervé, had migrated from built-in wall shelves to secure a perimeter around the edge of the table, like a corral of dominoes.

With a detachment that rang patently false, he indicated the polished white surface rife with black veins and said simply, "Voilà."

At first I couldn't fathom what was so significant. My aching, unsteady eyes veered haplessly from a blue enamel basin of water to the evenly split halves of a derby-sized hunk of coal. Nothing else leapt out at me. I stole a glance at Hervé. He was observing me keenly, in plain expectation I should be astounded. I blinked and reexamined the tabletop. In a reprise of my student days with him, the pressure to react appropriately was on.

Wait a minute. Something so subtle I almost blamed it on imagination or bleary vision was moving across the mineral expanse, gaining definition under my focus. And the sharper its outline, the more willing I was to shift that blame to the power of suggestion or the double whammy of pastis and exhaustion. Or had Hervé plied me with liquor and exploited my jetlag to soften up my incredulity, my common sense?

The thing was no bigger than a child's fist and had eluded my haphazard survey because it for the most part wore the white and striated black of its surroundings, camouflaged like an octopus or chameleon. That, however, was the extent of its connection to conventional zoology. Its top-heavy, wedgelike head most resembled a trilobite's, except for the curtain of feelers depending from it like baleen, and its hunched and banded body loosely mimicked that of a shrimp. Transparent legs like jointed straws, maybe ten, maybe more, held it aloft, in the posture of a daddy longlegs on tiptoe. It indecisively tottered around as if in perpetual daze at its circumscribed parcel of our alien world, conceivably suffering as much confusion as it inflicted. I hoped my gawking astonishment was up to the professor's standards. "What the hell is it?"

"What indeed?"

"Where did it come from?"

"You see that broken block of coal?"

"No. That's as impossible as the thing itself."

Yet there it is, his arching eyebrows challenged. "In the cellar is a bin full of coal not used up by some *ancien régime*," he recounted. "On rainy days for amusement I would fetch the bigger lumps and chisel at their seams to hunt for fossils. This I regarded as an idle pastime, with only poor chance to uncover anything. So when I pried open a crack in that block on the table, and met my little friend snug in a cavity, my expression must have been like yours just now. And when he began almost at once to awake, my head was spinning, believe me."

An eruption of coughing interrupted him, leading me to wonder if that vertigo might have resulted from inhaling some virulence that had survived along with its chimeric host. Which was as good as saying I'd already bought into Hervé's outlandish claims at face value, hadn't I? But I hadn't, damn it. "A live animal trapped in stone? Can you name me one reputable scientist who wouldn't laugh outright at that old wives' tale?"

He raised a coy index finger and essayed a mordant smile. "I am back on my native soil to be reborn as an old wife, then." Very funny, professor, and not getting us anywhere, and me wobbling on the brink of collapse.

"You alone have I called upon because I trust you most to accept the truth in front of your eyes. Nor do I guess you will reject the lesson this has forced on me, after decades spent defending my house of orthodox cards, for that is how I see it now."

"Fine, but aren't you maybe throwing out the whole deck because there's one joker in it?" I had just enough starch left to feel smug about winging a passable comeback.

"If you like to say so, you may." Hervé always had dealt patiently with sales resistance. "But these anecdotes of living toads encased in rock date to the twelfth century and recur independently of one another, in all corners of Europe." He shrugged diffidently. "I would only suggest reopening the book on these many cases, that was shut too soon for lack of understanding." He peered solemnly at his "farce cosmique," which had meandered to the phalanx of volumes bordering the head of the table, and was butting sluggishly against it, to no effect. "I might also submit that these prisoners freed from stone were not in actuality toads, but in spite of outward similarities may have been more akin to our present specimen."

"Before you go reopening any books, though, let's be clear on the kind of reception you can look forward to. Unless you can somehow safely transport your fragile pet from point A to point B, you couldn't offer any meaningful proof it existed. Any photographs would be denounced as a Photoshop hoax. And if you brought over a hundred eyewitnesses, it would only amount to a hundred instances of hearsay."

"Well, to counter you item by item, my miraculous pet cannot be as fragile as you suppose, or it would not have persevered through the terrible upheavals of many eons. However, I do not care to exhibit it to the public. I am showing it to you and not to *Le Monde* or the Smithsonian."

"But to play devil's advocate a minute, were you to ditch the academic integrity for a more P. T. Barnum approach, you might parlay your pet into a much more comfortable retirement than you'll enjoy in a rented farmhouse with Madame Clairette."

"Mademoiselle Clairette." He declined to dignify my mercenary pitch any further. Good man, as I well knew. "Besides, I would not dare inform our colleagues of my orphan from the coal, because I have not yet learned the most basic facts about it. Please, ask me anything, you will see my problem."

I sighed, hard-pressed to hide my petulance after running on vapors too long, but to begrudge my dear mentor a round of Twenty Questions would be the nadir of bad form, wouldn't it? "Okay then, what is that thing?"

"Ah, the second time you ask that. Of course, what more natural starting place for curiosity? I unfortunately remain ignorant after weeks of watching. Our guest is unlike anything alive today or in the fossil record. Dissection might be informative, but what a cruel end for this sleeping beauty, to be awakened after ages only to be butchered. I would also lose forever everything its behavior might teach me." Hervé's "guest" had refrained from breaking through the stockade of books and was torpidly patrolling the paper bounds of its exercise yard. It had yet to perform any actions I'd qualify as behavior, and perhaps it couldn't in this totally foreign context. I'd never have dreamed the thing knew we were talking about it, and had my doubts it even knew we were there.

"That incompatibility with the rest of the fossil record would damage your credibility even further, wouldn't it?"

"For some, yes." The professor unpocketed a handkerchief to muffle another barrage of coughing. "I might have been one of those martinets myself, not long ago. Sneering when somebody said, 'Absence of evidence is not evidence of absence.' Now my paradigms have necessarily shifted, better late than never. Uppermost for me finally is the truism that only a limited percentage of species had the luck to join the fossil record, and of those, how many will be discovered? I find myself aligned now with the partisans of yetis."

"I think you're a giant step ahead of them in terms of hard evidence, and you must've collected some specific findings by now. Any idea how old we're talking?"

"How old is coal?" he countered. "It began forming in the Carboniferous, after three hundred million years ago. But how long had our little iconoclast's species existed already?" I tried not to fixate on the sheer, staggering impossibility of that timeframe. "Moreover, if we incline toward that maximal age, we have a clue to our friend's lethargic movements. The air was a good deal richer then, and therefore I am not surprised at signs of oxygen deprivation. It may not be as stupid as its aimlessness leads you to suppose."

Was Hervé's tone a bit defensive, as if I'd unwittingly disparaged a favorite dog or cat? "At least it's still ambulatory, so you must be feeding it right." Did that sound vaguely conciliatory?

Hervé spread his hands to encompass frustration. "Again we touch on the dilemma of what to tell our colleagues. It does not eat, it does not defecate, not in ways I can detect. I provided raw meat of all kinds, in every combination of tough or tender, fresh or spoiled, including insects, and the broadest variety of fruit and vegetable material. Nothing won a flicker of its attention. It dips its head into the basin of water or climbs in sometimes, and perhaps on those occasions fulfills some alimentary functions. But in those as in other respects, it guards its mysteries impeccably."

I desperately wanted to sit in one of the brocade chairs and conserve my failing resources, but couldn't take my eyes off our Paleozoic foundling. "You haven't tried handling it, have you? Have you any idea if it's dangerous?"

"I am more wary about the harm my handling might do to it."

"I'm wary as well, but for your sake. How long have you had that nasty cough? Have you seen a doctor?"

"When would I find the leisure to do that? I am always monitoring the situation here."

"You went out long enough to send me that fax."

"Clairette drove to the village with my message. Besides, I often cough from dust and allergies. It is nothing." Another bronchial fit badly undercut his nonchalance.

"But would our genes still confer resistance to diseases dormant for three hundred million years? You must have asked yourself that once in the last couple of weeks."

Hectoring my mentor, and my distinct better in scholarship, in eloquence, in the art of living made me profoundly uncomfortable. Probing his features for signs I was getting through to him made matters worse, for then I discerned new redness encircling his nostrils, with tiny burgeoning granulations.

My gaze seemed to make him no less profoundly uncomfortable. He reapplied handkerchief to lower face, dabbing self-consciously as if at a runny nose, and then masking himself for the balance of our discussion. "What you said earlier, about misusing my discovery to procure wealth? I fully appreciate you endorse no such crass plan. Therefore you may appreciate why I keep this difficult discovery of mine to myself, as a lesson in humility after enforcing dogma upon too many generations. To you, however, I hope to impart a short cut to that lesson." By this indirect route he'd also exiled the topic of his health beyond the conversational pale.

Hervé's archaic plague dog had meanwhile slipped into the basin, where it floated apparently inert and prudently enamel blue. Hammerhead and glassy stilts and all, it had contracted to a seamless ovoid, an imitation cobble on the beach. The professor took this change in stride. Nothing new to him, I gathered, whereas I had to grimace at the lowbrow output of my guttering brain, which rudely likened Hervé's monumental find to a turd in the punchbowl. And no excuse for my vulgarity in being right, for how else would his animate relic be received by any mainstream biochemist or biologist or paleontologist? I couldn't altogether blame the professor if at heart he'd quarantined his "pet" to ensure a peaceful retirement, as opposed to endless controversy.

"Your eyelids have begun to droop, have they not?" he noted. Had he really been stone blind to my progressive deterioration since I'd arrived? Was this a case of that selective vision, a less endearing trait of his I'd forgotten in the past year? "Unless you object, let us retire. Mine is the room up the stairs, adjacent to yours. To access the bathroom, you go outside and to the right, and it is the first door around the corner. And tomorrow, who can tell? Our cosmic joker may have another trick or two for us."

Prospects of grossly overdue bed rest lent my feet rickety wings to help me fetch my toothbrush and otherwise perform ablutions around the corner. After I'd doused my doorway lamp and flopped upon the extra firm mattress, I wondered if I'd be too wound-up and full of revelations to fall asleep, and how perversely unjust would that be? In fact, I promptly shorted out, without a volt of energy for worrying about the vengeful mate of extirpated scorpion. I awoke more than once to the banging of shutters, but never for longer than it took to reflect that Clairette's bones had correctly forecast the winds in flux.

Then the sun was glaring through the slit between the shutters, goading me like an external conscience for sleeping in when Hervé must have been champing at the bit for further dialogue. I checked my Swatch at bedside. It told me 10 A.M., but adjusting for my normal longitude, it was only 4 A.M., really. From that perspective, I wasn't so disgraceful a slouch.

Anyway, first, most pressing things first. I made a blinkered rush for the bathroom and gave no thought to seeing Hervé nowhere en route. Clairette was fixing my breakfast when I reentered the kitchen. She gestured for me to sit and brought a bowl of café-au-lait and half a baguette smeared with Brie. I asked when the professor had eaten. As best I could decode her idiom, he hadn't eaten but had bolted outdoors on some unstated errand soon after she'd come in. "The mistral is always accused of fanning passions and rash actions." She threw up her hands at the inevitable. "Some people go crazy. It is capricious like a spirit." Her freighted language in regard to her employer running an errand puzzled me, and I'm open to the charge of mistranslating it and much of what she said thereafter.

Clairette had also sagely forecast the less oppressive temperature, though upstart breezes barging in through open door and tousling my hair were already becoming oppressive in their own right. But that was no real issue, was it? I'd be out of here in two or three days tops, loath to push my luck with Hervé's hospitality, and on to other scenic regions of France.

She accepted my thanks for the meal with an all-purpose "Très bieng" and commenced washing dishes. I excused myself and tossed a figurative coin. Heads meant a likely wild goose chase for the professor somewhere between here and Boulbon. Tails meant a second gander at his captive miracle. Tails won.

The dining room door was partway open. I could tiptoe in with an inch of clearance for my shoulders. But where was the distasteful mucky smell? Clean air should have tipped me off that I was wading into grief. A temperate draft was coursing from the entrance to the pair of windows in the opposite wall. The inward-facing panes hadn't been disturbed, but the green shutters were fastened straight outward, letting in broad shafts of daylight. I wouldn't need a glowing chandelier to find my fellow houseguest on the table. There was the bisected block of coal, there was the blue basin of water, and then I went weak-kneed at apprehending why Hervé had rushed outside. I squinted frantically at every square centimeter of marble till I was sure.

A vagrant surge of air must have scooped featherweight specimen up and out a window. Hervé had clearly assumed the same, since he'd dashed off to comb the grounds without first overturning skulls and books and furniture for hideaways.

Panic may have blinded him to something new upon the marble. I could now account for the second scorpion. It was the length of my index finger, not a strapping example of its biological order, and it was dead, literally belly up, stiff legs and tail askew. In its brown flank was an inflamed hole, like an inverted pimple, rimmed by tiny granulations that had radiated in a sunburst pattern. Nocturnal prowler may have easily scaled the palisade of printed matter, but then the feast on the table had proven far from defenseless. And Hervé, already ailing thanks to days of proximity to his "pet" and ignorant of its "new trick," was incautiously chasing it among weeds and bushes. Was he slated to end up as captor or victim? I wasn't wildly optimistic.

Meanwhile, I had to award Clairette yet more points for aptly comparing invasive wind to a "capricious spirit." It made as good an explanation as any for the quirk of the mistral that had freed the rarest of prisoners while sidestepping a defunct scorpion.

On the other hand, how many demerits should I assign her for aiding in the fugitive's escape? The professor would hardly have run the risk of parting the shutters on this blustery day. That leveled the blame at Clairette, who after unreckoned years here must have learned the secret to working the shutters from outside.

I hustled into the kitchen, fretting that she may have withdrawn to the undisclosed location of her apartment. No, not quite. She was draping damp dishtowel over refrigerator handle. I put it to her, aiming for a non-confrontational tone, "Were you aware of anything different about Professor Bayard's private study before he ran off this morning?"

She reacted as if I'd scalded her, or worse, charged her with heresy. She swore by a flock of strictly Languedoc saints how she would never disobey monsieur's instructions, and especially would never cross the threshold into "that chamber." But yes, when she passed the dining room door and the churning wind carried that "evil smell" to her, she had to open the door "un petit peu seulement" and go out to unlatch the shutters and start a draft to dispel the rottenness, because "you cannot eat in a place like that. You will fall sick just to breathe in there." She fiercely added that not one toe, not one finger of hers had entered forbidden territory.

When had she last seen "monsieur"? She pouted as if volunteering such information was not her job. "A couple of hours." Her rugged face contained no inkling that her conduct had influenced Hervé's. I couldn't marshal the French to insinuate it had. Nor could I picture what good that would do.

I conveyed my intent to canvas the Domaine for sightings of the errant professor. Clairette was none too encouraging. Everyone was on holiday except the nearest neighbor, but beware of her. She was a deranged old countess who kenneled a pack of half-wild foxhounds, "tout méchants," and Clairette was surprised their usual dawn rampage through the woods hadn't wakened me. I took her warning to heart, though as it turned out she needn't have bothered, because I hadn't finished searching the home acreage as of lunchtime.

In fact, I made my first and only relevant observation, if it were indeed relevant, the second the sun hit my eyes. The cicadas, strident as buzz saws yesterday, were mute today. The weather, the hour, any number of stimuli peculiar to cicadas may have shushed them. Or had scent or more esoteric signals from Hervé's stray anachronism startled modern insects into instinctive silence, according to mechanisms latent for eons? What did their hard wiring know about relict organism that the professor and I didn't?

For whatever reason, the morning continued unnervingly quiet while I scoured the landscape, shouting Hervé's name and poking into the underbrush. I watched my step lest I tread on the "cosmic joke" that had backfired so horribly. I had no desire ever to see it again. By noon, I'd arguably earned a break to rehydrate and refuel myself and reconsider how to proceed. I was disappointed but not at all shocked that Hervé hadn't meanwhile sauntered home under his own steam.

Had Clairette seen me coming? She dished out a fairly greasy croque monsieur as soon as I walked in, but hadn't prepared two servings. From this I inferred she took for granted I'd be lunching alone. I couldn't shake the premature dread he'd permanently disappeared, and did Clairette feel any differently? In any case, my plans to gallivant across France were null and void. I'd stay and search till Hervé resurfaced or I had to fly back for the fall semester. I owed him that much and more. It further dawned on me that to beat the bushes for him by myself was a fool's errand.

The black phone on the counter was a clunky rotary model, and I barely suppressed a patronizing double take when a dial tone affirmed it worked. Clairette's advice on reaching the police consisted of a laconic "Seventeen," which also worked.

The Domaine fell under Boulbon's jurisdiction. I reported an elderly resident was missing. Gone for six hours, I reluctantly admitted, leery the authorities wouldn't step in till he'd been AWOL overnight or longer. So when the French equivalent of a desk sergeant asked if this were someone suffering from dementia, I shamelessly said yes. Might as well play the dumb foreigner card for maximum worth and later claim, if necessary, I hadn't understood the question. Forgive me, professor, wherever you are.

I ended up joining the constabulary and their volunteer deputies on a daily sweep of the area. These were likable homegrown sons, good-humored and stolid, who preferred the sporadic excitement of law enforcement to cultivating alfalfa. The countess and her dogs were not as deranged and wild, respectively, as Clairette had warned, at least not in front of uniformed officers. The chorus of cicadas had gradually reconvened that first afternoon, and the mistral always tagged along. Of the professor, though, we recovered no trace, as I'd bleakly anticipated. His "cosmic joke" had also vanished like a mirage, whether it had holed up somewhere or met an ignominious demise.

If her employer's possible demise tapped any emotions, Clairette scrupulously bottled them up. Out of professionalism, I conjectured, or habitual reserve. Or else what? I've been coming to grips with that ever since. She was manifestly able-bodied but never made herself available for search parties. Could be she was avoiding me, or did my peregrinations from breakfast till supper have something to do with avoiding her? As if magically, meals were always ready on the stove when I tromped in. And her dealings were perfunctory but with good graces, as if cooking for me were an extension of her duties to Hervé. All told, she really owed me nothing, and her gruff exterior, I theorized, must have hid a genuinely nice core for her to feed and put up with me those two weeks.

Typically, sometime while casting about in fields and glades and family plots and ravines, I realized how I should have contested Hervé's presumptions about his captive chimera, that first logy, jetlagged night. Say the creature had been born into a much more oxygen-rich environment, wouldn't sealing it in rock have made its chances of long- or short-term survival all the more infinitesimal? Sealed its fate, so to speak? Why not posit microorganism instead that wriggled through a seam of coal into a cavity, thriving in isolation to fill its stygian house? Did it even have to be ancient or the beneficiary of suspended animation? If Hervé had released a Guinness-record specimen of amphibious plankton, a supersized mite, would that be any less extraordinary, freakish or provocative than a Carboniferous holdover?

I wished with all my soul I could dispute these points with the professor, but I had the morose hunch he'd stumbled on his "pet," and in the aftermath of that reunion, I shouldn't even count on recognizing his remains. Nor was it consoling to reflect that his first breath upon sundering the coal may have fatally infected him.

Hervé must have apprised Clairette of my departure date, for on my last evening, over a plate of coq au vin and frites, she announced that she would drop me at the airport. Maybe she'd been such a good sport all along because she'd always had the end in sight.

We had to get an early start, before the milky overcast burnt off. She drove the archetypal "bagnol," a sputtering Citroen that might have left the factory in 1948 or 1988. For fetching groceries it was fine, but illegal on high-speed autoroutes, obliging her to navigate tortuous back roads.

Half an hour along I'd heard nothing from her except the wheezing of her majestic nose. Content, was she, to wrap up our acquaintance in silence? Not I. Not in my now-or-never position to solve a nagging mystery or two. Should worst come to worst, I could live with alienating her for twenty odd minutes. "Did you have any idea what the professor had confined in the dining room?"

Her answer spent a good while percolating. "Did he have something in the dining room? I thought to have experienced that evil smell once earlier. But it was many years ago, when other people were in the house. They found an ugly little animal in the coal bin, and that one vanished also, as God required. It was unclean, profane. It could not be permitted in a decent home."

As always, my running translation might have been prone to error, though I'd hazard my ear for the dialect had markedly improved during this stay. And from the nuances, the implications of her statement sprang such a host of questions that I rode dumbstruck for the duration, which may or may not have been her intention. When the chugging engine ceased, so did my useless ruminations: what had Clairette done accidentally or deliberately, what were her motives, how attached was she to the truth? Hoisting the backpack from between my feet, I bumbled out the door and mustered the composure to thank her lavishly for everything and wish her the best. She restricted her valediction to "Très bieng."

Maybe jetlag's impact on my IQ, both coming and going, had been more chronic than I'd realized, or maybe I'm not as smart as I've been led to believe. After being home for days, the connotations of Clairette's reminiscence, as oracular as it was pithy, were still sinking in.

From blocks of furnace coal had emerged not one but two "profane" specimens. Why not premise a dormant third or more, waiting for the chisel? At the cost of another trip to Marseille, the honor of discovering "quelque chose incroyable" could be mine, with Hervé sharing in rightful credit, to be sure. Or else, like scorpions, the chimeras had traveled exclusively in pairs, and I'd have wasted weeks and self-respect pulverizing coal.

I did contact Clairette twice a month for any news of Hervé, then once a month, then bimonthly, and desisted once the effort of placing me seemed to annoy her. Neither a stitch nor hair of her old employer ever came to light, and about his "ugly little animal" I dared not inquire. So much for the elusive, essentially mythical beast of "closure."

I also never dared bring up revisiting the coal bin. The possibility of courting Hervé's kind of doom did stifle my initiative, and the landlord may already have packed his possessions off to next of kin and signed new tenants. And how would I justify all that hammering in the cellar to those newcomers?

No, I'd missed my opportunity, wasn't even aware of it till weeks afterward, and could never have exploited it unless I'd added 2 and 2 while en route to the airport, and had I done so, Clairette would probably have refused to turn around, particularly for the business I had in mind.

I'd wager, though, that nobody has ousted her from the property, or ever could. She's taciturnly cleaning and cooking for the occupants, whether they like it or not, and poised vigilant for a resurgent whiff of "profane animals." Even if her new employers are as Provençal as Clairette, I'd also bet they find her no less insular and enigmatic than I did, as if she herself were some anomaly hatched from a lump of coal.

welcome back

The banner next door proclaimed "Welcome Back" on expensive glossy vinyl, no spontaneous, affectionate scrawl of spray paint on a bedsheet. The colonnaded porch it spanned, like mine, fronted an overgrown bungalow meant for the aspiring blue collars of a century ago, and now the demesne of a family clinging by hangnails to middle-class gentility after latest banking bust. Those demographics were typical on one-block Greene Lane, our low-key side street bracketed by statelier, busier avenues.

Eerily quiet electric taxi pulled up by the neighbors' curb. Maybe nobody heard it and therefore nobody flocked out with open arms. Shelby disembarked on his own and weakly swatted at cab door, which fell short of closing by a few inches. He carried no baggage, at least none that anyone could tote for him. Unease furrowed the driver's brow as he guided his fare to the steps.

Of course Shelby was dazed, shaky, disoriented. He'd just come back from the dead. And I, not a nosy neighbor as a rule, had no handy explanation for my rapt (but not morbid or voyeuristic or empathetic) surveillance through parlor curtains. After all, resurrections had become common as luxury SUVs around here, both of them in differing respects vehicles, status symbols, displays of conspicuous consumption.

Maybe I liked giving myself the creeps. People, I'd venture, typically didn't, which led me to puzzle why springing for full-grown clones, memories and allergies and all, of defunct loved ones has caught on as it has. Ghoulish, I call it, and a major dent in the equity. Or do next-of-kin borrow against their homes to regain the providers without whom their homes were good as foreclosed?

Wait a minute. Poignant street scene had distracted me into a synaptic pothole. I'd initially peeked out scant seconds ago on the off chance of catching Cassie park in the driveway. She was due home this weekend, not from across the Styx, but from allegedly great outdoors. She, not I, was the glutton for blisters, dirt, bugs, roughing it in general. Separate vacations, I staunchly believe, are the best safety valve for marital stress. And godforsaken wilderness probably wasn't conducive to clockwork schedules and cellphone service. My nervous watchful habit accomplished nothing except, perhaps, funneling angst into a single neurotic channel.

Cassie, anyway, had a buffer zone of several days before she'd qualify as AWOL from the office. As for Shelby and me, we were out our doors in sync on Monday morning, bound for the bus downtown and "normal" workweeks. I wondered if more boisterous reception awaited him from colleagues than from the folks.

Like Tweedle Dum and Dee in Oscar de la Renta suits, we set off for the stop at the corner. I couldn't expect normal affability, had to excuse awkward pauses, searching squints during first chat after rebirth. He recognized me all right, but as if second-hand, through reports by a mutual friend.

To ride beside him as he stared glumly at gilded East Side fostered the impression we were on a prison bus. I'd stuck with safely impersonal palaver about baseball, the weather, national headlines, but flailing efforts to dispel his stifling mood threw tact overboard. My jaw clenched ruefully the instant I asked, "So how was your weekend?"

"Same as always." He answered promptly, betraying no indignation, and in flat affect I may have misread tightrope balance between casual and sepulchral. Had his family followed the tack of treating postmortem absence like no big deal (apart from the formality of front-porch banner), the better to reintegrate him into everyday routines? Was that more or less insensitive than cake and ice cream to celebrate retrieval from the grave? Assuming Shelby's memories were unabridged, how vivid, how distressing was his death to him, how much beyond his last breath had he retained, and how could that not be too private for even his wife to share?

Yes, this was a hefty bushel of wool to gather from a bland "Same as always." He disembarked first, and merged with the square-shouldered tide sluicing through the revolving doors of nondescript high-rise. Nobody cast a second glance at this trudging miracle whose original body was probably ashes on the wind. Maybe nobody around him worked at his firm. And who save I would have detected a vague looseness in his bearing, as if he were off the bus but still a passenger? Or was that purely an inexplicable figment of mine?

Shelby was out of sight and mind till Tuesday evening, at which point Cassie's no-show status verged on worrisome. I had to remind myself she'd flouted ETAs before, and a failed afternoon trying her number only meant she was roaming overlong where signals didn't go. When the bus from downtown dropped me off, I cherished hopes for clues out front that she'd returned, but half a block away my gut was positive she hadn't.

Shelby was on his granite steps, cupping pensive head in hands, bathed in Western exposure that lent a waxy, lucent complexion. He brightened as I passed, and waved me over. Well, if he could handle sun in his eyes, so could I. "Sometimes you really need a break from family activities, you know?" He jerked a thumb toward front door, and I nodded cautiously. We weren't such pals that I could tell whether he was pulling my leg or prey to partial amnesia, in light of recent ultimate break in activities. "I've always appreciated our in-depth discussions."

What "in-depth discussions"? How much was there to appreciate? Random banter across the fence, a few beers on his deck were kindling unfounded warmth and wistfulness. Was he wearing rose-colored lenses of previous-life nostalgia? I smiled pleasantly. Faulty cloning wasn't necessarily involved for two people to hold discrepant views on the strength of a friendship. Basic decency dictated I humor him.

"What I'm saying," he went on, "is you can't speak freely with just anyone." Why this hitherto secret bloom of rapport with me, though? Or did it even qualify as rapport if it wasn't mutual? I couldn't exactly cross-examine him on these particulars, not without destroying vaunted rapport. No special bond had to join us, however, for me to make a better sounding board than immediate family.

Free speech is typically more circumscribed among those nearest and dearest, isn't it?

Meanwhile, I hadn't mumbled a syllable, and was dangerously self-conscious about it, a loose cannon liable to spew crippling faux pas. "They're great people, of course," Shelby affirmed, repeating thumb-backward gesture.

"So how are the folks doing?" Thank God he'd been the one to bring them up, to steer small talk down a sanctioned path. But dubbing them "great people," didn't that demote them below the top echelon of intimacy, on a par with alumni club, blood donors, genial foreigners? Maybe they came to no more on the gauge of his affections. Beside me brooded an individual with the memories, the personality, the DNA of Shelby, except it wasn't genuinely Shelby, it was a surrogate, and the Shelby of woman born was dead.

I always had to wonder whether heartstrings or purse strings were foremost involved in reeling the dear departed out of oblivion. Into a vessel of synthetic flesh were deposited traits and trappings, obligations toward dependents and property, everything but innermost selfhood. Was that why Shelby's focus wavered and foundered as if his was a soul embattled, disconnected on ostensible home turf, a turf that included his body? At long last he addressed me with words that seemed to totter from interior desert, "Oh, there's been no change in them."

This pronouncement was too Delphic for off-the-cuff reply, its tone too ambivalent to peg as resentful or resigned. The essence of this man, this outgrowth of cells from a petri dish, wasn't that of the man shaped by Shelby's history, and I had to ponder the potential conflict between him and the Shelbyhood, the otherness, imposed on him. Beneath layers of Shelby was a core of blank slate, and how a blank slate expressed itself, let alone asserted itself, struck me as a mystery tantamount to the sound of one hand clapping.

I was also frustrated at how this tête-à-tête was undercutting the myth of "in-depth discussions." He regarded me earnestly, anticipating fellowship, good cheer, and the vein in my forehead throbbed harder every second I left the conversation dangling. What a godsend when his ten-year-old barged out, letting screen door bang behind him. He skidded in stocking feet to the edge of the porch, and flipped aside the cowlick overhanging his brush cut after the fashion of today's preteens, a whole generation accidentally impersonating quails. "Mom says your supper's gonna get cold."

The kid wasn't acting skittish or leery, not as if Dad had "gone away" somewhere without a snowball's chance of return, certainly not to hell or heaven. Nowadays when someone trots out the euphemism that family member has "gone away a while," it might well be only a while. Parents everywhere, without benefit of chart book, must have been navigating shoals of deceit, hiding funerals and changeovers to carbon copies from their children. Honesty would only be callous, traumatizing.

Meanwhile Dad, to my wary eye at least, was goggling dazed, adrift, as if waves of déjà vu bombarded him, as if his own son were familiar yet mystifying. The boy spaced out, apparently none the wiser as paternal circuits froze. Then some autonomic correction kicked in, circuits cleared, and Dad blinked and refocused on his offspring with a tic of reflex dissatisfaction, an ill-concealed undercurrent of feeling bilked as if the kid carried baggage of learning deficit or behavioral disorder. But for better or worse, Shelby was "himself" again.

"You kids and Mom are everything I have in this world," father somberly notified son who bolted back in as if nobody had said a word. I was halfway to my feet when screen door banged and made me flinch, despite watching it swing. Again, I couldn't quite read Shelby's tone, tinged with fatherly sentiment or maybe regret at his lot. Whatever the original Shelby had sown, his replacement had to reap, with no say in the matter. I saluted goodbye without looking him in the face. My empty house promised bleakness enough.

Yes, these clones were shaping up as one more innovation too initially irresistible, like heroin or fracking, for sober assessment of downsides. Even presupposing no dissonance between the imprint of Shelby and the man underneath who'd been born practically yesterday, Shelby had suffered fatal mishap on a business trip. He hadn't asked for reanimation, had no choice about awakening into grievous hock (between resurrection and household expenses), mired doubly deep in a domesticity from which he might rather have bailed.

He'd never, in my estimation, qualified as enthusiastic breadwinner, so why start now, a virtual indentured servant to kin and creditors? Sure, he could bail, providing he'd be happy dropping off the grid, holing up in Hawaiian rainforest. Where were the ethicists, the sociologists, the shrinks earning fat paychecks to foresee the impacts of new technology on society, on cases like Shelby? No red flags had caught my roving attention on TV, in print, or online. How could I be alone in willingness to put myself in the shoes of the counterfeit dead?

Meanwhile, discomposure of my own was brewing. I flung jacket and tie onto the bench in the foyer, breezed into the kitchen to plunk frozen lasagna in the microwave, and was naively upset that the light on caller ID box wasn't blinking. Well, who isn't overdue for a pleasant surprise?

Weeks of solo housekeeping had been daunting; not unlikely I'd misfiled passing mentions about where and why Cassie might be dawdling or detained. Amidst reviewing the day's snail-mail and e-mails, stripping down to bachelor-quarters undershorts, pouring a scotch and soda, I strove on and off to reconstruct Cassie's comments as she researched itineraries, booked hostels, packed. By the time the microwave dinged, I felt spent, as if I'd been tugging obsessively at locked bureau drawer.

I gave up on that drawer, but as I wrote checks for bills, watched TV, and played Wii, anxiety over Cassie floated behind me like a devilish balloon tied to a belt loop. Ill-digested lasagna churned around mercilessly, sending me to the bathroom circa 9:30 for Pepto-Bismol. In consultation with mirror above the sink, I rinsed hot pink dribble off my chin, and probed my reflected eyes to fathom a nagging impression that Cassie's whereabouts would still come to me, if I could only apply the will or energy.

I was consoled, persuaded that going to bed would serve some purpose, by a contrarily joyless sentiment that seemed to emanate from the disdainful man in the glass, and not me. Dad's discontented once-over of his youthful quail proved that the bedrock slate of newly minted substitutes definitely wasn't blank, for even if the former Shelby had harbored misgivings about his son, he wouldn't have advertised them on his face. Current Shelby hadn't the same emotional makeup, the same relationship to his world, as previous Shelby.

I had no idea why this insight comforted me. I dozed off like a carefree baby, tuning out Shelby's bellows of shitfuckpiss and worse (how un-Shelby-like) that carried through bedroom window, followed by juvenile crying jag. From the seabed of my conscience bubbled a final notion into the hypnogogic murk, Why not do something nice for Cassie in her absence?

And so upon shambling home Wednesday, I didn't bother going in, couldn't hack the foregone disappointment of echoes answering my hello, but knelt out front in jacket and tie to weed the nasturtiums and zinnias, something nice that Cassie had been after me to do since June. Thus I was at ringside when nuclear family achieved critical mass.

Funny, I'd just been mulling how Shelby's outburst last night had sunk like unnoticed pebble into the viscous pool of East Side quietude, a patrician quietude that made me heedful of grunting too loud as I uprooted a maple sapling. No such compunction muzzled the shrill anguish from Shelby's attic window, right below front gable. A crash, perhaps of someone tripping, scattering dishware, magazines, croquet balls upon impact, preceded a second and soon a third heartsick caterwaul, from male adult lungs I surmised were Shelby's, broadcasting grief and despair as if he'd gone out five minutes and come back to the one he loved best gruesomely slain.

I was fixated on the window, listening, maple stalk in sweaty death grip. Unbelievable for nothing but silence to inch glacially by after hellacious meltdown. Equally unbelievable, for all that ruckus to bring nobody on the run among busybody homeowners. Or was I sole witness, among dozens, minus drapes to spy through? To be part of their scrutiny, of the spectacle by mere virtue of squatting here made me unduly paranoid, shaky on the inside though stock-still to onlookers, till shooting pains skewered my stiff neck, my Achilles' tendons.

I'd also swear I hadn't blinked for the eon, or at most the minute, before Shelby's wife, somewhere on the second floor, began shouting to dissuade him of something, and then screeching because she hadn't, as punctuated by three heavy, crushing thuds. A gratuitous fourth cut into the renewed silence.

Cellphone was in hip pocket, and if I dug it out I could call 911, but no, in my torturous pose I couldn't free it, it might as well have been sewn fast, and I was powerless to move. What excuses, though, hindered neighbors behind drapes? Why weren't faint sirens already Dopplering into range?

Too late! The quietude was in smithereens again as the discord of two or three bawling kids burst from elsewhere on the second floor. Damn, I could never keep straight how big a brood Shelby had. One, then another, and yet another (or had the second briefly eluded blunt-force trauma?) stopped squalling as that godawful pounding resumed. And still I squatted like an effigy of useless, aching stone, and to further my inertia, the conviction seized me that any action of mine would only lead to blacker guilt later, to a worse end. But for whom?

I'd hardly begun to puzzle at my suddenly erratic cognition when I heard police en route, with an otherworldly resonance that may have been entirely in my own ears. By my subjective clock they were taking forever, as if squad cars were rising on slow elevators from remote subcellar to the main stage of this theater-in-the-round, where stasis had regained tenuous control.

My trembling ankles finally gave out and my gabardine-clad knees indented the soil and I was staring oafishly at inert phone in my hand by the time a pair of cruisers sped by from the east end of the block and another pair pulled in from the west, several heart-beats later. They parked diagonally with headlights toward Shelby's, in V-shaped formation, blocking half the street. Eight cops altogether piled out and hunkered, aiming semiautomatic pistols skyward, behind Chevy Impala doors.

Me they ignored as if invisible, scrupling neither to question me nor shoo me away, and in formalwear, I wasn't exactly camouflaged in the garden. Should I have been insulted or simply baffled at my negligible profile? In deference to jittery patrolmen waving guns around, I continued playing statue. I wasn't worried about stray bullets from Shelby's direction, as he'd told me at least twice he hated guns.

Identical uniforms endowed the cops, in my overwrought perception anyway, with faces generic as well, except for one from whose mouth sprouted a bullhorn. Throw down your weapons and come out with hands up! How the hell much armament had high-strung informants implied Shelby was hoarding?

Shelby, in spite of behavior that had brought him to archetypal no-win standoff, really didn't have it in him to play the hardened criminal, hadn't picked up reflexes for self-preservation in any event. A corner window on the second floor smacked open at firecracker volume, and as if to push bluecoat nerves closer to snapping, bloody-shirted, stricken Shelby lunged into reckless sight, no challenge to marksmanship. Too far gone to realize he shouldn't obey instructions so literally, or maybe banking on fatal result, he lobbed a shiny bulb-ous canister at the cops. In midflight it passed for jumbo cocktail shaker or low-caliber artillery shell. And as he let fly he screeched, "You can't take me alive!"

That did it. A hailstorm of bullets sketched a ragged fan shape on either side of the window, and slammed Shelby into the shadows, arms flailing as if boneless. Scary projectile had thumped anticlimac-tically into the lawn, several inches shy of the sidewalk, and despite blood like fudge on a sundae and the ghastly dents at that same ta-pered end, I had no trouble establishing the murder weapon as an ordinary funeral urn.

With paramilitary élan the cops charged the porch, kicked in the door, and deployed throughout the house as per SWAT training lest a dead man get the drop on them. They barked the all-clear back and forth as they "secured" each room.

Abused, forlorn urn soaked up lukewarm predusk rays, in spit-ting range of where Shelby and I had palavered yesterday evening. Since potential bomb had proved a dud, its value as evidence was discounted in the heat of action. I, no less a cipher in the law's my-opic view, could have filched it with impunity. But what would I do with it? And no easier to picture, what maudlin or dunderheaded impulse had possessed the missus to enshrine cremated Shelby in the attic where Shelby mark II would bump into him?

Too bad jumpy patrolmen had liquidated Shelby for no deadlier provocation than chucking his own ashes at them. Too bad they'd further demoralized me by contributing to self-image as a nonentity. I could have told them who was in that urn, why it had served as murder weapon, and how they may have played into mad, despairing

Shelby's hands. But I wasn't in the mood. Let the boys downtown figure it out as best they could. My tax dollars at work, right?

The dents in stainless steel caught and released fleeting sunset gleams. I wondered whether eyes behind drapes tracked my movements homeward, or if they bothered with me no more than the police had. Was I really the sort of non-person to blend into the background, and what the hell was wrong with me, what could I be missing that made me so easy to miss?

In my fragile mood, the welcome of a dark, empty house felt natural and proper. No e-mail, voicemail, or post card imparted Cassie's whereabouts, which also accorded with deviously redrawn normality. For a wife to sever contact with a husband, conceivably for good and all, didn't render him less of a nobody, did it? My feet by force of habit plodded to the window where I'd watched for Cassie, but I wasn't ready yet to touch the curtains.

To be a nobody wasn't, on reflection, without its merits. The siege at Shelby's implied I had a ghost's freedom of mobility around authority figures, and I was under no pressure to guard secrets, not even from myself. Confronting the worst in me could inflict no damage, if there was nobody to damage. My hands, on their own initiative, spread the curtains.

An ambulance was parked on the sidewalk beyond the cruisers, toward the west end of the street, tail and interior lights blazing, tenfold brighter than pallid streetlamps. Driver and EMT were presumably in the house, to whatever purpose after fait accompli of multiple homicides.

Verandas and pavement were unpeopled altogether, no surprise in the wake of gunplay, but what kind of expertise had I ever accrued to predict human behavior? My vision coyly receded from well-lit street scene to unlit driveway, which wasn't too gloomy for me to discern what I already knew was there, though only now would I acknowledge it. The scales of secrecy have begun falling from my eyes.

Cassie's Durango was crowding the driveway, crushing ferns on the left and pachysandra on the right. It hadn't budged in weeks. A pretty conspicuous bottleneck, I had to admit, for any but the most wilfully blind. I was under pressure to guard secrets after all. To balance selective vision and self-deceit was the crucial trick, and failure to master it had cost Shelby his second life. I'd almost upset that balance yesterday by rashly tugging at the mental drawer of most recent interactions with Cassie.

Stability for the likes of Shelby or me hinged daily on fighting the urge to unjam those drawerfuls of repressed memories, to weed out downright false history. My death, and subsequent homecoming, and Cassie's death, yes, such a mental drawer had yielded an inch to reveal those general contents, but I couldn't yank it any farther for details. Nor was I privy to why my cerebral cortex chose now to let on that Cassie was out back in the peony bed, under the sphagnum. Was every bereaved family in mortal danger of playing Frankenstein?

High beams diverted my vision down the block again. A morgue wagon was completing official vehicles' work of occluding the street. What a pity about Shelby, but fatal blow-up had come of slipshod discipline, defective insight, nobody's fault but his own. Not to deny a grave miscarriage of justice had transpired! He, and I for that matter, deserved better than summary execution, whatever our sins. Within mature flesh we were, strictly speaking, like Frankenstein's monster, swaddling babes in the woods, virtual newborns. How could we be arraigned as adults?

Or need it ever come to that? Let's say I grab a shovel, uproot the peonies again, disinter Cassie. Would I still be guilty of murder if I scrounged up the DNA to bring her back? Yes or no, I refrain from delving into what that says about the value of human life.

Oh shit, two cops are headed over, sizing up Durango as they go by. Did they notice my curtains rippling? How will I react if they ask about Cassie? Wishful thinking, isn't it, that I'll remain invisible once I open the door? Distance to the backyard might now be insurmountable.

I didn't expect to panic at the prospect of helping the police with their inquiries, but here I go into the cellar. Lean on the doorbell, knock till doomsday, nobody's home!

Nope, they're not buying that, are they? Frantic search turns up nothing better for self-defense than a grungy baseball bat with a split knob. It will have to do. Hold on up there, I'm coming! Anything to stop that infernal doorbell.

houdini fish

Catch me, find me, see me if you can
I am the guilt of an honest man.
                    —ROBIN WILLIAMSON

As a rule I washed up before lunch, especially after handling the luminous machine parts. Departmental men's room was all mine, aside from the mild funk of previous tenant. Something that swam in circles troubled the surface of pink liquid soap, about due for a refill. I pushed up on the nozzle of clear plastic dispenser. Into my cupped palm dropped a gob of fragrant goo and then a thrashing Houdini fish, of brighter pink than its medium.

It was the length of two knuckles and stick-figure thin, eel-like but for the flaring dorsal fin and tail that folded flat along slippery skin, virtually disappearing, to let it shimmy through the teeniest circumferences. Hence the allusion to Houdini.

Not so long ago, the discovery of a fish in liquid soap would have qualified as miraculous, but this was the third in two weeks for me. I acted humanely and unscrewed the dispenser's metal cap and tipped critter back into its habitat, and made a mental note to ask the janitor to please add more soap. Some people would have rinsed squirmy varmints down the drain, but that was callous in my book. Whatever lived and breathed in soap was unlikely to survive in the same squalid conditions as a goldfish. The present specimen just needed an inch more wiggle room to be content, I reckoned.

And why not be nice to the implausible fauna? None of it, on anecdotal evidence, had attempted even trial nibble at human flesh in lavatories across campus. Its proper diet defied speculation, unless soap were food as well as home. The dispensers never used to deplete so soon, to that much I'd testify.

How vagrant exo-species had infiltrated them in the first place was no less mystifying. Custodians swore they poured nothing "foreign" from ponderous feeder jugs into de facto fishbowls, and 24/7 racing round and round never churned up rosy gunk till days after a refill.

A thousand associated questions went begging. But to me, this mere slip of a fish, steeped in a pint of soap and a Sargasso of riddles, was foremost incredible for the lack of inquiry it aroused. I couldn't be alone among the faculty in wondering about its geographic range, or could I? The news media, university publications, myriad blogs, and the City of Providence website were uniformly mum on the subject of pink anomalies.

Today, moreover, was like any other in the refectory, where I overheard no mention of said anomalies while nudging my tray through stop-and-go lunch line or dining solo at underlit corner table. Not that people were in denial. The Houdini fish met with bland acceptance as if it had always been there, had maybe dropped off our radar awhile, but wasn't worth fussing over just because it was back.

To the best of my knowledge, nobody debated whether biologic upstarts were the product of genetic tampering or a breach between this world and elsewhere. Outlandish theories, yes, but this was an outlandish animal. Nor had anyone, in earshot or in print, expressed surprise that these creatures rated such meager curiosity, which was as perturbing to me as the creatures themselves.

My own pet theory contended that the fish had always been here, and only our power to perceive them had changed, coupled with the mindset that since normal perception now included them, it was ergo normal to perceive them. In this, I had what we scientists call "parsimony" on my side, i.e., I was positing simply a shift in people, and not in people and nature and/or the laws of physics.

But what had triggered this no less outlandish reboot in our brains? I believed the answer was literally under my nose eight hours each workday, though I had nothing stronger than coincidence and gut instinct to support me. And embarrassingly, weeks went by before it dawned on me that Houdini fish had appeared right after I'd supervised the exhumation of glowing smithereens.

Going into that project, I hadn't banked on raising more than potsherds, peach pits, and rusty nails, and I'd intended nothing more than teaching the rudiments of excavation to undergrads who'd never touched a trowel. The courtyards of the freshmen dorm complex West Quad were due for a reseeding, and the drainpipes under them needed replacement. With all that dirt slated for upheaval, what harm in letting Anthro 101 delve into it first?

The Quad had gone up in the 1950s at the expense of two historic blocks on Benevolent Street, between Benefit and Brown. With permission from University Hall and Buildings and Grounds, I had a week during spring semester to sink a trench and reclaim anything the Eisenhower-era bulldozers hadn't pulverized, before modern backhoes wrought their own havoc.

According to the deed in university files, the kids had dug their shovels into the site of former Crawford Tillinghast house, which a photo at the Historical Society depicted as a plain, snug domicile of bricks and black shutters, a product of the lull between Greek Revival and Victorian pretenses. It had huddled at the end of a narrow cobbled lane, behind a pair of Federal mansions that fronted the sidewalk. How sad that such venerable charm had bitten the dust for the sake of nondescript, hulking barracks, as it had all over College Hill. My wife would have told me yet again to get over it or go work for someone else, but she was too often out of town for Ivy League depredations to weigh on her.

From the tidbits I gleaned about Crawford Tillinghast, his relative seclusion within crowded neighborhood must have suited him well. City Archives, the Office of Vital Statistics, and tax rolls portrayed him as an unmarried homebody, with servants for company and no conventional employment. Several volumes of the *House Directory and Family Address Book* list his occupation as "philosopher," before he vanished from that and all other public annals after 1920. His was one of those founding families of Providence that had fanned out into every stratum of society, from statesman to hit man, and "old money" sustained his proverbial "shabby gentility."

A modern kinsman characterized him as an "eccentric inventor," but in keeping with fabled Yankee reticence, demurred from further comment on Crawford's personality, as if another century's black sheep were still a family embarrassment. During that phone interview, my request for access to a picture of Crawford was also handily rebuffed with the patrician drawl, "I've no idea where such a thing might be." Dead air followed as I cast about for a seemlier topic. He also pleaded ignorance regarding the balance of Crawford's life post-1920, and no paperwork or microfiche at City Hall or the *Providence Journal* enlightened me, as if the records were defective or had been expunged through familial clout.

After Crawford's departure from the *House Directory*, his property stood derelict for decades till the Tillinghasts bequeathed it to the university, which apparently didn't have to ask twice. In their correspondence to the Office of Gifts and Endowments, Crawford's heirs professed an enthusiasm for new dorm construction that read between the lines as relief at unloading the house and seeing it demolished.

True to New England form, everything of value down to doorknobs and light bulbs had been stripped before the house changed hands. Or so I gathered during the dig down to Crawford's cellar floor that unearthed little beyond the typical bottlecaps and hambones and shirt buttons. That little, however, was more confounding and compelling than a truckload of the usual detritus.

The shale foundation of the house had caved inward, back when heavy equipment had dumped and graded tons of fill, the blank canvas on which to create the Quad. On top of and among the fieldstones, and therefore previously entombed behind them, were brass and steel fragments of some custom-built machine, neither tarnished nor rusty. And plainly these remnants were all of a piece, based on weak but perturbing purplish glow from each least wringer and rivet divested of dirt. I sent someone to the Geology Department for the nearest Geiger counter, and it picked up nary a roentgen. The scraps moreover gave off no static charge or heat—though to judge by their hue, they might have been the remains of some economy-size violet-ray generator, still shedding wan residuum.

Those gizmos, basically elaborate joy buzzers, had captivated health faddists of a century ago, who bought into claims that tinted currents cured a range of ailments from cancer to frigidity. The fragments that my sophomores bagged and boxed and toted to the anthropology lab, though, were too numerous and miscellaneous to jibe with any online illustrations of patented snake-oil mechanisms. I imagined this debris would add up to some brainchild of the "eccentric inventor," but hadn't the foggiest why it had been hidden, and by whom.

Whenever I didn't have classes to teach or office hours or other obligations of untenured faculty, I'd tinker with my fluorescent jigsaw of a device, premising I could divine what it did and why it glowed if I could reassemble enough of it. A hundred percent restoration was impossible because several baggies contained slivers of glass, sorted by color, of deficient quantity to guess their original shape and dimensions. Nonetheless, undeterred by lack of aptitude, I'd refit roughly ten percent of the coils and baffles and cogwheels in a couple of weeks.

The kids didn't share my fascination. Unanimously, to varying degrees, they were nervous around the purple light, and I didn't force them to assist me. That wouldn't have been nice, any more than washing a Houdini fish down the drain. Admittedly, something was creepy about the ongoing glow, as if the machine, despite its destruction, were still running, performing its function, incapable of being deactivated once it had been turned on.

Yes, I could have brought in expertise from Engineering, and I might easily have lost control over my find, and credit for it as well. I've no naïveté about the level of respect a "soft science" like mine is accorded on this campus. Besides, did Tillinghast's contraption necessarily operate on a principle that a run-of-the-mill technologist would grasp any better than I would? Bottom line: an archaeologist unearths artifacts, and artifacts belong in an Anthropology Department for proper handling and conservation.

After locking up the lab come evening, I habitually strolled home and stayed put. Nocturnal crime has been on the rise of late around campus, predictably what with the lousy economy, and my Fox Point neighborhood of students, faculty, and blue-collar Portuguese families hasn't been immune. My wife and I are blessed with a comfy third floor in a quiet triple-decker, and too bad Phoebe's not here more to appreciate it. On the other hand, maybe being apart so often has saved us from growing apart, or at least from focusing on any expansive rift. As good a formula for wedded bliss as any?

I was, in upshot, quite used to holding the fort, which boiled down to dumping shrimp flakes into Phoebe's tank of neon tetras. Last Friday, that and surfing for less guilty viewing than 20/20 had been about the size of my dance card. I hadn't expected burglary to enter into it, but who does? Larceny, anyhow, was the apparent story upon eventually noticing what had happened. After supper I scattered fish food across aquarium surface, only to find no takers. The wife's lovely tropicals were gone. Stolen, I had to infer, yet nothing else was missing, and no signs of break-in were visible at doors or windows. This wasn't even the sort of theft I could bother the police with, for all they'd do was doubt my sanity or sincerity. I unplugged the tank's hood light, filter, and heater. Why waste power?

The hell of it was, as the night wore on, resentment at thievery cooled and ebbed away. The absence of fish in the tank rated the same blasé acceptance as the presence of fish in soap. Someone or something had poached a school of tetras, and so what? Phoebe didn't often ask about the fish when she phoned, and I'd be foolish volunteering anything. Her initial agitation, I figured, would lapse into apathy as quickly as mine if she got the news here first. Of course, the longer she was out on the road, the longer I could avoid controversy, but that was no way for a devoted husband to think.

Out to retrieve the paper Saturday morning, another untoward sight awaited me, and this one too I downplayed, far longer than did me credit. Twin heaps of clothing cluttered the sidewalk. From the porch I stared them down as if reprobates still occupied them, while declining to focus on specific garments. Were these the souvenirs of sex in the bushes, or of sloppy-drunk foray to the twenty-four-hour laundromat? I was young once myself, but good grief!

That evening, as usual, I courted disappointment by tuning in local news for any exposé on pink fish. Instead, I learned that a preppie and four East Side collegiates had gone AWOL in the past few days. Police weren't ready to assume or rule out foul play. Voiceover appealed to the public for information, as snapshots of the missing scrolled by. Those bundles of clothing out front did spring to mind, but only to the point of pondering whether their owners were still missing in action or had slunk back to reclaim sullied articles. My lukewarm concern didn't stir me to go check out the window.

I should have put two and two together immediately, yet shied from connecting dots between abducted youth and purloined tetras and unremarked Houdini fish and luminous debris. To fob off the human potential for monstrosity on some cosmic agency felt like flawed thinking, a copout, a throwback to blaming the devil and letting moral imperative off the hook. I was too much a man of science, "soft" science or not, to lumber into that pitfall.

I next ventured out of doors for the Sunday paper. The disreputable heaps of apparel lay unmolested. This is, after all, a sleepy side street, and who more than I would want to touch them? Upstairs, I unsheathed the *Journal* from orange plastic sleeve, and yesterday's snapshots of kidnapees dominated page 1.

At second glance, the gravity of the situation sank in. One path to peace of mind was open. I grabbed magenta rubber gloves from under kitchen sink and rummaged a sturdy, humerus-length stick from under the boxwoods screening the porch. Struggling into the gloves would have been easier after some coffee. I refrained from poking into the castoffs that contained a bra and tampon. In the other bunch I thumped a wallet and pried it out of Dockers pocket. It held three bucks, a RISD ID, and a Nordstrom credit card. The name embossed in plastic was not among those in the photo caption, but that didn't exempt me from step 2 toward a quiet conscience.

I called the cops. The desk officer picked up on the tenth ring. Evidence maybe pertaining to the missing young people, I said, was down on my sidewalk. "What sort of evidence?" he barked.

At his combative tone I drew a momentary blank before rallying to say, "Clothing and personal effects." Okay, he'd send a car. Begrudgingly, as if appeasing a pest. I sat with my coffee on the front steps to ensure no garments crawled off at the last minute.

During my third cup, two squad cars pulled up, a pair of uniformed cops in one and a pair of suits in the other. They glowered at the abandoned articles as if they'd seen the like before and weren't happy to see these now. The more rumpled, putty-faced plainclothesman directed the uniforms in their forensic chores. His lean, more debonair partner introduced himself, with a jerky handshake, as Detective Delacroix. He pronounced it "Della Croy." I presumed he dyed his hair and mustache to get them that exquisitely black. His chestnut eyes were taking continuous stock.

His questions soon acquired the character of hostile catechism. When had I first observed the suspicious items? Yesterday morning? Why didn't I report them right away?

I'd only heard about the abductions, or whatever they were, this morning, I argued, deciding I could fudge by twelve or fourteen hours if he was going to be such a hardass.

Did I touch any of the materials under investigation? Yes, I'd removed a wallet, and it was upstairs. Why had I tampered with a crime scene? Well, I wouldn't have considered it a crime scene had I not found the wallet, and to prevent contamination of evidence, I'd been wearing gloves, for which not a tad of gratitude was forthcoming.

Would I mind if he came up and got the wallet? I couldn't very well say no, though inwardly I vowed that henceforth someone else could reprise the thankless role of good citizen.

I couldn't interest him in any coffee. He proceeded straight to the wallet when I pointed at it, on a corner of the dining room table. From inner jacket pocket he produced white gloves and a Ziploc container. I'd have recommended a user-friendlier brand of bags, based on my own lengthy experience securing artifacts, but with his snippy attitude, the hell with him. I was already sorry for inviting him in.

Once he'd stashed his prize, he quizzed me on my term of occupancy in the apartment, my marital status, and my livelihood. In the meantime he strode around and rubbernecked, with the overbearing air of owning the place. I've no idea what keepsakes he'd have deemed proper to an archaeologist, but he ogled Phoenician oil lamps, Gallo-Roman priapic statuettes, and Egyptian faience amulets as if all might be used to hide or smoke illicit substances. Or as if I'd looted them.

He brightened on reaching the aquarium, till he discovered it was empty. "No fish in here?" His tone was accusatory.

"They were stolen. Sometime Friday." Damn, I'd rather that hadn't come out, but his zealous tour of inspection was too off-putting for me to ad lib a sensible lie. Thank God he was miles from ferreting out my quarter-ounce of stale cannabis.

His brown eyes narrowed dubiously. Was I joking? Trying to throw him off his game? Incredulous or not, he didn't grill me, thank God, on why I also hadn't reported that, or how much else was gone. I yearned for him to go jangle someone else's nerves ASAP, and I doubt he'd have disagreed that vanished youngsters rated more attention than burgled tetras.

Then I had cause to regret that burgled tetras hadn't distracted him. He approached an uncomfortable inch inside my personal space and demanded, "Where were you for the last six nights?"

"Monday through Friday, I left campus around suppertime and came back here. I didn't go out again. I stayed in last night, too." My eyes were fixed on his, with the steadfastness of the innocent.

"Who could verify that?"

"Nobody. I was by myself for the duration."

He nodded, maintaining eye contact all the while.

"Wait a minute. You're not implying I had anything to do with these kidnappings, are you?"

He didn't say. He stared at the threadbare Berber carpet as if embarrassed at my outburst. "So your wife's been out of town?"

"She's been away for the month."

"And when's she coming back?"

"Next week sometime. She's not sure yet."

His line of sight swerved from the carpet back to me. "Do you have any accomplices?" His delivery was casual, as if asking for a glass of water.

"What?" How dare he, after I welcomed him into my home? Offered him coffee? "What the hell kind of trick question is that? Why would I have accomplices?"

"Thank you. That should do it for now." He cast judgmental parting squint at the desolate aquarium and turned on his heel. Just like that, our interview was over. Except that my agenda found impulsive voice at the last instant. "At the precinct house, do you have pink fish in your liquid soap?" I called after him.

He brusquely about-faced with one foot out the door. "No, they're white. Like the soap. Why?"

"The ones in my department are pink." Not exactly a scintillating reply, and it convinced Delacroix that no further exchange with me was necessary. He resumed exiting as if I hadn't said anything.

He neglected to shut the door behind him. I stared out at the sunny landing while trying to absorb the ugly reality of becoming a "person of interest." And that, fundamentally, because I'd let my conscience get me "involved." Plus, dammit, I'd forgotten my cup on porch railing, where it had to be cold by now and perhaps peppered with drowning gnats. I went and retrieved it, tossed contents unseen into the bushes, and noted that the clothes were gone, with a pair of chalk outlines in their place, as if *corpora delicti* had indeed occupied them.

The cops weren't admitting yet that criminality was afoot, but that's how they were operating. And Delacroix, it dawned on me, was likely more on the ball than he realized. No, I hadn't waylaid people and stripped and disposed of their bodies. Yet if uncovering Tillinghast's debris had somehow brought Houdini fish into the world, it might also have snatched victims out of it, or brought in additional, man-eating species. In which case, yes, I was at involuntary fault, though in no wise conceivable to hardheaded Delacroix.

All the same, the onus was on me. I had a unique handle, right or wrong, on the wherefore of putative crime spree. I alone might be able to stop it. Since I no longer had tetras to trot home and feed, I burned nightly oil at the department, futzing with outré filaments and pipes till headache set in. Then I washed my hands, bid Houdini fish au revoir, and flagged down University shuttle bus on Hope Street. I had nine measly blocks to ride, but doorstep service these days was preferable to the lurking perils of nocturnal promenade.

My lab work was predicated on the theory that the intact device had projected an insidious radiation in which soap-dwelling fish, and worse, entered human perceptions, and vice versa. That radiation, with its short-range purple blush, had become intrinsic to each part of the device, regardless of breakage. Were I to rebuild enough for a control panel to present itself, pulling a lever might, I prayed, switch off the machine and kill its emanations and send everything alien back where it belonged. Yes, that was my best excuse for a plan.

I wasn't unmindful that earth had exerted a damping effect all those years on the violet radiance. I could rebury the entire load and maybe prevent further trespass from elsewhere. But would entities already here be expelled? And had any paired off yet to breed? I had to go with my gut, and it warned of time lost, lives lost, if reinterment accomplished nothing.

I also had to resist temptation to dump fluorescing miscellany on Engineering Department doormat, ring the bell, and run. Possessive pride had earlier kept me from sharing my find, and now engineering types, safe to say, would laugh in my face halfway through my alarmist spiel. This mission of mine was strictly solo, which was just as well if the device actually had no bearing on local felonies.

When Friday rolled around again, I'd reintegrated roughly half the hundred-plus bits, shed some pounds by skipping suppers, and listened to messages on home voicemail too late to return them. Phoebe was due back on the Acela next Wednesday evening. I'd have to insist she ride a cab up the hill. To let her walk would be reckless, and my driver's license had expired ages ago. Also, Delacroix was intent on a follow-up conversation, and would I stop in at his office tomorrow? Three such communiqués in as many days conveyed mounting impatience. Well, he knew where I lived, and where I worked. Why interrupt my vital efforts to indulge his petty bias against me?

Plus, I had to play catch-up with recent news. Two postdocs, a waitress, and a Whole Foods clerk had dropped into MIA limbo. The pressure was on, and it behooved me to chuck the whole frustrating mélange into cardboard file box and lug it home. Technically, yes, the material was University property and I was stealing it. But stealthy predator was unlikely to ease off for the weekend, and neither should I.

I slapped the lid on the box and exited into pale setting sunlight. Shuttle service wouldn't start for two hours, forcing me to hoof it with increasingly awkward, ponderous freight. Couldn't be helped. Purple rays escaping chinks and seams in cardboard container would prompt unwelcome attention on a nighttime bus, whereas spooky emissions shouldn't loom as garish on daylit sidewalks, when those sidewalks theoretically posed less danger.

But how well can mere theory model reality? I had the better part of my trek to go when the urge to rest aching arms asserted itself. On my left was deconsecrated Baptist church, repurposed as condos in the '80s. The square brick belfry's Gothic windows framed ventilation louvers, ineffectually shielded from nesting bats and pigeons by tattered wire screens. The light had relaxed into that lambent gold unique to this town, and the iron handrails flanking granite steps looked awfully inviting.

I was about to lower my burden onto the rail and balance it against my stomach, when the gilded ambience shifted to a seasick green. Meanwhile the belfry had apparently cast an arresting shadow on me. I shuffled backward without getting out from under it and belatedly grasped the obvious. The sun was setting not behind the church but behind the houses across the street, in the West as usual. I craned my neck toward the greenish heavens, faced with two dismal choices. Either something sizable had me in its oncoming shadow, or this wasn't a shadow according to Webster.

Too unnerved to govern my actions, I whipped around to confront anything sneaking up on me. Metal components slid and clanked to one side of the box, which would have tumbled from my hands if I hadn't hastily clutched tighter. As it was, the lid came loose and released a mini-aurora borealis. The shadow, or whatever it was, lifted, and the dusk faded to a more wholesome grey.

I hustled on, resolving to put up with sore arms for another five blocks. If I'd been in the same danger as previous fatalities, it had passed. Too bad that believing so did nothing to calm me. The purple radiance, I conjectured, may have worked as a repellant. Or I was simply keyed up and attaching false importance to atmospheric subtleties. That didn't, though, invalidate the principle I stored for future reference: we humans might be visible to things from elsewhere that might be invisible to us.

Another sort of predator was parked out front in a late-model off-beige Impala. The driver's head was tilted as he watched my approach through rearview mirror. He retrained his sights on me after he got out and tossed cold dregs from Dunkin' Donuts travel mug into scraggly grass below the boxwoods. Delacroix bypassed sociable greetings. "Ignoring me's not such a good idea. You academic types think you're above it all, don't you?"

I shook my earnest head. "Sorry. I've been tied up with urgent lab work every night."

He didn't bother disputing that, as if above such mealy-mouthed excuses himself. He opened passenger-side door, pitched plastic mug to the floor, and slammed the door. He nodded toward the box. "What's in there?"

"It's the project I've been losing sleep over." Why volunteer to show him? If he wanted a peek, he wouldn't be shy about it.

"You are looking pretty haggard. Okay then, go ahead up. I'll follow." Did cops study imposing themselves at the academy, or was Delacroix inherently gifted? "I'd like to see what you've been so busy with, if you don't mind."

I let brief eye contact serve as acquiescence and trudged forward. Venting my irritation wouldn't get me anywhere. He spared me further chat till the box perched on the table where the wallet had lain last week. I, at least, was uncomfortable in the lowering silence. Was I supposed to offer him a soft drink? A beer?

"Sometime tonight, please?" Fine, you overbearing bastard, I'll stop trying to play the gracious host. I'd hit every light switch on the way in, including the dining room overhead, hoping to render the violet emissions less blatant. I unceremoniously flipped the cardboard lid clattering to the floor. Delacroix bent slightly closer to the opening and his eyes widened. His newly mauve complexion made me wince.

"Is this an antique generator you're rebuilding?"

I brightened in spite of the circumstances. Very impressive! There was a brain behind the jackboot persona. Of course the pieces would add up to a generator, a term I'd never actually resorted to myself. "Why yes, I doubt it could be anything else."

"How come it's glowing?"

"That's what I want to find out. I've determined the artifacts aren't radioactive, if you were worried."

He shrugged. "You're the one with your face in it day and night. Anyway," he waved dismissively at the box as he straightened his spine, "not why I'm here."

From an inside jacket pocket he pulled and unfolded a sheet of Xerox paper. He watched me the whole while as if I might jump him any second. He thrust the paper under my nose. "Know her?"

I couldn't immediately tell what, let alone who, was in front of me. Head and shoulders in shaky resolution must have been downloaded, cropped, and blown up from a gallery in Facebook or the like. But yes, I did recognize her, and my heart turned to lead as I guessed where this was going. "She was enrolled in one of my classes."

"Was?"

"If she hadn't disappeared, why would you be showing me her picture?"

"You didn't notice she was absent the last couple of days?"

"It's a big survey course. Taking roll call wouldn't leave me time to teach."

"So you're denying she was a memorable student. You might be interested to learn you had the opposite effect on her. In fact, right before she vanished, she characterized you as 'creepy' and 'borderline pathological.' Any idea why?"

"No. I'd never even interacted with her."

"Are you sure?"

"Did she say I had?" Delacroix had to be quoting out of context, deleting pertinent verbiage just to faze me, and he was succeeding. Some stranger, a literal face in the crowd, had been badmouthing me, and to what end, apart from incriminating me in the eyes of the law? And I couldn't vent feelings of righteous indignation and betrayal, could I, because she was suddenly a crime statistic. *De mortuis nil nisi bonum*, right?

Delacroix was hanging on my next words, but he couldn't have entertained serious prospects of a confession. I inquired, "What did the other missing persons have to say about me?"

"Very funny." One fraught connection did not an airtight case make, did it? The only excuse for anyone to call me "pathological," and it was a stretch, would have been my febrile obsession to reconstruct Tillinghast's generator, and how ironic would it be if a casualty's catty statement had condemned me for doing my best to prevent further deaths? Especially if the outcome was my arrest as the serial killer? If she had ever focused balefully on me in the lab, I'd been concentrating too hard to feel it.

Delacroix had let up needling me and was resurveying my knickknacks and the vacant fish tank, as if they were new to him. He seemed to approve no more than on the first go-round, but abstained from comment. Confusion and uncertainty clouded his brow as if he'd been afflicted with déjà vu. He blinked at me and cleared his throat. "Anything you'd care to get off your chest?" He was merely going through the motions of harassing me now. Too disoriented, blindsided somehow, for his heart to be in it. I couldn't account for that, but I wasn't complaining.

A change of subject might be salutary for both of us. "I'm a little surprised there's no curfew in effect."

"Me too." He plucked the Xerox portrait from my grip, refolded and repocketed it. "You can't even tell me her name, can you?"

"I'm seldom able to match faces in the classroom with names on test papers. That's modern education for you."

"For you, maybe. Pretty sad." Something about my modest abode was definitely getting under his skin. The purple tinge escaping the box? "I've seen enough of you for one evening. Good luck with your doohickey. Stay in town." Again he neglected to shut the door behind him. Despite faulty manners, in Delacroix I did find encouraging proof that vanishing persons, unlike vanishing tetras, weren't yet "out of sight, out of mind." The influence of the "doohickey," so far anyhow, had its limits.

Nor did Delacroix have to fret about me as a flight risk. Skipping town was hardly an issue, since I was averse to leaving the apartment. And home wasn't necessarily a sanctuary, as the fishless aquarium reminded me. With a nylon cord I strung one of Tillinghast's luminous springs for a necklace, a latterday equivalent of my Egyptian faience charms.

Obviously I never disappeared, but impromptu talisman afforded me no help in my project. By Monday morning, my ambition was shot to hell. I'd progressed after forty-eight hours to the maddening stage of finding that the parts on the table were too interchangeable. Two thirds of the elements did constitute an abstract, vaguely Art

Nouveau sculpture, which left about three dozen loose items that wouldn't go with each other or with the partial restoration.

I'd wasted the bulk of a precious week after all and would have to start from scratch and pray I didn't make a fresh batch of errors. People and their accustomed world were meanwhile in jeopardy, and it was my bungling fault. Plan B resurfaced as more rational alternative. In hindsight, I'd have learned whether it was effective in much less time than I'd squandered on fruitless tinkering.

Behind the house was a forsaken, rectangular weedlot of a backyard, enclosed on three sides by weathered palisade fence, half of whose pointy tips were broken off. That was where, after breakfast, I carried shovel and a Stop & Shop paper bag stuffed with mechanical jumble. I cheated a bit by retaining the steel spring around my neck. Why not assess first whether burying 99% of the device banished Houdini fish from our dimension, before I disposed of my wearable "health insurance"?

I dug down two feet and some inches into rusty yellow sand. I gave no thought to laboring quietly, to scouting for witnesses in neighboring upper-story windows. Why should inhuming a load of scrap metal, or to an outside view a plain brown sack, rouse suspicions? Most likely and logically I was disposing of dead cat or parrot or hamster. Logic also recommended backyard burial for convenience's sake, in case I had to resume cobbling together the "doohickey."

A leisurely shower and lunch before my one o'clock lecture were still in the cards after completing the job. When I swung by the lab later, no one remarked on the absent artifacts, or on absent classmate for that matter. Noses to the collective grindstone. Except now, paranoia tugged at my sleeve and whispered, How many of these kids were feigning tunnel vision because they found me "creepy"?

More felicitously, no Houdini fish swam in the soap. That guaranteed me nothing, though. Someone might have rinsed it down the drain, but on mulling how to ask if anyone in the lab could remember doing so, my brain stalled out. Or had the device's output inhibited my wits, as it had inhibited curiosity about the fish?

In the interim till Phoebe's homecoming, I encountered no Houdini fish, no Delacroix, no malign nimbus hovering behind me. Delacroix, I surmised, must have had other leads to chase besides me, thank God, red herrings though they had to be. Nor did the lack of something stalking me, like the lack of fish in soap, mean that reburial had achieved its goal. The prophylactic magic of my necklace might simply have kept the bogy at bay.

Hence when Phoebe phoned to announce she was at the train station, I firmly reiterated that she hail a taxi, but needn't have bothered. She was already up to speed about the "East Side Snatcher," who'd made the *LA Times* and BBC News.

Would she perceive her fish were gone the second she walked in? After a minute? An hour? On other occasions, her approaching taxi had caught my ear. Not tonight. The trunk slammed, and a subjective instant later, the key jingled in the lock downstairs, and the wheels of her suitcase were ka-thunking rapidly against each step as she climbed. I managed to relieve her of luggage when she had a scant flight and a half to go.

On the landing we hugged and kissed and genuinely enjoyed the novelty of each other's presence. She waltzed in ahead of me while I dragged her luggage the last few yards. At the threshold I stopped short as she shouted while hanging paisley twill blazer in the closet, "What's that pile of clothing doing out front? That's not one of your suits, is it?"

I went racing downstairs, had almost made it to the first floor, and voted to plunge on, flinching, when I heard, "Where the hell are the tetras?" Chances were nil, weren't they, that apathy about the tropicals would take hold of Phoebe before I got back? Was I a heel wishing she'd postponed her return?

The garments were child's play to locate. Creamy seersucker fabric fairly shone in the dimness between streetlights. New bundle overlapped the smudgy chalk boundaries of old bundles. Even if beige Impala weren't parked across the street, my knees would have weakened with a queasy certainty of whom the invisible beast had disrobed, or devoured, or disintegrated. Whatever had transpired was, as usual, bloodless, which made it bearable to poke through jacket pockets for confirmatory badge. Brown Oxfords were, for reasons I didn't dwell on, pointing in opposite directions, and the folds of pinstripe shirt swaddled a bulging letter-size envelope.

Headache began to throb as I gazed on the envelope in my clammy grasp. Of course its contents would relate to me. A search warrant? An arrest warrant? I balked at undoing the flap. I couldn't picture anything it could be that wouldn't be too much right now. I dropped the envelope on top of Delacroix's other earthly remnants.

I turned my beleaguered sights toward third-floor windows, but the wife's silhouette was in none of them. Phoebe would be fuming, or tearful, or baffled, or reassessing our relationship. She had no inkling, and never would, of how lucky she was, of how she owed ongoing existence to the bare minutes by which Delacroix had arrived first. His demise at least served to suggest that reburying the piecemeal contraption did not get rid of previous intruders. Or did it suggest that my holdout of one measly spring made all the difference? And what if planting that single artifact with the rest made no difference except to render Phoebe and me utterly vulnerable?

Meanwhile, I must have been crazy to loiter this long by the "scene of the crime." The simple proximity of Delacroix's effects to my address was bad, and to be placed here by witnesses might circumstantially clinch my guilt. But dealing with this mother lode of incrimination was impossible till I clarified my status with Phoebe.

The apartment was devoid of any sign my wife had returned, apart from bedroom door, formerly open but now, no doubt, bolted against me. "Phoebe? Are you okay?" I called in vain, an inch from varnished paneling. "Can I come in? Can we talk?" In a couple of respects I was glad she didn't answer. The more she sulked, the more of an opportunity she allowed for detachment toward the fish to overtake her too. She'd also decide it was "just like me" to storm out for an hour, if she ever became aware of my absence.

The less she knew about my program of self-protection, the better. To save myself from wanton criminal prosecution, I elected to engage in flat-out criminal behavior. Rubber gloves were redeployed from under kitchen sink. On the porch I could discern no onlookers on sidewalks or in windows, and I dashed down, scooped up Delacroix's ensemble, and scrambled to his car. It was unlocked. His keys were in trouser hip pocket.

I cruised in low gear along the darkest side streets, meandering the quarter-mile to the road skirting the waterfront park. I'd avoided leaving fingerprints, but it was a poor anthropologist who'd down-play the difficulties in erasing all traces of my DNA. I also wanted to work fast and minimize chances of being seen. Or mugged.

The neo-Colonial Marston Boathouse and its marina surround-ings gave way to the alluvial terrain of India Point Park. I pulled over. No one was around, but that could change in a heartbeat. To crank down the windows and just ditch the Impala, and let salt breeze air out my dander and other vestiges, made for much less spectacle than rolling a car down grassy slope into the bay. Plus, if fortune smiled, some foolhardy delinquents might swallow the bait of keys in the igni-tion, and then where might official vehicle fetch up in the morning?

The loosely knotted wad of Delacroix's belongings I flung past the outsized pegboard of rotten, stubby pilings into the clutches, if fortune kept smiling, of outbound tide. The afterthought of magenta rubber gloves followed suit.

I slunk homeward, gawking left and right on high alert for pass-ersby to shun, and accompanied by a heckling awareness of my stu-pidity. Why hadn't I thought sooner that Delacroix must have logged tonight's itinerary somehow? Would I have done anything this dumb before the excavation of Tillinghast's mind-altering debris? Cops would come knocking, possibly before dawn, and though Phoebe might be none the wiser I'd ever gone out, she'd seen Delacroix's outfit, and her fine eye for detail would have absorbed telltale color and fabric.

I was screwed. I commenced to hyperventilate in anticipation of the third degree. How to protest my innocence? And of capital of-fense, I was damn well innocent. No, I'd only taken what rash, clod-dish steps I could to prevent entrapment by the legal system, though I'd thereby ensured the system had me hogtied. To my small com-fort, the state had the burden of producing a body, and chances of that were null.

Suppose I stuffed a week's essentials into a rucksack, hopped a midnight bus, vacated the state? Then when more East Siders van-ished, dozens of witnesses could testify I was in New York or Philly or wherever. Yes, that would be this sinking man's straw of choice. My feet picked up a more upbeat pace.

They carried me within three blocks of condos-cum-church where I'd almost been reduced to dirty laundry. The budget-minded owners of a nineteenth-century faux palazzo had enclosed their yard with plastic picket fence. Some extra color on a white corner post captured my attention and quashed my optimism. Streetlamps gleamed off a horde of tiny turquoise carapaces. I bent close enough to identify them as mites of freakishly star-shaped outline, a breeding population hundreds of times over, and whatever comprised their original diet, here they were feasting on plastic. The bottom several inches of the post had been ingested, and they were chewing madly on. It sounded like a thousand tiny dental drills.

Whether Tillinghast's machinery was under the soil had become irrelevant, as had fleeing town or defending my innocence in the long term. I had a gut-level pessimism that rebuilding the generator wouldn't help either, that enlisting the Engineering Department wouldn't have altered the consequences. Even if alien bugs didn't receive the same unnaturally bland reception as Houdini fish, they foreseeably spelled the collapse of modern culture. What the hell was my hurry? It was like racing toward the end of the world.

No squad cars were waiting by the house, a shallow consolation better than none. I should have savored it. I reentered quietly to sustain the illusion I'd never departed. Again, as with my entreaties that Phoebe take a cab, I needn't have bothered.

The door still stood between us, with no disorder to show for it if she'd sallied out. "Phoebe?" No sound or syllable emerged. Was she speechless with wrath, or with the apathy that should have been setting in by now? I dragged in a dining room chair and sat elbows on knees, chin upon fists, studying the glass doorknob. If I twisted it, would the door be locked? If it were or not, would the wife caterwaul blue murder? Or would the silent treatment go on forever because there was nothing of her in the bedroom but a bunch of clothes on the shag scatter rug?

I could have lent her my protective neckwear or culled another talisman for her from the Stop & Shop bag. But I hadn't, and was I to blame for not thinking of that? Had my unconscious plotted to reinstate permanent bachelor quarters? I never used to agree with Freud that accidents never happened.

My eyes are now aching and bleary from watching the door. My ass has been numb for ages. I ought to pack according to plan or reconsider trying the doorknob. But I can't conceive of moving, which binds me like a vacuum seal. Human decisions will soon carry no weight in any case, and Houdini fish will inherit the earth. Or actually they won't, because turquoise mites will have eaten the soap dispensers.

When the cops finally do turn up, they're welcome to bust their way in. Until then, my wife might simply be incommunicado and nothing worse, and I might not be complicit in her death. And the longer I can dodge that complicity, the longer I can delay facing my role in the grander scheme of insatiable chaos.

girl on a swing

I felt uncomfortably like a voyeur, but maybe that was the idea. The girl, ten years old at most, sat on a swing, alone in a minimal playground of swingset, seesaw, a slide. The treeless, grassless earth and ashen sidewalks of surrounding quadrangle were surrounded by dismal cement apartment towers, probably subsidized housing. The girl's tatty green dress afforded the only color in sight. Even her shoulder-length hair was a muted blond.

Despite the bleakness, she was smiling at me, loosely gripping the chains of the swing, slippered feet crossed and dangling inches above the dirt, no burden of loneliness or insecurity in armature-straight posture, as if something wonderful was bound to happen. VonFleet had her centered in the midground. There was no foreground, unless by luring me into the scene he'd figuratively incorporated me into the painting, coopted me into functioning as foreground.

I admired, I adored this portrayal of innocence, purity, spirit unfazed by crushing odds or blissfully ignorant of them. I also had to wonder what had gotten into VonFleet. He wasn't wallowing in sentiment here, but neither was he in tried-and-true form, synthesizing the *joie de vivre* of Edward Hopper, the warmth of Francis Bacon, into his own special cynicism that resonated profitably with disaffected "limousine liberals." For anything of his to exude this much positivity was unique, hugely boosting its collectability and my eagerness to corral the gallery attendant.

I tapped her on red padded shoulder. Arch those eyebrows to the ceiling, missy, you can always schmooze later. She tore herself away to plaster red dot below the frame on the clear tag with pointedly bland title, "Girl on a Swing." Hey, if I'm all excited about finalizing a sale, you should be too. The excitement, in fact, dispelled my qualms about voyeurism like a leaf-blower scattering the dew.

Then again, had it not been that snooty kind of a gallery, the opening would have been mobbed and someone else might have snagged my prize first. Moreover, VonFleet, who at least affected old-school etiquette, wasn't so beset by hoi polloi and sycophants that he couldn't sidle up, with an overfull goblet of sherry for each of us, to toast my purchase.

In tight black tapered trousers and loose tuxedo jacket he fit the bill of modern downtown romantic, updating the sallow complexion and sunken cheeks of Victorian consumptives with those of no less terminal junkies. But did he or didn't he shoot up? He'd parlayed much of his mystique from rolling up sleeves in front of no one, including his models.

He also sidestepped my curiosity at why one image of optimism bided amid canvases of standard angst and despair. Instead, for the duration of the sherry, he pontificated about the "fallacy of conscious intent" and went to congratulate me on my "taste and perceptiveness."

I pulled right hand from sport-coat pocket, and dammit, fingernail caught and expelled my worry beads, technically a rosary of lopsided pearls, *objet trouvé* of Greek vacation beachcombing.

"Oh, does it pay to pray?" VonFleet joshed, and suddenly it was my turn to equivocate.

I hefted adult pacifier like it was nothing to hide. "Yes, insofar as it's cheaper than therapy."

"Now you tell me!" We shared a dry chuckle before he ambled off and I plunged clattery pearls back into hiding and kneaded them for all they were worth. Good thing he never shook my clammy hand. Banter is such a strain.

The pearls also get a workout, and have likely become more lopsided, at the Foundation, where I hate writing letters of rejection, let alone denying applicants in person. I especially hate the association of my name, my face, with stifling dreams, with derailing careers, though I'm never sole decider and it's part of my job, pure and simple. Nor can I complain at how the Foundation has treated me, well enough anyway to afford the occasional VonFleet. Why feel guilty about being valued, as if anyone of sound mind protests at too flush a paycheck, as if less for me would translate into more for clients?

Beads unfortunately lay forgotten in office desk the evening I revisited the gallery. Shoulder-pad girl was on duty and played dumb at my tongue-tied astonishment after hauling out my VonFleet. In the few days since the show closed, the artist had gone and altered my art, had spoilt the absence of foreground by planting a post at far left, the height of a doorframe and girth of a guardrail, plausibly for hanging a ball from a rope. It was also about right for a whipping post.

Maybe any insertion would have violated the enticing, almost too deliberate symmetry, but this was especially disturbing somehow, changing the mood from innocent to ominous. The painted world still drew me in, though against my better judgment. Worse, my misgivings about voyeurism rebounded front and center. Was his secret agenda to perturb the viewer, and had VonFleet purposely sold an unfinished canvas?

The longer the attendant feigned ignorance of the problem, of deception and bad faith basically, the more agitated I became. I was a hairsbreadth from demanding her employer's cellphone number when, as if trivial afterthought had popped into her brain, she handed me an index card.

On it was scribble from VonFleet about his "mandate to correct flaws" by fostering "less transparent balance," "enhanced dimensionality," and "a more involving narrative." What the hell? I could decide at home, at leisure, away from this stressful context, whether VonFleet was bullshitting or not. Obnoxious hipster was at her perkiest bubble-wrapping and bagging my purchase to speed me out the door.

And if he weren't bullshitting, I soon concluded, so what? The unease of living with that post in the picture only increased. How extraordinary really that such a simple device, a mere dozen brushstrokes, could transform a salute to hope and resilience into a foreshadowing of atrocity.

Living-room sofa was the picture's provisional home till I had a chance to call VonFleet, and with every passing glance I was more "involved" with the "narrative," as he'd intended. But had his "conscious intent" been to show me a girl smiling placidly at her own undoing, at harm somehow guaranteed by the post in the foreground, able to get at her because of the post? Maybe he'd been bullshitting only when he dismissed conscious intent as "fallacy."

Such wild surmises in themselves implied his dozen brushstrokes were weighing dangerously on my mind. VonFleet had to remove them! Naturally he begged to differ. "This is not the artwork I paid for!" I protested into the phone, trying to blink away anxiety as my eyes met those of pale blond waif on the sofa. "This tampering with work no longer legally yours, it's . . . it's . . ."

"Anathema's a pretty strong word, isn't it?" Precisely the *bon mot* I was struggling to avoid! Christ, how could he know me that well? "You must understand money can't always call the shots. This isn't a case where your control of pursestrings can handicap me." An acerbic edge to VonFleet's suaveness upped my anxiety, as did the insinuation my "control of pursestrings" had handicapped him. When? How? Hell, I could brood about that later. I had to stay on message.

"But I liked the painting before, and I don't now!" I didn't specify why. Had I guessed his motives correctly, my malaise about the post would hand him ample excuse to gloat.

"A collector of your refinement surely appreciates that the artist must be sole ultimate arbiter of his work. You have to respect his prerogative, defer to his experience and vision."

I couldn't help noticing VonFleet's repeated use of "his." If he were a she, would I be up against this degree of pride and obstinacy? "Very well, but it's my prerogative to demand a refund from the gallery for your so-called vision, or initiate legal measures."

That at least evoked lip service in the direction of compromise. "Please, do us both the favor of striving for an open mind a bit longer. To let you dictate content like a CEO would be tantamount to cheating you. Take whatever time you deem fair, then tell me where we stand." He was plainly stalling, but with just the right note of entreaty to label me an asshole if I didn't humor him. An artist in more than one regard! Fine, I signed off, talk to you next week.

Uncanny how he'd homed in on a zone of my psyche I did my damnedest to shut out. Therein was etched in stone I was basically an asshole, no idea why, but that explained my chronically friendless, loveless, solitary status. Otherwise it should have mattered that I never dreamed of going Dutch on a date, and pulled my weight or picked up my share of checks on boys' nights out. Nor did I earn a salary by denying the worthy their due, just the opposite.

My social life deserved better. Not too much to ask, but how to ask was beyond my ken, presumably because I was an asshole. And worst, I've been saddled with this status via no actions or inclination of my own, to the best of my knowledge; not my fault I was an asshole!

Had I not been, I'd have allowed an extra day or two for amended painting to grow on me. But no, I lacked the decency to find out whether a new phase in my relationship with "Girl on a Swing" was transient or not. The "involvement" induced by passing glances now entailed stopping in my tracks and going blank for unremembered minutes, snapping out of it with lingering vertigo as if tidal forces from VonFleet's tempera realm had floated me like an insensible cork into and out of the frame. I owed VonFleet none of these worrisome details. Why brighten the smug light in his eyes? He, meanwhile, owed me three callbacks.

Not to say I was exempt from pangs of conscience, gratuitous or not. VonFleet's veiled accusation sporadically haunted me, despite bewilderment at how I'd "handicapped" him, unless I'd vetoed some Foundation proposal of his. No such recollection surfaced, but then I've processed thousands of applications. Suppose he did harbor a grudge, and stoked it by obsessively rereading rejection letter with my signature? Still, marring his own masterpiece to settle ancient score seemed unbelievably petty and ineffectual, and besides, I'd obviously done him no lasting damage. I also couldn't believe the amount of importance this would attach to me, to rate a celebrity stalker.

Contrarily, though, he was shaping up as a stalker who played hard-to-get. I realized the need to terminate his grace period, seize the initiative, when I emerged from a string of trances fixated on the indigent girl. The painting had ceased for good and all to be a source of pleasure because she aroused livid hatred in me, her nobler-than-thou pose, tatty green dress, vapid smile. I didn't question why; I only knew she had to go.

My id was probably responsible for waking me at 2 A.M. with course of action full-blown on my mind. I was grateful for that, even though it cost the rest of that night's sleep recapping the specifics lest I forget. Arriving late at work would doubtless be the lesser evil, compared to one more evening with heinous painting. Over breakfast I triple-checked that beads were in hip pocket, to rally focus and morale. Phoning ahead would be foolish, sabotaging any element of surprise, ceding golden opportunity to VonFleet for evasive tactics. I was ready to lean on his doorbell all morning in the event he were, or pretended to be, a sound sleeper.

To bag the painting without peeking at it was the tricky part. I unrolled and finagled open and laid out 20-gallon garbage bag and had only to slide the canvas in, managing to blur my line of sight an inch above the frame. But the hate compelled my eyes, damn them, like ball bearings to a lodestone. I glared at contemptible undaunted face.

As usual, I shook free of blackout with recent past a blank, no telling how long I'd been under. No less typically, I was dizzy and lurching, except the lurching didn't result from dizziness; rather, I was seated on a train accelerating around a curve. My palms were damp, in jittery response to this bouncy ride, or a touch of motion sickness. These hypotheticals, however, didn't clear up why I was short of breath, with burning lungs, as if I'd had to dash for this train, as if my life depended on it.

As mass transit went, I've ridden less grubby buses. Between threadbare upholstery, busted reading light above my seat, repulsive brown sunburst stain on the carpet, here was the kind of decor VonFleet might have envisioned.

The train was still gathering speed and must have left the station scant minutes ago. As for where it was bound, I'd either misplaced my ticket or hadn't bought one before boarding. And where the hell was I? I braved another bout of motion sickness and peered out dingy window. Cold sweat instantly swamped any stirring of nausea.

An expansive, desolate housing project, like America's answer to Soviet urban planning, was chugging by. Pretty as a picture it wasn't, but in a picture was where it belonged, where I'd previously encountered it. There was a dismal courtyard with apartment blocks on three sides, the fourth in direct view of the tracks, not even a precautionary chain-link fence alongside the embankment, and what insane luck or kismet ordained I'd look during that key second?

Like a snapshot, bygone scene persisted on my retinas, of bare-bones playground in the center of treeless courtyard, a nonfunctional post to one side, and no child in view, no sign of human habitation apart from a girl's slipper in dust beneath the swingset. I had to flinch away, in unthinking, visceral distress, though to no avail because my eyes took the afterimage with them.

Folded newspaper occupied otherwise empty aisle seat. I scanned it for distraction, and it failed abysmally. Celebrated downtown artist had been slain in home studio, headline proclaimed at top left on page 1. His model had found the door ajar and him inside; no word on whether his sleeves were rolled up or she'd rolled them up in search of track marks. Beyond that mystery for the ages, strangulation and not OD had been the cause of death, and the murder weapon, brazenly abandoned *in situ*, was a string of antique rosary beads.

What hour was this, what day, how long since I'd committed the crime, for that's why I must have been abjectly fleeing town, minus baggage and ticket? Enough time had elapsed for the grisly business to see print. Wherever I was, it was nowhere obliged to make temporal sense. Someplace where assholes go? I'd be consumed by guilt and shame, no doubt, if I could only remember what I've done.

Out of habit I thrust hand into hip pocket. Of course the pearls weren't there. My fingers were too slick with sweat for a good grip on them anyway, which wouldn't have stopped me from trying, because I desperately could have used them today, and for the foreseeable future. On the plus side, the law can never nab me in a painting. Or am I eluding a dragnet therein for the killer of the nobler-than-thou girl? Rickety train carries me ever faster toward one calamitous destiny or another, and right now it's moot whether the world outside is blurry with velocity or because it's composed of brushstrokes.

sinister illuminator

The drolleries came as such a happy revelation. Bret was resigned to stupefying months of "Rough Guide to Medieval Art" because his top picks for an elective had unfairly filled up in the lousy three days before he got around to registering. With soporific prospects of Madonnas, nativities, angels, and crucifixions till June, a fun instructor would be the one saving grace, and Bret had miraculously lucked out. Saint-Cyr fleshed out bone-dry dates and jargon and names with scandals and atrocities. He'd also introduced illuminated manuscripts with a slideshow of drolleries. Wow!

These were thumbnail images in margins or empty corners, and widescreen enlargement in pitch-dark auditorium made their details and vivacity all the more exquisite. Bret couldn't believe he alone was discreetly chuckling. Here was quill-and-parchment equivalent of those zany animations on Monty Python! Knights fighting giant snails, women in bed with dragons, bipedal fish out for a stroll, a horned, shaggy demon bowing like a maître d' beside a monstrous tongue doubling as open drawbridge, Bret didn't need Saint-Cyr to clarify these weren't mere doodles by bored monks.

In fact, the illuminators generally weren't even monks, though decorum often dictated they dress the part when visiting monastic clientele. They weren't always men either, these miniaturists with assembly-line workshops, international repute, and significant wealth. Alas, grand names now forgotten along with their specialty and the folkloric, allegorical, alchemical meanings of their depictions, too universal back then to bother writing down.

Bret hardly ever approached an instructor after class or elsewhere, any more than he'd attempt interacting with a character on stage or on TV. Yet today, in a rush of nervous excitement, he had to praise Saint-Cyr for showing what was "so cool" about the Middle Ages. And amazingly, Saint-Cyr had kindled scholastic ambition in Bret, who enthused about his brain-wave topic for a term paper, to decode one of those "surreal" motifs among the drolleries.

Saint-Cyr, transferring notes from lectern to briefcase, paused to nod vigorously, "Good, good!" He blinked and added, "Let's hope this is an occasion when fortune favors the brave!" He then hustled over to assist gangly grad-level aide, struggling to pack up the slide projector. Bret was elated at ringing endorsement of his proposal. Or was Saint-Cyr humoring him? Craftily cutting short their conversation? Bret wished he was better at construing nuances. Funny, too, how he'd assumed that adage about fortune favoring the brave referred only to flatulence, like on Dad's ancient T-shirt from the attic, with a broadsword cutting cheese.

Infatuation with pet project wasn't flagging anytime soon, though course load kept it from receiving optimal attention, and as usual afflicted Bret with chronic lethargy, blunted concentration, making him play perpetual catch-up with any given class at the expense of the rest. He scarcely had energy to party or chat up potential girlfriends. But everyone must have been in that same boat, right? Sometimes this truth seemed self-evident, and sometimes not, insofar as certain colleagues always had smart questions for teacher or an arm around a sexy waist, goddammit.

Conducting research at the Crock posed another grim barrier to scholastic excellence. He could seldom recall the official name of the humanities library; "Crock" was short for the moneybags who bankrolled it during the '60s, golden age of modernist eyesores. "Crock" was also what everyone must have called him growing up, poor guy! Hatching a profound thought, let alone staying awake, was next to impossible in humungous sterile milk crate, but the deluxe facsimiles of medieval documents, rare and valuable in themselves, were down in Sublevel C's noncirculating stacks, so that became Bret's main haunt.

A flasher at these secluded depths allegedly slunk from and back into darkness after exposing himself to girls toiling away at study carrels. Bret was skeptical, partly because it would lend the place too much undeserved personality, partly because it sounded like the kind of myth that persisted unconfirmed for decades. Maybe by now it was the ghost of a flasher!

Along with any ghosts, priceless originals were also entombed somewhere down here, and if Bret managed "some sort of break-through," Saint-Cyr would "see about green-lighting access to the real stuff." Okay, that would somewhat compensate for the unexpected wall of tedium he'd hit. Who'd have dreamed that reams and reams of feudal cartooning had survived, 90% of it mundane and self-explanatory, swordfights, coy damsels, jousting, musicians, kings and queens? Bah!

As for the enigmatic 10%, he'd plainly get nowhere without much heavy mental lifting, and the more he saw, the stronger his temptation to chuck it as idle nonsense, deranged cries for help. But the easy out wasn't for him, no quitter he, nor was blanket ignorance of European history, Latin, or art criticism an unbeatable handicap. He had the IQ to persevere in elite Ivy League, and *ipso facto* the inventiveness to assess drolleries in terms of adjacent graphics, English-language synopses of content. Weirdo artists were still people, and to paraphrase some ancient Roman, nothing human could be too alien, right?

Anyway, having bitten off this epic undertaking, Bret felt he had what he wanted from "Rough Guide to Medieval Art" and attended lectures as a necessary evil. Not even silver-tongued Saint-Cyr could enliven deadly-dull icons, tapestries, stained glass, flying buttresses, mottes and baileys. Then again, every wide-ranging session touched on manuscripts, imparting choice factoids as if purely for Bret's benefit. Miniaturists, apparently, were in unofficial competition for blank space with scribes who inserted pithy complaints of eyestrain, writer's cramp, cold scriptoria. Had drolleries been directed not just at the text proper, but also at copyists hogging the margins?

He put this to Saint-Cyr at their next one-on-one. Bret's ego soared at the opinion his premise was "intriguing," only to crash with the objection that "nobody had previously noted any such interactions." Bret mounted no defense; Saint-Cyr's office was an oasis of charm within another butt-ugly modernist slab housing the Art Department, though the musk of dusty volumes, the pantheon of African, Polynesian, Greek idols, the host of kitschy Mexican, medically aberrant, and bestially prehuman skulls scattered Bret's attention, immersed him in a bobble-headed daze. Not a place conducive to linear thinking!

"But you're not far off from a common interaction between the illuminator and the patron, whose portrait might turn up in a heavenly choir or a crowd scene, like a movie extra," Saint-Cyr expounded as if awarding a consolation prize. He leaned back in creaky swivel chair, hands folded over his girth, reminding Bret of an otter. For a prof, he was an awfully nice guy. Bret had overheard colleagues call him Quince, and while Bret wouldn't dare do that, they were on a first-name basis in his head. Maybe they'd be friends someday. Crazier things happen.

So how was the exegesis coming? Bret guessed what "exegesis" meant in context, and whether out of vagrant urge to impress Quince or the slippage of cognitive gears, found himself spouting he'd have to examine tons more drolleries before proceeding, even as inner voice screamed the well-entrenched opposite, that he'd already seen too many for a lifetime.

Did raised woolly-bear eyebrows connote Bret had impressed Quince with his initiative? Or did they insinuate Bret was dissembling, like in freshman year when he'd requested an extension on a take-home exam to fly out for Grandma's funeral? That instructor had obliged him, despite arching eyebrows of wry incredulity; the hell of it was, Grandma really had died. Saint-Cyr cleared his throat and restored Bret to the moment. "I understand how captivating antiquity can be, but bear in mind, midterm is next week."

Okay, so professorial eyebrows were indicators of a conscientious mentor. Not that he wasn't overstepping a little, to presume Bret needed micromanaging. Bret was voting age, fergodsakes, a full-fledged adult. "Well, Godspeed!" Quince bid him after penciling in their next appointment.

Of course, the brainstorm that definitely would have wowed Saint-Cyr didn't occur to Bret till he was out on the sidewalk, to wit, if patrons made cameo appearances on the painted page, why not artists too? But maybe he wasn't up to demonstrating that x number of drolleries were by the same illuminator, before detecting possible likeness among his works. Bret heaved a resigned sigh. Like so many inspirations, this one would wither in the pod, a dead end.

Or not! Sometimes the universe cooperated as soon as he threw in the towel. That night on Sublevel C, instead of dinky carrel, he snagged a cushy seminar room and its massive conference table. He'd opened oversize tomes to especially compelling reproductions, in bleary vision an overlapping spread like a rumpled quilt across mahogany tabletop. One design in the patchwork popped out as if somehow awry. It was at the wrong angle, didn't fit squarely onto underlying pages, had detached from the binding, was an oddly shaped foldout or simply the wrong dimensions.

As the truth dawned he was thunderstruck, overjoyed. Here was divine serendipity, A-plus guaranteed, passport to a career in academe, why not? A section of drawing in one book conjoined a section of drawing in its overlapping neighbor. Their perfect merge, in fact, fostered optical illusion that the right margin of the topmost book had disappeared, creating a unified tableau. At left, familiar shaggy demon invited readers across monstrous tongue of a drawbridge and through toothy portcullis gate. Background of leafy green tendrils and crimson flowers proliferated into the second book, approximating a bower or tunnel.

No, not exactly, for there the vegetation hooked a 90-degree turn downward, like a chute, enclosing a caped and cowled monkey beside a jolly crowned skeleton, capering together in freefall. Both illuminations were patently by the same artist, who must have intended they be combined, with putative missing pieces, into some meta-image, although these two facsimiles derived from monastic collections a continent apart, in Toledo and Salzburg. Bret was no closer to identifying self-portraits or cracking symbolic code, but to exhume this trans-European puzzle, this unsung genius operating on epic scale to no earthly end, was likewise monumental.

Bret's look darted, as it often did in the Crock after dark, to the murky sidelights of frosted glass flanking staunch oak door. He all too gullibly spooked himself with the suspicion that someone, flasher or otherwise, was lurking outside. Nobody ever was, and his jitters always dispersed in a minute. Tonight, though, he was extra paranoid at the notion that someone, theoretically, could bust in and poach his brilliant finding.

And along those larcenous lines, Bret may have felt more comfortable with Quince than with numerous uncles, which didn't make him an altogether known quantity. With sufficient incentive, who was above coopting the efforts of a vulnerable novice? Best to hold off trusting him till Bret had logged further results on his hard drive. That was friendlier than chucking temptation into a decent man's path. For now he jotted down his two books' titles, catalogue info, and germane pages, and for extra security misshelved them, adding their privy whereabouts to his notes.

Saint-Cyr's next lecture furnished yet another choice factoid. Behold the poster boy, he announced, for the demise of the whole illuminated tradition. On auditorium screen loomed the engraving of an outwardly rustic galoot in fur-brimmed cap and fur-collared mantle, and with gross sideburns hanging down to his chest. Ruthless cunning in his expression would have befit a snake-oil salesman, except this was the immortal Gutenberg, inventor of the printing press and a pillar of the modern world. Who'd have thunk he was also a destructive force, resented, despised on sundry cultural fronts?

This was the prevailing side of him in Bret's ruminations as he cast a wider net that evening among the ponderous editions on Sublevel C. All those poor copyists and artists, livelihoods down the drain, demoted from riches to rags! He hadn't heretofore dipped into *Selected Masterpieces from the Archdiocese of Mainz;* hadn't Saint-Cyr mentioned Mainz today? Stumped as to specific context, Bret shrugged and took dusky reference as auspicious.

As if to manor born he reoccupied symposium room, and as if rightful prize were playing hide-and-seek he leafed impatiently through *Selected Masterpieces.* Intent like a beagle on a scent, he opened to the middle and flipped one page forward, then one page back, again and again, convinced this method would soonest flush out whatever he was after.

Momentum might have whipped him right by that distinctive face, had he not begun watching for the one commonalty between his two pieces of the puzzle, the particular flow of green vines and red blossoms. Bingo! Pattern and colors caught his eye, and framed within were a cat on hindquarters, longbow in paws, and a jumbo rat on the run with an arrow up its ass. The rat had a man's head and sported fur-brimmed cap and dangling sideburns, and had absolutely been cribbed, down to the sneer, from the engraving Bret had beheld hours ago!

This graphic proof of ill-will toward Gutenberg couldn't have been on Saint-Cyr's radar, or it would have starred in today's slideshow. As for the enormity of coincidence? Tripping over that "off-putting visage" twice in short order, and with mocking version by the very artist Bret was after? Credit his guardian angel, or gift for tuning in cosmic wavelength, or brilliant destiny. At the ripe age of nineteen, he abstained from presupposing how the universe worked, accepted strokes of luck as blessed entitlement, shied from dwelling on them, questioning the odds, maybe jinxing future long shots.

Would Bret be pushing present luck to hope a suitably amazed Saint-Cyr might let him elaborate on Gutenberg-as-rat for term project and spare him further grubbing through the stacks? While crossing his fingers, though, that riddle of the interlocking foliage remained his to relinquish, his intellectual turf, and with third piece to enlarge his understanding, he couldn't help sallying down twilit aisle to retrieve the two others he'd squirreled away. The muted acoustics, the nighttime deadness down here always put him on edge. Never mind, a flutter of nerves was a small price to pay for laboring in peace.

Nor did nerves prevent rancor flaring up as he grabbed the doorknob to his sanctum and heard a dull smack, as of clipboard landing on tabletop. Some rude jerk was muscling in on the territory he'd staked with nylon jacket and study materials! Offhand he hated nothing worse, and stormed in wishing he had a fart or belch at the ready, usually good for repelling intruders from a confined space.

Huh? He was equal parts relieved and rattled. Nobody there! A couple of blinks later, the explanation came to him: clunky heating system was notorious for its banging pipes, which might well translate through a muffling wall as human activity. Bret relaxed.

In any event, segment three positively merited misshelving, but celebration would be premature. Johan the rat scurried along a bottom margin, and his background didn't connect with the vines twining across the top and down the left side of their respective pages.

No predicting the number of parts to complete the puzzle, and no sure bet they'd all be in the building. Bummer in the offing!

Funny, meanwhile, how Bret could thoroughly pore over something, and then plow into new details on reexamination. The drollery of dancing ape and skeleton wasn't quite flush with the edge of the parchment. It had to skirt a scribe's extempore two cents in faded brown ink. And in a cavity hemmed in between those two cents and the vegetation, and in similar lettering style, a vivid carmine "Sin · Ill · " leapt out at Bret, exuding importance for no overt reason.

He twisted around an impulsive second, annoyed that residual paranoia still insisted someone was peeking over his shoulder. He glowered at thin air. Okay, back to business. He had to scribble red inscription in his pad, as if invisible onlooker psychically commanded it. Whoa, he chided himself, curb that crazy talk! He riffled through the rest of *Selected Masterpieces*, on the laughable chance it contained more of the meta-picture.

It didn't, and he spent overlong verifying that, because miniatures of queens and maidens kept distracting him. They wore ankle-length coverage and bulky headgear, but some harebrained *je ne sais quoi* made him ogle them. No doubt about it, he had to scare up a girlfriend.

Before stashing *Masterpieces* in its own clandestine berth, he unpocketed smartphone to photograph four-footed Gutenberg for Saint-Cyr. Or did stolid professor even have means to view digital snaps? To err on the side of caution, Bret pumped quarters into Xerox machine by the elevator for several reproductions, either under- or overexposed. They'd have to do! During brief sojourn on Sublevel C the vibes had gone from disquieting to full-blown creepy; maybe he should devote some days to his other neglected courses.

That glut of classwork loosened Bret's emotional attachment to Gutenberg-related discovery, or follow-up with Saint-Cyr would have been more of a bringdown. First, as before, came the windup. Xeroxes weren't too smudgy to make their point, and Saint-Cyr lauded Bret's quick eye and wit for their masterly act of recognition, notwithstanding million-to-one fluke of that same day's premier sight of block-print face. Bret had pulled off some virtuosic sleuthing, and reinforced Quince's faith in his ability to achieve ambitious goal.

For all the visceral appeal of scurrilous lampoon, though, it was an isolated curiosity, without the game-changing possibilities of deciphering cryptic motifs. Bret's stomach rolled over and sank in dismay as Saint-Cyr exhorted him to stick to his guns, honor his commitment. Back to the salt mine! For a mentor and someday friend, Quince was perversely intent on inflicting toil and hassle.

And in the wake of this ambivalence about Saint-Cyr, about how kindly disposed toward his protégé he really was, just as well Bret hadn't spilled his bona fide thesis. Saint-Cyr would absolutely approve tracking down the meta-drollery, but Bret was currently less prepared to trust him with 24-karat idea. Simultaneously, he felt obliged to repay Quince's confidence in him, and resumed nightly delving on Sublevel C.

A vein of self-indulgence, frankly, colored his search method, good for ensuring he'd put in the hours, but it was nothing he could defend to Saint-Cyr, or even explain without rousting skeletons in Freudian closet. Nor could he account for his rapidfire fluky success.

Why, on evenings he could have spent chasing real skirts, did he instead zone out mooning over wenches on the painted page? He thumbed through glossy reprints till flirty eyebrow or sinuous gesture ensnared him, and in ensuing fantasies, the textures of ankle-length gown, fur cuffs, and clingy veils figured prominently. When he snapped out of reverie, he was still leafing away, and a couple of plates later, some ribaldry with crucial viny background always awaited. Often he was goggling at a book he couldn't remember yanking from the stacks.

Roving eye further led him in most of these instances to "Sin · Ill ·" in gaps between marginal text and visuals, or variations, depending on space, from "S · Il ·" to "Sinist · Illumin ·". They were always in the same loud red and imitated the preceding penmanship, both conspicuous and blending in, as if, Bret surmised, agape at his own brilliance, they entailed stealth signatures of the meta-picture artist. How amazingly prolific "Sin · Ill ·" must have been for Bret to extract a metaphorical pincushion's worth of needles from the illuminated haystack, and with blatantly undisciplined approach at that!

Ongoing fantastic luck was just Bret's metaphysically ordained norm, and his not to reason why; he'd already settled that. He was less cavalier about atmosphere of acrid musk, pea-soup fug of what had to be his sweat, for whose else could it be? To look at these 600-year-old coquettes, he shouldn't have been so hot and bothered, but his nostrils didn't lie. He'd never have pegged himself a sucker for a winsomely folded wimple. Funny, though, that his armpits were merely damp, when they should have been sopping, based on assaultive smell. A stronger deodorant, was that the ticket?

Not important! Midsemester was behind him, appointment with Saint-Cyr was tomorrow, and blanketing the table were eight compendiums in two clusters of interlacing greenery, a centerpiece shy of wholeness, despite which it was manifest they formed a maze, substantially no different from those of IHOP placemats or vintage *Mad* magazines. Remembering where he'd misfiled all those books was becoming a feat in itself. Don't get him wrong, Bret was profusely grateful for uncanny headway with Sin · Ill ·'s oeuvre, but anxious as well with the do-or-die urgency of unearthing final piece, forced to wager it still existed, since he'd done squat about deconstructing drolleries.

Aside from goofy pleasure, that oeuvre had given him nothing, no grounds for interpreting symbols via context because no two drawings by Sin · Ill · were similar. Astoundingly resigned or stoic monks simmered in cauldrons stirred by ebony devils, armored foxes fired crowned heads from bulbous cannons at fleeing knights, cloaked creature with the Quaker Oats guy's hat, round pince-nez, and birdlike beak and claws waved a winged hourglass at prostrate polka-dotted nudes. Great stuff, yeah, but obvious now he should have laid cornerstones for Plan B with examples of the same motifs by multiple embellishers.

Saint-Cyr chastened him to that effect, after heaping praise on his ingenuity in rooting out secret signature. He even concurred with Bret's half-joking hunch that the unabbreviated moniker would have been "Sinister Illuminator." "But don't assume the worst," Quince advised. "It might only mean he was a southpaw." It was also relevant only to the repertoire of a single artist, and not to Bret's higher purpose of translating pictorial language. "So have you anything to report?"

Why yes, it happened he had, after musings on anti-Gutenberg lampoon. Bret's vagrant urge to excel, to win approval, revived, and what a miracle in itself that his spiel recurred to him when it counted most. "Morphing Gutenberg into a rat, how comical is that? But beneath the surface, I see this as a cry of defiance against the writing on the wall, against becoming obsolete, and it shows the underlying place of humor for these illuminators in response to their awful lives, beyond any one crisis."

Should Bret slow down? Saint-Cyr was listening with crinkled brow, as if inspired floodtide were hard to follow.

"To me there's a keynote of defiance in all these drolleries, like there is in surrealism and Bullwinkle Moose and the Marx Brothers. Or in any humor, deep down, if you reflect that death and entropy are the way of the world, that doom is the one irreducible truth, then, well, to laugh at anything is one degree of separation from laughing in the face of eternal dissolution. It's a valiant stance, like a Spartan warrior's, with his back against the wall and not a snowball's chance in hell."

Bret was floored by his own unsuspected stores of eloquence. He hove eyes brimming with pride toward Saint-Cyr, who was gazing at the air between them as if spellbound, or shellshocked. Had euphoric Bret really gone over esteemed professor's head? Saint-Cyr finally arched his eyebrows and pursed lower lip under whiskbroom mustache, like a sommelier deciding whether the wine was corked.

"You have to be careful," he opined, "not to impose modern values on ancient minds. These people believed reflexively in a Christian cosmos, heaven and hell and whatnot. Even to bring up concepts like entropy and eternal dissolution would have made them candidates for the chopping block." Bret squirmed inwardly through exhortations to buckle down, heed the calendar, guard against sidetracks. He applied in vain to the skulls on the shelves for a supportive smile. Hey, he hadn't signed in blood to obsess about the first topic out of his mouth!

Taskmaster Quince was suddenly reminiscent of Dad bugging him to mow the lawn. Bret had toyed with broaching the matter of jigsaw maze, but forget it, he wasn't especially enamored of Saint-Cyr right now, of his stark, unflattering subtext. Bret's dynamic best had only prompted Quince to impugn his competence, and how could that not offend him?

Stress must have been taking its toll, wreaking havoc with his emotional thermostat, for spite began churning uncontrollably in Bret's gut, fermenting till he was logy with it, and then a Machiavellian pitch poured forth, and it belonged to that spite and not to him. He was at a loss for more cogent self-understanding.

"You're justifiably annoyed with my mediocre progress, so I'm afraid to ask, but weren't you ever cocksure a huge breakthrough was like an inch away, if only something gave it a tiny push?" Bret still couldn't see Quince's lower lip. "I can deliver an outline in a week, guaranteed, all I need is some fuel for my morale, to fire up the neurons, so, could you please let me at the primary sources, the genuine parchment?"

Fair to infer, from vein throbbing in temple, that Quince was deliberating strenuously, as if probing Bret under x-ray vision, with the grave demeanor of a judge at a sanity hearing. "I'll see what I can do," he hedged at last.

That much would have been fine for normal, easygoing Bret, who never held grudges, who didn't personally care about accessing genuine parchment. He bristled, though, in capacity as mouthpiece for uncharted inner zones. Well, if he couldn't tell where his words were coming from, who on Earth did conclusively know himself? "I won't let you down," he promised in parting, while from ungoverned inner zone emerged the perturbing non sequitur, *Living longest is the best revenge.* He suppressed it as he would a burp. Yes, a psychic burp, that's all it was.

He likewise didn't waste precious energy marveling at yet another lavish gift of coincidence from Saint-Cyr's next slideshow. The beaked, bespectacled creature in Quaker Oats hat and ankle-length garb, replete with winged-hourglass wand, had transitioned from miniature maze to big screen, except here he towered in empty foreground, half-obscuring a town on the horizon. He was a plague doctor, Quince expounded, an untrained quack in waxed hazmat suit, hired at public expense to treat infected multitudes.

"And here are his patients' twentieth-century counterparts." Transparencies of clinical photos were from the pre-digital era, when quaint black strips across eyes protected anonymity. Classmates chorused squawky disgust that resonated through Bret, but he resisted joining in. Each projection tarried mercilessly before worse replaced it: a hand with blackened fingers like charbroiled blood sausage; a thigh with goose-egg cysts crowding the groin; a girl's neck with inflamed, red-speckled knob oozing brown pus; cadaverous face with truncated black nose and black crater in cheek. "And the kicker is," Saint-Cyr declaimed, "bubonic plague, which is treatable, may be different from Black Death, which, if it reappeared, might not be."

Bret exited the auditorium with two fresh realizations. First, those spotty nudes in the maze with birdman were plainly plague victims. Secondly, beneath genial veneer, Saint-Cyr had a pretty major morbid streak. He'd presented gallery of disease sufferers and threat of future epidemic with arguably unwholesome verve, and what about office "décor" of skulls and sadistically leering idols? Bret couldn't absolutely rule out ulterior motives in Quince's guidance of term essay toward a fixed goal. Or by the same token, away from other goals?

All the more imperative, then, that Bret make the most heroic case for undeclared thesis, and scour the stacks for the fugitive heart of Sinister Illuminator's maze. Maximum impact or bust! Again, and he forbore letting it go to his head, favorite conference room was his, as if supernaturally reserved for him

Even more providentially, he entered the Crock as Saint-Cyr was traipsing toward the stairwell by the elevators, and Bret would have missed him had a racking cough at point-blank range not turned his head. Huh! Must have been some quirk of modernist-eyesore acoustics. The nearest person was yards away. Or had Bret himself coughed without realizing it? His throat felt like he had, but if so, it was news to him.

Bret's feet, without conscious intercession, voted to shadow Saint-Cyr, matching his pace half a flight back to muffle telltale footsteps. Stalking noiselessly was much easier after Quince pushed open the fire door to Sublevel A, and then Bret peeked from behind bookshelves at Saint-Cyr rummaging key to private study cell, a perk of tenure, classier than a carrel, cozier than a conference room. And on Sublevel A, a lot swanker than Sublevel C!

Bret gaped as if awaiting orders as the door swung shut, and then as an aid to memory he mouthed "Four," the number above its fisheye peephole. His feet carried him to favored sanctum, he draped nylon jacket over his usual chair, vowed to buckle down, and perceived no conflict with concurrent yearning for saucy ink-on-vellum wenches. Amorous impulses were stealing over him like a cloudbank as he set off to gather his miscataloged stash. That fog closed in and for a blurry interval he retained only snippets of prying at bindings on dim bottom rows, like highlight footage of somebody else.

He wasn't himself again till acrid, sweaty musk hit him like smelling salts, but with added ingredient most like musty rawhide, and he was blinking down at reassembled maze on the table as if at aerial view. Faux air-sickness had to fade before he discerned the centerpiece wasn't MIA anymore, and it was emitting the new miasma. It also wasn't any glossy archival reproduction, no, it was the worn, coarse condition of the real article, and Bret was initially too befuddled by its unaccountable, illicit presence to see straight.

But then he had to vent a few triumphant cackles. Mission accomplished! The big meta-picture was his; nothing trumped that. Legal, ethical ramifications could stew on hindmost burner. To prolong this momentous occasion, he refrained from homing in on the centerpiece, pledging instead to trace the maze from portcullis entry. "Hello, maître demon!" he joshed, uncertain a heartbeat later whether he'd spoken aloud or not.

Nor was he clear why his integrity rode on threading virtual route past capering ape, grinning reaper, feline archer, genius-headed rat, quack in bird mask, foxes firing human ammo, and other denizens of reconnected leafy passages. Surveying those passages in gestalt was like hovering above a lopsided crop circle, a smudgy thumbprint. Traversing them, however, neutralized his perspective, made overall image impossible to observe, as if he were literally in the labyrinth, powerless to foresee where next bend would lead, to expand field of vision and compass what was physically right in front of him.

Ability to distinguish minutes from seconds deserted him long before he crossed unawares into the centerpiece, where one last corner was under the grisly auspices of a decapitated knight with helmet in the bloody crook of steel-plate arm. And then Bret winced as ears popped painfully, as if at loss of altitude, and he weathered the disorientation of seeing from two vantages at once. A mural on a gritty wall confronted him, scant hopscotch away, but that was certainly rank illusion, overwrought nerves, for he was also cognizant of leaning against conference table, narrow gaze upon several square inches of parchment.

Regrettably, the duet Bret approached via breach in the bottom edge of rectangular flowery thicket was banal, incongruous with surrounding madcap figments. He and she had struck a pose from a pavane or somesuch courtly dance, side by side, hand in hand, kicking up their left feet, spines like plumb lines. Bret belatedly noticed "Sin · Ill ·" in fiery red below their feet, across the breach, as if it had just materialized or slid shut behind him like a gate.

If signature was intended to ID Sinister Illuminator, surprising he'd render himself so foppish for posterity! Floppy chapeau with ostrich plume, ruff collar, red cape, harlequin jerkin, puffy sleeves, cavalier boots didn't fit Bret's profile of scheming artistic mastermind. She, meanwhile, was the most bewitching slice of cheesecake in his oeuvre, flaunting bountiful red hair, robust cleavage and lithe waist under low-cut green dress, slender arms in flaring sleeves. Latticework slippers called attention to delicate ankles, but most compelling were black-rimmed eyes that challenged and enticed.

He lingered over her till a further nicety dawned on him, regarding special ink in which she and effete partner were delineated. It was sleeker, warmer, more vibrant, encouraging an illusion of gestures captured but not yet at full standstill, as if the medium were part alchemical brew. Spacy Bret reached out despite knowing he couldn't snatch away her hand, cut in on the dance. His fingertips brushed arid parchment and not hers, and his ears popped again at the reduction of double to undivided viewpoint as he rubbernecked patchwork maze on the table, swaying a bit like he'd been set down too emphatically.

Did fortune actually favor the brave? He hated leaving academic gold strike unattended, hated going public with his armpit funk, but couldn't pass up chance to show off awesome find when Quince was a figurative shout away. Luck was his lady all right! And she it must have been badgering him to the stairs, not an instant to lose, up three steps at once, neurotically mumbling "Four" the whole way to door 4, sublevel A.

No-nonsense knocking yielded no answer. Pretending to be dumb as an oyster, was he? To get his own scholarship done, Saint-Cyr maybe had a policy of ignoring uninvited visitors, and normally Bret would empathize, but not tonight. Fluorescents were casting brightness through the sidelight; Quince couldn't honestly believe he was fooling anybody. Bret's knuckles rapped more sharply. "Mr. Saint-Cyr? You okay in there? Please, it's important!"

Bret's straining ears detected a sigh, the squeal of swivel-chair springs, the rattle of doorknob. Quince, wary oyster in his shell, opened up no wider than necessary to squinch out. "Yes, what is it?" Uh-oh, this was going to be a hard sell. "And technically, it's Doctor Saint-Cyr."

"I've dug up something incredible!" Bret rhapsodized. "You have to come verify I'm not dreaming. I'm on Sublevel C. Literally seconds away. You'll be astounded!" He'd seen that look on Quince before, of presiding over Bret's mental-health evaluation. Finally, judgment still pending, the look relented, eclipsed by grudging capitulation, weariness at decades of imposition by spoiled, insubordinate youth.

"I'll be there shortly." Tone, in counterpoint to words, pleaded, "Let's get this over with!" Hinges groaned on slowly closing door.

"I'm in one of the symposium rooms!" Bret exclaimed into the vanishing gap. "I'll keep the door propped and watch for you!"

His jubilation while racing downstairs evaporated on the threshold of his rightful den. Ruckus inside was distinctly not a vagary of heating system this time, and he was royally pissed. Interlopers were potentially messing up his meticulous arrangement, defiling his serene domain with knockdown squabbling, in any case trashing his buoyant mood, his hour of glory. He flung wide the door to bang into corridor wall and charged in, ready to drive them off with harsher vitriol, more psycho attitude than they were hurling at each other. He wasn't ready for much rottener fug than when he'd decamped, nor for a pair of refugees from the Creative Anachronists.

Before he could stammer a syllable, they'd shut up, and tongue-tied him with haughty glowers of appraisal, and he gulped at late-breaking recognition of foppish artiste and his green temptress. Bret's cerebral gears jammed. These two had to be hoaxsters, nothing else was possible, but to prep a stunt like this for an upshot he himself couldn't have forecast, that flouted credibility too.

The *tableau vivant* shook off its stasis and spared Bret's problem-solving cogs further overheating. Ostensible Illuminator waved lace-cuffed wrist and dainty fingers at Bret and railed about "that whelp," at best guess, in what may or may not have been English. He then lapsed into a phlegmy fit of coughing and shivering, while she shoved him away from the table before he could collapse onto it, and past Bret who gagged at proximity to squalid putrefaction, and through yawning doorway, as she fulminated, "You sicken of me? Then sicken without me! Seek a doctor, gamble this age can cure you!"

A step or two outside, congestive attack resumed and arrested the fop's forward thrust. At this juncture, Bret heard Saint-Cyr amidst the bronchitis demand, "What the hell's going on? Bret?"

In the next split-second, green lady had Bret by the elbow and was carping, "I am done abiding his jealousy, his whining about our confinement. Come with me now or die of the pox!"

Bret in a flash understood how ingenious he truly was, because epiphanies careened into him like chain lightning, how he'd freed miniature couple by rebuilding the maze, how "Sin · Ill ·" should be spelled out Sinister Illuminatrix or Illuminatrice instead of Illuminator, how she and her paramour had fled a worse peril than the printing press. And incidentally, had ailing Beau Brummel been her first comrade-in-parchment?

Eye to beguiling eye with her, Bret realized nothing of the modern world was fazing her, no, she wasn't like that, and yes, she was drop-dead gorgeous, he'd never have another shot at anyone half as gorgeous, especially if everyone was dying of plague. There remained only the same mystifying riddle whenever an attractive girl paid him any mind: What the devil could she see in me?

This exuberance of cogitation flowed faster than a drowning man's lifetime of memories, and he came up for air, and the squeeze of her strong, imperious hand made him horny, and he gasped, "Okay."

She pulled and they tumbled backward into claustrophobic limbo, in which earthly sounds carried as through cardboard tubing. Saint-Cyr was evidently familiar with the book containing the centerpiece, for he exclaimed, "He shouldn't have this! I never would've let . . . Bret, where are you? My God!" A spasm of coughing stopped him from saying more in those heartbeats before her brushstroke eyes caught and held Bret, who could see nothing else in sandstorm whiteness. He, meanwhile, was congratulating himself for escaping in the veritable nick, and as for Quince, well, Bret hoped he'd be okay, he was old enough to take care of himself, some were always resistant, their relationship hadn't progressed to the extent he was ditching a pal.

Most importantly, horny Bret had temptress to himself forever, and even if he couldn't exactly ravish her, wow, drop-dead gorgeous she was. No, he'd never in a million years commit old boyfriend's fatal error and complain about their situation, would he?

dead city suite

introduction:
some homebrew from a
haunted cellar

How these specimens of juvenilia came to light is in itself one small remove from a ghost story. My mother died in August 2013 at the age of ninety-three and had spent the preceding sixty-one years in the house where I'd grown up. When I was a kid, my father, perhaps to "stimulate my imagination," gave me to believe the premises were haunted, and I can attest to garden-variety phantom footsteps on the front porch, lights in the barn switching themselves on, and piano music I could hear while "down cellar" (Swamp Yankee usage) when nobody was upstairs playing our piano. I won't go into the aftermath of that ill-advised Halloween reading of Bradbury's "The Emissary" to a circle of high-school friends in the barn attic.

That was 1972; I was privy to no more paranormal doings on the home front for the rest of my parents' lives. My mother, to the very end, was vehemently attached to the property and almost everything in it, hostile to mentions of downsizing or assisted living, selling precious little to our friend the antiques dealer. She became increasingly loath to throw anything away, as if amassing possessions as a buffer against mortality, in addition to the hoarded mementoes of my childhood, of hers, of her two husbands, her brother, her folks (going back to the 1890s). If a ghost can be defined most secularly as a "force of attachment," my mother had invested decades preparing for the role.

Well, make of it what you will that amidst those months of clearing out the homestead, a housekey unaccountably vanished from my wallet while I was at the back door, only to reappear a week later on the cushion of her favorite chair. Midwinter, a water valve for the furnace opened itself and flooded the cellar while I was on the first floor. And come the spring thaw, the living room where she passed the bulk of her last few years remained balefully cold. True, these were minor, inconclusive, purely anecdotal signs of postmortem displeasure at the breakup of an estate; other witnesses, arguably less reliable, had more daunting experiences.

As for the cache of juvenilia from which I've arrantly digressed? In salvaging the waterlogged chaos down cellar, I uncovered a sheaf of Xeroxed typescripts, dry but funky as hell, amidst completely un-related parental documents. Ghostly mischief (or whatever opened the valve) set in motion the circumstances that graced me with these four stories, which I'd most likely stored for safekeeping with the folks during that postgrad "age of migrations" when I moved every six months or so. Their address, anyway, was typed below my name in the upper left of every first page, another minor mystery since I'd have done so when I hadn't lived there for years.

I initially believed these were dupes of originals squirreled away somewhere in my own detritus, and mailed them to friend, editor, and critic S. T. Joshi as curios or "developmental milestones." Rum-maging through trunks and cabinets, though, I found only one of the stories in finished form. Two survived as rough drafts, and "Integrity" was altogether MIA. So for what it's worth, thanks, Mom (or the ca-pricious residue thereof), for at least indirectly making the second half of this book possible.

These tales date from 1977–79 during a somewhat troubled en-rollment in a "creative writing program" at a prestigious university. Chairmanship of the program had been volleying back and forth be-tween a tormented neocon and a hard-drinking elitist, and depart-mental scuttlebutt had it they hated each other. But they did see eye to eye in reviling genre fiction and "street" language (to the point of banning contractions; the program seems thereafter to have per-formed a breathtaking U-turn). Such were my suboptimal conditions for pursuing weird fiction, and regrettably, for reasons too boring to enumerate, the program and I were stuck with each other. Still, a so-journ in the academic snakepit was good for buying me three years to do nothing with my life except write, and this was definitely of value (whether or not the outlay and psychic turmoil were justified).

I was in my callow twenties then, which, for my money, marks these efforts as juvenilia, and that goes for everything of mine till the age of thirty-one. At that stage I began (erratically) producing material I'm not loath to show people today, whereas I'm much less reconciled to sharing younger work. To my happy surprise, though, S. T. declared these literal moldy oldies deserving of publication (after judicious pruning of clunky or unclear phrasing, naturally). Far be it from me to contradict him, but I, bearing in mind my green self, will always brand them juvenilia.

Writing some three decades later, in "Power of Midnight" (from *Tempting Providence* [Hippocampus Press, 2010]), I tried to recapture the inner and outer worlds of a character about the same age and renting in the same neighborhood that I had been when shaping these four novelettes. I conjured up a well-intentioned twentysomething oblivious to the gulf between his sincere conviction that he wasn't an asshole and the realization of when he was (but a lifelong labor, that). And now, rereading between those Xeroxed lines, it was nice to learn I did have some insight into the unplanned impacts of innocent remarks, naive behavior, even if I lacked the skills to prevent more-than-occasional blunders.

Maybe the Brit versifier Robert Wyatt was right to advise kindness to previous selves because they were doing the best they could. (Not that author and protagonist can ever be one and the same, even in autobiographies.) I can say my younger self was writing as best he could, whatever his other faults. . . .

If I'm a tad mystified at how well this "old stuff" has held up, maybe tenured naysayers' negative feedback had unduly, unconsciously influenced me over the long run. "Integrity" came in for a particular drubbing, and so I'm especially gratified it's the relic toward which S. T. seems most kindly disposed. It debuted inauspiciously as the upshot of a class assignment to devise a personal take on a canonical short story from a list of half a dozen or so. I picked something (title beyond recall) by Yukio Mishima, wherein love and suicide figured prominently. I recast it, very loosely (with sole nod to Mishima, ultimately, in recourse to Japanese folklore), in terms of Anglo-American idioms I'd been enjoying recently.

The supernatural, the hard-boiled, and the vernacular elements added up to three strikes right there. The antiestablishment, corporate-conspiracy gist in that pre-dawn of the Reagan era clinched my F for the semester. The noirish tone, the whiffs of cannabis beclouding a few scenes that had been such transgressions against "serious" or at least decorous prose seem a lot more convincing, and less uncouth, now (whereas "Immortality Sequence" and "Watcher of the Invisible World" bespeak schooldays fondness for the Romantic poets and prog rock and inventing moral conundrums).

"Integrity" also evokes the Providence of 1978, when its moniker was "Dead City"; hence the grouping of these artifacts as "Dead City Suite." "A Light in the Wilderness" is set in pre-suburban Maryland countryside, with the special pleading that I was describing that doomed '70s landscape from the vantage of my own. Stagnant economy aside, though, Providence was a "Dead City" with shops and proprietors Lovecraft had known, vintage diners, lunchrooms, and taverns galore, and downtown streets redolent of RKO backlot studios atmosphere. Dead but beautiful! The present city may have come alive in some respects, but it was never again such a wellspring of weird inspiration.

In their first blush, all these stories had their partisans among friends and faculty. None of these readers, unfortunately, included anyone connected with publishing, and none of the few markets at the time (or of which I was aware) were receptive. With aggravated wrongheadedness, I dove into the first of many drafts of a horror-fantasy novel that was to consume most of my resources and optimism for years to come, without satisfactory result.

Still, for my twentysomething self, here's a happy ending at last. It's taken thirty-five years, but that uncontrollable urge to thumb my nose at unsympathetic authority, to demand better for my student efforts than the landfill, has been rewarded. I never doubted that you never get anywhere unless you refuse to go away, unless "you persist in your folly till you become wise," to misquote William Blake (with no claims to wisdom on my part), and though that principle led me down a few primrose paths, I remain in its debt, and in debt to Phyllis and Alton Thomas for letting these stories age like homebrew in their cellar.

integrity

I'm holed up in this alley, my gun's out of bullets, I have no cover except some trash barrels, and the demons are gathering at the alley's mouth. It's around 3 A.M. I haven't a care in the world. I didn't plan to end it here and now, but I knew it would have to end like this. Pinball suicide, pure and simple. Once you put yourself in play, you have to roll down the hole eventually.

I almost feel good about the alley. The alley's a kind of corridor, and a corridor's an apt symbol of life. The opening at one end is birth, and at the other, death. Birth leads from somewhere, and death to somewhere. But this alley has a wall at my end, a good metaphoric touch, considering what the demons intend doing to me. They're cackling, making the trash barrels resonate, but not showing themselves yet. Killing me will be efficient. They're sworn to that. First they'll produce noises to make me sweat, but so what? Probably there's time to see my life replayed, the real life that brought me to this.

Like it or not, real life will kill you: my paraphrase of the ancient choice between a short, glorious life and a long, quiet one. I'm imagining an audience to help me order my thoughts, and that's the moral I want to impart. Even if I had a flesh-and-blood audience, it would have to be less real than me, because if it can sit back and be an audience, it hasn't lived as much as I have, hasn't lived at all yet, really. You couldn't understand unless you were here too, and then you couldn't be an audience at all.

Real life only walked in on me when I finally realized it was in charge of me, and not vice versa. In other words, I was so bogged down trying to run my life that I became its captive audience.

I was playing at private detective out of downtown Providence,

Rhode Island, a good facsimile of a rundown set from a *Thin Man* film, and maybe that's what had roped me in. Nothing else recommended my particular dump, a one-room office over the fleapit Strand Theatre, where the windows hadn't been washed for a good twenty years, plus the two years I couldn't afford to either. Not that Washington Street profited from a clearer view, looking more natural through dingy glass.

As for sensory input, I was treated to plenty by the porn soundtracks downstairs. At first I was amused, then annoyed, and finally it was no different from a constant background of Top 40. On that crucial afternoon, the culture downstairs was loud enough to rattle the windows, and I was investing attention in it to put off a decision. Twilight had already dimmed the office, and I could either up the electricity bill or go home to soybean casserole for the fifth straight night.

I was about to opt for bean destiny when she knocked and entered, as the door requested. I turned on my anglepoise lamp. Her hair caught the light, and hence my eye. Such hair was incredible, too good not to be true. Absolutely black, almost long enough for Godiva purposes, and with an air of life to it, as if you could caress it and it would caress you back and then some. Her face and features were thin and sharp, in a semi-exotic Eastern Mediterranean way, but her skin was white as lily-of-the-valley.

Her clothes were enviably snug on her, Frye boots, a navy-blue knee-length dress, and a skintight blue item that obviously wasn't a leotard because of the silver filigree neckwork that almost reached her breasts. Her moss-green velvet jacket was very tailored and didn't obscure the impression of a girl who was slim in the best slinky manner. My business forces you to assume whatever image will put the customer at ease about plunking down cash. Sometimes people need a Bogart or William Powell, but in this case, I was the one in need, at a loss over who to be.

"Arthur Kent?" Her voice projected both a childlike lilt and a grownup command. I nodded.

"I'm Selina Singer." I nodded again. She held out her hand, so warm and pliant it seemed willing to lie within mine indefinitely unless I let go, which I reluctantly did.

"My employers believe you may be of long-term service to us. I understand you've been here since completing an independent degree project in criminology two years ago?"

I nodded more cautiously, then remembered myself and indicated Miss Singer should take the seat before my desk. She smiled graciously.

"You also aided Providence police investigations part-time during winters and full-time between semesters." Once seated, she became so soft-spoken that the skinflick soundtrack threatened to drown her out. I curbed an impulse to stamp on the floor as if to quiet noisy neighbors. I tried to shift closer without coming off as hard of hearing.

"For the most part, Miss Singer, my police work involved documents, tracking them down or reading them well. Minimal risk of neck."

"But so far your clients have been satisfied with the results. Mr. LaPlante, Mrs. Schiller, Mr. Faig—"

"You probably also know I've had few other clients, satisfied or otherwise." To bolster a Bogart image, I fished a Kool from my top drawer, letting the cigarette hang casually, seldom inhaling. "Luckily for me, perseverance has been a good warmup act for competence."

Putting a fist to her lips, Selina coughed. "Could you put that out, please? My throat is rather sensitive." I ground the lit end in a tin ashtray and watched a paltry wisp escape.

"Cigarettes. I hate 'em, myself." Her puzzled look was fleeting. "You know, Miss Singer, you're the one paying me to dig. Why should you want me, since your investigators seem well-versed in the trade?"

"First off, we'll pay you to stop being a detective." Her smile was catty but no less enchanting. "That's not what we want you for, exactly." I arched my brows to imply she should continue.

"I represent Esoteric Research. We're tentatively nationwide, just setting up Rhode Island offices now. Ours is a scholarly pursuit of local arcane traditions, legends, phenomena, and practices. We try to trace their histories and factual bases, with special attention to surviving and resurgent spiritualism and witchcraft." As I took all this in, my grin cracked a tad wider to accommodate it. "A number of foundations have taken us seriously enough to allow us a certain liberality and freedom of movement. What are your usual fees?"

I sobered up. "A thousand-dollar retainer, and a hundred dollars a day."

She nodded as with confirmed assumptions. "Would you settle for a sure seven hundred a week?"

I tried to keep some caprice in my eyes as they widened. "Who, precisely, is endowing you, if they don't mind being disclosed?"

She reeled off some Waspy names ending in dales or fields or thorps, none of which rang even remotely like aluminum. I let her lungs empty out, and when she drew breath, I cut in. "All very well, Miss Singer, but my lease here runs another four months." The matinee downstairs was over, letting me tilt my chair back and make cathedral hands.

Her eyes followed me back into the shadows. "You'll be earning enough for this office to be a minor loss, but the organization may agree to absorb that cost for such a brief period." She said this more haltingly, as if it weren't in a brochure. I looked appreciative, and she relapsed into officialese. "I can't overemphasize your value to us, Arthur. You're familiar with the region. You minored in anthropology. You're ideal for both archival and field research, where many of our informants class themselves as criminal types and won't be easy to find. You'd have every chance for advancement in a young, growing company, and maybe for this one and only time you'd be able to pool all your resources. Are you interested?'

I wondered how a sphinx would smile and attempted an imitation as I leaned forward. The work appealed, the pay compelled, but two years of financial thin ice made me skeptical of instant security. I assured her I was interested, saying no more till she made one spot-on gesture to prove she was on the level. Brushing black strands off her cheek, she asked what I was doing for dinner. I told her, and she asked if I wouldn't mind dining at her place. That was clincher enough for me to take the job.

There was no sense humoring my office hours to the bitter end. I applied vindictive flair to "CLOSED FOREVER" on white notepaper and taped it to the door's frosted pane, then pointed at my lamp by way of polite request. Miss Singer obliged, drenched us in twilight, and slipped by as I locked up. I pictured the two years sealed up behind me as something alive, Fortunato without even benefit of sherry. My smile was pure and warm with spite as I ambled away.

On the street, Selina took my arm like a textbook lady, but with too much hold for mere formality. She answered my curious look with a fetching show of teeth, and I realized that she, inscrutably, was attracted to me. No complaints. In the dusk everything was dreamlike, still dingy but wistful within the gray, and my steps had that heavy, wading sensation common in dreams. But I felt more alive than I had in months, more a part of the world despite the moment's storybook simplicity.

I maintained the strong silent act until we climbed the granite steps of her Benefit Street mansion, an unattainable fantasy palace for someone like me who could hardly foot tenement rent in a punk section like Smith Hill. The outside was square, yellow, and Georgian, with the fancy trim in black. Inside, drastic modernizing had transformed each floor into an apartment of the sort beloved by the Mercedes set. Selina had the second floor, where everything had been upholstered and carpeted and cushioned until a hard edge or sharp corner would have been as shocking as the exposed bone of a compound fracture. She asked me to make myself comfortable while she got dinner underway.

When she returned, we chatted away the simmering time. We trundled out our shards of mutual taste, background, and attitude, tawdry things in the long run that fool people into thinking they're compatible, the modern mating ritual everyone dignifies as "getting acquainted."

The meal itself was something Southern European. I couldn't describe it more specifically except as mostly red and green. As with most great meals, my serving looked skimpy, but I could scarcely finish it. Selina seemed proud of making me full.

In one trip, Selina cleared the table but didn't return, neither acknowledging my offer to wash dishes nor running the faucet herself. Too glutted to move for a while, I contemplated my knees through the glass tabletop until something dropped softly into my line of sight. Selina sat down and placed rolling papers next to the ounce bag, and I, out of practice, fumbled through what used to be called a bomber.

My first greedy draw sent me lunging for the tumbler of water she'd wisely set out, and all the same I had to stifle a coughing binge.

Customarily, long exposure to mediocre dope casts doubt on the purity of anything stronger. Repressing the gauche question didn't purge the impulse to ask something. "Didn't you say your throat was too sensitive?"

"Only to tobacco smoke." She drew so deeply I winced, and held it with a feline contentment, and exhaled luxuriously. The cattiness abided in her smile. "Isn't that funny?'

I laughed, but not at that. The south wall's Palladian window was nearly dammed up with hanging plants on different lengths of wire. But half the plants were egregiously dead, and still up there as if nothing were wrong. That, to me, was funny, and I said so.

"What do you mean?" Selina looked bewildered. "They have as much right to be there as the rest of them."

"No," I insisted and took her hand as if for paternal effect. "They're not there, they're dead, don't you see? There's nothing left that can be deprived of its rights."

She looked at my hand, then at me, and at last she loosened up enough to let edginess show. We stood up and stepped into each other's arms as if we'd rehearsed. We kissed without hesitation or haste, lingered, and broke off. The rest was equally smooth.

I awoke contented for the first time in ages, though we'd slept little. The world looked fine, even if a little unfocused. That's how I reported to my new job. The euphoria persisted till I mentioned the scruffiness of the institute's neighborhood.

"We're not at all sensationalistic," she announced, the career woman again. We stood before the Blackstone Building, four stories of brick with Italianate cornice and lintel in white. Despite the Victorian ostentation, "Blackstone" itself was chiseled in simple block letters across the middle of the second story. The ground floor was mostly display window, long vacant. Our entrance was a modern glass door, surmounted by Art Nouveau stained glass, in the rubbishy alley off to one windowless side.

This was at the hind end, as it's usually conceived, of Westminster Mall, which runs like a spinal cord through downtown. Clustered around the head end are banks, public utilities, City Hall, while down here languish greasy-spoons, moribund shops, and outright dives. And also, avoiding "sensationalism," Esoteric Research.

Then and for the next few weeks, my employers declined to supplement the vague impression of the place Selina had fed me. Professional types led me through catacombs of little white cubicles occupied by indistinct, leisure-suited bureaucrats and secretaries about as receptive to eye contact as hamsters. I had no idea how many partitions or people had been stuffed into the building, or how they'd been regimented into floorplans. Gradually I realized I was being diverted from whole acres within the Blackstone Building's shell.

Suspicions of the company's real business first glimmered during my personnel interview, when the pruny man with the scrawny neck and wheezy monotone kept twisting the standard questions. Instead of requesting references, he reeled off a few dozen names and gurgled happily when I couldn't place them. He ignored my academic and vocational backgrounds and asked about religious and supernatural experiences, and knowledge of myth and occultism. On a one-to-ten scale he had me rate the plausibility of aliens, ghosts, and the ilk, and before the interview itself became more implausible, he handed me an ID and numbers to call if I were injured on the job. By way of cordial dismissal, he looked up and let a few teeth show.

My first field assignments seemed trivial, a waste of their money and my talents, and no "integration of all my resources," as Selina had promised. A typical case had me traverse an entire three blocks to Dick's Bookshop with orders to buy all his occult stock. I received an envelope full of tens and was advised to take a company car.

During college days I was a regular at Dick's, located in the heart of the soot zone amidst hat stores, bars, and a produce mart that had gotten away for years with the name "Majestic Fruits." Titles moldered untouched for eons on Dick's ceiling-high shelves, and the dust was thick enough for the silverfish to build bungalows. It was a timeless, archetypal bookshop. Dick had been there since 1930.

I could never tell if he recognized me. He always gave me the same squint, nod, and hello. A couple of his senior cronies shuffled aside as I approached the counter, inspecting me from coyly shifted faces. Dick was still intent on his pipe and a radio talk show. His mouth went grim, and he removed the pipe and poked it at me. "What do you think's wrong with state lotteries?"

I thought about it a second, but didn't have to.

"Well, I'll tell ya." For the several minutes he went on, the by-standers stayed out of it and I agreed politely. When he relit the pipe and started puffing as if to restoke himself, I asked if he had anything on the occult.

"What's 'at? Oh, yeah. Aah, that's a lot of bunk if y'ask me." His eyes welled up through lenses thick as false bottoms in shot glasses. "How old d'you think I am?"

I hazarded eighty-three. "I'll be eighty-five in two months. And d'ya think I'm scared to die?" He made a sour face. "Nah. Because, I'll tell ya, when you're dead, you're gone. Nothing. So what's there to be scared of? Ghosts, the beyond, that's all superstitious crap. Not one shred of evidence. Why, I found three boxes of that stuff in the backroom this morning. This woman came in here, must've been four years ago. Had this store on Washington Street, sold all kinds of hoodoo merchandise and books. Had to close down. Not enough interest."

He gloated some at this juncture. "She came in and sold all the books to me. Then I had that fire some kids broke in and set one night." The fire had been an old dependable topic when I'd last seen him two years ago. He ambled into the back and knocked things around. He was gone a subjectively long time, and I wondered what he was doing. His cronies were studying paperback titles and flipping old *Boys' Life* pages.

Dick returned lugging a melon crate full of hardcovers. He wasn't a big man. The load should have dislocated his shoulders, but he wasn't even breathing hard. He heaved the crate onto the countertop. "There's two more like that."

"I'll take them all. How much?"

He gaped incredulously from under his green visor and scurried away for the other two. He set a price that sounded fair, so instead of haggling I consulted my envelope. It contained just that amount. He counted it out, gave it a just-so look, and rang it up. I gave the first crate an experimental tug, and fought an urge to ask for Dick's assistance.

I never knew what came of this purchase, or any of my findings. Further items and reports went to Selina, whom I trusted more than an angel. An obvious lesson arises here that you, my imaginary audience, will certainly squander. If your ideal of love and beauty ever solidifies before you, and you want no one else and no one else has ever loved you so much, with no end in sight, then trust that person less than anyone else you've ever met, than even the sleaziest glowering drunk at the bus station. Like most truths I've discovered, it's too obvious and demands too much self-reliance to be believed.

Fool's gold though she was, Selina, salary aside, was the job's only reward those first weeks. We spent most of our free hours at her place "relaxing," with music, TV, reading, and little else to busy us. You can spend ages that way with someone you love and feel not a moment was wasted, and though you wonder where so much time evaporated, it's no big deal.

Hoarded privacy was the premium of our prior friendlessness, she too new in town, I too long there to retain any transient college pals. Some inconvenient phone calls and dead-of-night visits set me to pondering how high she actually ranked, since her input was in round-the-clock demand. Faking sleep when she answered the bedside phone, I overheard loud, guttural customers with kindergarten grammar and troglodyte accents. Demure Selina assumed a tone that should have left frost on the receiver, doling out decisions, always getting the last word. I wondered about these fellow employees and their exact duties, but only until Selina was beside me again, her arm coiled around me and her breath upon my neck.

After the sixth or seventh 2 A.M. doorbell, I indulged my curiosity as far as the Palladian window over the front door. Through the screen of hanging plants I listened to the typical queen-and-caveman exchange. The portico hid our caller till the front door closed, and then down the flagstone walk loped a dark form that would have confounded me no less at a more reasonable hour. On the man's back was a knee-length black trenchcoat, and on his head a wide-brimmed Stetson, during the first week of August when I was too warm standing in the draft naked.

He turned toward the door, and I went midwinter cold. Streetlight sufficed to show the face was gray, an inhuman hue as of city snow after a week of pollution. The face was leering. Selina's footsteps diverted me from the window, but before she'd reached the upstairs landing I couldn't resist another glimpse of the stranger. He was gone, when he shouldn't even have cleared the gate yet.

Selina entered, saw me across the dark living room, and stopped. Her face, I now realize, was choosing a mask, and settled on tenderness. She approached, took my hands, and fondled them. "I'm sorry that woke you, Arthur. An emergency consultation. I don't encourage them."

Either the hour per se or the residual command in her tone militated against humor on my part. She went to the window, checked up and down the street, and stamped petulantly. "I told them not to do that out in the open!" At my questioning expression she smoothed her pout and said, "That was one of our specialists. You'll be introduced in due course." For no excusable reason, that satisfied me.

If not for Selina, I'd have evacuated the organization by then. They, using her voice, claimed I'd be in on the ground floor, on the principle that the most blatant lie is somehow the last to be challenged. True pits are bottomless, and the Blackstone sheltered a Mohole for snakes, with a wafer-thin ground floor that broke as soon as I breathed.

The plunge was rigged so that both the institute and I would pretend nothing unusual had happened. That morning ceased to be like any other when we bypassed the receptionist who ordinarily relayed orders that took us our separate ways. Instead, Selina escorted me to a little white office with nothing to distinguish it, except for the man sizing me up from his desk as if I were his sole reason for being there. I felt like a wayward schoolboy.

Once the man was up and shaking hands, I could see he was teetering on antiquity, burdened by liver spots, slack jowls, and dunlap paunch. But when his blackish eyes blinked, I pictured vises snapping shut. He said I might like meeting a fellow employee from another branch of operations.

He leaned on the intercom button and coldly intoned a manifestly Japanese name. Its bearer immediately sauntered though the rear door, and I automatically offered a handshake, which seemed to confuse the newcomer, but didn't prevent him from reciprocating, to my instant regret. The flesh was gray and yielded unpleasantly like sponge under thin rubber. Vise-Eyes repeated the name, and its owner shuffled back.

The owner's looks were too distracting for me to retain his name. He could have been the same night caller I'd spied, or any member of his species; I could never tell them apart. Nothing in the facial features struck me as Asian.

The mouth preoccupied me. Ever since my moonlit glimpse I couldn't shake a feeling that the archetypal brutish gunsel had busted out of the Platonic realm, and the mouth foremost hinted why. Too wide in a sharklike fashion, it was stiff with a sneer both vicious and stupid. The teeth were bright and impossibly even, like a double row of blunted incisors. Rather than speak, the gray man was content to flash them at me and stare, and I conjectured whether each gray man's thirty-two points had been filed down to forestall panic among the stenographers.

For relief, I looked to Selina, which cued old Vise-Eyes. "He and his fellow Oni were recruited by our agents in Japan. The central office directs them to this branch, in whatever number we specify." Whatever number? I grimaced at the vision of Oni by the hundreds dropping off factory conveyor belts into huge baskets.

The eyes were glassy like two-way mirrors, and though nobody could look in, something was gazing out that wanted the spectator to squirm. The hair was black, combed back and slicked down. His black suit was loose and may have seemed less shabby some thirty years ago. An Imp of the Perverse made me ask, "So how do you get these Oni?"

"We conjure them up." The blackish eyes were devoid of mirth or irony. "We do not idly boast in asserting a serious, pragmatic approach to the occult. We find what myths and lore are based on fact, and we reopen ancient routes into the Invisible World to get at them. Then we literally employ those facts to strengthen the organization."

He waved at the Oni as if at a badly stuffed trophy. "We have uncovered his kindred spirits all over the world." He finally smiled, so we'd all know he was exercising his wit. It was a ghastly smile, and fortunately he couldn't keep it up. "Like most demons, the Oni prove little trouble to control and feed. They are completely subservient to us."

But I wasn't among that select "us" yet, and the demon was making the best of that. The mockery in the ashen face warned me only Selina and the fat man prevented him from tearing into me. I was uneasy all right, but smiled weakly and asked if the Oni ate raw meat. The fat man said no in a way that didn't comfort me.

The sub rosa message shone like magnesium strips between the elderly eyelids. My employers had lied outright to ensure my working for them, and after they judged me worthy of the truth, they'd dose me bit by bit. What they'd chosen to reveal implied how big and powerful they were, to scare me for my own good because they liked me, and because they needed loyal employees. Maybe I could go far with them, but I absolutely shouldn't try to test how powerful they were by irritating them. If I could locate my image in the fat man's eye, would it crack like a walnut whenever he blinked? I avoided eye contact.

Selina, though professionally cool, didn't participate in this workplace intimidation. She didn't have to, and besides, she did love me. Vise-Eyes did not, and wanted to underscore his point. "Despite patent shortcomings in charm and intellect, the Oni possess invaluable talents." He surveyed the demon as impassively as a flea-circus ringmaster surveys his performers, and commanded, "Demonstrate."

The gray man continued staring at me, occasionally flicking his eyes toward the ringmaster. Demon skin began to change, in the way an overripe peach gets soft and untouchable, only quickly, and with a methane stench that made me nauseous. Selina and Vise-Eyes must have been used to it. The putrescent flesh was running in greasy streamlets, melting right off the bones. Patches of white shone briefly on forehead, cheeks, and knuckles. The flesh paused at arbitrary ebb and then flowed into new arrangement, like a rising tide alive with sea worms.

The desk was close enough to lean on without being too conspicuous. I was afraid, not of the disgusting Oni, but of being sick in that clean white office. Even Selina's solicitous touch on my arm made me shudder reflexively, as if my body, at least, knew better than to trust anyone there. Vise-Eyes' smug smile was bereft of humor, and the Oni's lips were rolling back over skeletal grin to resume their sneer, red rather than gray.

As the skin reshaped it lightened, while movement at the waist showed off the baggy black suit's utility. The belly was bloating as if with stagnant gases, tightening the suit, and as the stench worsened, I leaned more feebly on the desk, weathering a new undertow of vertigo. The process, especially then, was the purest obscenity I'd ever seen.

When I looked to the face again, it, and demonic physique, had stabilized as another Vise-Eyes, marred only by the crumby suit and the wrought-iron stupid grin. Selina and the fat man talked business a few minutes, letting me contemplate a protean lackey's possibilities. The lackey stared back with a contempt too profound to take personally. Selina and her colleague ran out of conversation, and he glanced up and dismissed his grinning shadow. The departure was like a shark fin dipping underwater. The door never opened. I felt helpless, immobile, even after Selina tapped my shoulder and said, "He's gone, and we should leave too."

Without another word, Vise-Eyes sat down and studied his bare desktop. Selina led me out, and I followed complacently till the sight of a men's room door betrayed my suggestibility. I lurched in, and five minutes later Selina was waiting with whatever sympathy I needed.

In forthcoming weeks I joined with Selina in real work at last. We identified some Satanists in Woonsocket who'd been desecrating churches and who are still, as far as I know, blithely evading Woonsocket's Finest. In the second-growth wilderness of western Rhode Island we and our grotesque instruments staged an overnight vigil of a reputedly haunted graveyard, and though we arguably saw and heard things, we never found out for sure. The results, and the Satanist data, and everything else were consigned to another department. I was too infatuated with Selina, and too wary of the organization, to fuss about access to information.

The days of fixed innocence had to end despite every machination to prolong them. The organization's intricate bulk had too many holes to plug, and the innate corruption had to leak out. I could smell it walled up and waiting, but I, happy with Selina, was the last person who cared to deal with it.

In any setup so vast, oversights only hurt the hired help. The chance discoveries that put me in this alley were supposed to be dis-

closed gradually, so as not to overtax my tolerance, till I became utterly callous. And now chance may afford me my salvation, when
the Oni try doing to me what I saw them do when chance first
kicked in.

I was retrieving dossiers for Selina when the cruel, childish
laughter of Oni lured me to an open door. Three among the dozen or
so inside scowled at and then ignored me, which I interpreted as
carte blanche to snoop. Most of them were hunched forward on
built-in benches along two opposite walls, engrossed in four demons
cross-legged on the floor and playing chicken with a switchblade.

One would shake a fist at his circle of peers, holding the hilt so
that the blade seemed to bloom from the fist itself. His leer would
erupt intro chortling as he menaced the other three, and suddenly
the knife flipped at one of them, who had to disappear or be skewered. The point stuck into the floor, and the players grabbed for the
privilege of next toss.

The danger only made for fascination and childish glee, and as
the game grew feverish, they had to up the risk. Spectators slapped
players' heads and kicked their backsides, and the players pinched
and poked one another. One demon's head was twisted around
roughly, and he had an extra distraction seeing me for the first time.
He gawked a second too long, and the handle was quivering in the
side of his neck. Surprise expanded into shock before he fell back,
arms straight up, hands clutching at air that evaded his lungs.

The rest cackled louder and then went silent. Their eyes were
glossy with an unmistakable feral appetite, and they closed in, to
pound and kick at the dying body. They withdrew, one of them still
kicking at a twitchy arm, the others sniffing the air.

Eagerly they snatched at something unseen overhead, snagged,
yanked, ripped, and crammed it into their gaping mouths. They
flailed again while still chewing like dogs, and when swallowing,
their neck tendons bulged as if something wouldn't go down easily.
Their arms reached lower every time, as if something fluttered more
weakly after pieces were gouged from it. I couldn't hear their prey
suffer, but something at an unprobed depth within me shriveled in
response, making my stomach tremble as if it would crack into ul-
cers. Dizzy and enervated, I staggered off to Selina's cubicle.

She recognized the turmoil in my face, maybe from her own past, and made consoling noises. She sat me down and hurried out, and came back uncapping a quart of bourbon. I guzzled two shots from a Dixie cup and marveled at how incongruous liquor looked and tasted in these white rooms. Knives and demon gunsels weren't nearly as out of place.

She told me to show her what had upset me. The Oni were slouching at their benches or slumped against the wall, with sated, blissful mien. One noticed us, belched, and spaced out again. They were totally unconcerned with the gray cadaver stiff in contortion; it might have been a depleted antipasto platter. Selina said, "In mortal form, they can be mortally injured. Like humans, they have souls. The Oni eat souls." The scene seemed to make her more disgusted than horrified. "Now we'll have to conjure up another one." She turned and started away, expecting me to follow.

The organization had been careless, failing to segregate their ravenous henchmen effectively, and they extended amends agreeable to me and simple enough for them. Shamelessly I let them buy me off, despite the traumatic memory of what I felt inside me that day. That afternoon, Selina waved a pair of plane tickets at me. We had a week in Montreal, all expenses paid, commencing immediately. During that time I could neither block out nor fully accept that my employers had to be fundamentally evil, just to supply the Oni's diet. And Selina was with them all the way.

Montreal was all the more Edenic with tragedy lowering like thunderheads on the skyline. Halfway through the week I had one perfect day, a culmination of the last few months' dream life with Selina. Like a Renaissance cathedral, every plan, incident, and upshot cooperated to create a natural, harmonious gestalt, vivid to me yet. Selina had sensed the same, and we went to bed wistful that the enchantment, though lingering with us, would slip away in the night. The next days might be good, but we'd lost something unique. Back in Providence, I had only the fading illusion of those good days. I can't recall one measly image of Montreal now.

The first deceptive circumstance was of a fond reunion. I was finishing a lunch at Koerner's, another venerable glint in the soot zone, a bunker-like structure jammed like an afterthought between five-story neighbors. The frontage on either side of the entrance was mostly picture window, clogged with wire-hung placards of daily specials. Twin sets of day-glow green swinging doors opened onto separate breezeways, and inside were four rows of white enamel tables on black legs. The legs stood on alternating black and red linoleum with white inset squares, and the counter and walls up to tabletop height were azure. From there to the white tin ceiling, the walls were robin's egg blue.

The countertop radio's all-news station with its unchanging diction seemed to waylay time. The customer base and prices also hadn't changed since 1947, enticements in ascending order. As a student I'd often brought less snotty pals and instructors here, and now I was alone, viewing the codgers with frayed but adamant faces, dress sense, and voices. This was my sanctuary from undergrads, businessmen, and the 1970s.

When my long-lost college mentor trailed in on that thought, I dropped my spoon as if it had sprouted a joy buzzer. He reached the counter without seeing me, and looked as genuine and shopworn as anyone else in line. He was a big man who walked with a slight, humble stoop, though his eyes were bright and indomitable. While he ordered, I stared at him on the premise he'd eventually feel it like a homing signal. He paid, squinted around the room in chagrin, spotted me, and smiled.

No sooner was he seated with me than I pestered him for details of his last two years' adventures. Dr. Feder had a knack for storytelling and dining simultaneously, faster than I could do either. Tenure had eluded him for political reasons and he resigned, the same year I'd graduated. Glad to be shut of the game, he dipped into miscellaneous blue-collar gigs while developing quasi-mystical ideas on the ways environment shaped and arrested thought. Observation of small-town residents across the Northeast supported his hypotheses, and finally he'd lucked into an organization where his work had been anticipated, and where it could benefit the public.

He characterized his employers as wealthy but discreet unto anonymity, incorporated simply as Educational Research. I nearly choked on a mouthful of coffee, gulped it with a napkin to my lips. Perhaps he'd meant Esoteric Research?

He chuckled, but his eyes narrowed as he admitted I'd hit on a truer name at that. I asked for more details about his work.

"Well, consider the number of isolated communities even in so small and congested a place as Rhode Island. Dozens of them, between urban enclaves and backwater hamlets. Take into account the state's total population of circa 900,000. Statistically, a lot of good minds must be wasting away in isolation. Far too many become sticks in the mud after high school, maybe selling insurance or shelving library books, but never suspecting, let alone realizing, their potential in the wider world.

"And before they settle down, or stagnate rather, these thinkers show striking originality, without a mainstream to conform to intellectually. My employers have the manpower and funding to locate brilliant children in elementary and middle schools and finance their private, non-restrictive education. The children I've found were headstrong, unique, and creative, in reaction to stultifying environments, before they could 'grow up' and give in to them."

"What happened to the kids who enrolled in this program?"

Feder scratched a wispy sideburn. "I don't know. Other people act on my findings." Feder studied my face and rummaged vest pockets for his pipe and pouch. On the third try I lit a match for him. His eyes roved the lines on his big red hands. "You've reminded me of some sad news I happened upon in today's obituaries. A very likable boy I recommended for aid died yesterday in an auto crash." He waved impatiently at my sorries and asked about my work.

I deleted Selina and the Oni. Feder was good at concealing worry within his bulk, but some escaped through gleaming eyes and an itch under thinning salt-and-pepper hair. After I swore my bosses really were called Esoteric Research, he got up for another cup of tea.

We traded more data. He punched in on Washington Street, I on Westminster. He'd been working three weeks, I'd put in two months. I described all the personnel who'd made a distinct impression, and some sounded awfully familiar to him. Educational Research had also baited him with talk of a Rhode Island ground floor in a nationwide venture.

I was especially curious about his recruitment. "Coincidence," he said, a one-word hedge for the misgivings that hovered around us.

His graveyard factory shift in Albion was becoming onerous. One midnight he found the evening paper at his workstation, open to the classifieds, an overhead bulb shining directly on Educational Research's five-line come-on. Next day they hired him. He remained somber, presumably over the boy's death, and I was glad he hadn't crossed paths with the Oni. As for my recruitment, Feder heard an abridged version wherein the cordiality, and nothing more, of a company rep visiting my previous employment had won me over.

We were both still uneasy, but could do nothing for it. Feder yanked out a pocket watch and went hmph. "Any minute now, someone should be waltzing in here with my new assignment."

"And we'd both feel better if our mysterious bosses didn't see us together." We shook hands.

"At least not till one of us figures something out, or proves there's nothing to figure."

As I rose, he scribbled on a paper napkin. "My address and phone number. Can you drop by, say, Thursday evening?"

I nodded, took the napkin, and shrugged on my jacket. Feder mock-saluted and pondered his teacup as if it held loose, prophetic leaves.

After the first swinging door I paused, hearing someone bustle through the other side. Had Feder's lunch date arrived? I peeked through my door's porthole. Gentlemanly Feder stood to greet a woman whose movements were so clipped as to seem like propaganda for muscular economy. Any grace or beauty was encased in efficiency. Something about her puzzled me till I caught her in brief profile. It was Selina.

I couldn't have backed off faster if she'd shot at me. I staggered back to the Blackstone, in a daze, unable to think. At 5 P.M. I was worse, and told Selina I was coming down with something. She believed me, and into the week I improved at faking insouciance. I preferred not to confront her. She was still the love of my life till I informed her of what I'd learned too soon. Two years playing at shamus had taught me ugly facts seldom bowed out gracefully, but I still loved Selina more than truth at whatever cost. Feder was more skilled a digger than I and lacked my compunctions. Thursday night I went to him like a charlatan courting blind justice.

Feder had cloistered himself on Weybosset Street, around the corner from Dick's, two flights above a billiards hall. He was among the few people I'd met who could be disliked purely because of their ideas, which made some colleagues jealous, and threatened the cozy little paradigms of others. Intellectually, Feder was always on the defensive.

He first entered my mind as a physical target as well when knocking on his half-open door produced no response. I poked it hard, stepped to one side, and waited. I peered in. The room was dark, and bright rectangles outlined drawn shades. I groped out the wall switch, blinked away the glare, and winced. The Spartan furnishings had been wrecked, even the stove door wrenched off, and the radiator upended.

The backroom's door was stuck, but gave too quickly when I shouldered it, as if someone had withdrawn. Off-balance I crashed into a desk and apparently bruised my hand on a sharp corner. This room was also dim, but by the light through the door I discerned, instead of black-and-blue, bloody tooth marks below my thumb. I cussed and glanced around, but the demons must have vanished at my entrance. Odd outlines where furniture should have been suggested a continuation of rampage here.

There was no overhead light, and I wasn't anxious to see too much too soon. En route to pull the shades I slipped and cursed again, stumbling against the wall. A feeble voice called my name the instant before the shade snapped up. My slide across the floor had been recorded in blood streaks that had spread from a broad pool beneath Dr. Feder. His bulging eyes were on me, and his hands wavered helplessly over his broad chest. The shirt was soaked and shredded, and I drew blood biting my lip at the thought of what was under the fabric. I couldn't speak for a minute. To make matters worse, Feder spoke first. "You're a tad late."

To me it was already a voice from beyond the grave. "Who killed you? What happened?"

"Lights went out, and they were just there." He turned his head and retched blood. "In bad light they looked gray."

I started shaking. It wouldn't have helped, but I regretted telling him nothing about the Oni.

"Played games with me. Knew where it was, but pretended to search so they could destroy the place." His arms sank to his chest, then rose back in revulsion at the mess there. "When they found it, one with knife to me pointed at one who made begging motions on knees. One with knife made mock stabs while other laughed. Then he just tore into me. They were waiting for me to die. They looked . . ." Horror managed to glaze over the pain in his eyes. "They looked hungry."

"Then I came in. What did they take?"

He didn't go on. I left without touching anything.

Both our organizations were limbs of the same inconceivable behemoth, but that was the most someone at my rank could nail down in a lifetime. Their ultimate policy was so well-shielded, they could keep their enemies on the payroll till they'd served their purpose and then lower the boom. Feder had understood his situation and been liquidated all the sooner for letting on he understood. I was probably safe. Even if the assassins had recognized me, they likely hadn't said anything, out of contempt for their masters.

Within twenty-four hours, Feder was avenged and I was a dead man too. I'd continued spending a few nights per week on Smith Street, and better there than Selina's for a bout of insomnia. I didn't see her till 5 the next day, determined to know her actual work, and how evil she was when we weren't together. After supper I used her dope so I could simulate detachment, but it made me distant and curt until Selina excused herself for some sort of courier rendezvous. To no avail I rifled her desk and bureaus for solid information. In all documents, knowledge of the organization was assumed, and I could connect nothing on paper with the Selina I loved. In minutes she'd become a stranger.

I had the jitters, paced the room without losing them, and sequestered myself in the spare room I'd converted to a study. My revolver from Washington Street, including ammo, was earning its keep as a paperweight. I saw it for the first time in months. I wanted it to panic Selina into talking. I heard her call my name and through my unlit doorway saw her listen, then stash a long envelope in her living room davenport. She doused the lights and shut the bedroom door behind her.

Absent-mindedly holding onto the gun, I turned her desk lamp back on, extracted the envelope, and undid its flap. I dumped out some two dozen obits and headlines, each concerning a small-town quiz-kid and untimely demise. A yellow lined sheet contained two lists of names under the headings "Deceased" and "Extant," though several of the latter were crossed out. A sheet of typewriter stock with Feder's return address in the upper right bore several false starts at an apparent warning letter to parents. For the first time, Feder seemed small and pathetic.

I hollered Selina's name and barreled into the bedroom. She was just exiting the en suite bathroom, dabbing makeup off her eyelids with a facecloth. She asked, "Did you call me?"

I shook the papers at her like a mute ghost, furious, with chains. She wasn't remotely rattled. "Why, what's wrong?"

"You had him killed!" I snarled and flung down the papers.

Without them, the gun in my other hand was much more conspicuous to both of us. Selina stammered a little. "You mean the man who compiled that material? Well yes, of course, he was an enemy of the institute. If you read any of those pages, you know that."

"He didn't know he was an enemy!" Part of my mind was hysterical, and it determined what I said. But something else inside was steady and planning what to do, and its pathology frightened me.

"No matter. We'd intended to eliminate him all along. He forced us to act prematurely." My hysteria persuaded her I was harmless. I'd been waving the gun like Punch with his rubber cudgel. Selina, beaming endearment and sympathy, slunk toward me, reaching out. "Did you know the man?"

My backhand left a red blotch on her milk-white cheek. She was more bewildered than stung, wiped away a couple of tears, rallied her charm and tried again. "Arthur, please don't let it torment you. I was in charge of the liquidation, but you can't imagine where my orders came from. Who has a choice anymore?"

I didn't care. My grip on the gun had become more businesslike, and though Selina hadn't lost her composure, I could have pumped her for no end of privileged information. It wouldn't have done me any good. I'd henceforth only do what was necessary, what my innermost calm demanded.

I was no hero who could save the world, or help it in the least. I was even too late to make my own clean break with corruption. I loved Selina too much to let go of her, but I knew too much to accept her unvarnished self. "Smile. Show me how you smiled that night in Montreal, in bed next to me, after the lights went out. I've always wanted to know."

She obliged me. It was the easiest thing to do in her position. I shot her through the heart. She crumpled forward whimpering, and I sidled away as she hit the floor. Free will, a swirling fog around me, lifted at last, and I pocketed my gun and the bullets and hiked over to Smith Street, wondering how long the organization would need to catch up with developments. That was last night.

Idle curiosity coaxed me out of bed this morning. Tracking me down and blocking my escape would constitute a brief annoyance for them, an inevitably rigged game I'd play only out of spite and pride. I couldn't guarantee I'd die well, but so what? At this stage you, my imaginary audience, clamor to know what I'm going to do for you. Why not warn the world? Reduce the organization's menace to some degree? Find out something crucial and squirrel it away for your future use?

Save yourselves, dammit. Guard your own acre of reality. Mine came into fruition and exhaustion thanks to Selina. Loving too much commits you for life, bestows a basis for faith and reality, and no substitute will do. It's bigger than your own life, and nothing else matters more. Too much knowledge of Selina corrupted that reality for me, and my sacred duty was to kill her rather than let it languish corrupt.

What more to do afterward than refuse to cooperate? A few minutes early on Westminster Mall, I ducked into the shadow of a black marble alcove kittycorner from the Blackstone. Familiar bureaucrats passed without a word or nod. After half an hour, the sight of another familiar figure, strolling from the direction of College Hill, hit me like venom. Tingling and sluggish, I had to force myself into deeper shadow. Selina, her walk awkward and her smile more of a leer, entered the Blackstone, and my nerves quieted. I checked my wristwatch and inspected my reflection in black marble for any bulge of shoulder holster. I wasn't sweating.

In about fifteen minutes the alleyway door flew open and a dozen trenchcoated Oni poured out and scattered. I slipped into the black marble lobby. A few loped by without seeing me, glass door reflecting morning glare at them. I waited another minute and left, fully aware that for every Oni on the sidewalk, a legion could be airborne. By way of small comfort, I knew the quick pounce wasn't their style.

I went through the motions of skipping town. Ten minutes of crowded pavements and empty bylanes brought me to the cavernous train station. I looked sidelong at the cabbies out front and pushed by the oaken doors that whooshed behind me as I stopped short. Dour executives and Amtrak workers in blue jumpsuits made echoing footfalls as they crossed my view, and then my coast was clear.

Across the grand lobby and up a long ramp was the platform, the launchpad to anywhere. At the bottom of the ramp was a snack counter, and slouching against it, a steaming Styrofoam cup in one hand and the other buried in trenchcoat pocket, was a gray man, his complexion unobtrusive in the shade of black Stetson. When he saw that I saw him, he growled so wickedly that an undergrad approaching the counter kept his distance, jaw hanging.

As the Oni straightened up and strode forward, the forgotten coffee sloshed over his hand and he stiffened, his snarl drowned out by the garbled announcement for an incoming train. Enraged, he crushed the cup, roared as more coffee scalded his hand, hurled the cup away, and wagged remnant drops off his skin. A gaggle of foolhardy businessmen was openly staring, whereas citizens in the pews were making a point of looking somewhere else. I was already backing out, groping for the door behind me.

I made a beeline for the Greyhound terminal. Winded, I turned around on the steps, but the Oni hadn't followed. Photo booths and phone booths in the narrow corridor to the waiting room were empty, which encouraged me to forge on, and then inertia took over. A trenchcoated man was bent over the pinball machine, scowling at every footfall in earshot, then resuming his game, manically slamming the machine between bells. Without intercepting me, he began pounding on the glass top steadily, cackling at top volume between motionless lips.

I glimpsed two old security guards by the magazine rack looking thoroughly overwhelmed at him. I checked on the demon again, who started toward me, still cackling, and pointing at me. Before he'd entered the waiting room, I was dashing through it, diverting stares from him, stumbling past a door to the bus bays and around the corner. I slowed down and caught my breath. I didn't like providing a show for the nervous people in the bus station's black bucket seats, and I didn't want the Oni gloating that my flight was wild and panicky. Dignity remained an option in this game, which wasn't nearly frenzied enough yet for the Oni to close in.

After several more deep breaths, I meandered along side streets to Kennedy Plaza, a depot for public-transit buses, none of which were currently in. Any would have done. From the shadows of the Art Nouveau octagonal shelter, I noticed a gouty derelict eyeing me from his bench in the scruffy park across the street. With too much agility he sprang up and waved to a geezer at another bench; then both started wading among the cars braking for a red light. I retreated across the street, void of traffic between lights, on the other side of the plaza.

More alleys, then cobblestone streets and parking lots, brought me to the edge of downtown and the entrance ramp for Route 95. I stood before the traffic light at the intersection preceding the ramp, one foot off the curb, thumb held out, wondering if I looked cagey or impatient. Sun on windshields prevented me from seeing the drivers, who had the green light and sped by.

A black Cadillac was first in line at the red, and when it beeped twice, I ran to it naively exhilarated. I had the passenger door open and was leaning in when I noticed the driver's gray face. He chuckled and patted the seat beside him. I staggered back and slammed the black door.

Suddenly the traffic flow on 95 was super loud, and the cars behind the Oni's were all honking. Shaking a fist at me, he shot forward, leaving black streaks on the curve. From the highway came another outburst of horns as he merged, doubtless with poor grace. As the other drivers went by, frowning suspiciously at me, I grinned and walked away, trying to think.

Step two in the ritual, since escape wasn't happening, was hiding out. Both my place and Selina's were too obvious, which wouldn't stop the demons from staking them out. The organization didn't necessarily know why I'd killed Selina, nor would it care, rightly judging me no more threat than a blemish to be dissolved, a cosmetic matter. Then too I was exercise for their bloodhounds, none of whom confronted me en route to Feder's. Remembering a fire escape out his window, I trotted an extra block to approach from the alley's rear and boost myself to the steel ladder.

The window was unlocked, the electricity was out, and nobody jumped me when I inspected the rooms. Everything had been replaced or repaired. I left the Frigidaire open to dispel the reek of spoilage, came back after locating the farthest seat from windows, and threw together what wasn't rotten into sandwiches. I had no appetite, but ate for the sake of keeping up strength, ritual defiance again.

By my watch it was eleven when I hunkered down to dispose of the day. Brushing crumbs off my shirt, I contemplated how any quarry, man or beast, would best hold up while holing up. Not by thinking, or he'd go berserk or crack quietly. Any toad or hare would conserve energy, in stasis but not off-guard, intolerant of extraneous input. I could only achieve the rudiments of this state before the ticking of my watch distracted me. Finally I sighed and saw it read 11:45, unstrapped it, and whipped it into ruin against my fauteuil's wooden armrest.

My breathing relaxed. I draped the smashed watch over my thigh, surveyed the shadows lengthen from out of my corner, felt the traffic vibrate the floorboards, and noted the clearing of the thick inner-city air toward dusk.

When the front door's lock jiggled, I leapt from the chair to the square arch between rooms. Light from the hallway emphasized the apartment's darkness and silhouetted the big man shambling in. His lizard voice called out something with the inflections of a name, and he flipped the switch by the door to reveal Dr. Feder's stolen likeness. I shot it through the face, removed its gun from corduroy jacket, and pocketed the bullets. Nice that we all carried .45s.

From the backroom I heard something scraping. By the wall opposite my seat was a dusty velvet armchair, which thank God I hadn't touched all day. It was melting, its arms striving to rise and stretch like a waking man's, the feet elongating. Deep inside was a muffled cackling, but before a mouth surfaced, I fired. The thing shuddered and sagged as it was, while from the corridor cautious voices and footsteps approached.

I ducked out the window, down the fire escape, and through an alley. The streetlamp at the mouth of the alley came on the instant I glanced at it. I stopped, frightened for the first time all day. I skulked around its white circle as from a judging eye and ran for the nearest side street.

Hat shops and variety stores were just revolving backdrop before Dick's snagged me, probably because it was my only personal connection with this street. I wasn't resigned to the lot of a running target yet. I looked around, hustled inside, and noted that though the posted closing was 4:30, the darkness set the hour at 7 or later. The automatic buzzer annoyed me. When it cut out, Dick's dim outline sauntered from behind his partition.

"Well, what can I do for you?" He was too cheerful. I drilled him through the chest and he toppled over soundlessly. Dodging one aisle to the left, I stooped over and neared the counter, deciding no other Oni would have remained undercover while a good meal flapped away. Others had certainly heard the shot, if every potential storefront refuge hid a demon. Watching the sunken chest bubble, I smiled morosely at Dick's morning surprise if the Oni didn't clean up their mess. I scavenged more bullets from the body and navigated the dark storeroom to the rear alley.

Directly across the street from the alley was a tavern, and I thought about sanctuary there. But I felt like an exile, with a moral constraint against mingling with humanity. I knew too much for that, I knew death wasn't the end, at least not for the entirety of a person. That was the good news, and the wellspring for however much courage I had. The hungry jaws of the Oni were the long and short of the bad news.

I listened at the pub's gaping doorway, but out of it came gibberish. I belonged inside no more than a ghost or an angel. I was living in a microcosm now, with room for no man but me.

The practical downsides of tavern hideaway surfaced once I'd

slipped away. The Oni could infiltrate any human gathering and capture me, impersonating cops, or drunken pals, or asylum nurses. A
shootout was inevitable, and a crowded bar was the worst place to
be cornered.

Trudging along, I realized I'd no longer have cared about shooting any number of bystanders. The possibility of having murdered
the real Dick interested me briefly, but sparked no concern.

Even this amount of thinking was too much. Something clanged
inches behind me, and I turned for a casual look. Streetlamps gave
the cobblestones a cold brightness, and shivering in the seam between two stones was a shiny blade. Above the lamps, warehouse
windows were black and impenetrable as the sky, as if the walls
were false fronts. But from behind them, echoing back and forth
across the street, more and more demon throats took up the imbecile
cackle. Knives began raining down, aimed so carelessly I could sprint
zigzag to avoid them, like a GI in an occupied village. Breathless, I
rounded on them at the corner and fired into an upper window. The
laughter paused a minute, then resumed uglier than before.

Past the corner, a straight, short street would terminate on
Weybosset. One story up, a fire escape leveled out onto a catwalk
the length of the building overshadowing me. Footsteps on the slats
clunked toward me, and I aimed just above the railing. Pursuer
sprang over the railing to pounce almost before I could shoot, his
twisting body knocking me backward. I cursed and pumped two
more shells into the twitching thing at my feet. My ears were ringing
with the last few seconds' exertion and fury and gunblasts.

I stumbled down the street, red brick wall to my left, white wall
of St. Francis Monastery to my right. Stained glass cast warm colored
patches on the sidewalk, and I pictured contented monks snoozing
within. On the portico, the welcoming mosaic of St. Francis in Ap-
ennine terrain was obscured by a huddled shape that flattened need-
lessly as I fired wild and blinded St. Francis. Cursing some more, I
careened onto Weybosset, seeking a nook where I could reload.

The first gloomy doorway that caught my eye was good enough.
I paid no attention to the long cliffside of wall across the street, with
its rows of drawn venetians or black panes. Why kindle fresh anxie-
ties about demonic impatience with the chase? In their clumsy but

vicious way they were starting to close in, and some might be trying to organize. With no past left or future to speak of, this game of killing and evasion meant continuity, a life in quintessence, everything. I wasn't reconciled to making a stand.

Running zigzag again, I got across Weybosset and slowed within the shadows. A shabby man whose teeth and white hair had both gone yellow hobbled from out of the streetlight and asked me something in a dog voice without consonants. Reflexively I shot before he even saw the revolver, and he folded up whining. I weathered a brief wave of shock that, likely as not, I'd executed a genuine drifter. Maybe he'd saved me while I reloaded, if the Oni wanted to attack without the amenity of changing form for bystanders' sakes.

My remorse passed. The man was an intruder. My microcosm had its laws of survival, with no more room for conscience or morals than in the jungle.

The nearest alley's brick walls were painted black, sawdust covered the ground, and the windows had heavy bars and grates. The brilliant pod of a streetlight was bracketed to the wall a few feet overhead and powered by a long metal stalk from underground. I stopped to stare as at a long-lost idol. A jabbering turned me around in time to yelp at a stone against my cheek, and as I reeled back, the light burst and showered me with slivers. When I lowered my arms, the Oni were gone, probably waiting for the shabby man to expire. I pressed on.

I crossed Westminster Mall and kept going. It was too wide and well-lit for evasive maneuvers on my part, and too late did I realize the first alley off it was little better. High walls on both sides were thick with fire escapes and were linked overhead by a plain plaster-sheathed gangway calling itself the "Tri-Store Bridge." I stopped, unwilling to backtrack or advance, dipping a shoe in a puddle that never dried, fed constantly by gurgling pipes low in the walls.

The stench of pigeons and piss annoyed me. I heard angry whispering from above. Why hadn't they attacked? Their hearts were no longer set on a moving target. Over the voices of demons and drainpipes rose the caterwaul of a police siren. On the fire escapes, silhouettes were rattling to and fro like chimps in cages. The siren that made them cringe goaded me into scrambling headlong.

I dove into the porn shop toward the corner. Panting for breath in the G-rated anteroom, I focused on the comic books, refusing to turn and acknowledge the manager in his inner sanctum. My reality had no room for him.

After the siren faded, the Oni would have me trapped. If they hadn't dragged off the shabby man's corpse, the police would be searching for a gunman on foot, but the double whammy out there of cops plus Oni was better than game over if I stayed put. My final standoff wouldn't be here. At worst I'd end up demon bait in a jail cell. I inhaled and bounded into the shadows of Washington Street.

At a glance, the building I faced was vaguely familiar, as if from decades ago, and I wasted precious seconds staring till I recognized the site of my detective bureau. I felt nothing, but then the name Selina came unbidden to mind like a wilful ghost. I got the shakes and took off running, and to throw off tender memories tried pinpointing where echoing sirens were coming from.

The forsaken mass of the hulking Biltmore Hotel brought me short. Kennedy Plaza was on the other side. The Oni could easily nail me there before I'd reached any cover, and two squad cars were always stationed at each end. I turned on my heel, up Eddy Street, toward the mall again.

I passed the Miles Building. Its walls up to the eaves were of aqua vinyl, and then Second Empire dormers and minarets emerged, with dense ornament like tropical fungus. New decorative touches fidgeted impulsively. Oni were perched like gargoyles on every peak, glaring down at me. They still postponed attacking while the sirens threatened complications, so I cackled up at them and headed onto the mall.

I had to rest. My legs weighed tons, my lungs were spent, despite unflagging willpower. I needed a vantage in a building that afforded the demons negligible cover, and where it wouldn't be obvious I'd ventured in. From there I could decide how much longer I wanted to live.

After one more block of the mall, the street counterintuitively narrowed for normal traffic. I staggered along the sidewalk in the throes of fatigue. Several dozen yards ahead hung the bright circle of the Arcade clock, suspended from a long wrought-iron bar. It was only 8:01. The sirens were obnoxiously loud, maybe sending the demons into hiding or into a careless rage, sneering jealously at those mortal others hunting me. If the cops missed me in the next few seconds, they'd be a godsend.

Here was my ideal building, a Greek Revival temple of commerce from the 1820s, allegedly America's first roofed galleria. The entry was locked, and the three levels of balconies were too open for demons to hide effectively while spying on passersby. I gathered the sturdiest empty crates from the alleys on either side of the Arcade and piled them under one of the curly iron rods from which dangled an unlit spherical lamp.

I climbed up, jumped, caught the rod, traversed its length hand-over-hand, and clambered frantically onto the second-floor railing. I wormed over, hit the floor, rolled flat, and looked streetward. The distance down seemed much greater than the distance up. I noted gratefully that my leap had scattered the boxes into outwardly purposeless rubbish.

Headlights approached, and the sirens were deafening. I rolled farther in, more to escape the volume than the police per se, and listened as the cruiser stopped and its doors slammed. Men spoke, but my ears were disoriented, unable to arrange the inflections into English. They kicked the boxes around, laughed, got back in the cruiser, and drove away, siren at full blast. I didn't understand or care about their behavior. They were no immediate menace and didn't matter. I was thinking without foresight, like any four-footed prey, and accepted that without qualms.

I slid back several yards down the aisle before standing up, momentarily safe. Any Oni in the building would already have attacked while I was down. The galleries were silent as a vacuum, easily absorbing my careful footfalls. The roof was all tinted skylight and lent a bluish glow to the Ionic columns upholding it. Each of the three levels had a continuous aisle and was recessed slightly from the level below. Hanging plants brushed my face every so often, and hanging black-and-white shop signs receded like dominoes.

I passed a goldsmith, antiques, a photographer, a handwriting analyst and spiritual counselor, a travel bureau, all rendered congruous in this matrix of antebellum architecture. The wooden floors, slanting enough to test my balance, accentuated my fatigue, and I sought a door nobody would bother to wire against burglars. Maintenance Department looked good. The lock was too old to put up real resistance.

Without resorting to the lights I located a chair behind a nicked, battered desk and sat in darkness and silence a while. On the desk was a radio. I doubted a reasonable amount of background sound would pose any harm. Words and music rippled out incoherently. I grew curious about the Oni, whose ranks seemed coordinated only by uniformly increasing amounts of impatience and frustration. After sufficient time, all might wonder at once whether any of the others had spotted me. I sat a little longer, then went out to listen, leaving the radio on.

The radio faded as voices from the street came into range, cuing me to drop upon knees and crawl toward the rail. I didn't have to get close enough to see the speakers. Through the railing slats I could discern the dark reflections of Stetsons and trenchcoats in the shop window across the street. Apparently we'd arrived at the hour they felt safe in stalking openly, no more ambush, sniping, or lurking in depots. I beat the urge to join their game and leap like a beast among them. My superiority lay in making them come to me.

About half a dozen deliberated in dog language for a while, and several more showed up, the glint of pistols in their reflections. About time the Oni reached the conclusion that the night was too quiet for me to be out walking among them. Like the police, they were kicking the crates around, drawn to them without recognizing why, till one booted one box to land atop another, and he goggled at it and started jabbering.

The surrounding Oni glowered at him for interrupting their conference till he pointed at the pair of boxes, and then up in my general direction. They all peered up and then at nothing in particular while they concentrated. Simultaneously they glared toward me, baring teeth, and instantly tiny globes of light floated in their places, spiraling up to my gallery. I stumbled up and back into the Maintenance Department.

I switched off the radio. I'd make nothing easier for them. For the foreseeable future I'd kill so many that survivors would snarl aghast at all the souls escaping uneaten. I sighed and waited. Contemptuous and hushed I sat, while demons singly and in couples crossed the doorway's dim light like shoppers. Some strolled, some hurried, some scrambled to false alarms. A few doors were kicked in and locks yanked off, leading me to ruminate over the outcome if police overheard and barged in. I didn't ruminate long. Police, law, interference had become idle fantasy, as had everything outside the moment.

A demon paused at my door. I didn't move. The silhouette in frosted glass tugged at the doorknob and became flesh. Only my hand moved, aiming and firing before he could yell. Without premeditation I was bent over the quivering body to relieve it of pistol, and up on my feet again in the doorway. The shot had brought the pack running, but I hadn't been cornered, and I had the inspiration of the casualty at my feet.

Demonic modus operandi of capture and humiliation before the kill worked to my advantage. A gun in each fist, I trod squarely into the aisle, fired three times into one oncoming stampede, about-faced, and did the same to the onrush from the other direction. While the unwounded scattered, I cast my empty guns to the ground floor and looted new ones from the dead and the injured who lacked strength to vanish, pulsing in and out of translucence as they writhed.

No sooner had I pocketed two revolvers and reloaded two than more demons spewed out of doorways and dark corners. After the third try they learned, and left me alone while they cobbled together a plan.

At either end of the gallery, the Oni as globes of light roiled like a cloud of gnats, their language reduced to twitterings. Irritated I paced back and forth, feeling caged, then realized I was caged and didn't like it. I refused to be cornered while I had any choice and strode to the railing, brandishing pistols, to lure the Oni out of the air. They'd stop me and kill me, but at least I could push them into killing without capturing me, a moral victory, to style the inevitable into giving them no satisfaction. What more could I do?

From above swished something too fast to follow, and my forearm was snared in a lasso, half a dozen demons doing their best to haul me up and dislocate my elbow. I swore and fired the gun in my free hand at them, their fingers already clawing at my sleeve. Some howled and they rescattered, and the drop onto my back stunned me for a second. I craned my neck, but the demons on the topmost level were gone. The Arcade was silent, as was the world outside.

I got up unsteadily, battling vertigo and a ringing in my ears that sharpened into the droning of more Oni than before, swarming around both ends of the gallery. I started toward the teeming lights again, groggy enough for them to dazzle me. From a doorway thrust a demon like a barracuda, slashing hard at my nearer hand. The pain cleared my head as tendons snapped and the gun fell from useless fingers. I snarled and hissed as well as any demon, emptying my other gun into the assailant before he could do anything more. He fell back twisting like a snake; grinning, I traded my spent gun for the one he'd dropped.

No more snipers were visible above or ahead, but the three-story chasm within the galleries churned with globes, thicker than dust in a sunbeam, tinted an icy blue by the skylight. Gritting my teeth against their chorus, harsh and loud as a chainsaw, I advanced again. I had to pull off my tie and loosen my collar, dizzy and breathless in the wet, tropical heat the demon horde was generating.

The Oni at the end had some reason for hovering farther out above the street, but that didn't stop me. Once I emerged from under the third floor's balcony, my railing was in reach. Something clicked overhead, and an arc blasted into the floorboards a pace away. The world was mute, my ears numb and throbbing, and above me leaned three demons laughing noiselessly and cradling tommyguns, one of which was smoking.

Meanwhile Oni slunk toward me from the acute angle beneath the staircase to the third floor. Again I forged ahead, assuming the tommyguns were meant to fence me in now and kill me later. When I ignored a second strafe at my feet, the gunner had to swing wild. A few demons behind me went down clutching at surprise wounds, and their cohorts hopped back, barking curses loud enough to hear through the tinnitus. In this brief lull, the pain in my gushing hand irked me like the first nausea of a suicide full of pills. The only remedy was oblivion.

More Oni grabbed my jacket as I bolted for the rail. I pulled out of the sleeves, roaring as my gash tore wider. The gun in my good hand I flung to the street, and I vaulted over the rail after it. En route down, my good hand tried closing on a spherical lamp but couldn't hold on. My bad hand managed only to slap the globe. I rolled with the impact but heard an ankle crack and prayed I wouldn't have time to feel it.

I limped over to the gun and looked up. On the white globe was a smeared red handprint. Beyond it were demons leering over, with hundreds more droning behind them, setting the whole Arcade aglow. More buzzed directly over me, then whizzed back to join the swarm.

I emptied my gun at the balcony and lurched away without seeing if I'd hit anyone. That too had outlived its importance. Out of habit I kept the gun as I made for the next alley, several buildings away. After ducking in, I saw the brick dead end, ten feet high. I wasn't disappointed. I was tired. The back of another building behind the dead end loomed ethereal like a vision. Turning back to the alley's mouth, I slumped against trash barrels and waited, and watched the demons gather and gloat, and thought of you and the past.

I'll play it through for you like a newscaster. Some two dozen Oni are squirming for a view past the three who sneer at me, brandishing tommyguns. A car door slams and the Oni are in sync as they look and scatter or vanish. The three executioners hold their ground as a cop shambles over, not even glancing in my direction. My heart beats faster despite my better judgment, my hope an unwanted reflex.

Cop and demons converse, with the artillery of no concern to either party. The cop yawns, takes off his cap to scratch his head, and replaces the cap. He says something at which the demons nod obediently, and he waves good-night. In seconds there are more spectators than ever.

Why should I resist the vice of dividing humanity down the middle? Some ultimately obey others, the rest, ultimately, themselves. The present moment is the undisguised price the latter eventually pay for their integrity.

Maybe my soul has a sporting chance. Keeping the mob at a distance also forces the gunners back, and none are flitting overhead yet.

The mob is getting pushy, though, and for the privilege of the kill, the gunners will have to act. I drop my pistol and stand up away from the trash barrels. The killers take aim, and by reflex I hold up my hands as if to ward off bullets. I laugh at myself, a little too loud, and staccato enough to make a segue for the guns.

the immortality sequence

At least they no longer accuse me of Professor Shale's murder. The only fingerprints on the pistol were his, and the landlord, on regaining his composure, remembered hearing my ascending footsteps after the shot. In fact, he initially mistook me for the police he'd just called. Otherwise he'd never have mustered the courage to enter the "scene of the crime" and discover me burning the professor's papers.

I still face severe penalties, academic and legal, for my impulsiveness, and though I understand why, I can't help feeling indignant, if not hurt, at the insinuation I acted out of spite, for less than the greater good. I did the wisest thing, and had I been hastier, I'd have circumvented any repercussions or anger over purged documents. As it is, all men are free of a temptation, almost as costly as a deal with the devil, that can never recur, any more than could a mind like the professor's. Perhaps the university and the Shale estate will believe that, if they believe my story.

Tomorrow I stand before the campus disciplinary council for my preliminary hearing, and unless the past month's events are outlined cogently, I will lose what slight credibility I retain.

When Shale's students received the mimeo'd notice that we'd have to choose new courses because he was on a special leave of absence, I especially was disappointed, or really, dejected. After all my coursework with him, all our discussions in his office, all my dinner invitations to him, I'd hoped to be regarded as a friend, close enough to hear his plans and tribulations. Obviously he was always busy, but I assumed he was mentor enough to warn me of his departure.

Through September I tried contacting him, to be sociable, to counterbalance his aloofness. Nobody answered at his previous address or phone number, no new listing was available, and the English

Department withheld the whereabouts of faculty on leave. The secretary did confide that the chairman himself didn't know where Shale was. She also reminded me Shale was eccentric, erratic even, and I should relax until he chose to reemerge, like some migratory dolphin. She annoyed me, but I smiled courteously. And then what could I do?

I didn't worry unduly. My semester was the duller without Shale, and I often pondered his disappearance, though never long enough at once to count myself preoccupied. The intervals between musings increased until, toward winter, the professor's image was faded and uncertain.

With January's final papers and exams, the mystery of Shale was forgotten, and only then did it resolve. The first bitter cold snap had followed a minor Providence snowfall and deterred me from exiting my Hope Street apartment for the library. I had the requisite notes and reading for one paper and no excuse to delay writing, except for the street view from my tabletop desk.

Everything was fascinating and uncanny, as with a new photo of a globetrotting friend. Dusk was almost night, and the snow's thin crust was tinged like old paste with a coating of dust. The trees and roofs of my nearby horizon were limned as in stencil by the wan hemispheric glow of downtown light, and the street itself was glistening with ice like froth eddies in a black flow. But something more, something elusive, contributed to the view's uncanniness, deriving from neither the hour nor the weather.

My wandering sight was drawn to the house at the corner of Hope and Power. Previously unimpressive, it was pell-mell Victorian replete with narrow-windowed turret from which, for the first time in memory, light was spilling. This disoriented me, as if the teapot on my desk started shooting out beams from its solid surface. But the man's silhouette that occasionally blocked the light was further disturbing, suggesting the egregiously cramped space was inhabited. As my unease dissolved into pity, I felt less bound to watch the errant shadow, and soon I was at work.

My first paragraphs were disagreeably stubborn, leaving me unsatisfied after several hours. I was verging on fatigue, but refused to quit at such a shamefully unproductive stage. Brewing tea only worsened matters, for I was still too logy to write, but too wired to sleep. Again I contemplated the lit turret. What could anyone do in there? Who would make it his home? I'd already assumed the chamber served this purpose, not imagining elsewise.

The motion across the light, sometimes abrupt, sometimes hovering, reminded me of a fish in its bowl. Whatever determined how and when it moved was equally inscrutable, and neither turret-dweller nor fish acknowledged onlookers. And even as fishy undulations exert an entrancing effect, I felt myself nodding off. Astonished at staying up till 2 A.M., I heaved out of my chair, pausing to glance out the window once more, just in time to see the turret light wink out.

I awoke half-heartedly fending off euphoria and redoubled my efforts when bedside clock came into focus. My morning class was half over! It was a lost cause, but I was too jolted not to spring out of bed. To deplete my nervous energy, I went for groceries at the corner milk store.

Stepping off my porch, I heard the door of the Victorian house creak open, amplified in the frosty air. Still in the shadows, I stared in hopes that here was the turret-dweller, who would have to be an extraordinary character. Moreover, we'd both gone to bed at the same small hour. Why shouldn't we rise and venture out simultaneously? His back was to me as he slammed the door, and as he turned and descended the steps a wall of hedges still concealed him. On the sidewalk, his head was lowered while his hands brushed windborne snow off his coat, but a gray, untrimmed beard caught the sun. The silver crescent's familiarity startled me, but I couldn't quite place it. He proceeded, eyes on the treacherous paving, his face uplifted just enough.

"Professor Shale!" I exclaimed. Instantly I hoped my voice hadn't carried, something I'll never know because the next second I was racing toward him. He pushed his hands into coat pockets and stopped, cautious and perhaps put off. He didn't seem to recognize me, and greeted me as if surprised anyone would recognize him.

Once I came within handshake range, his eyes glinted with recollection and he spoke my name, albeit coolly. Undaunted, I talked about attempts to contact him, and how much I missed his classes, till my breath ran out. He smiled wanly, and twisted his face away from a gust laden with powdery snow.

"You're not the one renting the turret, are you?"

"As a matter of fact, I am," he rejoined brusquely, as if I were prying at intimacies. Evidently he'd speak only to reply, so I groped for another question. Not till now did I feel the cold, and dug my hands into navy-surplus peacoat pockets, worming fingers into the gloves within.

I was so anxious to converse that I broached whatever occurred to me, without vetting its tactfulness. The professor admitted to leasing the room since September. The landlord, who lived downstairs, was reluctant but was receiving a very handsome rent. There was no better place to work on a special project. The project would take some time to explain. He was also going to the milk store. No longer did last night's restless silhouette connote anything sinister or eccentric. It, and the turret, had become enchanting, attractive.

On our way back, my persistence began to open cracks in his reserve, and a little of his old geniality welled up. I kept walking with him past my house, feeling our talk was not yet properly over. At his own door, he'd have to invite me in or we'd have to part more ceremoniously. From the granite steps, he looked down at me and warmed a bit more. Apparently he wanted to speak, but a wariness, or maybe hauteur, prevented him. My affability undermined his barriers, and the daunting prospect of chatting any longer in the cold probably collapsed them.

He asked if I were really interested in his project. I nodded assertively. He still wavered, but a need to reveal something, easily suppressed only in the absence of an audience, seemed to possess him. Shale couldn't help being a teacher, and to encourage him I asked point-blank to see his work. He nodded slowly, then more definitely. "When?" I asked, and this seemed to throw him off-balance. His forehead creased as with bafflement, and as if on autopilot, he intoned, "Tonight."

I repeated that to be sure he meant it, and with slight hesitation he nodded. I smiled, thanked him, and cradled his grocery bag while his pink hands struggled with the key, and then I awkwardly assayed to hold the door from the outside while he barged in.

My anticipation till nightfall was steady, but no more distracting than if I were awaiting a favorite class. After supper, my concentration crumbled. I'd planned nothing for that evening but the visit, and buckling down to anything else was like clutching at fog. I had a cup of tea, left the cup in the sink, and hastened to Shale's.

Squinting through gray streetlight for names under doorbells disclosed only that his was not among them. I advanced to the locked inner door, and in the foyer's darkness imagined Shale could be a ghost. He'd materialized here, but I had no witnesses, no solid indications, of his presence. Rather than deliberately ring up the wrong person, I knocked so that whoever was in earshot or most kindly disposed could answer. From deep inside, footsteps approached and someone demanded, "What the hell?"

I shouted, "A visitor for Professor Shale!"

The footsteps ceased and the voice muttered searchingly, "Shale?" The door opened and a fiftyish man with salt-and-pepper slicked-back hair eclipsed the somber hall light. He was gripping a newspaper folded to the TV listings. "Oh yeah, in the garret. Up three floors, then more stairs behind a door on the right." Without another word, he trudged through the nearest doorway into a family living room; my nosiness made me self-conscious till the long, steep climb winded me.

The third-floor landing gave onto an ill-lit corridor and girls conversing behind a door at the far end. The meager light came from a 25-watt bulb hanging in a glass shade with a grape-cluster-and-leaf motif. To the direct right of the lamp was a door with its own buzzer, which proved dysfunctional. Knocking on the door's painted-over glass panes silenced the girls, and their blatant eavesdropping bothered me. Shale called down for me to enter, and the girl talk resumed after I shut his door. I couldn't make out whether they were discussing the professor.

I peered upstairs and grinned. The Victorian extravagance below rarefied into a more seventeenth-century air of starkness. The winding stairwell was tight as a closet, with bare plaster walls and paintless, narrow treaders. As I shambled past the first twist, my overhead light winked out, and Shale's shadowy face stared down from a wooden railing. I stopped. He smiled, and I continued up. Backing off as I rounded the railing, he remarked he thought it would be me.

I briefly lost track of the professor himself amidst his ambience pervading the Spartan room. In these cramped quarters I had a counterintuitive feeling of lightness and expanse as if in an aerie, and my lingering tension dispersed as Shale pushed his chair toward me and bade me sit. He perched on his desktop, for want of another chair, and I wondered how he could be at all comfortable.

"So you want to learn of my work." I nodded avidly, and in his eyes ignited a spark of challenge. "In effect, you'd serve as my apprentice." Mulling his choice of words, I nodded more slowly while he issued his last caveat. "And you'd have to live in constriction like this."

He laughed at my poorly masked bemusement. "Forgive me. I need austerity for my research. You shouldn't need it to learn from me." A gale rattled every window in succession, and though the room was warm, I sidled toward the Franklin stove at its midpoint. "Would you like some tea?"

Foreseeing a long discourse, I nodded again. He slid from the desk and removed a jug of Poland Spring from a fridge no bigger than a fruit crate. "In this space I could best renounce our mundane, consensus reality and start fresh." He poured water into a tea kettle, which he set on a double hotplate's burner. Atop the fridge were two cups, into which he spooned loose tea from a purple canister.

So far his words affected me less than his household arrangements, and he noticed. "The logistics here are interesting. Kitchen, bedroom, study all in one. That's about everything, isn't it?" He entertained second thoughts. "I use the third-floor bathroom and wash my dishes there, usually before the tenants are awake or when they're out for the evening. Do you mind if I lie down while we speak? I've been prone to headaches lately." I shook my head and turned my chair toward his mattress on the floor. He directed his words to the blank ceiling and folded his hands upon his chest. The kettle was beginning to gurgle.

"Let me first warn you, I can't prove I am sane." His voice did not project well, obliging me to loom over him. "At the least I'll free you from the cultural context where sanity and insanity form a meaningful dichotomy." His face turned from the ceiling, to see if I was balking yet. But I remained as receptive as at any of his lectures. He could have been introducing an ode by Shelley.

My quietude heartened him, and his eyes receded to the ceiling. "Do you appreciate how arbitrary and limited our organization of reality is? Our pyramid structure of science, theory stacked on theory, only works insofar as our few accredited disciplines yield a consistent system. The entire pyramid is more of less of the same material, because others would be troublesome to adapt. They could imply the old structure's obsolescence." He glanced at me, and my attentive look met his before checking on the kettle, though it hadn't yet whistled.

"Our rational system, especially our classifications of"—he waved impatiently before he settled on the catch-all—"things relies on some basic arbitrary assumption. What is a platypus? What distinguishes a bush from a tree? The logical man, when pressed, must finally admit he is logical because it makes him feel better." I nodded agreeably although he wasn't watching, then gazed expectantly at the hissing kettle. Weathering a first wave of fatigue, I was craving my cup of tea, but the professor, I found, was staring at me. Our eyes met, and he went on.

"Our society's vision of reality is rooted in the Renaissance's classical revival, which compromised, then displaced the medieval Church's cosmos. Though this inclination toward science comported with the era's exploratory spirit, it was not the sole possible choice. Likewise, the early Church competed with cabalistic and Celtic traditions, among others. Celtic assumptions, in particular, lay dormant in Western culture till the spread of Romanticism." His voice faintly quavered. "Then certain arbitrary tenets of the Rationalists at least came into question."

He paused, and his silence, and the wind's, and even the kettle's, rattled me. "But it was already too late for the Romantics, who had early on acquired a fascination for science. Contrast the trans-rational spirituality of Wordsworth's 'We Are Seven' with Shelley's cruel bell-jar experiments, asphyxiating doves." I smiled, for I'd anticipated a recourse to Shelley.

"Our culture had its last true choice of directions at the outset of the Renaissance. Poetry and language then forfeited their chance, thanks to science and rationalism, to determine their own principles of universal order, except in stubborn enclaves where the rudiments of my studies were pursued as incantations, a branch of unabashed magic." He checked me for signs of scorn, but I had no objections to magic. He cleared his throat, a bit bewildered.

"Renaissance-era poets came closest to rediscovering their latent powers of physically altering themselves or their environment through words. I have tried to purify and build on their implicit precepts." He propped himself on his elbows, seemingly more intent on my expression than on his own message. "One arbitrary duality they nearly exposed was that between past and present. The mutability sequence was a popular genre, describing how time decays beauty, and how poetry, albeit metaphorically, can stave off this decay. That was their fatal concession. I do not accept the scientific, rational submission to aging and death."

The words were vehement, but their delivery was calm as an underground lake. "I am formulating an immutability—in upshot an immortality—sequence. I seek literal immortality through words." Shale's tense, smoldering features conveyed both enthusiasm and entrapment. I could reject his ideas, his very sanity, and perhaps crush the fragile eggshell of a new reality in which Shale was encasing himself. But his scholarship had always been trustworthy, and I was nothing but inspired.

Once I smiled my approval, the professor, stammering with relief, proceeded. "By breaking the barrier between this and every other moment of our existence, we can select, relive, any of those moments ad infinitum. Within the range of one's own years, one could live forever." He seemed to drift off for a second. "The body would age and die, but that would matter nothing to the unfettered mind, which could seek refuge anywhere in its body's past."

"Might you remember back to previous lives?" I blurted, thrilled that I had an idea to share.

"I'm not a Buddhist by nature," he remarked as if that resolved the issue. In his self-established reality, I supposed it would.

He lay still a moment, and I leaned in to see if he were dozing. As my shadow overtook him, he gasped. "Scientific method and mine parallel each other, such that I'm not creating new dualities so much as reversing the servant and master roles of language and science. My initial assumption, basic enough to fit into any system of thought, is expressed in the simplest verse."

His round glasses caught the desk lamp's brightness like coins, and he scowled, removed them, and rubbed them clean on his shirt-front. "Concise poetry is the most efficient use of language in terms of lucidity, memorability, and least appreciated, incantability." He reaffixed his glasses. "These allow one to reinterpret sensory input and grasp, emphasize, and manipulate channels of a more comprehensive existence, ordinarily inaccessible. In effect, one has entered a different reality."

Shale's forearms came up and his hands wavered, as if he wanted to gesture but considered it déclassé. "Once a concept is assimilated and becomes a constant in my thoughts, I carve the next, you could say, and compound it to whatever preceded." His hands made less restrained molding motions. "As the structure grows more complex, passive understanding shifts into manipulation, and at present my world already looks quite unlike yours, though they were the same a few months ago."

"You've done all this in a few months?" I feared that if Shale's mind were great enough to progress so swiftly, I'd never be able to put his ideas into practice, at any tempo.

Shale laughed. "No, this apartment is the tip of the iceberg, so to speak. I've spent the last forty years, two-thirds of my life, contemplating this. Only recently have I dared commit myself to writing, and merely in notes, experimental drafts, prose expositions of premises. My academic schedule allowed time and energy for no more. I've been unmarried many years, never had children, so when my project could go no further among people, no obstacles barred me from bringing it here."

His hands fell back upon the mattress. "Another couple of months and I'll be ready. I'll speak the words, my mind will make the connections, and I'll be free. My past becomes a resort, a refuge, a paradise."

He paused to rein in his excitement. "Up here, without scoffers and diversions, I've composed years of verse in a paltry span. And it flows ever more easily." He scratched his white skullcap of hair vigorously, patted it back down, and flicked dandruff from under fingernails. "But I've lacked something lately, perhaps the classroom situation I'd quit."

I nodded understandingly.

"I don't know. In this tower, all alone, I've felt ever more like a sorcerer." His fingers lifted to stroke his chin, then recoiled as if nipped. "And I haven't trimmed this in so long, I probably look the part. Yes, I've been rather absorbed in that image, almost compulsively. I've become what Hawthorne referred to as the inseparability of the symbol from the thing symbolized." He regarded me gravely, and I couldn't help fidgeting. "Perhaps my self-image, if nothing else, requires I take an apprentice. You're in the right place at the right time." If Shale were confessing to exploitation, I was too flattered by my role to care.

"And maybe for your first lesson, you should inspect one of my spells. The first poem of the sequence should be on top, there." He waved vaguely at his rolltop desk, and I pushed back my chair to rise. Shale, however, sprang up with startling agility. "I might as well get it, since I know exactly where it is. Besides, high time someone poured the tea water."

I swung around in amazement, to watch him grip the kettle handle with a potholder. Steam geysered and dissolved into a frail mist. Then the kettle's sudden silence summoned tenuous perceptions of its shrilling for the past five minutes.

Shale handed me a steaming cup and, holding his saucer out dangerously, scattered several layers of paper around the desk with his other hand. He snatched up one sheet and dropped it in my lap.

In the upper right was the typed number "one," and nothing else save a quatrain on the upper half of the page:

> Memory is the vault of heaven,
> Anguish is the coin of hell.
> Why men hoard up tainted lucre,
> Baffles every sage to tell.

I must have looked unimpressed, for Shale retrieved the paper anxiously, mumbling, "I found this a convenient sentiment from which to diverge into my own channels. Intentionally simple. Doggerel. The optimum amount of relevant content and length, for my mind anyway. You'll need much preparation before you can assimilate this simple verse's impact. Like most specialized literature, mine is an acquired taste." Almost piously, he replaced the sheet atop the paper disarray.

He asked again if I wanted to know more and, without awaiting my reply, set up several nights a week for me to join him. Gulping my tea, I was imbued with an energy that made me want to shake the professor's hand briskly, uncoop myself from these tight quarters, dash out and laugh in the cold night air. He proffered me a notepad page containing our session times and wished me good-evening, explaining he had little leisure between his delvings and their dissemination to me. I did shake his hand.

I enrolled in only three courses for the upcoming semester, treating Shale's program as a fourth. Unable to picture a man as enlightened as Shale needing companionship, I tried maintaining a student's attitude toward him, rather than patronizing him as a friend. Though my follow-up visit didn't change this, he was oddly solicitous of my sincerity and, in some oblique fashion, my health. He declined to share any more finished poems, instead outlining a regimen of his explanatory prose and some rough drafts.

At first he contended that each mind perhaps reacted to its own formulations, so that studying another's poetry would be worse than useless, especially without firm grounding in preparatory theories. He moreover refused to involve me in real incantations till he'd completed the process, lest anything go wrong, or as he amended it, prove undesirable. Shale was beyond turning back by virtue of ideas already fermenting in his psyche. His manner would have chilled me then, if not for every previous experience with him.

As it was, he saw me press deeper into the swivel chair he'd newly acquired, and smiled to reassure me, and then his eyes were reflective, as if he were reassuring himself.

He then pressed deeper into his seat, his eyes cloudier. Fascinated, I watched him lapse into meditation, then brooding, then melancholy. His lips scarcely quivered as he breathed, and I half expected him, as if hypnotized, to divulge some precious hint about his past and admit me, accidentally or not, into himself. Whatever had entranced him with its vividness was entraining me with its mystery. Maybe I couldn't be his friend, but now I was compelled to understand him.

I rolled back my chair and approached a window, wondering how long Shale would doze. Between my footfalls I heard a long sigh like a pressure drop, and turned to see the slouching professor stare dazed at my empty chair, then up at me. His posture straightened and his smile beckoned, so I reseated myself.

He extracted his wallet, and I wondered what sort of memento he was going to confer. He removed a two-dollar bill, and before my confusion found voice he said, "The milk store won't close for twenty minutes. I'd like some tea, a hundred bags of whatever's cheapest, and English muffins, and a can of beans." My confusion must have showed, for he added, "Traditional apprentice duties, to be sure."

By my return, his abstraction had herded him to the same window out which I'd been peering. His eyes evaded mine while he put away the groceries and set one teacup on the desk. Turning up the heat under the kettle, he looked toward me without focusing, repeated my week's lesson plan, and went mum with a finality I could only react to with a good-night.

That coming month, these interruptions, and their hints of a revenant past, became ever more frustrating. Rather than abridge an evening, he resumed after my errands with so fine a reserve that his personality hardly trickled through. He remained too wary to show even that he knew I knew something was driving him. He needed me and hence grew more accustomed to me, as with a servant or labor-saving device. Nonetheless I was too fond of, and intrigued by, the professor to feel used.

Meanwhile he was ever more consumed by his endeavor, or his past, so that most nights his lights were on when I went to bed, remote like the shine of a neighboring city. Whenever I couldn't sleep I'd pace my dark room, and often the turret still sent its beams to unsettle me. Especially after our meetings, the light would burn for extra hours, and I deduced the professor had become unconcerned with day, night, and sleep as reference points, and with no signs of enervation. Nor could I influence him, and this felt like a denial, leaving me dejected but not spiteful.

Superficially our meetings were the same, even lengthened and fired with a sense of urgency that worried more than enthused me. If anxiety impelled him, did he suspect some danger to himself, to me? Often he dismissed me long after midnight, his body quivering like an overheated engine, and I wondered if he ever passed out once I'd gone.

Despite my longer tutorings, not they, but Shale himself, chiefly inspired me. I kept awaiting a sudden plunge into understanding, or a gradual hindsight epiphany about what he'd imparted. When neither transpired, I began worrying about my capabilities, though my other courses went well, almost of their own accord.

And so I studied regularly with Shale till the city's most tedious season devolved into its generally bleakest week. Hordes of students used April vacation to escape the raw, gray weather, but I was almost desperate to stay and maximize my chances of seizing elusive revelation. Besides, I didn't want to leave the aging man alone, and in this I proved wise.

Shale's outpourings that night were so eager that he remembered my errand run when only the all-night store was open, fifteen minutes away. The air wasn't terribly cold, but thick and clammy with mist, which wafted like ghosts of decayed little heaps of snow along the curbs. With one hand at my coat collar to keep out the damp, I grimaced as black puddle water began seeping through my cracked soles. Relieved to be back at Hope and Power, I swung open the door of Shale's stairwell and heard him cry out, "Now who's there?"

I answered and traipsed up, uneasy with an unfamiliar, incongruous quaver in his voice. The room appeared no different, but the professor, who apparently hadn't budged, was pale as the mist outside, and my careless foot nudged the shards of his teacup. I tracked its dregs along for a few paces and was as queasy as if I'd spread blood. Dragging over the wastebasket and a roll of paper towels, I looked to Shale for an explanation.

For a few minutes he seemed displaced, hard-pressed to reorient himself, and then he spoke cogently. "After you left, I thought to rest my eyes a while, so I turned out the light and sat back. I was half drowsing, I couldn't say for how long, when I heard faint steps in the third-floor hall." Shale kept glancing behind me, as if an unpleasant afterimage lingered.

"Since the other tenants are gone for the week and the landlord's family is always asleep by now, I assumed you were back. You were taking a long time though, and I could make out doorknobs being jiggled. In my half-adrift state, I couldn't really localize the footsteps, which were attempting to be subtle, till they were halfway up the stairs. I snapped out of my fatigue and turned on the light." His arm groped as if restaging the moment, and a rivulet of sweat glistened on his brow. "I could see the boy, about seventeen, from the waist up, and he was holding a crowbar."

"What did he look like?" I desisted from gathering up broken crockery.

Shale waved impatiently. "I don't know. It was all too sudden. He wasn't a student. He was as shocked as I, but that didn't mean much to me. My eyes homed in on his crowbar and couldn't look away, and a tension mounted in me for what felt like a long time, though it couldn't have lasted ten seconds. Then instead of even trying to yell, I threw my teacup at the crowbar. With that the boy bolted, and I could hear him all the way to the backdoor." Shale unpocketed a handkerchief and wiped his forehead.

I didn't speak, awkwardly grasping the wastebasket, trying to figure out how to help. I turned around and discerned my own wet prints on the steps, and another set alongside them. Some of Shale's fear seeped into me.

"Listen," he said, and posthaste I faced him again. "I want you to get something so I'll feel safer. At my old house I have a gun, a souvenir of a sadder time. A box of bullets is in the same drawer." I could conceive of nothing less desirable to fetch at that hour, especially for someone like Shale, but there was no refusing him then. He gave me keys, the address, and directions inside the house. Neither of us had more to say.

En route, I belatedly realized how Shale had opened his past to me. Scarcely a gaping doorway, true, but it was a foothold, past which I could glimpse sorrow, violence, perhaps unconfessed crime. Whatever he'd striven for and lost, and had driven him to academic refuge, still exerted some pull on him, impelled him as literally as possible into the past. I had to understand that passion, I envied it, and above all, vicariously or not, I wanted it.

My pace quickened at the thought of my destination, a virtual museum of Shale's history, though he must have trusted me not to treat it so. I wondered how ironclad my ethics were, how impervious my self-respect. Before I could weigh the value of unrewarded honor, my shadow startled me, bending toward me in abrupt clarity. Instead of blending into the sidewalk further greyed by condensing mist, it stood in sharp contrast against a picket fence whose peaks undulated like stylized whitecaps. I was surprised to gaze upon Shale's Cole Avenue property already.

A foggy night best suited, or least disfavored, this house. It, too, was white and spare of detail, except for an entrance with enough pilaster-and-fanlight ornament for the whole place, which otherwise seemed like unfinished Colonial Revival. An amorphous row of black bushes crested halfway up the first-floor windows. As I unlocked, then shouldered, the sticky door, I imagined myself infiltrating the machine responsible for the mist.

By streetlight through the open door I found the stairs at the end of the front hall. On the second floor I felt out the lamp on the telephone table in the corridor. While my eyes adjusted, a car stopped nearby. Wary of anyone's presence so late, I paused and listened. My fancy, or my intuition, placed two people at the gaping door, and after a moment's indecision I cleared my throat loudly, as if in warning. That dispersed the impression of intruders, and I hurried to the professor's library.

I rejoiced at my simple proximity to Shale's mementoes, an unparalleled opportunity. Why had the house seemed eerie? Mystery would be dispelled, not generated, here. Gooseneck lamp brightened his desk, at the window facing the next house, enough for me to retrieve gun and bullets from their drawer. The lights from the bay window next door had also been on for an indeterminate time. I set the gun beneath the lamp and reconsidered my need for stealth.

I scanned the walls and shelves. The edge of lamp-curtailed darkness masked the heads in framed photos, and my haste to behold any especially compelling face only blurred them more. Objects in cabinets or earning their keep as bookends seemed nothing more than tourist debris. The books themselves constituted one homogeneous mass, and from the highest lit row I yanked the oldest-looking brown binding. Why not? A library was not normally an inviolable sanctum, and I detected nothing to the contrary. No loose papers fell from between the pages, which were void of marginalia, and I reshelved the book, at once disappointed and relieved. With a start, I realized I hadn't even read its title.

My unsteady hand reached for the gun, then hovered spread-fingered as I scanned the desktop. My eyes were drawn to legal-pad sheets with short messages for a housekeeper. Surely the desktop had nothing on it Shale wished to hide if the cleaner were able to inspect it. I riffled through some loose piles and found only university bulletins and lecture outlines. My reservations about trustworthy behavior had basically shouted themselves hoarse by now, and in their place nagged the urgent admonition I'd have to depart soon and squander this educational opportunity.

The drawers couldn't be sacrosanct if I had permission to go through one of them. Just then that was sufficient pretext, and I explored the gun drawer, and another, which merely yielded more academic ephemera. The bottom, though, was full of letters, some quite yellowed, but none cried out for perusal. My fingers trembled and would not invade an envelope at random, and I flicked through them despairingly to the end.

A photo lay beneath them all, and I extracted it by the edges with five fingertips; my hand reminded me of a hunching spider. The breath caught in my throat as I goggled at a girl's coyly smiling face. Her eyes were lively, her cheeks were broad, her copious hair was imperfectly clipped into a loose bun. Without an inscription, I couldn't tell if she'd been wife, daughter, or lover. Like the black veil of Hawthorne's minister Hooper, Shale's past was opaque and maddening to its witnesses. They and I knew, and shared, only its effects, its outcomes, without access to the motivations underlying those effects.

I looked outside and dropped the picture. A doughy, fortyish couple was watching me from the bay window. They were focused below my face, however, and upon the gun gleaming in the lamplight. I grabbed it to conceal beneath my coat, and when I looked again they were gone. I began to blush and shake, hastily refilling the bottom drawer, snatching the box of bullets, killing the light, and lunging out and down the stairs. My arm flailed behind me to catch and pull the front door, which presumably locked, its concussion speeding me away.

Previously the streets were unpatrolled, but on my mazy return route squad cars were always one block back, or cutting across too far ahead to spot me. I stayed in shadows and behind lines of trees, aghast at prospects of explaining a sidearm, yet unwilling to waste time hiding it up a sleeve. When I heard a car behind me, I'd slip past the nearest wall or shrubs before headlights pinned me down, and I'd wait motionless till the engine died away; golden chance to conceal the weapon never crossed my mind. At last the turret beckoned me with its mist-filled beams, and I relaxed enough to feel how frayed I was outside, and how drained inside.

No sooner had I entered the streetlight's circle below the house than a pair of high-beams approaching from a block away dazzled me. The high-beams quickened toward me, and I heard a CB sputter. So close, I felt cheated, not afraid, and indignantly scrambled for the driveway. Gun and bullets nearly tumbled from my fumbling hands, and the box opened. Angrily I clutched the box, partly crushing it, and a bullet hit the sidewalk. Breathless I reached the backdoor, but paused on the stoop, curious at whether they'd chase me up the graveled drive.

Two doors slammed, but I heard no more till a voice caromed from the street, "Oh Christ, look at this." Another grunted and said, "Fool kid's really begging for trouble. Do we go after him?" The first cop drawled, "Nah, what's the point? He probably lives around here, knows the area. Could be anywhere by now." I heard a cigarette lighter's tiny click. "Some night. First break-ins around Hope, then that one on Cole. Think it's all the same kid?" "Who knows? Is there a full moon tonight?" "Did you get a good look at him?" "Not good enough. Give me a baggie for picking up that slug." There was a pause. "Let's go." Car doors slammed again, and I meekly entered the house.

Since I'd dropped only one anonymous bullet, the police worried me much less than explaining the street commotion to the professor. I climbed slowly and rested on the third-floor landing. I knocked

twice and tried to simulate my usual rate of ascent, debating whether my breaths were too hard or too shallow.

These precautions were for naught. For all intents mesmerized
over a book, Shale was unaware of me until the gun lay in front of
him. He twisted around as if he were the one caught short without
an alibi and slammed the book shut. I read the name De Quincey on
the cover, and my eyes hove back to Shale, who still struggled for a
thought. Something ironic here made me smirk helplessly, with jaw
muscles hard to unknot as barbed wire. Rather than take umbrage at
my expression, Shale seemed to subside deeper into himself, and only then did embarrassment sober me.

He picked up the gun, cradling it reverently. As if his strength
had gushed into it, a new weariness left him blanched and brittle,
and he intoned, "Thanks. I will see you next week." On the stairs I
turned, line of sight level with the floor. Shale's face remained downcast, benighted.

For the next two weeks Shale no longer seemed embedded in his
work, but to have broken through its bottom. His enthusiasm lapsed
into an airy rapture, from which he could not fasten on anything
tangible, and which seemed involuntary inasmuch as his eyes, after
tea, sometimes flashed, as if fighting dreaminess. He could move neither objects nor himself without visible effort, as if matter had
gained unaccustomed weight. Even pens and papers resisted his
grasp. Much quicker to tire, he cut back to one shorter meeting per
week, which ended with his arms dangling, head drooping, and eyes
fluttering between vision and slumber.

This sudden aging weakened his grip on his emotions, and once
he muttered, "I have seen my life's structure too well. Its long incline, its apex and steep decline, with a single crowning point in
space and time, loom too large on my interior landscape. The pyramid maddens me because I am locked outside its glass walls, and I
cannot outdistance its shadow, overtaking me on these barren flat-
lands of my eventless life ever since."

Then he addressed me as if I hadn't heard him. His teaching, un-
fervent and automatic, symptomized his detachment. I was one
more tedious distraction, an arbitrary imposition on his time, like
eating, sleeping, and washing. His words were a scant remove from

monologue, and I felt depersonalized. This depressed me, and worse yet, his behavior hinted at failing health. But his rapture meant the Sequence neared completion, and this too depressed me because I couldn't predict how that would affect him.

I knew Shale's principles only intellectually. I hadn't absorbed them through experience or learned to apply them in my life, such that wherever Shale's conclusions led, I might be powerless to follow. Already he'd withdrawn his warmth, and I sensed a more crucial desertion was imminent. During the third week, my worries were justified.

My mood was already burdened by the weather, a downpour in its fourth day, typical of a Providence spring. Almost slipping on Shale's topmost step, I clutched the rail and my eyes lit on the window over the landing. It was wide open, and a pool on the floor was dripping onto the upper steps. When I shut the window, Shale looked up questioningly. "It was raining in," I said, but he gave no sign this was reason enough for closing a window.

Such bemusement dominated while he taught, and he constantly fell into distraction, after which he briefly regarded me like an intruder. He often lapsed into Delphic mumbling and, upon catching himself, gave no excuse, but inhaled deeply and continued. As his spirits became more vaporous, mine grew heavier and more hopeless.

Within an hour, his spirits seemed to have fled altogether, and his body quaked like a hollow gourd hanging in a draft. Handing me a list in careless scrawl, he sent me to the store, and when I returned, he sat staring where my face would rise above the floor. All his resolve, including much that was not sympathetic, seemed to gather in his eyes and jolted me. I smiled sheepishly, expecting him to do somewhat the same. He didn't. His eyes were fixed grimly on me as I set groceries before him. His hands pulled the bag closer and did not let go while he spoke. "I'm sorry. Maybe I should have foreseen this, but there's nothing to do for it now. I'm calling off our sessions indefinitely."

My worst suspicions, far from preparing me, intensified, dramatized the impact. I had to ask why we were through.

Shale's jaw shifted stiffly as if begrudging words. "Finishing touches are going into the Sequence now. In about three weeks I will recite it. Until then, and during my first expeditions, I cannot have any interference." His features struck me as defiant.

All my resistance, which I'd theorized would subside into deference and resignation, flared up. Meanwhile, Shale's concise, rehearsed statement had consumed his guttering energies, as if his last reserves against debilitating age had fled like smoke. He appeared cold and shriveled, his head bowed, hands folded in his lap.

"But I can't leave you now, don't you see?" I said. "This place isn't healthy for you. You're already weakened, and if you couldn't take care of yourself, who would know it?" Shale's lassitude goaded me. "I should visit more often, if anything! You're not a young man!"

His head rose, and I saw hostility. His hands clenched into fists. If I spoke quickly enough, could I crash the wall thickening around him? "You have to get out now, before it's too late. Conduct your research elsewhere. Or let it go a while. This isn't worth it!"

Shale reared out of his chair. "Out! Out! You've never understood. You can't help. I won't have you meddling. I won't have you betray me!" I could hear his echoes downstairs, and they frightened me. His face was red as if about to burst with blood, but only tears leaked out, and I saw that his frustrations, and not his faith, had made him a child again. This regression was more terrible than his anger, and I was at the stairs with my coat before I could think. But when I hesitated and turned to him, he inhaled and ordered, "Go!"

Before closing the stairwell door, I observed the girls' apartment was spilling light from its gaping doorway, and all too quiet. I couldn't see them, but I could separate whispers in that direction from the rain pelting the window beside me. As I grabbed the stairwell doorknob, Shale feebly shouted, "Wait!" Hoping he'd apologize, I gazed up with a compassionate expression.

There came a shriek, a heavy thud, bumping sounds, and fearful cries. Shale slid into view at the stairs' turning and sprawled at my feet, clutching the notebooks and loose papers I'd forgotten. He groaned and shook his head sluggishly, but when I reached out, he waved me away. He flung my things at me and pounded the wall with his fist. His ire assured me his injuries weren't serious, and the glistening instep on his left shoe reminded me of the pool I'd slipped in.

As Shale rested his head on a treader and breathed deep, a hand brushed me on each shoulder, and the two girls, prim and unmemorable, jostled by me. They were horrorstruck, and one exclaimed, "Oh my God, the old man's fallen! Somebody get the landlord!"

The floor already vibrated to heavy approaching footsteps, and I turned as the landlord rose into view, stopped at seeing the girls, put on a shirt bunched up in one hand, and joined us while buttoning it. "What happened?" He addressed me.

To my relief, his voice behooved Shale to speak, face still downcast. "I fell down. My fault. Stupid of me. That's all."

"Are you all right?" The landlord pressed forward and bent over Shale as if to examine him, one arm reaching uncertainly.

Shale's voice was steady and acerbic. "I'm okay, goddammit. A little shaken, but you all insist on seeing I'm unhurt, so here, I'll prove it." Waving us back, he put his weight on a trembling arm and got up. "Whenever you're done, close my door, please." He eyed each of us and tarried on me. "And don't forget your papers." While Shale clumped off, the landlord was staring at me, and my whole body felt constricted as I stooped to collect my notes. I glanced at the girls, and the same distrust glared from them. I said good-night, and only as I closed the front door did I hear Shale's door close.

For days I wondered if I'd shown any smugness when Shale's infirmity tumbled him to my feet. I couldn't recall any, but such a natural reaction may have registered unintended on my face, for all to see. That would explain the bystanders' unfriendliness, and why I contended with obscure guilt. Whatever they thought of me didn't matter, except for the useless soul-searching they'd prompted, diverting me from figuring out what to do about the professor.

I kept vigil on the tantalizing garret, depriving my other coursework of as much time as before, as if this were just another phase of Shale's instruction, and no less strenuous. Much concentration I invested in remaining still and single-minded, subduing the thought that inertia was burying me as under sediment.

To ease the tension, tedium, and finally drowsiness of my watch—for I could hardly outlast Shale's longer hours—I invented games using my view's few elements. I pursued effects of opacity and light with my gossamer curtains and desk lamp. With the fabric taut, the light formed a blind disc over Shale's windows. Behind loose curtains, the tower wavered as if submerged or dissolving. In clement weather, the curtains strained toward me from the open window, and I couldn't decide if the veil were dispersing, or trying to absorb me.

After several nights I noticed my reflection in the glass, winning my attention till I was mostly concerned with my face behind the drifting veil, or how I looked when lit from below or from the side. Though the turret was always in front of me, I'd forget about it for hours.

Only Shale's silhouette disrupted my games and the underlying monotony; nothing conscious alerted me to it, but nothing conscious could deter me from it. Each glimpse, brief as a spark, was invigorating and lent a sense of justification. Every sighting has left a photographic impression, yet all I saw was hulking and black, no more defined than photos of ghosts.

Such bleary rewards eventually bored me, and when I awoke cramped and queasy in my chair at dawn, Shale's panes were still yellow against the pale sky, and by day the light shone on, deflecting sunlight from the panes. By the third night of round-the-clock illumination, it was perversely more comforting, even as I grew more haggard. The glow's constancy told me Shale was still laboring and vital, perhaps at once wholly sustained and consumed by inspiration.

Around nine the next morning the turret went dark and stayed dark for almost a week. At first this stunned me, as a rabbit must feel when its burrow is blocked. For several nights I was more anxious than when the light was always on, and I paced my room, casting quick, sidelong glances at the window. I yearned to investigate, but prospects of Shale's wrath were more fearsome than finding him disabled or the turret empty. When insomnia and worry harried me to the verge of illness, merciful nature took over. As if by remote control, I'd suddenly be lying in bed at a reasonable hour. And a new consolation occurred to me, irrational or not, that if anything had happened to Shale, I would have known.

On our former meeting night, the light returned. It brought my nervous meanderings short, and I pressed my forehead against the glass, as if to amplify a psychic ability. In about ten minutes Shale's face floated into view, pressing itself against his window, and I felt like a fish awed by a lure. His features were searching, and when I saw that he saw me I shuddered as on a hook.

At this distance his outline wavered, and if his face hadn't been so close to the glass, I wouldn't have recognized him. Especially in his yellowing light, he seemed bloodless and collapsed, as if he'd punctured and too much of him was billowing out, blurring the air. The face receded from clarity and a hand emerged, beckoning weakly but insistently. The hand paused and the face reclarified, more desperate. I banged on the glass twice and dashed for the stairs, as if to save a drowning man.

Outside, while putting on my jacket, I sneezed and then the apparent response of a much louder concussion reverberating down Hope Street made me stop. I dismissed it as the backfire of a car in some echo chamber of a driveway, and hurried along to the Power Street backdoor, which was never locked.

Despite the ominous hush inside, restraint was beyond me till I burst past Shale's door, bewildered by a brimstone whiff. More warily I climbed into ever smokier air, and unsure of all the beclouded outlines and of my wisdom in resolving them, I heaved open the window at the top of the stairs. Once I'd lurched to the opposite window and set up a draft, the smoke uncoiled from where it was densest, around Shale's desk. The chill breeze made me shiver.

Shale was not at his desk. His chair was overturned, and he was outstretched between its feet and the desk. His arms were flung wide, and the gun lay about a yard from one hand. His eyes were bulging, but seemingly with dread and not pain. Blood still rilled from the edge of his grimace down his emaciated cheek, and more was soaking through his white shirt above his heart. I gawked at the red circle's regularity, as if the body weren't real. My equanimity may have been shock.

My eyes, of their own accord, hovered over the desk, where I gradually acknowledged all the papers neatly stacked for the first time, with a mostly blank sheet atop them all. In its center was my first name and nothing more. On the sheet beneath was a sort of farewell letter:

I was not strong enough. I succeeded in losing myself within my past's countless moments, to dissipate my ceaseless longings into a self-contained omniscience. But as my helplessness of almost a week has proven, the past is a terrible slow vortex. As soon as my mind hung in the void below which every past event was spread in panorama, I realized that, though any moment I could isolate was mine to relive, so long as I surveyed them all, I felt them all. This alone made any of them impossible to isolate. Every pang and grief was mingled with every joy and comfort, all of them with the intensity of the present.

Eventually my will would have buckled, and I would have sunk into the turbulent current of specific moments, an eternal hell rendered more unbearable by the certainty that each moment would be repeated infinitely, with each exacerbated pain, and each dulled pleasure, grinding an ever deeper rut into my soul. The inevitable outcome would have been a madness in which I forever fled recklessly from moment to random moment.

By a greater willpower than I knew I possessed, I have wrested myself from the past. Otherwise I would have lingered both trapped and immortal, for my body, as you see, verged on starvation, but my consciousness would have had eternal range, and a spectator's ownership, of all my bodies, young, tired, or dying.

But I am restored to the present and struggle to stay afloat on it while I write this, and then do what I must. If I can only obliterate myself in the present, my awareness will not plunge back, but pass away like my body. The peace I sought through infinite reverie can only be mine now through true oblivion. Perhaps that is what I always sought. Do not imagine my last act will be difficult. I know, as you can never know something, that this is the easiest decision of my life.

I ask only that you burn my notes and the sequence itself, that is, every paper below this letter. It involves too much time and distraction for me to do so. If you desire a second opinion, you must resort to De Quincey. For once, he is admirably concise. Good-bye! May you never need the same peace that I must seek through death.

Beside the papers was the paperback of *Suspiria de Profundis* I'd earlier caught Shale scanning. Its binding had been split so that it lay flat open, and red ink circled several lines:

"Death we can face; but knowing, as some of us do, what is human life, which of us is it that without shuddering could (if consciously we were summoned) face the hour of birth?"

A minute later the landlord barged in, and he goggled at the flames in the wastebasket, and me standing over them, blinking when the smoke drifted into my face. He lunged reflexively to save the wastebasket's contents, the importance of which my raptness alone betrayed, but he pulled his hands away before they could singe. Then he saw the body at my feet and made a few choking sounds, regarding me wildly, and flew down the stairs yelling for the police. I stayed, since I'd easily be traced to my apartment.

I cannot feel too upset, or even concerned, about tomorrow. My mood, on the whole, is optimistic. I kept Shale's note, and that may help somewhat. I also preserved the first few and last pages of the Sequence itself. I will not disclose these, but if I ever feel a strong enough urge, I may try to reconstruct Shale's work. The professor need not be lost to me forever, after all.

a light in the wilderness

After three days at his new farmhouse, Sam Gog still stared off its porch at the breasty Maryland countryside as if at an unconscious titan. Sam, though awestruck and goggling, wasn't ill at ease because the land awake in upheaval was beyond his imagination. To accommodate the thought of life's total profusion was strenuous enough, even overpowering. Everywhere life blossomed, chittered, chirped, flew, rustled, hissed, entwined, hung, reeked, and whistled.

There went some now! From a wall of trees and tangle between properties a good half-mile away charged a white rabbit, almost too blurred to recognize, across a meadow. Hoping for its getaway, Sam wondered what was chasing it, when the sharp glissando of dogs redirected him to the foliage. Right behind the black and brown pack dashed three big, brawny men sporting workshirts and crewcuts, and waving bats. The mongrels overtook the rabbit, strafing it with snapping jaws and gabbling in exultation; the rabbit skipped around frantically, like a toy worked by a squeeze bulb.

Howling and whooping, the men smacked the dogs aside with their bats, to leave the rabbit cowering and bloody in a wide circle of flattened, red-streaked grass. While the dogs yipped and paced back and forth, the braying, cackling men moved in and smashed the rabbit boneless. As another man ambled from the house on the hill above the meadow, the three brutes waved, grinning, and ignored the dogs rushing at the little carcass, shredding it merrily. The fourth man stopped halfway down the slope, spat a brown wad into the grass, and asked rhetorically, "Get that rabbit?"

One exhilarated man raised his bat overhead and hollered, "Yup!" The other two leaned indolently on theirs. He added, "Won't get none o' your crops either, no more!" The other two nodded sagely.

"That's what I like to hear. Do appreciate it." The newcomer trudged back while the hunting party rounded up the dogs and sauntered away from the remains, which weren't gory to Sam because he couldn't connect them with the remembered rabbit. But the whole scenario had left him astonished, disgusted, and trembling.

He retreated into the house, rubbing the slickness off his forehead and striving to fidget loose his underwear, sticky with sweat and humidity. Moving his electric fan from floor to table, he flicked it on and sat at the table's far end, to catch the fast air in his face. He opened his mouth, and the slight electric taste blowing in reminded him of New York.

That's why Father had bought the farm from a distant cousin in the first place, to give Sam's nerves somewhere to reknit. Neither he himself nor Father ever faulted Sam for failure and breakdown on Wall Street. At least he'd tried going it on his own—that's what mattered. The pressure and congestion and maelstrom of city streets and offices were simply too much, as if conditions had bred an intangible predator specifically for him, as nature cursed sparrows with sparrowhawks. Father would let him stay here till Sam sensed the predator had left New York, or till he felt ready to face it.

But Father wasn't familiar with everyday pastoral shocks and horrors, obviously. Death, cruelty, and coarseness, no strangers to the city, were never hailed with such zest and devotion there. Still queasy, Sam had to tell himself the neighbors killed only out of necessity, to save the harvest that directly and indirectly fed their families. Life, because of its profusion, rated even less reverence here than in the city.

Tiring of the fan's ozoned air, Sam paced around the room as one of his grand insights, especially rare after the breakdown, surfaced from Delphic depths. The fashioners of stereotype and propaganda have always been the urbanites, and they were responsible for setting up the rustic as essence of provincialism. Sam, formerly so naive of country ways, knew better now. Perhaps the hardcore New Yorker, Sam for example, was in truth the most offensively provincial.

The farmer had to understand the city at least to the point of realizing how much his produce was worth there. He had to bargain over what he sold. The urbanite didn't question price tags, had no awareness of where foodstuffs came from, really, and how they got to him.

If goods became too expensive, he struck for higher wages. He'd never try to quibble down the total at the checkout counter. Sam sat down again, a little tuckered out from so much cogitating. The wave of insight receded and left Sam feeling hopelessly ignorant and defensive. Silos, cornfields, and cows were as foreign as Samoa to him.

And the neighbors, so far, seemed no less remote. He could appreciate their shyness, independence, preoccupation, even wariness, but they apparently couldn't work up an ounce of curiosity about him. Yesterday he'd found this insulting, but with today's onset of stifling June heat he was more vaguely peevish. He deserted the fan's soothing draft for the window in the rear wall. His own house and the nearest, hardly an insect's morning away, had backyards separated only by platte map lines, but he hadn't even overheard the women guessing about him while they hung out laundry. Why, hicks were no less insular than city folk!

Sam's eyes had been following some commotion in the neighbors' yard several minutes before his mind acknowledged it. While two leisurely Golems of hired hands shoveled a narrow, shallow ditch from the foundation of the house on out, a short, turnip-shaped farmer and his stunted cornstalk son, with vegetable blandness in their similar faces, were setting up what seemed a lantern atop a collarbone-height pole. Sam gazed devoid of thought, as if the natives were performing a ceremony that referred to nothing in his experience. It could have been impenetrable crayon nonsense drawn by a bored child.

Once the ditch extended up to the pole, the Golems sat on the back porch as father and son connected wiring from the house to the base of the pole. Bouts of cussing interrupted the operation, but soon they were satisfied and buried the wiring. Without comprehending any of this, Sam withdrew to his fan-cooled table to write father a cheery, uninformative letter that somehow took all afternoon.

To reward that perseverance, he fired up the Buick at dusk and braved miles of ravelly Maryland roads to the local tavern. Farmers unshaven, unbathed, weary, and restless muttered and hawed at one another along the Olympic-length bar without a word or eye for Sam, who drank enough to fluoresce with friendliness in the gloom. Tapping shoulders and asking for a light got him a lit match and the

shoulder's return, in one move. The barkeep took his money and answered in grunts. Sam sobered quickly in the social chill and drove
home. On the upside, he hadn't smoked enough to backslide into
addiction; quitting was hellacious the first time.

The effort of holding the road against alcohol fatigue convinced
Sam he'd sleep the second he lay down. And he did relax, and drift,
and watch dreams begin to fall kaleidoscopic into form. But the beer
still warmed his blood and wheeled dizzily in his stomach, a nervous
energy, an interior cork that wouldn't let him sink but bobbed him
about the waking surface. Sam groaned, and groaned again because
he never remembered how drinks before bed always did this to him
till this stage in the game.

As usual, he tried to quiet his abdominal gyrations by recalling
the day's events, the feeling of drowsiness, and the first jigsaw pieces
of dreams. If nothing rippled into his reflections, sleep would rise
thickly around him until morning. Otherwise Sam would roll back
and forth in bed for hours until he chanced on some quasi-mystic
cue and dozed off toward dawn. The last two nights had been deathly tranquil except for bug sounds, trivial after teeming Manhattan
nights, and the silence lured Sam from behind a final membrane of
tension, leaving his ears fully open and vulnerable.

The neighbors' station wagon rumbled up their gravel drive like
a scourging steam shovel. Sam shuddered as soon as silence resumed,
but then car doors slammed like shotgun fire, and Sam grimaced as
sweat welled out all over him. Parents and children singly and together exercised robust tonsils en route to their house, and Sam denounced them as Huns, boors, and morons. He took their backdoor
to be the last shot, encouraging him to breathe deep and cool down.
A steady humming too low to bother him slipped into his awareness
as he verged on oblivion.

The humming paused and something crackled, a shade too loudly to ignore, frustrating him more than a real bang. The neighbors'
house disgorged voices and giggles that would have been too gleeful
at a party. Sam was awake and hot like an ember, flaring up at another sputter and acclamation seconds later. He sat up, muttering
like Popeye, sensing perdition settle over the night.

He peeked past the back window just as the new lantern, glowing blue, sparked and crackled again, longer and louder than before. The whole family, seated on the back porch, looked wonderstruck as if at fireworks, then after each burst seemed to gloat. The lantern, at its inconceivable work, became all the more arcane and iconic, and the neighbors loomed more barbarous. For all Sam knew, they were savoring visions of their gizmo jolting him into insomnia.

Dread mingled with his outrage without diluting it. Before formally meeting these people, he dared not disrupt their ritual. Moreover, something sinister and corrupt about it warned him away. He slunk back to bed and lay listening to the lantern and its cultists, resigned, and unable to tell when the noise began to muffle and fade, softer and vaguer, till he was asleep.

Waking up didn't seem so bad. Sunlight gilded the room new and clean. Even the window's sunlit dust shaft, as it blinded him, enticed him to swing obligingly lightweight legs to the floor. Morning brightness demoted the silent lantern from an idol to a toy. In the bathroom, though, the toothbrush was unwieldy, and the sink water he scooped at his face landed on his stocking feet. On second thought, the painfully bright sunshaft reminded him of the final dust settling after a cave-in. Disabused and leaden, he forged on to the kitchen.

Caution and deliberation saw him through breakfast, and at last he could approach the rear window without aching eyes. The son was shuffling around the lantern's base and whistling "Louie Louie." The mix of lethargy and reverence in the boy's manner persuaded Sam to shelve his pride and go investigate the lantern and its adherent. Contact was not such a concession when the contactee was off-guard, idle, and alone.

Though Sam in dressing gown and sandals trod casually, coffee mug in hand, the son gawked and stumbled back as if Sam were an utter alien. Discreetly halting beyond handshake range, Sam nodded and said, "Morning. Sam Gog."

The contactee squinted suspiciously as if accused of being Sam Gog, but caught on and answered, "Sean Saxe."

"I'm the one, or it was my father actually, who bought the farm from his cousin Charles Doggett," Sam stumbled, fearing pause.

"We know," said Sean with the authority of tribunal, studying Sam yet apparently focusing beyond him. Sam drifted a little and confused the coffee's rising steam and the fog lifting from the hollows into one phenomenon. Night's tenacious chill was burning off, and Sean had gone back to watching his feet disorder a black crunching wreath around the lantern's pole. Sam noticed Sean's jeans had no knees, sipped some coffee, and swallowed his pride.

"Sean, what's that gizmo anyway?" Sean looked up at the cup extended toward the lantern, stopped shuffling, and beamed. Sam hadn't seen such enthusiasm and openness in days, but sobered at Sean's lack of several prominent upper teeth. He pictured a temperamental Yanomamo from the *National Geographic*.

"Why, that's a bugkiller." Sean perked up as if Sam had galvanized a pleasure nerve. "You hear it goin' last night? Every time you heard it, that was maybe a dozen bugs gettin' cooked. The blue light brings 'em in and then, zap!" Sean's chuckle was pure fiend, and his eyes expected Sam, who smiled bleakly, to join in. Sam regarded the wreath more carefully and lowered his cup. Black moth wings, beetle shells, and legs among the ashes made the rest of his coffee a cue for nausea.

"Yeah, that's something," he agreed.

"Yeah," echoed Sean.

Sam was too stunned to fake an off-the-cuff excuse for escape, and grew desperate as the sun heated the nape of his neck. Sean, still grinning, resumed scraping among the carnage. Looking around, Sam was startled by Sean's father white with sun against the black of his barn's open doorway. The older Saxe's eyes quarried Sam lovelessly, then swerved to the horizon as he hollered, "Sean! Get over here!"

Before Sean had trotted far, Sam called out, "Sean, why doesn't your father come say hello?" Sean's eyes assumed the grimness of his father's.

"The farmers around here got to farm. So they can eat, you know?" Without another backward glance, he followed his father into the barn.

After crossing presumptive property line, Sam tipped his coffee to spatter vulgarly in the grass. The day was already too hot and Sam consigned himself to reading indoors, with the past five minutes guaranteeing ruminative fodder for the duration.

The bugkiller was too horrible to contemplate yet, except as a signpost of attitude. What disdain these people had accrued for their closeness to nature, happily reducing myriad species to cinders with Nazi abandon! Ecological depredation was no more their concern than the next Ice Age, and Sam could no longer pretend the farmer killed out of necessity. The Saxes were overjoyed to massacre whatever had tried their patience. Sam couldn't conceive of the insect toll from just one night. Far from ensuring harmony with nature, the farmer's attitude decreed genocide for whatever inconvenienced short-term interests.

The sun was shy of zenith, still laminating the room with glare, but Sam felt chilled as if he'd been perusing a grimoire at midnight by candlelight. How safe was he, minus phone or friends, among this tribe where one interaction refined aloofness into lurking animosity? Given the chance, would they humiliate, injure, or get rid of him? Sam was disinclined to stand or raise his eyes. How could his mere presence have offended them? Sean's spiny retort and Mr. Saxe's dagger stare were stuck in Sam's memory.

He felt helpless and adrift. He would not have New York, and Clayberd County would not have him. Somehow he had to fathom the neighbors' grudge without provoking them. He focused on the title of the book he'd grabbed at random, a history of King Philip's War. Sliding a hand under each cover, he slammed the book shut and thrust it across the table.

Eavesdropping, since he had nothing better to do, wouldn't waste his time and resources and promised the frankest confessions. From window to window he skulked, more for effect than effectiveness, going through the motions to inspire schemes on how to proceed. He peeked out front, and indignation supplanted craftiness. Saxe senior was herding a dozen cows across Sam's lawn down to the road. Confronting the man now amounted to self-defense, an assertion of territorial propriety. Sam barged from the house, but slowed to gather his breath before blocking Saxe's line of sight.

The farmer kept strolling, and Sam had to keep up alongside. Saxe gave him the entomologist eye while Sam introduced himself. "My father bought this place from his cousin Charles." Though Sam was in perfectly ordinary T-shirt and chinos, Saxe's narrower squint insinuated he looked outlandish, or perhaps weak because he hadn't bought the farm himself.

"Dirk Saxe," the farmer finally admitted. "My family's been here a hundred and fifty years. So were the Doggetts. We were always good neighbors, them and us." Dirk's eye became accusatory, as if Sam were Charles's usurper or murderer, or worse yet, already not a good neighbor.

"So what brings you here?" asked Sam, doing his best to brace up.

Dirk's almost blind squint indicated Sam was either stupid or pathetically ignorant of the Saxes' inalienable rights. "The Breyers across the way share our pastures, and we share theirs. Our property has that wire fence along the road, so Charlie always let us use his yard to get back and forth." Dirk, citing local custom, had cannily snatched the stuffing from Sam's righteousness, and now that they were in the middle of the road, no longer in Sam's domain, he felt powerless.

"You must have done him favors in return," Sam meekly prompted.

"We helped each other out." Dirk's cloudy blue eyes fixed on the horizon. "Too bad he couldn't resist all that money. Hate to lose good neighbors." On Breyer land, Sam felt as insecure as an archery target and prayed that Dirk, staring hard as if restraining an outburst, wouldn't turn on him.

"Well, I must be going," Sam quavered, dropping behind. "Nice talking to you." Dirk strode on as if meeting him had been a daydream.

Back indoors, on home turf, Sam saw his way clear to pent-up anger. The farm wasn't Doggett's anymore, it was Sam's, but that obviously didn't matter to the natives. Without the least how-do-you-do, they thought they could just carry on as always and make Sam feel guilty in the bargain. Feeling helpless only stoked his umbrage. Socially, if not physically, Sam was a mere cipher.

They condemned him for his money, reducing him to a stereotype as if he had no heart, no personality. He, who'd never snubbed a poor man, was a victim of poverty's snobbery against the rich. The only excuse a snob needed was consensus, and Sam's resentment collapsed into embarrassment as he realized his isolation made him feel deposed. And feeling deposed betrayed his own covert snobbery, saddled him with guilt. Hiding inside for the day, he resorted to his book and sided with King Philip for a change.

With nothing to rekindle his energies, Sam tired and went to bed early. Precedent had taught him always to anticipate the worst, so he wasn't surprised by the resurgent hum and sputtering. Instead of tensing up and cursing, he lay supine and listened, groaning as insidious tension stole over him anyway. He imagined cartoon moths, with buggy but cute faces, frisking round and round the lantern, gradually spiraling in. Inevitably the blue flash in his head coincided with a real incineration, and his hands twitched as if with electric shock. After each sizzle, the cruelty of killing so many likable creatures enflamed him closer and closer to running out and kicking the Frankenstein down. Only fear of reprisal constrained him.

Each insect had a life, an awareness, a capacity for pain, and a right to that life despite its natural brevity. How wasteful and lonely was death in the callous lantern! Like the insects, he too was an undesirable, a nuisance, but in their innocence they never foresaw mortal danger. He envisioned the instant of panic and suffering and his breath stuck as if his heart had stopped.

He tried tallying the death toll until, at 240, it struck him as a macabre variation on counting sheep. His fingers groped for the lamp chain and pulled it and he regarded bedside travel clock. The hour wasn't nearly late enough to hold this many deaths. He watched five minutes grind down before lying back and reaching for the lamp chain. Aiming high, he squeezed the light bulb during the loudest burst yet. Yow! Enraged, he swore and sucked his fingertips, initiated into the outermost chambers of the pain inflicted nightlong. Without conceiving how, he vowed to overthrow the lantern and, finding the chain with his unstung hand, dozed off under the momentary blessing of conscience.

Sam awoke restless, primed to garner data for his scheme. Determination freed him of yesterday's clumsiness, and he went, fully dressed this time and already caffeinated, to today's deeper black wreath. Before more point-blank inspection, he discerned Sean frowning suspiciously from behind the back screen door. Sam smiled. "Come on out and say hello, Sean."

The boy grimaced and scuffed as if busted red-handed, glumly shuffling out and on over till Sam asked, "Sean, is that bugkiller legal?"

Sean straightened up with the indignation of an evangelist. "Course it's legal." After an excruciating silence, Sean, as if making up for Sam's unneighborly faux pas, remarked, "I thought about it, and I got a better word than bugkiller. It zaps the bugs, right? Like those ray guns on *Star Trek*. From now on I'm gonna call it a bugzapper."

"Is it expensive to run?"

Sean sounded impatient with dumb, boring Sam. "Don't know. It's worth it, anyway."

Sam's eyes had wandered the wreath and braked at something briefly confusing only for its size among the insects. It wasn't as charred or crumbly, but it was dead. Sam exclaimed, "Sean, that's a sparrow!"

Sean, bewildered at Sam's temper, fixed an eye on him, nodding slowly.

"Doesn't that disturb you in the least?"

Sean shook his head warily. "There's lots of sparrows." He guffawed experimentally. "Except now we have to call it a birdzapper too. Or a sparrowzapper. That sounds cool, don't it?"

Too furious to answer, Sam strove for pokerface, waved goodbye, and marched home, leaving Sean to clean up his smirk, scratch his nose for whiteheads, and wonder what made city people so moody.

Examining the lantern directly would be no help without some mechanical acumen, and he'd only arouse hayseed distrust. The pitiful bird's image repeatedly closed like a stage curtain over his efforts at writing letters and reading, until he succumbed to sentimentality's demands for reprisal. Once all the Saxes were too deep inside their house for Sam to detect from his window, he scurried to the Buick and hid there to overhear any Saxes who emerged. By and by they'd have to bleat something useful.

Lying on the gritty floor, it delighted him to feel like a kid again. Then as the situation's novelty staled, he heeded the songs, pristine and sacred, of birds and insects, reconciled to nature's sporting chance revoked by man. The Saxes' backdoor banged and broke Sam's reverie, and he assumed the women lamenting the grudges of menfolk were Mrs. Saxe and a daughter. "Now take how your pa badmouths the city man who bought Charlie's farm," expounded a husky mature voice that cracked without pausing. Sam twitched as if he'd been nabbed, but the discussion was too far away and the land between houses too level to betray him.

"Who is he anyhow, Ma?" The younger voice was slow and enticing as ketchup.

"Nobody knows." Sam puzzled at a rusty squeak. "He's not overly friendly, so he might be an embezzler, or a millionaire recluse, or a runaway mobster. Then again, city people aren't overly friendly from the get-go. All I know is, your pa's not one for the benefit of the doubt. The big city man had the misfortune of fitting your father's notions of what's wrong with big city men." The metal mouse sound repeated.

"So what's wrong with him?"

"Well, Pa was watching the TV, talking right through the shows as usual like he was watching a fireplace, and he got this sad look. Said the farmer's days were numbered here, because of what that city man started, someone who didn't know how to work the land nor care to, and he'd just attract more of his type." Sam was fuming at his status as scapegoat of one stereotype too many. He wasn't callous, and he wouldn't, especially with their attitude, live there long enough to threaten their benighted ways, which they were welcome to forever.

"Got to admit, that land will go to waste, but a little rest won't hurt it. Your pa was seeing beyond our time, anyway. Once he got going, he imagined all these rich bastards forcing everyone to sell out, and when the rich got sick of it, they'd turn it into shopping malls and tract housing."

"Ma, that would be awful!" Something squeaked again. Sam, conceding it would be awful, risked a peek from the window to see what made the sound. Two short women with long braided hair were transferring a basket of laundry to a clothesline, pulling free rope toward them by means of a steel wheel fastened high on one wooden post. Sam nodded and ducked down. "Think we'll ever get friendly with the man?"

"Not likely with your pa's stubborn streak, if I understood him right. I guess that's what he was talking about. He does tend to ramble late at night in front of the TV. Why don't you go ask him yourself?"

Sam heard nothing but the squealing wheel till the back door banged again, and silence thereafter. He'd learned enough for one morning, so upon scanning the house for more internal motion, he scrambled back to his sanctum. Officially or not, the neighbors had declared hostilities, and Sam ditched all compunctions about sabotage. In any event, wherever he went, and New York still made him cringe, he couldn't tarry much longer beside the Saxes. He had to strike an immediate blow for humaneness and then, doubtless necessarily, flee. Dirk, for his part, might well have been mulling some nastiness for Sam. Mrs. Saxe had to be downright thick to second-guess otherwise.

Electronics couldn't be too difficult for Sam, a college man, if the cloddish Saxe had wired the lantern. With a little application, he mused, the lantern might submit to his remote control. This day he wouldn't fritter into torpor and lollygagging. Whistling in defiance of thunderheads douring the sky, Sam jaunted to the Buick and down the dozen two-lane miles to the nearest hamlet. At a loss for a bookshop or hardware store selling manuals, he joined the village library, snug in its whitewashed cottage, and borrowed a few textbooks.

Home again, he plowed through the two thinnest volumes, ignoring suppertime and sunset, till sneaky lightning's brightness left a dark room in its wake. Rain and thunder lured him to the front porch; after so much nonstop reading, he needed diversion. The knowledge he'd absorbed would percolate quietly till something clicked sometime when he was contemplating the lantern. Barring that, it had sunk beyond conscious retrieval.

Daytime rain was depressing, but at night, especially with lightning and a scenic vista, the worst storm was delightful, even soothing. In the city, rain rounded and softened all the sharp noises, a cosmetic treatment for crass technology. Out here, would the less numerous machines be drowned out altogether? Would thunderbolt justice defang the bugzapper, if it hadn't already?

Sam hurried to the back window where the lantern, mute and

dripping, sparked his keenest elation since childhood Christmas mornings. Hoping the rain had completely ruined it, as water often rusted or dissolved movie monsters, Sam pulled up a chair just to behold the lantern being inert. The future, his eventual return to the nightmarish city, couldn't nag him while he feasted eyes on the lantern's lifeless shell. After a long sardonic gaze he retired and, for the first time after his breakdown, dozed off content, proud of optimizing a day.

Awakening had to be a comedown. The day refused to brighten past a predawn drear. He must have been deluded to believe any of yesterday's self-schooling would ever resurface to help him, and further reading promised to mothball him. But cram he must, for sooner or later the bugzapper would be resurrected. He forced himself to put on clothes and swallow a joyless breakfast, sure he faced a slew of unpredictable disappointments. The same storm system could embellish by night and tarnish by day.

He glanced out front, desperate for something counterintuitive, and raced cheering into the wet toward his roadside mailbox, its red flag raised. Eyes to the ground kept rain out of them and steered him clear of puddles, but allowed him no warning that Dirk must have ventured out the same moment, for there he was, flouting the downpour by extracting his mail envelope by envelope, sour, deliberate, and shivering. Dirk's demeanor was off-putting as barbed wire, but Sam stood his ground, plucked out one flimsy envelope which he secured under his shirt, and said, "Good morning."

Dirk shut his mailbox and trudged down the road toward his driveway. Nettled, Sam strode up the lawn, vowing to squander no more tact on enemies without the breeding to be civil. He was oblivious of the dank state of his outfit, first because of Dirk's snub, then with excitement at father's return address, and finally with shock at father's plainspoken, casual betrayal:

> Dear Son,
> Your mother sends best wishes, as do I, certainly.
> We hope you are happier, and that the country is proving restful. Soon, I trust, you will feel ready and strong enough to tackle responsibility at home again.

As a port in this particular storm, the farm was indeed a godsend, but I would advise you not grow too attached to it. The natural course of things would seldom, if ever, bring us out there anymore, and the house would deteriorate and the land lie fallow.

I have been talking to Mr. Koffler, the developer, whom I suppose you have met once or twice. He claims that your stretch of country is one in which suburban expansion is imminent, and that I could profitably sell off the land for housing in the short run, or hold out until there is a demand for malls and plazas. Better, I think, to dispose of the property quickly than retain it for sentimental reasons and let it become an eyesore with which our name would be associated.

Do let us know how you are faring, and if you have already written, don't feel bound to wait for our reply to write back!

Love,

Your father

By the time Sam could stop rereading the letter, his clothes had dried. Father's reduction to Dirk's clichés shamed Sam and made him the villain that Dirk suspected. He felt like a cat's-paw, a plant. Though the Saxes were peons, he couldn't very well look them in the eye, guiltstruck yet with no touch of sympathy for them. Nor could he face Father and his New York, their unconscionable priorities writ plain at last.

A tiny tan beetle careened into his shirtfront and clung there as if for succor, inspiring him. Only the innocents, with four legs or six, deserved his concern, and like them, he was hemmed between local and urban wantonness. The creatures that did only what they had to do needed no higher impulses because they had nothing to make up for. In that sense they were perfect. Only men were deliberately malicious and unable to separate livelihood from transgression. Sam wanted to forget he had a father and tried to read expression on the beetle's face.

At a knock on the back door, he brushed the bug to the table, clenched Father's letter into a ball for the wastebasket, and opened up hastily, with jitters. The missus, Dirk, the daughter, Sean, and a younger daughter, bearing toothbrushes and facecloths, scuffed miserably on the back porch. Mrs. Saxe spoke up: "What with our pipes clogged on account of the rain, we thought we might borrow your bathroom, if you don't mind. This happened sometimes when Charlie was here, too. Soon as we can afford it, we have to get new plumbing." She smiled disarmingly.

Sam mumbled, "Yeah, sure," and they trooped in with soiling feet, their colossal nerve towering over him like a leering ogre. Mrs. Saxe shut the bathroom door behind her, and the rest, forming a line, thoroughly rubbernecked the place, paying no specific mind to Sam. He chalked up hypocrisy along with the Saxes' other offenses, seething that his company was good enough when they wanted something. Grasping, devious Philistines! It almost served them right to lose their heirloom dirt to condominiums.

Still, that was of no satisfaction to Sam, watching the bug caper around the table. Of all his company, only the insect, who never presumed, was fit to ask a favor. Dirk pushed past his exiting wife, who dallied to console the impatient younger daughter, weedy, toothy, and freckled. When the older daughter's eye meandered by Sam, he beckoned to her, and she grinned shyly.

"Your father's not a very talkative type," Sam discreetly informed her. "It's funny he didn't mention the plumbing when he saw me at the mailbox."

"Pa? Oh, he's just in a foul mood today," she said too loudly for Sam's comfort.

He glanced around, and the other girl chimed in, "Oh, we knew you were awake before Pa came out. We were waitin' on you from the kitchen window." Mrs. Saxe shushed her, and Sean grinned sheepishly at Sam's hard look.

Sam began to sweat. Had they spied on him sufficiently to guess his saboteur intentions? Were they actually here to intimidate him? "What exactly happened to the plumbing, Miss Saxe?"

Mrs. Saxe stepped in. "Her name's Juliet. We just got what comes of too old a cesspool." Sam nodded as with insight, and Mrs. Saxe went back to shushing the kid sister.

"Juliet," Sam pressed on, making the most of Dirk's seclusion, "I didn't notice your bugzapper going last night. Is it okay?"

Juliet blinked giddily before adjusting to the change of subject. "Oh, Pa's fit to be tied about that too. Some water got into the wiring and it short-circuited. We got to take it all apart now." Sam's pokerface almost shattered into guffaws, but something in Juliet's look alarmed him.

She reached out and flicked the tiny beetle to the floorboards, and though it tried scampering down a crack, and though Sam shouted at her to wait, Juliet ordained, "It's a bad bug," and stomped it under a wet heel.

Atrocity under Sam's own roof, in the sanctuary! "That's one of God's little creatures!" Sam snarled, then gloated at the terror, or at least stupefaction, that calcified criminal and witnesses. To the rescue emerged Dirk, whose sullen departure from the house, without a word to Sam, reinstated the flow of time. The little girl sprinted into the john and slammed the door.

Sean, the rightful next in line, grabbed for the doorknob, thought better of it, and hollered "Shit!"

"Sean!" scolded Mrs. Saxe. "Next time don't stand gawking in a strange house."

Sean moped around and gradually fell in with his ma and sister, who mostly stared at the floor but seemed huddled in self-defense when they checked cagily on Sam.

"Sean," Sam called, enjoying Sean's squirms at being singled out, "why didn't your father speak to me at the mailbox?"

Sean channeled Dirk's gruff inflections along with his analysis. "Pa was mad because he had to go the long way in the rain, down the driveway and down the road, to fetch the mail. He likes to fetch the mail, but Charlie always let him cut through the yard, and now Pa don't feel right about doing it."

Sam mouthed Oh, without offering the "neighborly" shortcut, miffed that Dirk was grumpy about Sam's ignorance of customs Dirk didn't care to explain. Mrs. Saxe's sidelong focus on Sam seemed to simmer with disapproval. As if he were the unreasonable one!

The girl dashed from the bathroom and outside, with a wild, speechless gander at Sam. Sean plunged in as Mrs. Saxe warned, "Shake a leg in there, you got work to do." Sean's mother remained as sole Saxe in the kitchen, doing her best to avoid meeting Sam's look.

Once he'd flushed, Sean crowded awkwardly behind Mrs. Saxe, who bustled off, tendering anemic thanks. So now they were a tad afraid, dubious of Sam's stability. Served them right! They'd smelled up his bathroom, stampeded all over his privacy, and forced their profane value judgments, fatally, on his six-legged protectee. But spite mellowed into smugness, for Juliet had blabbed how water, true to movie monster form, defused the bugzapper.

As in medieval feuds, the rain dictated a ceasefire, during which Sam pored over technical literature when not fantasizing about digging secret irrigation tunnels to the zapper's vital organs. High spirits proclaimed that any tidbit of knowledge might prove handy, and inveigled him into memorizing theorems and diagrams. The rainclouds vacated at dusk, and overwrought Sam had trouble falling asleep in the unlanterned night, its hush hearkening to ancient pavilioned camps tense for dawn battle.

Sam awoke groggy, overhearing Sean and Dirk cuss, dismantle their monster, blither about insulation, and cuss some more. Progress may have been nonlinear, but their brightening tone conveyed success was in the offing. Sam would have to forgo sharp-force or blunt-force assault on the lantern or its overhauled electric supply; impossible to disguise, it would surely give him away. Juliet, their unwitting Benedict Arnold, had provided the answer. Water left no clues, even hid the fact of intentional damage.

But how to inject the poison? Midnight infiltration would backfire if his weapon were too noisy or cumbersome, like a garden hose or bucket. A watering can was too dainty, inefficient. Adopting father's bullish approach to situations wouldn't work here, and seemed inappropriate after Father's letter. For once he dwelt on what Mother might do. Sam had nothing against her, but he had no idea how she and Father had ever connected, and her happy-go-lucky wiring left little to emulate.

Sam marveled at the helter-skelter kitchenware she'd literally pitched into a valise for him, in effect the only tools on the premises. Amidst balloon whisk, spring-driven ice-crusher, turkey-baster, nutmeg-grater, and sundry whatsits, the few knives, forks, and spoons were lucky stowaways. The turkey-baster pestered him into fondling and pondering it. As he flexed the plastic squeeze-bulb and felt the nozzle's spew of air upon his cheek, revelation dawned slowly till he was roseate and agape. His weapon had practically pounced at him!

He vented a nasty laugh, thrashing the baster around like Excalibur, before subjecting it to the formality of a test. He leaned a plate upon the shelf above the sink, plucked off the black bulb and loaded the tube with water, replaced the bulb, and strode to the opposite wall. With a duelist's pomp he lifted his arm, glowered at his target, and squeezed. A bolt of water rocked the plate from side to side, and a curt nod rewarded his arm's good job done. Sam refilled and refired until the plate resignedly slid into the sink and resoundingly gave up the ghost. He consigned major pieces to the wastebasket and washed splinters and powder down the drain.

To stay intrepid for his midnight raid, he took it easy, furthering his electrical studies and, for fun, squeezing off shots at more crockery. He wondered how the Saxes were managing for sanitary facilities and, toward twilight, spied them trudging across the road to the Breyers. After supper, he chugged a pot of coffee and maintained an antsy vigil from window to window till all lights were out next door.

Meanwhile the lantern's renewed activity baited him, with every burst, to show his hand too soon and save a few more innocents. He grimaced, he winced, but he resisted. The impulse that propelled Sam had to be irresistible, like destiny. He paused in heroic stance, cradling the baster like Che's tommygun, before he sneaked out. Sam's clock read a mere 10:54, but how could the righteous urge err? He seemed to be watching himself in a movie, and the clockface numerals hung overhead as if engraved in historic red flames.

As Sam's silhouette prowled forth, the lantern's sputters alternately challenged him and gibbered for help. Cool breezes egged him on, to grip the bulb authoritatively, aim it point-blank so that the glow tainted it blue. Moths and mosquitoes swooped from the darkness and dove crackling into the color, to Sam's horror, disrupting the dramatic buildup. Sam flicked one more glance at the farmhouse, listened to the infernal humming, and, on the heels of a protracted burst, clenched the bulb to drown the noise. His squirt hit the mechanical heart. But when the voltage lunged back through the water, Sam's astonished howl melded inseparably with the machine's tortured white noise.

For a while Sam couldn't move, though bedroom shades went white and Dirk's outline blustered, "What the hell's going on out there?" Sam, still tingling like a tuning fork, knew he had scant seconds before the shade flew up and light spilled out and nailed him. But to escape back inside was a nonstarter. Whether the door slammed or only creaked, it would out-and-out incriminate him. Sam shook off his daze and scrambled for the Buick's underside, farther off but not hopeless.

Headlong Sam had flattened beside the car and was snaking under it as the Saxes' screen door slammed and Dirk charged out, flashlight beam too single-mindedly on the zapper to spotlight half-hidden culprit. What a miraculous reprieve! Sam resumed breathing and watched from between the front wheels.

Poking his light into the lantern like a doctor with a tongue depressor, Dirk swore louder than the circuits, which fizzed as if lamenting. The only distinct word in his torrent was "Water!" He swiveled a full 360° with the beam at eye level, overshooting Sam by inches. Dirk carelessly illuminated his own feet while glaring at Sam's bright windows, worrying Sam into a cold sweat.

Muttering, Dirk let his eyes wander to the light at his feet and grunted at the downtrodden grass. Frantic Sam thrilled as if reliving the zapper's sting as Dirk, grinning fiercely, followed the stomped grass toward the car. But since Dirk kept trying to follow a presumptive beeline to Sam's house and the trail always veered away, he gave up in disgust halfway to the fugitive. After a last leisurely scowl at Sam's, Dirk headed back.

Long after lights out for the Saxes, Sam's limbs reluctantly unfroze and he slithered from under the Buick, to seek refuge on all fours like a crawling tot or, as he saw himself, a pelt-mantled Indian stalking Anglos on the prairie. He opened and closed the screen door with the subtlety of a minute hand. For another goodly span he sat on the floor below windowsill level until the nerve possessed him to douse the lights and turn in.

Sam was stuck, and not only with old bedfellow insomnia. The Saxes would be on their guard, and informed of his specific target. The lantern must be snuffed, definitely, but the impracticality of a direct hit militated for striking at the Saxes instead. Sam trembled with the new depth of his commitment, including the slipperiest trick—to convince the Saxes of his repentance, if innocence was too much to ask. His campaign, and his show of harmlessness, had become especially urgent with the newly aggravated likelihood of Dirk scheming against him.

Sam was too jumpy to sleep late, and then his concentration was altogether put to rout by an invasion of saurian, grinding vehicles apparently at his doorstep, as if phalanxes of artillery had been brought to bear on his innocuous cottage. From midmorning till noon, he hunched in a corner like a hare in a besieged hutch. With the resurgence of quiet he braved the window, to gaze upon the Saxes' yard transformed into earthworks.

Surrounding a sierra half eclipsing their house were pumps with mucky siphon coils, predatory scoopers, and ponderous transporters of pipes and fittings. Boyish derring-do tugged him toward the dirt heap, where some unabashed horsing around might make him seem like less of a guilty skulker. Seeing no workers to chase him off, he revved up his nerve, plunged out across the border, and scrambled upslope, with too much momentum for the soft dirt to swallow his feet.

King of the hill, greedy for breath, he was stunned to survey, sitting against shady farmhouse wall, a row of lunching, shirtless bruisers gawking back bewildered. Dirk, seated with them, said nothing except with acetylene eyes. But before Sam could feel like a fool, his narrow summit slid out from under him, and he, landing on his back, slid too. Dirk sprang up and swore a long, rapid lexicon.

Sam yelped at the impending pit, acrid enough to choke him before he could see to the bottom. His gouging fingers and heels were averse to grabbing at slick, spongy soil, but recanted when the void framed his toes. His first deep inhalation, corrupt with fecal stench, almost jarred him loose and left him faint and sweaty. It was less a smell than a force.

Shallow mouth breaths helped at first, without restoring the strength to let him hold his ground, dwindling by torturous millimeters. For incentive he inspected the deadly drop and the crusty pipes sticking out of pit wall. A higher glance revealed the loungers had evacuated, and hearing commotion from above, Sam tipped his head back, though it squooshed into the foul stuff. Dirk and the workers were climbing from behind the crest, with shifting stance to keep from sinking, confused and grim save for Dirk, whose wolfish, vengeful glare made Sam feel trapped.

Once Sam had eyeballed Dirk, the others did as well, and only then did he trim his dreadful glow and bark, "What are you waiting for? Pull him out, goddammit!" After some bickering, one hero agreed to lie on his belly and slide down, while another, digging boot heels into the summit, held his feet. The prone rescuer was unnecessarily loud. "Hey, mister, when I say when, reach back and I'll grab your wrists, and you make it fast!"

"Oh, yes," Sam promised, aghast at the eons that ticked by before the cue. His arms flapping back pushed him down, and the slippage's half inch seemed to engulf him, whole and tiny, in midair terror before godsend hands yanked him up. With one, two, three jerks as the foot-holder eased down the leeside, Sam was rescued and hauled to his feet, head throbbing and ears chiming.

Merciless Dirk was on him, eagerly, in a trice. "You damn fool! Don't you know you could've been killed! Prancin' around a cesspool like that! If the fall or the pipes didn't break your head, you'd asphyxiate in a minute. That air's poison!"

Shame had commenced worming through Sam, but Dirk's tirade inexplicably made him grin. Still speechless, he lost interest in Dirk and watched the workers shake their heads and drift back to their lounging wall.

When Dirk, complexion like cranberry sauce, ran out of vitriol, Sam cockily said he was sorry and that Dirk should thank the men for getting filthy on Sam's behalf. Only the slime drying in his scalp, caking upon his hands, and weighting his feet sobered him, but soon aroused happy reflections that he, at least, could take a long, cool shower.

After a leisurely cleansing, Sam brewed a pot of coffee to stimulate strategic visions. In the third cup he regarded his reflection, which brought to mind Dirk's bloodthirsty features, huge, inescapable as if in Cinemascope. He'd wanted Sam dead, and if the workers hadn't been there, he'd have let Sam drop. Wasn't that in upshot like trying to kill him? On first spotting Sam atop the heap, Dirk, rather than warning him off, seemed to will the downhill topple.

Sam's assault on the zapper must have cemented Dirk's killer incli-
nations, despite lack of concrete evidence against Sam. To survive long
enough to fulfill his anti-zapper mission, he had to eliminate Dirk and
whoever would side with him during a showdown. Death was both as
immediate and abstract as a redheaded pin on a map. Whatever he
devised would have to be flexible and comprehensive, to deal with
Dirk and any allies alike, and dramatic, savory with justice. But further
rumination was useless, for plans, he realized, would linger in the
realm of fantasy until circumstances commended something specific.
He had to be on guard against Dirk seizing opportunities till then.

A premise hovered, teasing him, but refrained from perching,
when Dirk, late in the day, drove his herd across Sam's yard from
Breyer's pasture. It would look better, and he'd feel better, if he
could goad the Saxes into attack and then lay them waste in self-
defense. Frustrating the Saxes' cavalier disregard of property lines
played the major role in Sam's bare-bones idea, but he couldn't picture
anatomy around it yet. He couldn't afford to indulge impatience and
anxiety, obstacles to crucial insights. Calm and confidence would pro-
vide for him. A sound sleep was essential and therefore came easily.

Sam awoke alert and purposeful. Deliberate as a hunter or priest,
he breakfasted and made the round of windows to monitor the Saxes' migratory patterns through the neighborhood. Unfortunately,
Sean and Dirk disappeared over a ridge into their fields and hadn't
returned by noon. Mrs. Saxe and the girl drove off and mulishly
strayed away, and Juliet never left home. Restlessness and distraction
crowded in on him. Yesterday's cesspool operation was finished,
plugged with sod and deserted, leaving neither workers nor disorder
to busy his eyes. Hungry for motion, his gaze ransacked the terrain.

Sam didn't care to curb increasingly brattish petulance at the oaf-
ish view. The front yard was boring from one window; but in the
next, Sam twitched with the mild vertigo of beholding something
known formerly just in stories and art. A deer stood within whistling
distance, as if the deadpan ground had coughed it up to startle him.
The deer looked appropriately lost, trembling, revolving its ears, advancing one step as if lightning would strike a wrong move. In all its
charm and timidity, the deer was less an autonomous creature than
an antidote for doldrums.

While Sam, under the dim influence of a grade-school primer, grabbed a fistful of sugar cubes because deer liked them, Dirk Saxe, topping the ridge that overlooked Sam's, sighted the deer and beckoned Sean to catch up. Dirk shushed him, pointed at the deer, and whispered instructions Sean ran to obey. Figuring the deer's home was the Allegheny range an hour away, Sam bolted out with blurry notions of shooing it off in the right direction. Already tensing at a faraway telephone bell, the deer swung around and went deathly stiff at Sam's lummoxy intrusion.

Sam thought twice and stopped, but his abrupt entrance, sugar in hand or no, spurred the deer to race into the road between Saxe and Breyer lands. Pursuit was hopeless, but Sam, winded before he'd passed the Saxes' driveway, couldn't accept that the deer's fate was already out of his bailiwick.

Saxe and Breyer doors slammed, and Dirk and a tall, ruddy man with a crayfish's jerky motions charged across their respective yards to the road, baiting Sam's righteous indignation because they, coarse and mean as they were, would overtake the deer first, they had shotguns, and the deer was oblivious of them. Sam was driving the poor critter into an ambush! They were making him an accomplice, and he refused to shoulder any guilt.

"No!" he cried hoarsely, staggering, almost abreast of the men poised and aiming from opposite roadside bluffs. The shot within seconds of each other, and the deer kept going, but the noise arrested Sam, who surmised the men would fire whether or not he blocked their target. He'd afford Dirk no happy accidents.

The farmers shot some more, and on the third barrage, the deer somersaulted as if tripped and didn't get up again.

Sam joined the killers' rush to the spasming body and barely restrained a suicidal pummeling at them. In defiance of Dirk's eyes mocking and Breyer's judging, Sam raged, fists shaking helplessly and sight blearing with tears. "Why the fuck do you have to kill everything you can't appreciate? What did that deer ever do to you? Don't you have any reverence for living things? You're no closer to nature than sewer workers!" Sam was too proud of his steam to care about off-target oratory.

While Breyer's look hardened into contempt, Dirk only grinned, chortled, and snapped, "It was a damn thievin' animal and didn't belong here." The last three words hit with ominous emphasis and Dirk, as nonchalantly as if he'd dispatched a fly, turned to Breyer and discussed where and how to divide the carcass. They ignored Sam, fuming and frothing to himself, till Dirk, dragging the deer by front hooves while Breyer took the rear, looked up and smirked. "Thanks for getting out of our way before, or we couldn't have gotten a bead on that animal." With a curt nod he and his good neighbor pulled their quarry toward the Saxes' driveway like a couple of pismires. Once they were past the mailbox, Sam, dignity intact, strode home.

The deer's death, Sam knew, would stir the pogrom master plan to surface and coalesce, if he sat down and let it. He also knew that any of his manuals, open to any page, would be indispensable. Electricity, property lines, and revenge with impunity swirled through his meditations, but evaded his grasp like minnows riding the currents that groping made. Dirk could pick him off anytime and plead mishap or perhaps suicide. If a rabbit, then millions of bugs, then a deer met ruthless ends, Sam was just another minor escalation.

But had the deer not fled Sam's yard, he could have saved it. Sam's chair toppled back like an awestruck lackey, as the brainchild full-blown breached Sam's temples. A fence along the Saxe-Gog property line would both fend off and provoke the Saxes' aggression. And an electric fence couldn't be a more poetic punishment. If Sam improved his acres as he saw fit and neighbors went manic like lemmings and recklessly overran lawful construction, he wasn't responsible. Stranger things, familicide, ball lightning, rains of frogs, reputedly occurred out in the boonies.

Tomorrow was Saturday, a day sacred in the country, Sam suspected, to visits and outings. To ensure he wouldn't run afoul of Saxe acquaintances, he ascertained the Yellow Pages' remotest fencing company, somewhere in the next county. For a weekend rush job, he guaranteed triple pay, gas and incidental expenses, and a hefty bonus for finishing by suppertime. With justice in the balance, hesitation at deploying the God-given Gog fortune was foolish. Sam suppressed the vagrant fancy that Father would be proud of his bullishness. Fuck Father, after all!

The night was surprisingly bad. Each bug combustion seemed a cry for help, until he distinctly heard each zap as "Sam!" Only brooding about the pathos of each victim this night weighed him down upon the bed. All were so close to salvation, could they but resist the blue glow. If only each bug's random foraging veered it away from the lantern, put foliage or other barriers in the way. Chance spared so many insects of a night; why did it demand sacrifices?

Sam's helplessness reminded him of film noir detectives hiding, outnumbered, compelled to witness gunsels rubbing out likable finks. He thought of all the cars that would have safely crossed bridges had movie monsters or tsunamis been an instant slower. He'd read of a downed planeload in the Andes trekking out and directly away from a hotel within three hours' hike and resorting to cannibalism before survivors were discovered. Scorning the death-wrought sound of his name, he wept himself to sleep.

Urgency ousted him from bed and stranded him in desperate readiness an hour before the crew's 9 A.M. ETA. Alarmed that the Saxes hadn't departed when the hirelings arrived promptly, he raced out and shooed the trucks into his heretofore locked barn. Sam's furtive glances toward the Saxe residence went unwitnessed, and when asked by the houndish, slouching workforce what went on, he hemmed and hawed about giving them a shady place to mix cement and get organized. Dubious stares didn't soften till Sam offered coffee, and even then the men's reassurance was tentative.

He and they talked a little, but Sam mostly squinted out the window, and in forty-five minutes brought the slack faces up with a gleeful "Aha!" Dirk was sitting stolid at the wheel of the station wagon as Sean, leaning on the passenger side, yelled and waved at the others to hurry up. Mrs. Saxe, pretending not to be rushed, huffed out the front door, nudging Juliet before her, while the kid sister yanked her mother's sleeve, caterwauled to no avail, and pointed back at the house for something.

When Sean and Mrs. Saxe were done arguing who should ride shotgun, Dirk sighed and drove off. How charming that the family excursion still flourished, Sam leered, how obliging that the Saxes lived up to pastoral stereotype.

With a zealous quaver, Sam turned to his game troupers slumping against posts and exhorted them to toil like ants. Without meeting his eyes they complied, though not snappily enough for Sam, who'd have nagged if not for fear of antagonizing them. Genuine Dixie torpor burdened their every move like deep-sea pressure, and Sam suspected they snickered when he vented his chagrin by scrambling to get whatever one of them asked for.

He kept them in coffee and ice water, depleted his ham and eggs for their lunch, and warily trusted them to forge on while he flaunted the speed limit for ten miles to fetch beer. What did it matter if pawns took momentary advantage and ran him ragged? Within twelve hours every investment in money and humiliation would pay off explosively.

Sam's generosity did kindle some genial curiosity in the men, but when one asked why Sam wanted the fence, Sam worried about letting slip any of the scheme, about the men siding with the locals. With suspicious pauses aplenty he eked out a Saxeless story of craving seclusion after frenzied, epic business campaigns in the city.

The men nodded judiciously and ceased to probe when one of them asked what Sam meant to do with the land and was informed it would revert to nature, that cultivation may have been a necessary evil, but only wilderness seemed healthy, uncorrupt, invigorating. Once Sam made himself clear, he was happy to find the men at last toiling like ants, silent and steady, except to ask for water or the time.

The sun was balanced on a western hilltop when the fence reached the road, and the foreman presented Sam with a red control panel, roughly the dimensions of a bathroom scale. When the foreman squinted doubtfully at Sam's checkbook, Sam outlined what his father did and owned. As the foreman backed away with the check, he explained that the grey dial would go up to 110 volts.

Sam's mordant cheer crumbled. "Is that all?"

"House current." The foreman's delivery sounded like a slogan in a detergent ad.

"Will that kill anything?" Sam quavered.

The foreman shrugged. "Bugs, snakes, small birds, maybe squirrels. Nothing it shouldn't kill."

Sam was glad he'd somehow spooked the crew into hasty de-

campment. They couldn't dawdle anyway, because Sam had an unexpected task to tackle before the Saxes or panic deterred him. Sam
cogitated, till it hurt, for something that drew more than 110 volts.
At last, again, he had to bless Mom, who couldn't see him hand-
washing clothes and had a washer and dryer installed in the cellar.

Unearthing the fence's cable connection to the house, Sam, with
the relevant manual propped on the windowsill over him, scissored
the plug and shoved the neck end through the cellar window. Down
in the cellar, his eyes followed manual diagrams while his fingers
pulled, cut, and spliced, and his mind bore spellbound witness, not
daring to interfere. Sam was thrilled. Here he was, doing something
deftly the first time, though he felt close to delirium.

Half an hour later, the dark at the top of the stairs surprised him.
It was too soon, and out of his control. His sense of staging was
threatened. He rushed indignantly to throw every light switch. In
charge again, gently as a granny with a hot pie, he laid the control
panel on the windowsill overlooking the fence. Ghostly figures stood
mute at different distances behind the barrier, and the bugkiller
hummed and cackled like their conjurer. Sam sallied forth to play his
role fearlessly, unable to conceive of failure.

The Saxes, Dirk foremost, said nothing while Sam, gloating,
paced back and forth. He slowed to watch the younger girl yank her
mother's jacket hem and ask what they were going to do.

"Not a whole lot you can do," Sam cut in, and Dirk trod forward,
with Sean more timorously following suit. Sam chuckled and dashed
into the house and out with a plastic bucket from under the kitchen
sink. He filled it from a hose spigot and lugged it within arm's length
of the fence. Without guessing what would happen, he exulted at
how he spontaneously hit upon the right moves, and how he sensed
the imminence of denouement.

"Goddamn you, Gog, what's the big idea?" Dirk snarled, fists
clenching at his side, while the younger girl, sneering, shook a fist at
Sam more overtly.

"I'm defending my little friends, Dirk, and I'm defending myself."
The bugzapper caught Sam's attention, taunting him with more victims. As he stared, his lips rolled back doggishly. He snatched up the
bucket.

"What the hell do you think you're doing?" Dirk bellowed. Mrs. Saxe looked around nervously, and Sean stepped up beside his father. Juliet asked her mother what was going on.

Sam thought of the lantern's millions of cruel, underhanded murders and weighed them against the lives of five stupid, callous reprobates the world would never miss. They weren't even people so much as bumpkin stereotypes.

"What are you gonna do, Pa?" Sean whispered.

Sam knew in this situation his aim would be true, so without careful sighting, he swung the water from the bucket, over the fence. A good third of the contents slammed into the lantern, which flared up brilliantly, on and off, dunking the appalled family in and out of blueness. The lantern chattered rabidly, Sam roared triumphantly, and Dirk, looking from one to the other, growled and charged.

Sam went silent and wide-eyed, briefly shocked like a green recruit at the reality of Dirk's speed and fury. But once Dirk had fingerholds in the chain links, Sam lunged to the windowsill and twisted around with the panel. For a second he savored the scene, Dirk clambering up, the rest fidgeting toward Dirk and back, as if afraid to cross him. Taking a deep breath, Sam dialed full voltage. In the cellar the washer chugged on, the fence sizzled, and Dirk howled, eyes, nostrils, and mouth jolted into circles.

The family's immediate reaction was obvious as magnetism. The bratty girl ran wailing to her father at the same time Sean, idiotic with rage, pounced at the fence, roaring at Sam. Sean grabbed chain links and the girl grabbed her father, and no sooner were they screeching than Mrs. Saxe dove for the girl and caught her too late by one last breath. Meanwhile Juliet, her timing also off as she stumbled at Sean, missed him and the fence stopped her. And there they all were, as Sam gaped in dumb wonder that he'd actually done it.

The washing machine gurgled along, the dying lantern squelched more and more weakly, the fence sounded like a sizzling grill, the Saxes keened until their lungs gave out, and Sam found himself babbling about bugs and justice. The spread of Saxes across the fence was reminiscent of flypaper casualties, and that at last aroused a twinge of pity, but he shrugged, as it was probably too late anyhow. When the grisly but rewarding reek of singeing skin and cloth wafted over, he cut off the voltage gripping the Saxes so that they collapsed. The washer stuttered off, and the lantern spat and flashed its last and darkened.

Sam left the panel on the sill and breathed deeply, to maintain calm, until the breeze swept away the burnt odor. He was managing not to think about the Saxes, or anything in particular, when he registered a tiny sting on his arm and slapped at it. His quaking hand brought away a flattened mosquito, pasted to him with its life juices. A dizziness passed, and he flicked the tiny corpse off. He wouldn't bear any guilt. He was still different from the Saxes. He wasn't blameworthy for reflex or instinct, he insisted, with a final survey of the bodies, in clumps like snipped puppets.

He ambled into the house, and in kitchen brightness couldn't avoid seeing the brown smudge on his palm. He still defied guilt, but felt more obliged than a minute ago to flee the house forever. At last he'd learned how to stand up to the world, to function in it, to satisfy a desire. All he had to do was discard guilt, regret, and the businesses of both city and country. He'd hardly begun to realize who he was and what he could do. The mystery of what would happen next, or in six months, didn't unsettle him. Forward motion would establish and actualize his goals.

After washing up, Sam crushed clothes and everything from the bathroom cabinet into suitcases and dumped suitcases into the Buick's trunk. He paused to disown, formally, family and wealth. Grandfather had started modestly, and Sam no longer wanted more than he needed. He could always find short-term ways to make a modicum of money, for the world, he finally recognized, was large enough to contain the solution to every situation he handled resourcefully. Too much money would only adulterate the joys of flight, concealment, and day-to-day survival.

While letting the engine warm up a minute, Sam unpocketed a penny and flipped it into his other hand, heads for Mexico, tails for Canada. Then he rolled along the gravel drive and onto the enticing dark road, and headed for the interstate, humming a tune whose name he'd long forgotten.

watcher of the invisible world

Dear Mr. Nagel,

   Please do not disdain me for my tone of supplication. I appreciate your concern for historic renovation, and in general I applaud your plans for Transit Street. But I must implore you to exclude my tenement from them. Doubtless the clamor and commotion of your work would aggravate my condition, but an intenser, possibly irremediable trauma would ensue if I vacated. I fully understand the seriousness of your property investments, and my family will agree, I am sure, to whatever rent increase you deem appropriate. Before Mr. Gulditch closed the sale with you, he assured me you would be sympathetic to my position. Perhaps he forgot to explain that to you, or felt I could better explain it myself. In any case, I remain convinced that your eviction notice was an unhappy oversight, and that your sense of decency will guide you.

Yours sincerely,

Vergil Pendergast

The script was tremulous enough to seem a right-hander's attempt at using his left. Impatient Peter Nagel sought more light by the window, squinted, swore at the leaden Providence sky, and retreated to his desk lamp. His lips formed each word while he strove to decipher it, the rest of his face grim in concentration. After the second go-through, the contents resolved into coherence, and Nagel's mouth relaxed into a series of dry chuckles as he crumpled the note.

   He shook his pitying head. If this Pendergast's sob story contained any truth, it made his removal all the more imperative. Even if he didn't interfere with contractors in the rest of the house, his ailment, if mental, might escalate into mania, and if physical, might be contagious. And how could he sign upscale new tenants with a quarantined lunatic on the premises? By that time, the man could be a living legend throughout the East Side. In long and short runs alike, expedience called for Pendergast to go.

Nagel gingerly unballed the letter and smoothed its wrinkles with the heel of his hand. Should the affair go into litigation, God forbid, here was a signed confession that Pendergast was irrational, quite ready for involuntary commitment. But Nagel didn't consider himself inhumane. Since an obviously old, solitary, perhaps senile individual was involved, why be unduly harsh? In essence the fault was Gulditch's, making worthless promises, leading the geezer on till he was the new owner's problem. Nagel wouldn't forget to devise some suitable payback for Gulditch.

Meanwhile he'd visit this Pendergast, assess his mental and bodily status, and persuade him he'd be happier elsewhere. The compassionate approach! Feeling his conscience warm up in approval, he gazed out his Westminster Street aerie to College Hill, hoping to locate Transit. Unable to remember where the hell it was, he snorted in annoyance and rummaged in desk drawer for a street atlas.

With atlas on the passenger seat, he was in the vicinity after lunch and, recollecting his neighborhood tour with Gulditch, easily singled out the house. Parking the Beamer was another matter. Not another moving vehicle was in sight, and only a few pedestrians, but stock-still congestion produced the impression he'd driven into a sepia tone of an Old World bazaar. The street was scarcely two cars wide, and on both sides vehicles straddled half the sidewalk, bumper-to-bumper, into the soft-focus distance. Trees of likely a century's growth shadowed the already overcast scene, and the houses, supposedly from the early 1800s, loomed over the street and seemed to compress it further, their walls bulging unpleasantly out.

With a grunt of relief he noticed a side lane that seemed fitter for a driveway and swooped in, effectively plugging it. He couldn't imagine such an obscure alley going where anyone had to go.

On the flagstone stoop he paused, hoping a glance at Pendergast's quarters from outside would prove informative. Gulditch's trans-

ferred records listed a ten-year denizen of a "monitor-roof apartment," so Nagel craned his neck until it creaked, to no avail. How
sheer and high the frontage was, as if it enclosed a city rather than
rooms. The house was too massive, improperly so, and he felt uneasy
as he backed off.

Across the street he finally attained a clear view and clucked
mournfully for the poor soul who'd exiled himself up there for his
sunset years. Prying him out was tantamount to a charitable act. Like
a vault heaving from the soil, the apartment was a low excrescence
from the roof, begrudging enough height to stand. He tried envision-
ing a floor plan of the interior space; the usual tally of rooms resolved into little more than closets. Flush above the interrupted
slope of the hipped roof were two-paned windows like a row of
eyes, but rendered opaque, figuratively blind, by some agency beyond wholesome reflected daylight.

The very inscrutability of the place, as distilled into those blind
eyes, mesmerized him, suggesting morbid images of dotage and solitude. He dispelled them roughly and returned to the door. He finally
noticed the warmth exuded by his soppy underarms.

On the third-floor landing, he gaped breathless at the companionway to a square ceiling hatch and questioned the infirmity of any
regular traveler up all these stairs. So steep were these last that he
took them with hands as much as feet, but before his head poked
through the unlit opening a gruff voice proclaimed that no visitors
were expected today.

When Nagel identified himself, the following pause implied confusion, and more hesitant voice bid him enter. He rested on the top
step, straining to survey the layout ahead via weak light trickling
from a back room. He inhaled, gagged, and almost reeled off-balance,
for the air was thick with the must of crumbling newsprint, and the
stuffiness was like a blast from a kiln. He made himself inhale and
shakily enter the oppression.

Such conditions were normal for a rat-infested attic, not a home.
Scornful Nagel deplored his tenant's submission to decay and squal-
or, and the gloom suggested this could be any crawlspace where forgotten things moldered.

Rhythmic creaking impinged on his awareness, and with an equally subtle metallic ping the room was aglow like a brick oven's ashen interior. Nagel cursed his eyes for dazzling so easily, and as they adjusted, they were drawn to the brightest source of reflection, a motionless set of tubular copper chimes, suspended inches from his head. They held his bewildered attention till a quavery voice apologized, "I didn't mean for the poor light to bother you coming up. It's my customary amount, unless I'm reading. It's just I've grown disused to interacting with people."

Apprehensive Nagel's sight proceeded across less and less dim floorboards, anticipating a disfigured, cringing photophobe. He relaxed when Pendergast smiled at him, a gaunt but uncommonly preserved oldster, bobbing contented in his rocking chair. The low wattage from battered pole lamp beside him showed fine creases as if they were the remnant gray traces of ivy torn from brownstones. These spanned his forehead and fanned from his eyes and mouth. His jowls, though, were firm, his cheeks and eyes unsunken. Gray beard and thinning hair were his only other signs of age. "I wanted to phone you first," Nagel explained, "but your number's unpublished, apparently."

"I have no phone," Pendergast intoned as if it were common knowledge. "I conduct all business through correspondence. I can't hold your forwardness against you, however, since I imagine you can't indulge in leisurely transactions."

While the recluse spoke, Nagel scanned the room, finding no furniture except an unkempt pallet, and windows thickly swashed with grey paint. And in stacks along every wall to the windows, and crammed into the recess created by the roof slope, were countless newspapers and magazines. Nagel's unease revived, and he asked, "Why all the paper?"

"I don't go out," Pendergast replied curtly, "so I don't discard them. About every four years I hire students to empty the place, and they take it all somewhere to be recycled." His head twisted owlishly, and his perturbed eyes focused on the air before him till he looked up meekly. "But you were inquiring why I read so much. That brings us to your reason for visiting, I daresay. I've always fantasized explaining my situation, so this should come easily, though I've never rehearsed aloud. Whatever the case, I must be eloquent now, or you won't be convinced to let me stay." He smiled.

Nagel said nothing.

His host gasped with embarrassment. "Thanks to my solitary habits I've neglected to get a chair for you. There's one in the next room. I'll—" He made a clumsy effort to rise, gesturing toward the murky doorway even as Nagel waved him down and strode over like a good sport.

Again he had to fend off dizziness amidst a more potent backroom fug of moldy paper, while shielding his eyes from a naked light bulb on a chain. His vision adjusted, then narrowed with fresh scorn at more floor-to-ceiling newspapers. His nose would not adjust to the pungency, in which he came to detect mildew, whose point of origin was a rickety shower stall and a toilet crammed together, with a black-streaked plastic curtain half-concealing them.

On the other side of the room, a cabinet under the sink over-flowed with papers, and Nagel could hardly squeeze between it and a massive mahogany table to the chair beyond. A double hotplate occupied the table's far end, with cleaner circles where dishware must have rested in the chronic dust. Disgusted Nagel hauled the chair away.

Pendergast peered anxiously at the audience sitting down in front of him, till Nagel asked if they couldn't open some windows. Pendergast's gray eyes grew distant and morose, but his jaw firmed up as if he were bracing himself. "Very well, if you must. Only you do it, please. Any window to either side of us, but none I'm facing directly."

Annoyed at this diehard quirkiness, Nagel lurched over to the paper barricade and grabbed a window's handle. After several tries knocked the wind out of him, the paint seal cracked and the win-dow flapped up. He propped it open with a rolled-up *Newsweek*, re-seated himself, and waited flintily for Nagel's story. The shut-in's eyes flicked nervously toward the floor, and Nagel, doing likewise, was startled by a shadow movement. In the purging breeze, dust co-hered in balls and rolled across the boards like crabs on sand flats.

Very deliberately Pendergast began to rock, raising his eyes from the floor with a theatrically strenuous effort. When they reached

Nagel, the tenant's whole body twitched as if with surprise that the visitor hadn't vanished. Nagel thought he heard him mumble, "How foolish of me." Then Pendergast cleared his throat and commenced.

"From childhood I was apart, alone. I saw what others never saw. These discrepancies were not so frequent when I was very young. Still, unique observations influenced me so that the mundane world no longer affected me as strongly as it would anyone else. Thus I was judged a cold, uncaring boy, but that wasn't strictly true. It was more that by the age others had developed the imagination to see a cloud resembling a demon, I'd seen a real demon."

Pendergast expectantly regarded his audience. Nagel only ogled back and said, "I don't understand you at all."

The tenant's stonier eyes and tightened lips betrayed irritation, but he rallied his serenity and sighed. "My talent, or affliction perhaps, is a recurring auditory and visual access to what Cotton Mather termed the Invisible World. I can see entities who do not inhabit what we call space, who are not composed of what we call matter. Am I plainer now?"

"You mean ghosts?" Nagel ventured.

"Among other things," Pendergast conceded. "But specific stimuli are necessary. As I grew older, access came more freely, despite familial attempts to discourage my purportedly 'distracted moods.' Psychiatrists, boarding schools, travel, finally college—nothing could hinder my developing powers. After two hellish years fighting off my unearthly perceptions in environs that aggravated them as I built up associations there, I quit the university, friendless and exhausted. I rented this apartment, where I've remained ever since. My ability strengthens its hold on me, but I've at least slowed its progress. Though it enervates me, I've managed to keep my senses within this world."

"My records show you've only been here ten years." Nagel leaned forward imposingly. "And you claimed to move in after your sophomore year of college?"

"I'm thirty-three years old!" Pendergast snapped, and added apologetically, "I started late, because my parents sent me overseas several years."

Nagel shook his head as if stunned.

"I gather you are still confused." Pendergast rocked thoughtfully till the resultant breeze grazed the chimes into faint commotion. He shuddered as if the jangling were unnatural, but as he listened to it, his features brightened with inspiration. "Perhaps a metaphor will help. Usually I strike the chimes to disrupt a dangerous line of thought before it can go too far. The irony is, they also work much like my mind when my senses are redirected. Consider any force that moves the chimes an influence on my mind, and each of its tubes, an association in my memory. Any resultant sounds represent the perceptions shaped by my thoughts."

Pendergast stretched out an arm and pawed the air below the chimes, which shivered minutely and silent. "Too weak a stimulus, and there is no collision of the tubes. The thought dies harmlessly, without arousing further associations. But suppose there is more provocative input." Pendergast lunged up to swipe one finger across a single tube and thudded back into his seat as the rest ricocheted into discord.

"Out of control, my associations tend toward the unearthly, and then my broodings prevent me from blocking glimpses of the Invisible World. If a man thinks constantly about doorways, he will be more observant of them. Once I have dwelt on supernatural beings, I have no choice but to behold them. The climactic perception is as alien to the first as the cumulative dissonance is to the first pleasant chord of the chimes. And the process is likewise unstoppable, barring drastic measures." For a second, Pendergast looked resentful, as when normal people feel the first scratch of flu in their throats.

"So you're always having these hallucinations of ghosts?" asked Nagel smugly.

"No!" Pendergast thundered, thrusting crimson face toward the blanching landlord's. "How can I make you understand? These things are real!" Breathless he sat back, rocking vigorously and glaring at Nagel, who sat braced as if to flee. "You want to hear something reasonable, clinical. Very well. Recently in one of these news magazines . . ." He pointed at a modest pile beside his pallet. "Let me try to find . . ." Heaving himself up, he blinked at the periodicals and settled down again with a dismissive wave.

"Never mind, I'll just tell you. In everyone's blood is a chemical almost identical to psilocybin, a psychotropic drug. Those with a higher percentage allegedly embrace a more comprehensive reality, like William Blake and Martin Luther, who saw what they considered angels or devils. And they did indeed see things endowed with autonomous, conscious existence. Our everyday senses are too inefficient to detect them. I may produce a record amount of this chemical. Too much for me to interact with the outside. Hence I cannot leave here. Too many stimuli. Ironically the mortal world would plunge me perpetually into the occult realm." He ignored an irregular tic below his eye.

With a sly smirk Nagel leaned forward. "If knowledge of the world is so dangerous, why read so much about it?"

"It's dangerous only inasmuch as I can't control the quality and quantity of stimuli. I must be where the fewest associations present themselves. This place is therefore so sparsely furnished, though I'm still too prone to unhealthy reverie. Unless I constantly steep myself in the tedium of current events, I'd be lost even here. Most of my waking hours I devote to reading. Only thus can I limit the influx of the unstable world." As his voice trailed away, his eyes tried to bury themselves in Nagel's, as if to hide in their aloofness.

Unsettled by Pendergast's intensity, Nagel lowered his sights and asked, "Couldn't you go back to your family? Wouldn't they take care of you?" When he looked up again, the tenant was rocking mechanically, eyes blank as if he were thoughtless and adrift, except that tiny globes of sweat sparkled on his brow.

Pendergast spoke very deliberately, still expressionless. "I have not seen a relative since college. They gave up finding a so-called cure then. I decided that removing myself permanently would alleviate their despair over me. In correspondence I sound like the ordinary son they wanted, and I will not hurt them by uprooting that belief." His reserve briefly abated. "My years have changed me too much. I cannot let them see me now." He began to sigh, but his features tautened, lower lip twitching.

More urgently he explained, as if words could wash away the distraction clouding his eyes, "My family is dear to me in a way you might find too abstract. Though they can't understand me, I maintain that they respect me, and are tolerant enough of my impositions on them from afar. My parents' allowance is my sole support, you know. Food and rent, and whatever living expenses." He indicated the barriers of paper. "And they've resisted any impulse to visit me, or even mention the idea in a letter." Pendergast went quiet, and the creaking of the rockers loudened, as if he were bearing down on them harder.

Nagel was skeptical of any man's ten-year isolation from his parents, but maybe such offspring they'd want to keep at arm's length. He'd have to snoop around some. He positively couldn't accept that the graybeard was scarcely middle-aged, with living parents. Since the tenant was at least a partial liar, Nagel could annul his pity, however pathetic the recluse appeared. Besides, his first duty was to empty the building. "You can't be happy here, all by yourself. And I can't have anyone in this house during renovation. You'd be better off moving in where people could take care of you."

Pendergast struck the rocker's arms with his open palms. "When will you realize, I'm not old and feeble?" He leaned forward with shaking fists, gaped at them in turn, and more gravely sat back. "Nerves, the stress of my vigilance, have made me this way."

Nagel nodded, unimpressed. "I don't know why you're so afraid. If these are things you just see, they can't hurt you. I'm sorry, but you've given me no reason to let you stay."

Before Pendergast could vent the anger darkening his brow, the distraction took hold again, and he paled into quiescence. "It is dangerous for me to brook this at all," he whispered, "but apparently I cannot change your mind otherwise. The perceptions are traumatic enough, even when they're not horrible, but my relationship to them is changing somehow. I can't be much clearer, because I don't understand it myself." The landlord noted with surprise that Pendergast's eyes seemed sightless, no longer staring at anything. The codger spoke on, oblivious of Nagel's wary approach to inspect his pupils, as dwindled and distant as twin stars.

"My power has been taking me over more persistently, enwrapping me, as if it is my chrysalis, and I am about to be transformed. I've felt a change coming, which I've tried to deny. My human existence has been a mere larval stage." His words came more rushed, slurring together, and sweat drenched his face. His body quaked like an overheated engine. "My spiritual experiences have dangled me off this world and over infinite others. I have held on to this world. I have fought."

He slumped as if his bones had softened, and his breathing was more labored. "I fear letting go more than anything else. My body would be here. My mind and senses would float adrift forever among those terrible others." His voice briefly rallied, like the last of a dying man's. "I would be completely helpless. I fear it. I fear it so!"

Nagel sat dumbfounded as the tenant stiffened like drying clay into his slouching posture, eyes unbearably wide as if about to burst, unable to contain all that flowed in. "Too late. Too many images in mind," he rasped, hardly parting his lips. "Each image puts me in a different realm, invokes a different denizen. Must concentrate on a benign one. Please, let it not be unpleasant. Please." Held immobile himself by Pendergast's motionless struggle, Nagel realized only as an afterthought that the appeal was not to him, forgotten completely in plain sight.

The tenant gasped with what could have been either ecstasy or torment and, exhaling, seemed to relax, but retained an unnatural steadiness, as if sustained by interior props. His eyes were of almost normal width again, radiating wonderment instead of dread, but as he smiled disarmingly a weariness suffused his face and voice. "Have I ever seen this fine couple before?" Nagel opened his mouth to ask who Pendergast meant, before it registered he'd referred to a couple, and that his gaze aimed somewhere behind the landlord. "I think not. But no matter! You are friendly little guests. Come here and let us converse." Nagel couldn't bring himself to turn, as if restrained by electric charge in the air.

Before he could overcome that restraint, Pendergast's words increased the charge. "Here, here now! You two haven't met my other visitor. It's not gracious to pass through strangers uninvited." A chill hit Nagel, but he insisted he was reacting to the eccentric's speech, nothing more. Pendergast's gaze had lowered to his feet, and he spread his hands as if in delight, and his grin widened. But a stiffness underlay his gestures, as if he were in their thrall.

He bent forward and fondly stroked the air to his left and right, carefully inspecting the space below his hand. "Can you speak at all, my friends? Ah, but you can smile!"

"Pendergast, stop this fooling around and be realistic." Nagel was involuntarily squinting toward the floor, blinking, jolted by a wispy wriggling that must have been some turbulence of dust. "Pendergast, what are you talking to?"

As if able to answer only obliquely, Pendergast went on, "Are you young, like tadpoles, or ageless, like cherubs?" His hands seemed to be tickling under a pair of chins. "You don't mind that, do you? You do remind me of children. Please don't think me condescending. No? That is good." Again Nagel lapsed into squinting at the disturbed air. "Would each of you like to sit on my knees?"

"What kind of trick are you playing? We have serious business."

Oblivious Pendergast settled back and parted his knees, patting them. "Gently, that's right. Don't sink through them."

Nagel crossed his arms and sighed. "How much longer do you intend to keep this up?" He shook his head sullenly. Why had he wasted sympathy on this faker?

Pendergast glanced at the chimes. "Do you want to hear them? Certainly, but be careful hanging onto my legs, or you'll go spinning off." Pendergast lunged up, and his arm arced into the chimes. Nagel's displeasure dissolved into angst at the noise, as if one of the creatures had caused it. With hands growing cold, Nagel stared at the recluse chuckling as if to echo another's contagious laughter.

The laughter, before lapsing into open-and-shut hysteria, was drowned out by a blaring car horn, startling Nagel but short-circuiting his tension. Pendergast's throat wheezed into constriction, and he fought for oxygen, nostrils flaring. "The phases shift," he croaked, "and bring a new conjunction. And it will be unpleasant!" His head lolled and he groaned as if gnawed from within, while Nagel, disgusted by the dramatics, strode to the open window and tilted his head out.

To his amazement, his car blocked an idling newcomer's, fender confronting fender. The horn blasted again, and Nagel wailed, "I'm coming, goddammit!" Warily the landlord turned toward his tenant.

With deeper breaths, Pendergast groped hopelessly through the air above his knees, then yanked his hands away as if they'd wallowed in mushy putrescence. "My dear little friends are gone!" he shrieked. "And now you!" He screened his face with trembling arms, but his eyes, bulging now with affliction, could not flinch away. "Don't look at me like that! Not like that!"

"Pendergast, I definitely can't let you stay if you're going to carry on like this!" Backing toward the door, Nagel finally understood that the recluse wasn't pretending. He shivered in revulsion at the tenant's wild visage. "You've got to get out of here!" Nagel yelled in desperation at Pendergast, who moaned loudly and whimpered. Through the jagged outcry, Nagel heard the car horn once more and staggered headlong down the ladder stairs. "I'm coming!" he shouted again, though he knew nobody outside would hear him.

In the next two weeks, Nagel's eviction notices escalated from patronizing to subtly threatening. The sole response was a curt scribble requesting he address the specifics of any rent increase to Pendergast's parents, since Nagel's harassment had triggered a marked worsening of his condition. Such gall dispelled Nagel's dwindling compassion, and this epistle he felt no qualms about crumpling. Evidently Nagel had to convince him he wasn't playing games.

His two dropout nephews were the handiest excuse for strongarm goons, and they came cheap. To make his point they'd only have to lug Pendergast's meager possessions to the third-floor landing, whence Nagel would supervise, to curtail unnecessary roughness. Legality barely entered into it, for Pendergast was doubtless too addled to conceive of lawyerly assistance, and no other renters remained to think for him. Nagel's fingers drummed restively on the phone receiver, as if they were themselves sentient, itching to proceed.

Next day the nephews' lummox footfalls masked stealthier Nagel's up to the third floor. At the companionway they caught their breaths, and then Nagel jerked his thumb toward the open hatch.

Before the first nephew's fireplug head encroached, Pendergast repeated his erstwhile greeting, that no visitors were expected today. He received no reply till both enforcers loomed over him, and then Nagel listened hard, to nod approvingly as his agents concisely explained their task of helping Pendergast vacate. A second later, a miserable screech beset Nagel's fine-tuned ears. He winced, and on looking up found his nephews trudging down with the pole lamp and kitchen chair. Their self-conscious smirks served to emphasize rather than downplay mixed feelings about bullying a defenseless senior.

Nagel expected a cascade of raving about ghosts and whatever; the deathly silence puzzled him. But he had no time to ponder with his henchmen awaiting orders. He waved them back up and made himself comfortable in the usurped seat.

Again he strained his ears and overheard a nephew ask Pendergast why he was cringing in the corner. At the lack of response, Nagel concluded Pendergast had succumbed to another fit. The other nephew commented how the geezer was simply cooperating by vacating his chair so they could take it. Nagel frowned, planning to reproach their sarcasm as bad form.

He heard the rocker scraping across the floor, a couple of grunts and some laden footsteps, and then an alarming thud. His eyes darted to the hatch, where the nephews were silhouetted an instant before pounding down the steps and scrambling past him, eyes and mouths round with ineloquent terror. Astonished Nagel twisted about to follow their panicked descent and wavered between checking upstairs, deathly silent again, or on the nephews, already safe on the street. Well, family came first. It was only right. And best to be informed about whatever had spooked them before going up himself.

They were huddling in the Beamer's back seat, quaking and blue-lipped as if half-frozen. He goggled at their whey faces, cast an uneasy glance at the monitor's blind windows, and slid into the driver's seat. "What happened?" he demanded as if they must have screwed up.

They told him in tandem, each inhaling and then jabbering till his lungs were empty. Finding the codger dumbstruck, they couldn't read his fear at first because he was in such a zombie trance, which made them no less anxious to extract the chair and themselves ASAP. Halfway to the hatch, they gave in to curiosity and peered into the shadows where the codger was focusing. They dropped the chair.

Something humongous, with jellyfish body and froggy hindlegs, was both puffing and hopping toward them. It grew drastically as it approached, as if crossing miles more space than the room contained. The light slanting in from the backroom penetrated the monster like sunshine through dust, and it was silent like a 1920s movie, but that made it no less harrowing when a mouthful of peglike teeth and a wagging anteater nose and shaggy-lidded goggle eyes popped from the jellyfish body. On their breakneck way down, the nephews glimpsed the beast glide through the upended chair.

Nagel sighed resignedly. Pendergast had rebuffed this siege. Lifting his nephews' husky mitts, he pressed money into them and let them fall back upon tremulous knees. He fired up the car and drove these pushovers home. Well, at least he'd lucked into parking right out front this time.

For a few days Nagel was at a loss. Intimidating a feeble codger had failed wretchedly. Were Pendergast's fits an act, and had he cunningly hypnotized his adversaries? Or was he sincere in his delusions, and his fear contagious enough to endow shadows and dust with shuddersome forms, all the more credible in the gloom? Fortunately another letter from Pendergast cut short his speculations:

> Mr. Nagel:
>
> I am almost awestruck by your inability to listen or understand. I have been as cordial and patient as possible, with results worse than useless. Your hoodlum antics have pushed me over the edge into the dreaded next phase, or at least heralded that phase's arrival, as your hirelings can attest. Happily for me, little is different, but on outsiders the effects are traumatic. The outcome of your rash provocation should underscore the gravity of my prior instructions. Leave me alone, Mr. Nagel. Deal with my family. They will make all needful arrangements with you. Sincerely hoping to avoid any more distasteful incidents,
>
> Vergil Pendergast

At first, Nagel was confounded. He laid the notepaper on his desk, smoothed out its folds, and reread it several times. After Pendergast had twice demonstrated his derangement and confessed to its aggravation, in writing no less, he flouted the further insanity of taking for granted his continued residence. And the landlord himself had no more say in the matter than a scrubwoman. He could only blink in disbelief.

Gradually the edict that Pendergast had to go kick-started his thoughts into motion. Vinyl siding was on order for the outside walls and plywood paneling for the interior, and contractors had their start-date for modernizing a vacant house. He couldn't afford delays. Aboveboard channels wouldn't be practical, as he'd learned once before by schlepping in and out of court for six months to oust deadbeats. Fright tactics were also out, since Pendergast had proved himself a pro at fighting fire with fire. Desperate Nagel scanned the letter for any solutions it might unwittingly suggest.

His eyes lingered at the mention of Pendergast's family and assumed a predatory gleam. He looked up the party responsible for the rent and was nonplussed to discover a Mr. and Mrs. Horace Pendergast. Still, Nagel doubted the tenant's claims of middle age, suspecting Horace was a son or brother. He'd simply have to word his way around referring to Horace as any particular relation. He wrote out a check for the amount Horace had sent his office last month and had the secretary type a heartfelt plea.

To wit, he couldn't in good conscience accept Horace's money because the building was no longer open for occupancy. Renovative work was underway, and for safety reasons the ancient, subcode house had to be untenanted. Mr. Vergil Pendergast, however, had misunderstood this concern for his welfare and could not be persuaded to relocate. The Nagel Corporation would greatly appreciate the Pendergast family's cooperation in helping Vergil make the wise choice. Hah! Pendergast's resistance would have to crumble with the defection of his only earthly supporters. Hopefully he'd be able to move in with relatives, but that wasn't Nagel's concern. He rubbed his palms together vigorously in anticipation of an empty attic.

A week hence, Nagel received a letter signed by Mrs. Pendergast and was mystified that she alluded right off the bat to her son Vergil. How old were the folks? How old was Vergil? Lest this line of thought put him on the slippery slope of buying Vergil's claims, he shelved misgivings and read further.

Misgivings, anyhow, vanished under a wave of elation at news that an upbraiding missive was en route to wayward son. Mrs. Pendergast confided how Vergil was often difficult, and though she and Horace had always respected his privacy, they would step in on Mr.

Nagel's behalf. They'd informed their son with loving patience, but firmness, that Mr. Nagel was only doing what he deemed best for his property. And if he refused payments of rent, Vergil could scarcely expect to stay. They'd encouraged him to seek out new dwellings immediately, and did Mr. Nagel have anything available in his other buildings?

Nagel grimaced at that. Or, with reimbursement for his efforts, would he kindly supervise Vergil's moving operation? Nagel chuckled gleefully. There was nothing he'd rather do, reimbursement notwithstanding. His delight was clouded by the coolness with which mother wrote of son, as if preferring not to deal with him more than absolutely necessary. Vergil was an odd one, but after all, family ties shouldn't be so nebulous. It troubled him till he shrugged it off as none of his business. Eviction was finally imminent, that's what mattered.

Assuming a parental note would also reach Vergil that day, Nagel geared up for a visit. In the bathroom mirror he calibrated his expression to proper empathy, since Vergil must have felt let down by his next-of-kin. To appear less than benign, to let the slightest gloating creep in, would be unprofessional. He'd offer to make arrangements with a moving company and help Pendergast direct the crew. At the thought of Vergil's new address, Nagel grinned. Gulditch had any number of nice apartments open.

Pendergast had retrieved the pole lamp, its glow trickling down to the landing. But the kitchen chair had remained, and Nagel sat down to rest and listen for any sounds to indicate Pendergast's mood. Soon he made out a weak and forlorn sobbing, and weathered a reluctance to intrude at all. Well, if a stubborn, belligerent troublemaker couldn't deter him, why should a blubbering, defeated one? Nagel clumped forthrightly up the steps, correctly surmising Pendergast would be too distressed to pull himself together on hearing anyone approach.

Wretched geezer didn't even notice when Nagel's shadow draped over him from behind. The rocker was closer to the hatch, presumably on the spot where the nephews had dropped it, and the lamp stood beside, its cord stretching across the floorboards. When Nagel cleared his throat, Pendergast turned slowly as if fragile. One hand clutched stationery with Mrs. Pendergast's florid script, and the other quivered weakly, like a dying sparrow. Pendergast's red, unfocused eyes didn't pause at Nagel, but roved around the room, as if he were one mere presence among a more compelling many. The rocker wasn't budging.

Nagel decided Pendergast had come unstrung in earnest and warily called out, aiming for a balance between solicitous and domineering.

With no sign he'd heard, Pendergast spoke in barely audible gasps, amidst long silences when his abject voice gave out. Eventually his face hove toward the landlord's, though without evident recognition. "They've never understood me. But I never dreamed to what extent. It is obvious enough now. They couldn't love me because I was too foreign to them, my needs too irrelevant. My experience partook of theirs, and I could understand their worldview, I love them. But they could or would not see past the edge of their world into mine. I trusted they could. That has been my tragic illusion, has it not?"

Pendergast's sobs grew convulsive, and as he struggled for breath his head drooped as if he were expelling vitality with each cry. Alarmed, Nagel tried barging through the tenant's isolation. "Pendergast, pay attention! It's all right! Be more realistic!" Elderly eyes narrowed toward him, but still without recognition.

Pendergast unclenched the note so that it covered his lap, and his eyes lowered as he said, "Listen to this. Can't she see what a betrayal it is? 'We put up with a lot of eccentricity from you, but it isn't fair to inconvenience strangers the same way.' Why do they turn against me?"

Nagel sincerely pitied the codger, almost pleading as he strove to make contact. "Pendergast, I want to help you. I'll help you find a new place. I'll even make sure your things get there safe." Though Nagel felt unguilty, he couldn't be entirely immune to the miseries of this frail, heartbroken headcase.

Pendergast mumbled on, oblivious, scanning the room more slowly. "They were my only ties. Now I am too alone here." He bent nearer the letter. "'Mr. Nagel was nice enough to refund our last check. Your father and I think he's been more than fair. Now you're still our son and we pay your rent. If we think it's right for you to move, and if we don't pay the rent where you are now, then you'll have to move. Mr. Nagel will help you, if you're polite.'" Despairing Pendergast seemed to cave deeper into himself by the minute. And why were his eyes fixating on the dark back wall? Nothing to see. The kitchen light was off.

"What is left for me here? Why should I go on?" Pendergast's weeping became louder, but his gaze was all the more absorbed. "Perhaps this is the final push." His words were more distinct, as if he addressed a receptive audience. Nagel assumed Pendergast had noticed him, till he heard a faint jangling and found the wind chimes trembling together. Bewildered, he tried to guess the source of a sudden draft and discerned a soft pulse of air against his cheek. He looked where Pendergast's eyes led, and then Pendergast was forgotten.

Nagel's fear did not mount swiftly or steadily because he couldn't be sure he saw anything for a while. Dim movements were too widespread and rhythmic for dust currents; homing in on one midair locus, he bore passive witness as his optic nerves built up a motile pattern like some 3-D connect-the-dots. Whether or not overtaxed imagination outlined a lazily flapping pair of membranous wings, a giant sturgeon snout, and a leonine body, he then couldn't help perceiving this pattern duplicated across a broad swath.

He counted a dozen of these shapes in repose like lions, in a semicircle facing the men, and creating the rhythm by beating their wings in series, from leftmost in the pride and back again, like sea fans. Still he watched more fascinated than afraid, for the wall of stacked newsprint behind the shapes was no less visible, and manifestly more solid, than they.

Then Nagel realized he saw the beasts at all only insofar as they reflected light from Pendergast's pole lamp. They did have substance, and the longer he stared the more substantial they appeared. Worse, they seemed as aware of him as he of them. He couldn't tear his gaze away till he distinguished round, glossy eyes, egregiously predacious, zeroing in on him.

Nagel's fright was bolstered by late-breaking awareness of his kettledrum heartbeat, and he turned to Pendergast, still weeping, studying the brutes, but without a hint of anxiety. He pitched one more appeal to the tenant. "Listen, Pendergast, this place isn't good for you. I promise to put you somewhere you'll be happier." At last Nagel brought himself to reach out and lightly shake Pendergast's shoulder.

Only then did Pendergast seem to acknowledge the landlord by uttering, "No use, no use." Nagel backed away from him and toward the open hatch. The beasts couldn't be real, or Pendergast would be afraid of them, right? This gave Nagel oddly little comfort. Pendergast would probably get over his crying jag by tomorrow, and Nagel could do nothing with him in the meantime. Repeatedly peeking over his shoulder, he did his weak-kneed best to exit calmly down the hatch.

Come morning, memories of the winged phenomena had faded into clear-cut stress-induced mirages. Nagel again paused for breath before the companionway. The echoes of his footsteps had rung uncannily harsher, as if the house were emptier, deserted. From above came no shuffling about, no weeping, no squeak of the rocking chair. The silence had a stifled air, as if the attic were sealed beneath thick sediment. Nagel was uneasy without understanding why, and bracing for something without understanding what.

His calls to Pendergast went unanswered, and somehow he wasn't perplexed. If the silence surrounded the tenant in new mystery, it also ruled out the presence of big, tromping creatures. All the same, discretion was the better course, and he ascended furtively.

He hesitated just before attic floor came into view, and his nostrils quivered instinctively. The stale newsprint odor was nigh undetectable. Something new overwhelmed it, outside his experience yet unmistakable. Squeamish Nagel climbed the top steps, face downcast till he capitulated to the inevitability of looking.

He was appalled but unsurprised to find deceased Pendergast slumped out of the rocking chair. Dead weight had tilted the rockers forward, and the head had fallen back upon the seat, blue face toward the ceiling. Stiffened face wore instead of sorrow an austere resolve, with little of grimness in it, scant comfort though that was to Nagel. Mom's letter, warped by Pendergast's sweaty fingertips, had landed halfway past the lamp's yellow circle. He'd apparently clutched it till he died.

Before nausea drove him out, Nagel sought to determine cause of death. No marks or blood marred the face or body, nor were implements or pill vials on the floor. There was nothing informative in the odor that prompted gagging Nagel to open every window and hastily depart.

He was truly sorry about the codger's demise, but balked at temptation to blame himself. If suicide were involved, he certainly hadn't hounded Pendergast into it. He'd only been doing his job and wasn't responsible for anyone's latent instability. And if a physical defect like a bum heart had been triggered, why hadn't one Pendergast or another informed him? He wouldn't lose sleep over a crotchety stranger's death, but the whole affair really was regrettable.

From his office he phoned the coroner and rummaged up the number for Pendergast's folks. Mr. Horace was at work; Mrs. Penelope was speaking. Nagel identified himself, and she asked civilly, if a bit curtly, what she could do for him. He chose to get it over with directly. Her son was dead. No obvious cause. Could she come right away? After a spell of dead air she agreed and in a businesslike tone requested directions. Nagel spared a moment to ponder how any mother could take such news so impassively, and then he rushed back to Transit Street, where the coroner was waiting.

By the time Mrs. Pendergast arrived, morgue wagon and squad car had made parking even dodgier than usual, and the coroner had ascertained what he could, short of performing an autopsy. Maternal entrance was agitated but not without calculation, and the men subjected her to a brief once-over before the coroner introduced himself. She seemed the epitome of reserve and privilege, of well-tended "old money," and a facelift or two shy of the border between "handsome" and "senior."

Her cobalt eyes drifted to the corpse on the mattress, and she examined it with less grief than indignation. She didn't want to believe her son was dead. Who would? But she especially didn't want to believe this was her son. Both the landlord and coroner looked from parent to child and to each other, amazement writ plain in both their faces. The son appeared older by thirty years.

Minus any preamble, Mrs. Pendergast protested, "This can't be Vergil! He had some gray hairs, but he wasn't geriatric!" Her composure began crumbling, and she backed away from the mattress. The coroner dove in with self-conscious efficiency and extracted a wallet from trouser pocket. He produced a student and more recent state ID, with decline conspicuous from snapshot to snapshot. Mrs. Pendergast frowned at them, surveyed the body again, and flinched away toward the men. "Horace always said we'd never had a son, but I didn't believe it until now." Her patrician monotone quavered.

Rather than framing a tactful reply or even parsing such a statement, the coroner confessed, "We don't know what happened. His heart just stopped. That's all we can say right now. Emotional stress? I don't know. We can't say how he got to look so, well, aged, either. An autopsy—"

"That won't be necessary," Mrs. Pendergast cut in. "It would only raise more questions." She shook her head decisively, and then tears bleared her eyes. She assured Nagel she'd see to removing Vergil's effects after the funeral, provided she had a key, and she assured the coroner she'd make arrangements with his office for transporting the body. The coroner searched Vergil's pockets again and passed her a keychain with a single key.

Mrs. Pendergast snapped her purse open, dropped in the key, and snapped it shut. The coroner's and Nagel's sorries-for-your-loss awkwardly overlapped, and without further ado Mrs. Pendergast withdrew at a measured pace. Above the clacking of her sensible heels, Nagel discerned an occasional smothered sob.

Though Nagel labored under a solemn cloud for the day, life's new simplicity next morning restored joie de vivre. The house was his, and the means, however tragic and controversial, were academic, a fait accompli, receding ever further into the past. Till he returned to the attic and gazed on Vergil's shallow impression in the mattress, yesterday's death had been out of sight, out of mind.

Tapping pencil against clipboard in waltz rhythm, Nagel lapsed into a brown study. A funereal mood set in, intensifying as his eyes wandered back to the mattress. Someone had closed the windows, leaving inadequate lamp to supply all the light, rendering freighted atmosphere doubly burdensome. Despite the fuggy warmth, Nagel was chilly, and edgy too, as he discovered when a dusty updraft fostered the semblance of someone rising from the pallet. He lurched away, surprised at how firmly he'd been rooted to the spot. His every inch of skin was sensitive, on the alert.

Again a fragment of motion, near the rear wall, startled him, after which his body reacted to nothing he could consciously apprehend. He was weak and trembly, and the clipboard tumbled from nerveless fingers. The instant it crashed, a burst of laughter resonated from the rear wall, in a voice damnably familiar, but hard to place because laughter had been so incongruous with it. More puzzling, the laughter was reverberant and muffled, as if from a crypt. A second outburst, its echoes fading, seemed to mark an exit from the crypt. Simultaneously a figure emerged from the dark, but without physically advancing.

Nagel was too stunned to be afraid, even after the silhouette had filled in enough for recognition. Pendergast grinned triumphantly, naked, fists on hips. His body was aged and wizened, but bolstered, literally glowing, with uncanny vitality. He had the demeanor of a divinely touched prophet.

"But you're dead," Nagel whispered.

Pendergast laughed again. "A mere formality," he bellowed, "and for that I must thank you. I do thank you, honestly." A numbness pervaded Nagel, leaving him more powerless to move than ever. He wasn't even going to be terrified, no, he was skipping straight ahead into shock. Meanwhile Pendergast, for a specter, seemed bigger than life, no more the brittle recluse.

"Yes, Mr. Nagel, I never suspected until the end that death, such a trifling business really, was a prerequisite for my next step. I cannot overemphasize how your scheming and harassment drove me to it. I also never suspected how wonderful the aftermath would be. My transformations are finally over." Pendergast stretched his viny arms luxuriously.

As last-ditch consolation, Nagel babbled to himself, "Ghosts aren't solid, they're just like mist, they can't hurt you." Besides, Pendergast, despite his gloating tone, didn't sound hostile.

"My destiny was," Pendergast resumed, "to become, how shall I put it . . ."

"A ghost?" the landlord hazarded.

"A bridge," Pendergast resumed, "between this and every realm of the so-called Invisible World. Perhaps all men shall be so endowed someday. Perhaps it's the next stage of evolution, into which freakish genes have vaulted me." Pendergast shrugged with affable disinterest.

"But a bridge," he expounded, "must touch down on both sides of the river, so to speak. Unless I were also part of that other side, I couldn't physically convey denizens from place to place. Just one of those realms, and one which looks to me for leadership because of my endowment, shelters earthly spirits after corporeal demise." The glow around Pendergast had widened, like a full-body halo, and it had acquired depth as well, like the mouth of a tunnel.

"And so you see, I had to die. It is, indeed, the only way to conquer death. Isn't it exhilarating to imagine someday all men might become, in a fashion, immortal like me? Death, at least, will lose its sting." Far from being heartened, Nagel perceived his mouth was bone-dry, his tongue adhering immobile to his palate. He was shivering, mildly but uncontrollably. The halo's depth was increasing, till it reminded him of a cornucopia.

"Just think, Mr. Nagel. There are some realms whose inhabitants I can command by simple willpower. They, too, are anxious to visit, though they don't know anyone here. Yes, soon all fleshly men shall enjoy new company, new neighbors. I would invite them to reciprocate and sojourn beyond, but I've learned they cannot well be trusted. Can they, Mr. Nagel?"

Nagel couldn't shift a muscle to reply.

"Now, about my lease. I would like to stay here and use this attic as a base of operations, or a terminal, or what have you. It is home to me, if anywhere is. You and your workmen, of course, are free to refurbish to your hearts' contents. My friends and I won't interfere."

Nagel gazed helpless into the cornucopia as a blizzard of motion began decelerating into shapes, into milky people regarding him with flinty appraisal. Even worse were shapes that absolutely weren't ghosts, peering out with greater fascination. Nagel felt dizzy and faint, but his body refused to collapse.

Pendergast strode forward, unhooked the wind chimes, and tossed them at him. Finally Nagel budged, reflexively dodging the chimes before they hit him. "Maybe you will have some use for these. I certainly don't, not anymore."

Nagel tried to speak, and barely managed a croak.

"Surprised, Mr. Nagel? Once we're here, we can be as solid as anyone else." He laughed again, and added, "As for the key you looted from my body and gave mother, don't worry about it. It's not really necessary, either."

Nagel was able to take one step backward, and then, more easily, another. He felt as if his body were water, and his skin a membrane ready to burst, but when he began to move, there was no stopping. Ever so slowly he turned toward the hatch. Pendergast laughed on, and Nagel heard other voices, less garbled every second. These goaded him into stepping livelier before he could understand what they were saying, especially if, heaven forbid, they were discussing him.

But then he almost toppled off-balance down the companion-way at the tremblor footfalls rattling the whole house, as if the slabs of Stonehenge had uprooted themselves to take a stroll, wreaking God knew how much havoc with antique house frame, except slabs never smelled like putrid, liquefying bread. And even as he puzzled at how anything so evidently bulky could squeeze through Pender-gast's arms'-width gateway, he had to cope with that abusive smell probing in and out of each nostril and his gaping mouth, like tendrils or an elephant's trunk. Insofar as smells couldn't behave like organisms, though, what the hell was going on?

As his body disobeyed his foundering mind and turned back toward the alien bedlam, he harbored one last coherent thought, banal but too much to accommodate, that his tenant problems were only beginning. The very last sound he processed with mind intact was of copper chimes crunching under a piledriver hoof.

acknowledgments

"Three Dreams of Ys," first published in *Searchers After Horror: New Tales of the Weird and Fantastic*, edited by S. T. Joshi (Fedogan & Bremer, 2014).

"Down the Hatch," first published in *A Darke Phantastique*, edited by Jason V Brock (Cycatrix Press, 2014).

"We Are Made of Stars," first published in *Black Wings IV: New Tales of Lovecraftian Horror*, edited by S. T. Joshi (PS Publishing, 2015).

"A Quirk of the Mistral," first published in *The Madness of Cthulhu, Volume 1*, edited by S. T. Joshi (Titan Books, 2014).

"Welcome Back," first published in *Weird Fiction Review* #5 (2014).

"Houdini Fish," first published in *Black Wings III: New Tales of Lovecraftian Horror*, edited by S. T. Joshi (PS Publishing, 2014).

All other stories are previously unpublished.